MW00879144

Silenced Justice

Silenced Justice

A Josh Williams Novel

By Joe Broadmeadow

Copyright © 2015 Joe Broadmeadow

All rights reserved.

ISBN-1506182704

ISBN-13:978-1506182704

Dedication

... to those who pursue the truth...
Without truth, there is no justice.

BURIED SECRETS

Chapter 1

"Do you have a busy morning?" Keira Williams asked her husband.

"Nope," Josh said, finishing the last of his breakfast.

"Can you drop my car off for an oil change?" putting on her suit jacket and picking up her briefcase. "I'll take your truck to work."

"Of course, isn't that what a husband is for?"

"Glad you know that. I gotta run, call you later," kissing him on the cheek. "I'm in court this afternoon, but I should be home before you, any dinner preferences?"

"Ha, you're not going to cook, are you?" Josh laughed. "My stomach hasn't recovered from the last time." He ducked as Keira threw the dog's toy ball at him.

Cassidy, their eighty-pound Labrador, assuming this meant playtime, charged at Josh, fighting for the ball.

"Great, now she's going to want me to amuse her," Josh said.

"Learn not to insult your wife's cooking," Keira smiled. She grabbed the slobber-soaked ball from the dog and threw it at him again.

"Hey, you got dog slime all over me," Josh said, using two fingers to remove the ball from his lap.

"Good, serves you right."

Cassidy danced around in front of Josh, maneuvering to entice the ball from him. Josh opened the sliders to the deck and tossed the ball, sending the dog scurrying outside to chase after it.

"There, problem solved. Now back to me avoiding food poisoning. How about I cook so we both have a chance of surviving?"

"Suit yourself," Keira said, folding her arms across her chest. "I am getting better. I made a delicious dinner last week."

"You heated up a plate of baked stuffed shells that I made. Then, you called me five times to ask me how to set the oven. That is not cooking, that is following simple directions," Josh said, pulling her close and kissing her.

"I'll take the car, go shopping, come home, and make dinner," Josh said, hugging her. "You can just sit there, look pretty, and watch me."

"I'm glad we settled that," Keira said, looking at her watch. "Talk to you later, I gotta get out of here." She opened the cellar door, smiling back at Josh, and walked downstairs to the garage.

They built the house in Rehoboth three years ago after Josh's trial, and acquittal, on civil rights violations. Keira fell in love with the area. They hid the house in the woods to enjoy the more private, rural environment.

For Keira, it was a short drive to her law office in Providence. For Josh, it was an even shorter ride to the East Providence Police Department.

Josh waited until he heard the garage door opening, then reached into his briefcase and took out an envelope. Opening the flap, he withdrew the letter. No matter how often he read it, he could not wrap his mind around the words.

Preliminary indications... potential for cancerous... inconclusive, requiring more testing...

Josh reread the letter, disbelieving the words. He didn't hear the cellar door open. Sensing something, he looked up, surprised to see Keira.

"Forgot my phone," she said. "Is something wrong? You have a weird look on your face." Her eyes narrowed, hands on her hips.

"What? Oh no," Josh answered. He tossed the letter face down on the table, hoping the casual gesture would quell her curiosity. "Reading a report from a case I'm working."

Keira eyed him for a moment, "You can't fool me. You do realize that, right?" glancing at the letter. "If it's one of your surprises, I'll figure it out." She went to the living room and grabbed her phone from the coffee table. Walking past him, she brushed her hand over his cheek. "You can never fool me, Mr. Williams." Her eyes darting again to the letter, she headed down the stairs.

He watched the door close.

Well, maybe just a little I can.

Josh let out his breath and waited as his heart rate returned to normal. He put the letter back in the envelope and slid it behind the Bluetooth keyboard in his iPad case, hoping she'd never look there.

Cassidy clamored for Josh's attention, bouncing up and down on the rear deck, ball in her mouth, demanding to come in. Josh opened the slider. Cassidy thanked him with an enthusiastic shaking of wet fur from the romp in the woods, pelting Josh with water.

"Dammit Cassidy, I already took a shower," grabbing the dishtowel and wiping himself off. "I gotta go. Go take up your guard dog position."

Cassidy ignored the order, dropping the ball at Josh's feet, trying to get him to throw it again. She followed him around the room, dropping and retrieving the ball several times in her quest for more playtime. Failing that, she sulked to her dog bed, curled up, and went to sleep.

Josh opened the cellar door and looked back at the snoring Cassidy. "You have quite the life there, Cassidy. Stay off the couch." He locked the door and headed to the car.

Cassidy's ears went into full alert status. She kept her eyes closed, tilting her head to listen as the garage door opened, then closed. Her eyes opened one at a time. Lifting her head, she stood up, stretched, walked to the front window, rested her snout on the sill, and watched Josh drive away.

She hesitated a moment, moving her ears around listening for any sounds and sniffing the air. Satisfied she was alone, she bounded to the soft couch, jumped up, circled several times to make a proper nest, and went to sleep. She would stay there until the sound of the garage door sent her scurrying back to the dog bed.

* * *

September 11, 2009
7:40 AM
Route 44 West
Rehoboth and Seekonk Line
Massachusetts

Keira climbed into Josh's Nissan pickup, adjusted the seat and mirrors, and headed toward the main road. She changed the SiriusXM radio to the Coffeehouse channel. She could never listen to the Gregorian Chants channel Josh enjoyed, unless she wanted to go to sleep. Josh had the oddest tastes in music.

Driving along Rocky Hill Road, she spotted two deer grazing along the edge of the woods. A flock of turkeys ambled across the road, the huge tom leading the way, forcing her to weave around them. She loved the daily exposure to nature and the quiet serenity of the woods.

Turning onto River Street, she saw two people standing next to a motorcycle stopped along the side of the road. She noticed the helmeted heads turn and watch her as she drove past.

Must have broken down.

Keira continued to the intersection with Route 44. Waiting for a gap in the steady morning traffic, she joined the flow.

Glancing in the rearview mirror, she noticed the motorcycle pass two cars on the right just behind her. The bike swerved to the side to avoid hitting the back of her truck. *Idiots, gonna scrape those two off the road one day.*

She made her usual stop at the ubiquitous Dunkin' Donuts. No matter how many they built, they were always crowded.

Forgoing the drive-up, Keira parked in front. She noticed the motorcycle pass by her, stopping at the far end of the lot.

Both riders wore black leather riding suits and helmets, hiding their faces. They stayed with the bike.

That's the trouble when you marry a cop; they make you suspicious and paranoid.

As she waited in the line, she kept glancing back. The two riders sat on the bike, still wearing their helmets. After placing her order, she took out her cell phone to call Josh.

"Keira, hey, how are you?" a voice called to her.

Keira turned, recognizing one of her neighbors. She put her phone back in her pocket. "Hi, Marie, how are you?"

4

"Okay, I guess. We're off to Boston again, John needs another round of chemo," Marie said.

"Oh, I'm sorry to hear that," Keira replied. Her order arrived. After paying, she headed back to her truck. "Tell John we are hoping for the best," she said, patting Marie's arm. "If you need anything, anything at all, just let Josh and I know."

"I will, Keira. You take care as well," Marie said, turning to place her order.

Keira returned to the truck.

* * *

September 11, 2009
8:00 AM
Route 44 West near the
Massachusetts and Rhode Island border

The motorcycle passenger watched Keira leave the coffee shop. As Keira drove away, they followed, leaving distance between the bike and the truck.

As the bike pulled out, the passenger removed his helmet; tossing it away. *Better to aim this way.* "After she passes the next light," he yelled over the engine noise, "pull up on her side." The driver nodded.

Traffic was heavy, the roadway crowded with commuters. The driver moved close to the center of the road, ready to make his move to catch the truck.

* * *

Motion in her rearview mirror drew Keira's attention. The rising sun behind her made it difficult to see, but she sensed the bike was still following her. '*Just because you're paranoid doesn't mean they aren't after you,*' Josh's voice echoed in her mind.

The sun disappeared behind a cloud; she caught a glimpse of the bike. The passenger was no longer wearing a helmet.

Pushing the Bluetooth button, she said, "Call Josh."

"Contact not found," came the response.

"Josh, dammit, call Josh," the tone and tempo of her voice rising.

"For help, say help. For more options..."

Flicking the command button off, she fumbled with the phone and brought up her favorites list, pushing the call button.

"Miss me already?" Josh answered, his voice coming over the hands-free connection.

"Always, my dear," she said. "Look, I know this is nothing, but I think there's a motorcycle following me."

"Where are you?"

"Just left Dunkin' Donuts at the Seekonk line."

"Okay listen, I am not too far behind you. Drive to the police station. Don't stop for lights. Just look and go. If it's nothing they won't stay with you."

"I'm not going to run any red lights, Josh. You've made me psycho over nothing."

"Keira," Josh replied, "you noticed them, your instincts are good, and you're driving my truck. Humor me. If it's nothing, it's nothing."

"Okay, okay," she answered.

"And stay on the phone with me; I'm heading your way. I'll call the station on my portable, see if there's a cruiser nearby."

Keira came to the light at Route 44 and Arcade Avenue; she stopped as the light changed to red. Glancing in the mirror, she saw the bike still behind her, two cars between them. She wondered about the passenger no longer wearing a helmet.

"Where are you?" Josh asked. "Sergeant Armstrong is sitting on 44 at the Rhode Island line. After you pass him, drive to the station."

"I am at the light at Arcade Avenue, there's a big truck in front of me. I can't get by. And Josh.…."

"What, Keira?" Josh asked.

"The passenger took off his helmet, the driver kept his on. Weird, huh?" Keira said. "Just the driver has a helmet on."

"Where's the bike now?"

"Back a ways, two cars between us. Josh, forget it. I'm fine."

"I'm sure you are, just humor me a bit until you get to the city. Armstrong will stop the bike."

As the light changed, Keira started to move. Glancing in the side view mirror, she saw the bike pass the cars, moving to catch up to her.

Then, she saw the gun.

"Oh my God," Keira screamed. "Josh, there's a gun, he's got a gun."

"Go, go," Josh yelled, "just go, don't stop. Weave back and forth. Don't let 'em get alongside you." Still a half-mile behind her, he shouted into the portable radio, "271 to S1."

"S1 go 271"

"There's a gun, Keira says one of the guys has a weapon. They're trying to catch up to her."

"Where is she, Josh?" Armstrong asked. This was personal now.

"She just left the light at Arcade."

"Okay, I'm right at the line. Seekonk PD has a unit coming up behind her." Armstrong reached behind his head, releasing the shotgun from the cage-mounted lock. He chambered a round, checked the safety, and then parked the car at an angle to the roadway.

He had the perfect firing position.

Once Keira came by, it would give him enough time to aim and end this. He would not arrest anyone.

"Keira," Josh said, "talk to me."

"Passing PriceRight, the light is green; the bike is back a ways." Her heart was racing as she weaved the car back and forth, preventing the bike from approaching alongside.

Josh could hear the tension rising in her voice. He tried to reassure her. "Okay, Armstrong is right there. Just keep going, keep weaving, he'll get them."

All the excited radio traffic caught the attention of Steve "Chubby" White, tow truck operator and cop wannabe.

Chubby tried several times to get on the department. However, his love of food, and inability to complete even one sit-up, prevented it.

He did the next best thing. He bought a tow truck and a scanner. He then secured a city towing contract by contributing money to the campaign funds of several city council members. The way of the world....

As Chubby sat in his garage, listening the radio conversation, he saw his opportunity to be a hero. The garage sat on a dead-end street, right at the point Route 44 entered Rhode Island. Positioning his truck facing the roadway, he waited for his moment in the sun.

Timing was everything. He waited for Keira to pass by.

As Keira's truck flew by him, he stepped on the accelerator, and put the truck in the path of the motorcycle.

* * *

Armstrong watched as Keira came flying over the rise, the truck's tires losing road contact. Once she passed his cruiser, he aimed the shotgun toward the sound of the approaching motorcycle. A flash of movement entered his peripheral vision. A large, fast-moving object blocked his sight picture.

The bike driver, focusing on catching up to Keira, had no chance to avoid the heavy-duty tow truck now blocking the road.

The operator reacted to the sudden change; the involuntary turn away from the truck forcing the bike onto its side.

The sounds of screeching metal and shattering glass, the violence of a high-speed impact, echoed in the street. A cloud of dust and smoke obscured Armstrong's view. The odor of fuel, hot oil, and burning tires enveloped him.

The force of the impact separated the driver from the bike and his right foot from his leg. Sliding and tumbling along the roadway, the former driver came to rest against the curb. He was unconscious and in no condition to try to escape.

The passenger did not fare as well.

The momentum tossed the passenger headfirst into the side of the tow truck. With a helmet, recovering the pieces of his shattered skull would be simpler. Without the helmet, the head disintegrated.

There was a benefit to the lack of a helmet- instantaneous death.

* * *

Keira heard the crash and pulled onto Commercial Way.

Sergeant Armstrong, at first cursing the tow truck, now realized it solved the problem. An unorthodox, yet effective, solution.

Josh arrived in time to see the bike go over and the resulting death and mayhem.

Chubby White, ecstatic with his intervention, was less so with the sizable dent and blood on his tow truck.

Josh pulled up to Keira. She stood next to the truck, shaking. He hugged her and looked her over. "You okay?"

"No, I am not okay. I start out my day chased by a gunman. That's not okay."

Josh looked in the truck. "What, no coffee for me?"

Keira punched him in the back and held him tighter. "Interesting life we lead isn't it?" as her shaking subsided.

A few moments later, Chief Brennan arrived on the scene with just about every on-duty, and some off-duty, officers.

"You okay?" Brennan asked.

"Fine Chief, fine," Josh answered.

"Not you, I meant Keira. I don't care about you. I can see you're alright."

"I'm fine, Chief," Keira said, forcing a smile.

Brennan hugged her. "We'll sort this out. Why don't you let Lieutenant Akerley drive you to the station? We're going to need a statement. I'll have your car brought there for you."

Keira nodded and walked with the Lieutenant to his car.

Chief Winston Franklin Brennan served as Chief of the East Providence Police for the past 15 years. Even in small cities like East Providence, weird stuff happened, but nothing like this.

"What the hell happened, Josh?" Brennan asked.

Josh told the Chief what he knew.

Brennan waved for Sergeant Armstrong to come over, Chubby in tow. "Listen to me, gentlemen," Brennan said. "This means you too, Chubby," grabbing the man's arm, stopping his waving to the gathering media. "I am going to try to put a lid on this. We need to keep this out of the news until we figure out what's going on."

"How we gonna do that, Chief?" Armstrong asked. "You know some asshole in the PD is gonna try to win points by giving them the story."

"Here's how," Brennan said. "I'll tell them it was a carjacking gone bad. The two guys on the bike tried to steal Keira's car and she managed to get away. We let them know one of them was a gang banger. They'll buy that. The problem is controlling the story about our dead mystery man. We'll just have to keep a tight hold on anything we find out until they lose interest. Any ideas?"

"Let's make Chubby the hero," Josh said. "He did stop them. Let them focus on our friend here until something else happens."

"Hmm, that might work. We can hope for a murder in Providence or a State Senator getting locked up for drunk driving to draw their attention away," Brennan said. "Okay, I'll deal with this. You two go figure out what the hell happened here."

The Chief turned to Chubby. "Chubby my boy, you are about to have your fifteen minutes of fame. But I need you to remember something."

"What's that?" Chubby said, the smile covering his whole face.

"You keep to this story," Brennan said. "You heard the scanner about the motorcycle chasing Keira, that they tried to steal her car and had a gun, and you were trying to block them from catching her. Is that clear?"

Chubby looked confused.

"Is there a problem, Chubby?" the Chief asked.

9

"Ah, no. I mean, what else would I say?" Chubby replied.

Josh and Armstrong chuckled.

Brennan shook his head, "That's my boy. You have police supervisor material in you, if you ever pass the physical. Come on. Let's go meet your adoring fans."

Armstrong and Josh watched as the two headed toward the cameras, Chubby raising his hands like a champion boxer.

Then they tried to put the pieces together.

Josh looked at Armstrong. "This is quite the little mess, isn't it?"

"I'm glad Chubby took 'em out. I just washed my cruiser," Armstrong laughed. "And, it's less paperwork for me."

The results of the investigation, one unidentified dead guy and one living MS-13 gang member. The gang banger no longer had two feet to stand on with his 'some assembly required' leg. They also recovered an unusual handgun none recognized, with no serial numbers and of an unknown make and caliber.

What they had, in Sergeant Armstrong's words, was a giant nightmarish shit show.

The Medical Examiner, Dr. Edwin Porter, arrived and processed the body. One of his latest toys was a live-scan fingerprint system equipped with a secure link to the FBI database.

The ME lifted the right hand and scanned each finger. He tried to do the same with the left hand. Two of the fingers no longer bore enough tissue, so he settled for the thumb and two remaining fingers.

A short time later, the preliminary inquiry produced no match.

"I'll run a more in-depth database query when we do the autopsy," Dr. Porter said. "Sometimes we get lucky with military or foreign data."

"Military? Foreign?" Josh asked, as he and Armstrong looked at the ME.

"My guess is he's Latvian or Ukrainian by the tattoos on his neck and what's left of his hand." The medical examiner smiled, "Won't be counting to ten anymore."

Josh watched as the ME bagged the man's fingers.

What the hell is going on? This doesn't happen here. This is East Providence, not New York.

Chapter 2

One month earlier
Wednesday, August 12, 2009
8:00 AM
East Providence, Rhode Island

Josh walked into his office. Before he sat down, the phone rang. *Christ, I haven't even had coffee yet. Bad sign.*

"Special Investigations Unit, Lieutenant Williams."

"Wow, big words now. What's wrong with just SIU? You think you're some big freaking deal now?"

"Hey Cheeks, to what do I owe the honor of this call?"

Josh listened as retired Detective Lieutenant Chris Hamlin laughed on the other end of the line.

"Can I buy you a drink after work? I should say, once you leave the PD after pretending to work."

"Oh shit," Josh replied, "this is going to cost me more than the price of a drink, isn't it? I've gotta start paying attention to caller ID."

"Now, now, my former protégé, have I ever steered you wrong?"

Josh replied, "I don't think I need to answer."

"I kept you out of prison."

"Well, to be more accurate, you pointed me toward an attorney who did. However, I won't argue semantics. Where will you be?"

"Amsterdam's on South Main work for you?"

"Oh shit, this is bad. Should I bring a fake passport and unnumbered weapons?"

"Nothing of the kind, just looking for a little help," Chris answered. "Not to worry."

"You know what Brennan says about those three words."

"Oh yeah, okay. Slight worry," Chris added. "See you there."

* * *

Josh left the SIU office at 5pm, heading to Providence. He wondered what this little favor for Chris would entail.

Chris Hamlin retired from the East Providence PD two years ago. This opened a Lieutenant's position and the job of SIU commander. Josh worked with Hamlin for several years as her assistant commander and now ran the SIU. It was, he believed, the best job in the world.

After retiring, Chris opened a private investigations company called Alpha Babes Investigations. The agency was a consortium of three women, Chris, Vera Johnson, and Margaret 'Maggie' Fleming. The last two made rather unusual private investigators.

Vera Johnson retired after thirty-five years as a librarian for the City of East Providence. Vera and Chris served together in Vietnam treating and transporting the wounded. Margaret Fleming resigned as an Assistant United States attorney after Josh's civil rights trial, citing her unwillingness to work for the former US Attorney, now Senator, Robert Michael Collucci.

The trio developed the idea over a dinner fueled by several Ketel One martinis. It became one of the most successful PI firms in the state. They handled cases ranging from the standard domestic fare to international clients.

Josh parked on South Main Street. He walked several blocks to Amsterdam's, a small, pub-style restaurant. The pub offered seating along the river.

As he entered the pub, he spied several Judges sitting at the bar. One of the Judges waved, the others looked and then turned away. The rest of the crowd was a mixture of people solving the world's problems.

Josh ordered a glass of wine and found a table outside, along the river. He preferred being outside enjoying the waning afternoon sun warming the view of the walkway and riverfront, a central part of the Providence Renaissance.

Chris and Vera walked into the pub, and then spotted him through the window. Walking over, they sat with him.

"Nice of you to make it, Cheeks," Josh said. "Don't worry, I got my own drink."

"Poor boy," Chris answered, "I see you found a spot away from all your friends inside. Nobody invite you to join them?"

Josh laughed. "Bastards almost ran out when they saw me."

"Well, can you blame them?" Chris smiled, "You do associate with an unsavory defense lawyer who helped you beat the rap."

Josh shook his head and smiled, "Okay, you've dragged me down to your part of the world, what, pray tell, do you need?"

Chris looked at Vera and nodded.

"Josh," Vera spoke, leaning on the table, "I am the one who needs the favor. It's my niece I want to help."

Josh looked at Vera, "Anything you need, Vera. If I can help, I'll be happy to."

"You might want to hear the whole story first," Chris added.

Josh looked at Chris and back at Vera. "Okay Vera, let's send Swiss Cheeks here for drinks, I think she can handle that, and you can tell me the story."

Chris earned the nickname, 'Swiss Cheeks', during a violent confrontation with two armed robbery suspects. A fellow officer accidentally shot her. The bullet left several extra holes in her ass. Few could call her that; Josh was one of the few exceptions. She flipped Josh the bird and headed into the bar.

Josh turned to Vera, "Tell on, my lady, tell on."

Vera smiled, sat back in the chair, and looked out at the river, "How old are you, Josh?"

Josh's face grimaced, "Old enough to listen to anything you have to say, I hope."

"No, I mean... indulge me. How old are you?"

"Thirty-seven."

"A mere babe...," Vera replied. "Okay, then you wouldn't remember this story. So, I have to give you some background."

"I am all ears," Josh answered.

Chris returned with the drinks and sat next to Josh.

"I was just about to give him a history lesson, so he understands the background," Vera said.

"Talk slow and use small words," Chris answered.

"Nice," Josh added, "this from an old, shriveled up, prune of a former cop."

"Okay listen," Vera began. "About three months ago my niece, Loren, came to me asking for help in finding information about her biological father. Her mother died, and she wanted to know more about her dad. Chris and I tracked down some information," taking a sip from her drink. "Does the name Darnell Grey mean anything to you?"

Josh shook his head.

"Providence Police arrested Darnell back in 1972 for a series of rapes and a murder. He never made it to trial. Two inmates beat him to death in the prison."

"So, what do you need me for?" Josh asked.

"How about you speak when we ask you to?" Chris interjected.

"Oops, sorry I'll remain silent your majesty," Josh answered, bowing his head.

"That's a good boy."

"This will take all day if both of you don't shut up," Vera added.

Josh looked at Chris, "I see this one has some teeth to her. I hope she's had all her shots."

Vera laughed and returned to the story. "I remembered her father from way back. Loren isn't my real niece. Her mother Chantel and I were close, and I always thought of Loren as a niece. Over the years, we lost touch. I think her husband's arrest for those terrible crimes embarrassed her. She didn't want it to affect her daughter."

Chris picked up the story.

"We contacted the AG's office and the Providence Journal. The AG's said the file was missing. The Journal gave us a ton of information on the cases. There was a lot of fear in the community," putting her drink down.

"The first one occurred in Providence, near Brown. The next two happened in East Providence. The last one started with a kidnapping in Pawtucket," leaning forward in her chair, elbows on the table. "Providence PD got a call for a suspicious car near the Brown University boathouse. When the officers arrived, they spotted the suspect rolling the body into the river. One officer went in the water to get the body; the other chased the guy down and arrested him."

"Okay, so you guys have your niece, right?"

Vera nodded.

"And you find out daddy got killed in prison. What do you want from me, to give her the bad family tree lesson?"

"No," Vera answered. "We think there is more to this."

"Oh, of course you do," Josh answered, hands spread out. "You want me to work on a thirty-seven-year-old case with a dead suspect? Hmm, sounds like fun. It's not even our case, Chris."

"Yes, it is," Chris said. "Two of the rapes occurred in East Providence and, since no one was convicted, it is still an open case."

Josh chuckled. "I can hear Chief Brennan now," rising in his seat to attention, hands flat on the table. "So, Lieutenant, let me understand. You want to reopen a case from before you were born, with a dead suspect, why?"

"Don't tell him," Chris smiled.

"Oh sure, that's a great idea. I enjoy working midnights. Are you nuts?"

"Look, all we need is for you to pull the old case files, so we can go over them. If Darnell did it, so be it. But if he didn't, I'd like to give Loren a better memory of her father."

"All you need me to do…," Josh rested his chin in his hand. "Okay, let's say I pull the files and you find something, then what?"

"Then you'll help us, won't you?" Chris answered.

Vera reached over, taking Josh's hand. Josh saw tears in her eyes. "Come on Josh, nobody understands searching for the truth more than you."

"How many times did you rehearse this?" Josh replied.

"Rehearse?" Vera smiled. "I would never do that, Josh."

"You might not, but she would," pointing at Chris.

"We need your help," Vera said.

Josh looked out at the river. *Vera was right; the truth won my acquittal.* He knew he had no choice, but it would come with a price.

"Okay, I'll pull the files. Give me a day or so."

"Told you the teary eyes would work," Vera said, laughing. "He's such a soft, sentimental type."

"Played by a couple of pros, wasn't I?" Josh said.

"You, my former protégé, are putty in our hands. That and your wife told us how."

"My wife conspired against me with the witches of Alpha Babes Investigations. So touching." Josh took a long drink as he looked at his two friends. *I would do anything for them, no matter the cost.*

Chapter 3

Thirty-Seven years ago
March 23, 1972
12:30 PM
 East Providence, Rhode Island

Darnell Grey was an angry man.

Rubbing his fist, wiping off the blood, he stormed out of the Warren Avenue Shell station. He would not be back. The rage, taking control of him once again, made sure of it.

His wife would not be happy.

He wouldn't let them push him around. Nobody pushed him around. He'd find another goddamn job.

He knew he needed to control this anger. Yet the nightmares haunted him still. Sounds of the Ia Drang Valley echoed in his head, robbing him of sleep, depriving him of any sense of peace.

No one understood.

All they saw was an angry black man.

Darnell Grey was an angry man, with good reason.

Chapter 4

March 23, 1972
7:30 PM
Detectives Squad Room
Major Crimes
Providence Police Headquarters
Providence, Rhode Island

The two Providence detectives dragged Darnell Grey into the squad room. Pushing him onto a wooden bench, they handcuffed him to a pipe attached to the front. Old blood, sweat, and other unidentifiable stains covered the bench and wall.

Grey sagged in the seat, one eye swollen shut, dried blood on his cheeks. The side of his head a purplish-blotchy discoloration, hair matted down; his body wracked in shaking spasms of fear.

The lead detective, George Weslyan, went to his desk and typed out the complaint forms.

"That the stovepipe that killed the girl?" the Detective Commander, Captain Anthony Gemma, asked.

"Yeah," Detective Alfred Georgiana answered. "Uniforms grabbed him trying to run from the stolen car. Piece of shit just dumped the body." He lashed out, kicking Grey in the legs, causing him to recoil back, straining at the handcuffs, the fear rising in his face. None of the other detectives in the smoky squad room paid much attention, beyond a couple of chuckles.

"Get the lineup paperwork done and take him down to the cellblock until we're ready," the captain ordered. "No phone calls. Let the intake center deal with it."

Georgiana stood in front of Grey. "So, asshole, you like fucking white broads, huh?" slapping Grey across the face.

Grey looked up, his one good eye glaring. "I told you man, I had nothing to do with that girl. That uniform guy came running up to me and grabbed me. I was just sitting there, doin' nothin'."

"We'll see about that, asshole. We got witnesses put you there. You're going away for a long fucking time."

"I want a lawyer," Grey demanded.

The detective turned and smiled at his partner, "He wants a lawyer. You hear him? This piece of shit wants a lawyer," turning, he grabbed Grey by the throat. "And who's gonna pay for it, nigger. You want it for nuttin', don't you? Fucking mulignan, no fucking mouthpiece for you here. We own your ass, like the good 'ole days."

The complaint finished, the detectives unhooked Grey from the pipe. Cuffing him in the back, holding the man's handcuffed hands high behind him, they forced Grey to bend forward at the waist. The detectives paraded him through the squad room. "Anybody interested in a broken-down nigger?" Weslyan asked, laughing. "I'll sell 'em cheap. No? Okay, then off to the cages he goes with the rest of the monkeys," heading out of the office.

The entertainment over, the other investigators returned to their reports.

Hauling Grey into the cellblock, they stood him in front of the booking desk. The sergeant in charge glanced up, looking him over. "Have rescue come take a look at him," he ordered, returning to his newspaper.

"Sarge, the asshole killed a white girl and raped a couple of others. Screw him, no rescue."

"Oh, this is the prick, huh?" the sergeant replied, now more interested. "In that case, put him in A-5. Are you guys doing a lineup?"

"Yeah, just waiting on East Providence PD to bring their victim here. She's a cop's kid, a retired trooper."

"No shit?" the sergeant said. "We should just give the trooper a few minutes alone with the cocksucker. Save us all some headaches."

Weslyan removed the handcuffs and pushed Grey into the cell. Closing the door, he looked up and pointed above door. Georgiana looked and saw the words *Monkey Exhibit* written there.

"Perfect," he smiled.

* * *

Two hours later, Weslyan and Georgiana brought back Grey from the cellblock and took him to the lineup area. They put him in the first position. Five other black men completed the array.

"What about the blood and the swollen eye?" the assistant AG, Robert Collucci, asked. "A potential problem don't you think?"

"Want me to go smack the other five?" a detective suggested.

"No," Collucci replied, "Go clean him up first."

A short time later, the prosecutor's concerns satisfied, the lineup was ready.

Five men waited in the viewing area, Collucci, two detectives, the uniform officer who arrested Grey, and Captain Gemma.

Two East Providence PD detectives came in with the twenty-five-year-old victim from one of their cases. Collucci explained the procedure as they opened the curtain covering the view window into the lineup room.

The victim, Sheila Monson, looked at the six men. She studied them, one by one. "I'm not sure; I don't think he's there."

Collucci looked at the Providence detectives and shook his head.

The door to the witness area opened, slamming into the wall. The victim's father, retired Rhode Island State Police Lieutenant Alfred Monson, barged in. "Which one is it, Sheila? Just tell me. Which one?"

"Why is he here?" Collucci asked.

"Hey," Monson said, stepping toward Collucci, fists clenched. "This is my daughter that piece of shit attacked. You wanna try to keep me out of here? Go ahead, try."

Captain Gemma stepped between the two.

Collucci backed up, raising his hands, "Okay, okay. Just let her look them over. We don't want the lineup thrown out." Turning back to Sheila he said, "Take a good look again, Miss. Take your time."

Monson looked again, shaking her head, "I'm not sure. It might be number three, but I can't...I'm just not sure." Looking to her father for help, all she saw was his disappointment and rage.

"Give me a minute with her," Alfred Monson said. "She's just nervous."

Collucci looked at Captain Gemma. He shrugged his shoulders, nodded, and they both walked out. Monson and his daughter walked to the squad room. The two Providence detectives followed, standing with Monson as he talked to her.

Weslyan tapped the father on the shoulder and made a head movement to follow him. As they walked outside to the hallway, Captain Gemma saw them, raising an eyebrow. Weslyan smiled. "No problem, Captain. We're all set now."

Gemma walked away and Weslyan turned to Monson. "Tell her to pick number three. She thought he was the guy. I'll move the son-of-a-bitch to the third spot. No problem."

Monson smiled. "Thanks, can I have five minutes with the asshole after?"

"I'd love to, but that fucking AG would shit himself."

"What about him?" Monson asked, motioning toward Gemma's office. "He gonna be good with a second look?"

'What second look?" Weslyan replied. "Only one lineup happened here, that's what the reports will say."

22

Returning to the squad room, Monson sat next to his daughter, speaking to her in a soft, yet insistent tone. She looked at him, wide-eyed, afraid. "But I wasn't sure."

"Yes, you were, Sheila. You were just nervous. You don't want that piece of shit to get away with this do you?"

Sheila shook her head, "No, of course not. But I want to be sure."

"I'm sure," Monson said. "Go back in there. You know what to do. Listen to me Sheila; do the right thing for once in your life."

Weslyan came back into the squad room. "All set Sheila, come on back and take a look."

The group returned to the lineup viewing area, Collucci and Captain Gemma absent this time.

Two minutes later, Weslyan and Georgiana took Grey back to the cellblock.

"She didn't pick me out, did she?" Grey said. "She couldn't, I didn't do nothin'. I wasn't there."

Weslyan smiled, "She picked you out, asshole. We made sure of that."

* * *

Detective Weslyan called the shift commander. He asked for a wagon to transport Grey to the Adult Correctional Institute, known as the ACI. A short time later, two young Providence patrol officers walked into the cellblock.

Grey, chained to a wall, face bruised and swollen, watched the officers. There was blood on his shirt. He was having difficulty breathing.

"Hey, Sarge. What's up?" one of the officers asked.

"Take that fucking stovepipe over to the hospital," the sergeant ordered, looking up from his desk. "Tell the ER doc to just clean him up. When the ER's done with him, take him to the prison," handing the officer some paperwork.

The younger of the two officers walked over to Grey. He looked at the man's injuries, "What the hell happened to him?"

The sergeant slammed his hands on the desk and rose from his seat. On the job 35 years, he didn't feel the need to explain anything to this snot-nosed, slick-sleeved, boot patrol officer. Backing the officer into the wall, he smiled. "He fell down. Twice. That fucking okay with you?"

The officer swallowed hard and said, "Ah, yeah, sure. The hospital's gonna ask how this happened. I didn't know what to tell them."

"How about you don't tell 'em a goddamn thing, stand there like a dope and smile. Think you can handle that? Just let them patch 'em up. Now get the hell out."

At the hospital, the charge nurse took one look at Grey and called for the resident on-duty. "I am not letting any of my nurses near this. That man needs to be admitted and the two cops are insisting they're not leaving here without him."

"I'll deal with it," the resident answered.

The doctor examined Grey and then called the officers outside the exam room. "Listen to me. I do not care what some sergeant at the police department thinks. I am admitting that man," turning from the officers and reentering the exam room.

The officer got on his portable radio and told the shift commander.

Fifteen minutes later, Detective Weslyan and another detective charged into the ER. The uniform officer pointed to the exam room. Throwing the curtain back, Weslyan had a short and angry exchange with the resident. The pasty white looking resident left the room, went to the desk, and spoke to the charge nurse. She glared at the officers, shook her head, and turned away.

Weslyan had Grey back in cuffs and pushed him toward the uniforms. Turning to the young detective he said, "See, nothing to it. We decide, not some fucking fairy doctor."

* * *

The Providence paddy wagon pulled into the sally port area of the ACI Inmate Intake Center. Dragging Grey from the back of the van, he fell to the floor in front the admitting desk.

Glancing over the desk, the guard looked at Grey. "Let me guess, unpaid parking violations?" laughing at his own humor.

"Nope, rape and murder," the officer answered.

"No shit?" the guard answered. "Okay, got my paperwork?"

After handing the guard the forms, removed the handcuffs. Two guards came out of the backroom and took Grey. The officers headed back to their van.

"Well, that was a fun field trip. What say we stop somewhere for coffee and kill the rest of the shift?"

"Sounds good to me, as long as I don't have to deal with that fucking sergeant anymore." The young officer looked out the window, "So do you think he did it?"

"What do ya' mean? Of course he did."

"I heard the guys in detectives talking; the girl got coached by her father and they did two lineups."

"So what?"

The officer didn't answer. *If I ever get to detectives, I ain't doin' this shit.*

Chapter 5

August 12, 2009 7:00 PM
East Providence Police Headquarters
East Providence, Rhode Island

Josh returned to the East Providence PD headquarters after his meeting with Vera and Chris. *No better time to poke around old files than in a closed Records division.*

Unlocking the archive storage room, he searched through the case files. After an hour, he'd found some of the investigative reports. Placing the files in his briefcase, he walked out into the corridor and back to his office.

He read the file, fascinated by the differences in the language used. Case reports were different back then. One report, by Joe McDaniel of all people, caught his eye.

Joe McDaniel was a legend in the department. Josh, and many other cops, learned a great deal from working with him. McDaniel had retired six months ago. Josh made a note to call him about the case.

After an hour of reading, he realized how hungry he felt. This was usually a late night for his wife, but he thought he'd take a shot and see if she'd like dinner.

Picking up the phone, he called her.

"Law offices, Keira Williams."

"Hey, how you doing?"

"Fine, sitting here reading files and you?"

"Funny you should ask," he answered. "I am doing the same, reading a case file. Want to meet for dinner, or should we try to cook at home?"

"That would involve shopping; I'll let you take me to dinner. I can leave here in five minutes. Bonefish okay? Meet you there."

Josh packed up the files and headed out the door. *Nobody better to discuss a screwed-up police file than my wife. Her Innocence Project work might be just what I need for this.*

Arriving at the restaurant, they sat at a table in the corner.

"Tell me about this case that commands your attention," Keira said.

"A thirty-seven-year-old rape case in East Providence with two victims. Connected to two other rapes and a murder in Providence."

"A bit of a history lesson isn't it? What spurred your interest?"

"This is the case Vera and Chris asked me about. You told them how to get me to help them."

"I thought it was just to find some info on her niece's father," she laughed.

"Yeah, well. Nothing is ever easy with those two. Would you look at the file for me? Your perspective might be helpful."

Keira feigned shock, hand covering her mouth. "Are my ears deceiving me? You want my perspective. The jaundiced, distrusting, suspicious of anything official view?"

"Yeah, because if you don't see anything wrong, then it's not there."

Keira's work with the Innocence Project had sometimes caused issues between them, some of them severe. No one understood how they remained together. But they did. It worked for them.

"Well, my dear, I'd be happy to look them over for you. What do I get for this?" her smile having the wanted effect.

"The fee is negotiable," returning the smile. "Perhaps a retainer after dinner?"

"My retainer needs are high."

Josh laughed. "I'll see if I can measure up."

"I'll be the judge of that," reaching over and taking his hand.

Chapter 6

Friday, August 14, 2009
9:00 AM
Alpha Babes Investigations
Providence, RI

Two days later, Josh and Keira met with Chris Hamlin and Vera Johnson at their office. Just as they began the discussion, Maggie Fleming came in.

"Well, this seems like quite the group. Can I join in?" Fleming asked.

"Grab a coffee and sit down, Maggie." Chris said. "We're going over the case for Vera's niece."

After getting coffee, Maggie joined the group as Keira reviewed the case.

"First, the witness statements from the civilians are terrible. They saw a shadow run by, nothing more. None of them could identify Grey. There is no statement from the first victim. The primary investigator reports the victim's identification of Grey in the Providence case. There is no mention of a lineup; all the detective's report says is the victim identified Grey from a picture. I'd say that's dubious at best." She finished her coffee, raising her cup to Josh for more.

"Hmm," Chris said, smiling, "maybe she has found something useful Josh can do," raising her cup. "Oh waiter, I will take some more as well."

"Get your own f'ing--"

"Josh," Keira interrupted, "be a good boy and do as you're told."

Josh shook his head and went to get the coffee.

"You have to show me the trick," Chris said.

"Don't you dare," Josh yelled.

"Sorry, just for me," Keira smiled. "Look at this, another East Providence detective's report. All he says is the victim identified Grey in the Providence lineup," handing the lineup copy to show around. "Grey's face shows evidence of a beating. The other five aren't even close in stature or appearance. I'd love to talk to the AG who handled this lineup."

Josh returned, handing out the coffees. "Who was the AG?"

"There are initials, but I can't make them out. Maybe we can find someone from that time who might know who they belong to?" Keira replied.

"I know someone I can ask," Chris said. "George Tucker was a special assistant back then. He might know."

"Tucker, as in the Presiding Justice of the Supreme Court? The one who just received the Thurgood Marshall Memorial Award for Judicial Excellence?" Josh asked.

"That would be him," Chris said.

"Well, he might recognize the initials, but I doubt he'd know anything about the case. You know what they call him right?" Josh asked.

"No, I don't," Chris said.

"When they tried to transfer all the black gang members from the prison to other states, he ruled against them. He ordered the prisoners returned to the ACI. They gave him the nickname Reverse Oreo."

"Oh my God," Chris said.

"He's right," Maggie Fleming said. "I've heard it as well. He has a huge reputation in the civil rights area. Some people think he's gone too far on many decisions. The Reverse Oreo nickname caught on."

"That's so nice," Keira added, shaking her head. "Look, you need the Providence PD file to be certain, but I'd say this has all the earmarks of a railroading by the police. You have a conveniently available black guy and all white victims. If this were a conviction case I think the Innocence Project would take it." Turning to Josh, "Didn't you say one of the victims was the daughter of a police officer?"

The three other women turned to Josh, wide-eyed.

"Yeah, I recognized the name from when my father was on the State Police. Sheila Monson was the daughter of a retired State Police Lieutenant, Alfred Monson."

"I am surprised Grey made it as far as the prison," Chris said.

"Okay," Josh said. "I think I can get the file from Providence. I'll tell them some bullshit story about writing a book or something."

"Ha, writing a book?" Chris chuckled, "Shouldn't you read one before you write one?"

All the women laughed, although Keira tried to hide it.

Josh just looked at them. "Nice group I've got here. Anyway, I know someone who may be helpful. I'll reach out to him. Next, we need to talk to Tucker. Chris, since you know him, you and I will do that. Maggie, how about you dig around the prosecution community. Vera see if you can find news stories on what happened at the prison."

"Sound good?" Not waiting for a response Josh stood, glancing at Chris. He took two quick steps toward the door. Chris took a drink of her coffee and spit it back into the cup.

"The son-of-a-bitch put salt in it," trying to get around the table at Josh.

Josh opened the door. "Was that salt? So sorry my friend," slamming the door behind him.

Chris looked at Keira, the others were laughing. "You still have serious work to do on him."

Keira smiled. "I know, but he can be funny sometimes."

Chapter 7

Monday, August 17, 2009
2:30 PM
Rumford, Rhode Island

Giovanni 'Fatso' Bellofatto, the consigliere of the Patriarca crime family, was not your typical mobster. Bellofatto, educated and stylish, prided himself on his sophistication. He mirrored the style of John Gotti; designer suits, $500 haircuts. He admired Gotti's manner and tried to copy it. He once served as a conduit to New York during the time Gotti was killing his way to mob leadership. The difference was Bellofatto's fondness for food and loathing of exercise. Gotti was the Teflon Don. Fatso was the Donut Don.

In 1969, Bellofatto went to prison for conspiracy to commit murder for the execution-style slaying of two bookies. His conviction secured his position within the organization's hierarchy. The bookies made the error of refusing to pay protection money to the family. Bellofatto took the hit and made his bones.

The informant who testified disappeared into the Witness Protection program. He resurfaced in California trying to return to his old habits. His bullet-ridden body, absent a tongue, washed up on the shore of a lake outside Los Angeles several months later. State Police suspected two people of killing the informant. One was a frequent visitor of Bellofatto's in the prison the other, one of Bellofatto's soldiers. Authorities charged no one in the informant's murder.

In 1973, Bellofatto's lawyer lobbied the General Assembly to approve a request by the Governor to pardon Bellofatto on humanitarian grounds. The lawyer, who would someday become the Presiding Justice of the Rhode Island Supreme Court, had persuaded the Governor, his former law partner, to seek a pardon for Bellofatto.

The attorney argued that the diagnosis of terminal pancreatic cancer was a death sentence. The diagnosis, rendered by the state's own prison physician, confirmed by the medical reports. The attorney's emotional plea garnered much sympathy for Bellofatto. The Bishop of the Diocese of Providence testified before the General Assembly in support. He touted Bellofatto's generous support of the Church and genuine remorse for his past.

The Governor issued the pardon on a Friday afternoon before a long holiday weekend. By Monday, it was yesterday's news.

Days after his release, a fire in the prison hospital ward destroyed the records. The prison doctor left state employment a short time after the fire. Claiming an inheritance from a distant relative, he retired to a Caribbean island.

Bellofatto remains one of the longest known survivors of this fatal prognosis. He credited his longevity to his fervent prayer for intercession from the Heavenly Saints.

Only in Rhode Island is such a miraculous intercession possible.

The patron saint of Rhode Island. Saint 'I-Know-a-Guy.'

Josh had several encounters with Bellofatto over the years. Fatso owned an Italian restaurant on Pawtucket Avenue, near Bay View Academy. The restaurant was a favorite of Academy parents for birthday and graduation celebrations. Fatso's twin daughters graduated from the school in 1968. The school benefited from Bellofatto's generous donations.

Josh drove to Bellofatto's home in the Rumford section of the city. Bellofatto's home was huge, but not ostentatious. No marble statues of nymphs peeing in the pool or lions guarding the driveway. It is a Victorian style mansion, secluded by surrounding woodlands along the Turner Reservoir. Equipped with better security than the White House, the house was a virtual fortress.

Josh pulled up to the security camera at the front gate and pushed the call button. The camera zoomed in on him and, a moment later, the gate swung open. *No need to ask why I'm here. This guy is a piece of work.*

Pulling up to the covered portico, Josh saw Fatso, and his bodyguard, waiting on the front steps.

Josh got out of the car.

"Sergeant Williams, how are you?" Bellofatto asked.

"It's Lieutenant now, Mr. Bellofatto," Josh answered. "I am well. And you?"

"Lieutenant, ah, a well-deserved promotion. Please, call me Gino. We are among friends here, I hope." Trying to gauge Josh's behavior and body language, Bellofatto was cautious but charming.

"Gino, I was hoping to speak with you in private for a moment," eyeing the muscle, who was staring him down.

"This is as private as it gets, Lieutenant. Speak freely."

Josh gave the bodyguard one last look, "I was hoping I could test your memory. In 1972, while you were in the ACI, they brought a guy in, a black guy, on a rape and murder beef. Two inmates beat him to death a few days later. Do you recall the incident?"

Bellofatto made a slight motion with his head and the muscle walked inside the home. "Is this of an investigative nature? That would affect my memory," Bellofatto smiled.

"This is off the record." Josh answered. "I am asking for a friend. They tried and convicted the inmates responsible. It's not about you. Just looking for background info." He saw the bodyguard watching from the front window.

"In that case, yeah I remember when they killed the mulignan. Bastard deserved it," Bellofatto replied.

"The what?"

"Mulignan, it's Italian slang for eggplant. A nicer form of nigger if you will," smiling at Josh.

"Ah. So, did you hear anything about why an inmate held for trial was in the general population, especially a rapist?"

Bellofatto paused a moment, studying Josh. "Let's just say none of the guards worried too much about following procedures," Bellofatto said, "or what would happen to the guy," folding his arms and smiling. "I heard someone in the State Police put the arm on the warden to make it happen. We all have our ways. You have yours and we have ours. You have to remember, those were different times."

Josh listened, taking in the information. "So, you think it was intentional?"

"What I think doesn't matter. They put the guy out there and let nature take its course. Far as I can see, it worked. Son-of-a-bitch raped a bunch of white women and killed one," hesitating a moment, eyes narrowing. "Or he didn't and you're out to find out who did."

"Something like that."

"If you did your research, then you'd know the rapes stopped after the guy was caught. The cops made a big deal out of it. They acted as if they caught the Boston Strangler. You're sure he wasn't the one?"

"Let's just say there is some doubt. About a month after they arrested Grey, Massachusetts State Police made an arrest in Seekonk. They grabbed a guy in an attempted rape at the Ramada Inn. The guy matched the description of the suspect in the RI cases."

"Well," Bellofatto smiled, "you know them mulignans all look alike."

Josh shook his head. "Thanks, Mr. Bello...ah, Gino. I appreciate the information."

Bellofatto nodded, "Look, no one appreciates the cops looking to help an innocent guy more than me. If the mulignan," pausing a moment, "sorry, force of habit. If the guy didn't do it then I hope you can help out whoever you're doing this for."

"It's his daughter," Josh answered. "She'd like to know he wasn't a rapist and murderer."

Bellofatto nodded and motioned for the bodyguard to open the security gate, the conversation was over.

Josh went back to his car and headed out. As he pulled onto the roadway, his cell phone beeped with a text message from a blocked number. "Ask Jimmy Calise from Providence PD."

Guy is a piece of work.

Chapter 8

Tuesday, August 18, 2009
8:30AM
East Providence Police Headquarters
East Providence, Rhode Island

Chief Brennan was reviewing files when his assistant paged him. "Lieutenant Williams is here to see you, Chief."

"Send him in, Donna."

Josh walked into the Chief's office and sat on the ledge near the window. "How's your day going, El Jefe?" he asked, smiling.

"Up until a moment ago fine," Brennan answered. "Now, I am not so sure."

"Well, good news for a change."

"I'll be the judge of that."

"Okay, I was wondering if you had a problem with me taking some unplanned time off. I know the requests are supposed to be fifteen days ahead of the date, but I found some cheap flights to Fort Myers. I figure Keira and I can use some time away."

Brennan smiled. Williams was a favorite son of his and he was happy to hear things were back on track with the young couple. "If it means you'll be out of my hair, then by all means go. Go now if you like. But please, go."

"Thanks boss, I'll miss you too."

Josh walked out of the office. *One down, one to go. Now to convince Keira to take the time.*

Stopping at the aide's desk on the way out, Josh asked, "Hey Donna, how do I convince my wife to take time off to go with me to Fort Myers Beach?"

"Try asking," Donna replied. "I bet it would be a good place to start."

"Genius," Josh answered, "You are a true genius."

Josh called Keira on his cell as he walked back to the SIU.

"Hey, what's up?" she answered.

"Are you busy?"

"Not at all, just finished a motion I argue tomorrow. Why?"

"I want to take you to dinner," Josh said.

"Uh-oh, what did you do now?"

"Nothing, can't I just decide to take you to dinner without raising suspicions?"

"Not usually, but I'll give you the benefit of the doubt. Where would you like to go?"

"How about the Canfield House in Newport?"

"Now I know you did something spectacular. Okay, what's up? "

"Trust me, you're gonna enjoy this."

"I can't wait. When will you be here?"

"Five okay?" Josh answered.

"Will that give you enough time to think of an excuse for whatever it is you did?"

"Hey, have some faith in me will ya."

"I know you too well Mr. Williams, too well. See you later."

* * *

Arriving at Keira's office just before 5:00 PM, Josh walked toward the front entrance. As he got to the door, his cell rang. Looking at the caller ID, he felt his face turning red. The display read, Kristin Volpe AG's Office. *Uh-oh, not taking that one.* He sent the call to voice mail. When he looked up, Keira was walking toward him.

"Who was that?" she asked.

"Oh, no one, the office. I sent it to voice mail. Tonight, there are no interruptions."

"Oh my god, now I know you did something. Just tell me and get it over with."

"Nothing to tell, but I do have a surprise for you."

"Yeah and… "

"You're going to have to wait until dinner. Keep you in suspense a bit more," Josh said.

"Oh, I cannot wait to hear this one."

A short time later, they sat in the restaurant. Josh ordered a bottle of Cakebread Cellars Chardonnay, Keira kept looking at Josh.

"What?" Josh asked.

"I keep waiting for the bomb to go off," she said. "Cakebread Cellars, dinner at Canfield House, just unbelievable."

"Okay, here it is… " Josh began.

Keira leaned forward. "Shouldn't you remove any sharp objects from my reach?"

Josh shook his head, "No, okay. Just listen, I want to take you to Fort Myers for a week. Take some time off. Just you and me."

Keira looked at him for several moments. "Okay, what have you done with my husband? You are an impostor."

"Okay, okay. You made your point. I should do this more often. So, are you in? Can you take the time to go?"

Keira smiled, "I would love to go. Why Fort Myers? Not that I'm complaining, but it's not on the list for the top ten destinations."

"Ah, yes... um. Well, remember the case I had you look over... "

"I should have known," folding her arms across her chest, leaning back in the chair. "This is a working trip. Unbelievable."

Josh put his hands up, "Just one quick stop to talk to a retired Providence detective sergeant. I don't even know if he'll talk to me. The rest of the time is just us," reaching over and taking Keira's hand. "We don't even have to stay there; we can go anywhere you like."

Keira smiled, and then laughed. "Well, you are improving there, Mr. Williams. I take this as progress. "

Josh smiled back. "Thanks, I knew you'd come around."

Keira smiled, "Wait, what about Cassidy? She doesn't like to be left behind."

"I'll get Chris to stay at the house with her. I'll have to lock up all the liquor, but she's somewhat housebroken," Josh laughed. "The two of them can watch each other. That work?"

"Like I said, it's a good start. You'll need to start planning the next vacation, without any work-related matters, so you can surprise me again on my birthday. Always remember jewelry is your best friend. *David Yurman* in particular; I'll make a list for you."

Chapter 9

Monday, August 24, 2009
11:45 AM
Fort Myers Beach, Florida

The Southwest Airlines flight began its approach to the Fort Myers International Airport. Josh looked up from his iPad. Keira was asleep, lying against his shoulder. Josh nudged her. She opened her eyes.

"Time to stop snoring and put your seat up," Josh said.

"I do not snore," Keira answered, stretching as she adjusted the seat.

"I bet the people in the row behind us would disagree," Josh said, smiling and taking her hand.

"Are we there yet?"

"Just about, I got an email message from Sergeant Calise. He sent me his address, wanted to know when we'd be there."

"Did he ask what it was about?" Keira asked.

"Nope, just said he'd be there all day."

"Hmm, you'd think he'd be curious."

"You would, wouldn't you?" Josh answered. "Oh, and I got a picture from Chris. She took Cassidy to Barrington beach. Look," turning his iPad for Keira to see.

"Oh my god, she's covered in seaweed and sand," Keira said, hand over her mouth. "It will never come out of her fur." Keira smiled and shook her head.

The plane landed, taxied to the gate, and the flight attendant opened the door, jumping out of the way.

Josh and Keira watched as the twenty-seven people who boarded by wheelchairs could retrieve overhead bags and walk from the plane. Known as the *Miracle of the Jetway*, it is the best therapy in the world.

They followed the miraculously healed from the plane, and then found the rental car counter. After getting the car, they headed to Fort Myers Beach.

* * *

Driving across the San Carlos Bridge gave them a spectacular view of the beach and island. Fort Myers Beach is a mix of hotels, motels, condos, houses, beach bars, restaurants, and businesses.

Some of it is the redneck heaven of vacation spots, some of it quiet and reserved.

Jimmy Calise lived alone in a mobile home just outside the area known as Times Square. Josh pulled into the lot and followed the directions to a small, rundown, faded white, rusting trailer.

The front of the trailer overlooked the beach; but the torn awning drooping over the windows blocked the view.

Parked next to the trailer was a 1987 Chevy with RI plates. The car was as rusted as the trailer. It hadn't been in Rhode Island in a long time.

Parking next to the Chevy, Josh got out of the car. "You want to come in with me?" he asked.

"Nah, I'll go walk on the beach. I saw a coffee shop just as we came over the bridge. If you finish first, come get me there. Or I'll just walk back here."

Josh walked to the door of the trailer, watching as Keira strode down to the beach.

Knocking on the door, he heard a voice from inside. "Come on in, Lieutenant."

Josh opened the door and walked in. The inside of the trailer was beautiful; handmade hardwood table and chairs, some oil paintings of the beach, spotless kitchen.

Seeing the reaction, Jimmy Calise said. "I keep the inside nice and let the outside look like shit. Keeps my tax appraisal down. I don't go out much anyway."

Josh nodded. "Smart, I guess. Nice location though, right on the beach."

"It's a pain in season. Too many drunks on the beach and traffic sucks. Not that I drive anywhere much."

"Ah, yeah. I saw the car."

"It runs great. I just use it to go to the liquor store and for food shopping. Speaking of which, you want a drink?" pouring himself a water glass full of rum.

"No thanks, little early for me," Josh replied.

"Used to be for me, I got used to it. Suit yourself," taking a seat on one of the stools near the kitchen counter. He did not offer Josh a seat. "What can I do for you, Lieutenant? I've been gone a long time."

"Josh, please, call me Josh. This isn't anything official. Just doing a favor for a friend."

"Must be a good friend to travel all this way," raising his glass, "So, ask away," his eyes studied Josh's face.

"Do you remember a case, a rape murder investigation, suspect was a guy named Darnell Grey?"

Josh saw the recognition in Calise; eyes squinting, jaw clenched. *He remembers, and he didn't expect this.*

"Yeah, I know the case. Guy raped four women and killed one. What about it?"

"He was killed in prison, couple of weeks after he got locked up. Did you know that?"

"Everybody knew that. Hell, it was the fastest way to deal with the bastard," dropping his eyes to his glass. "Should happen more often."

"Was there anything about the case that, well, wasn't right?" Josh watched for more reaction.

Rubbing the back of his neck, Calise studied Josh for a long moment, "There were always things that weren't right. Witnesses aren't worth shit, can't talk to the suspect without his lawyer, no case was ever perfect."

"But with this one, anything you can think of might help."

"What are you looking for? Why ask about ancient history?" Calise asked, pouring more rum into the glass.

"Grey had a daughter; she wants to know if her father did this. She just wants to know the truth."

"Well, I guess I can understand that. But I don't know how I can help. I was on the job just a few years then. My role was to keep my mouth shut and learn," taking another drink. "That's what I did."

Josh looked past Calise and saw a frame with a Ranger Battalion Emblem and Ranger Tabs.

"Were you a Ranger?" Josh asked.

"101st."

"Did you know Grey was in the 1st Cavalry at Ia Drang Valley in 1965?"

Calise glanced at the picture frame, "No, I didn't... not a good place to be."

"Look, this isn't going to go anywhere except to satisfy his daughter's curiosity. Nobody's gonna get jammed up. She just wants to know the truth."

Calise took a drink, staring into the glass. "Let's just say you should check the lineup reports," looking up at Josh.

"You mean report? There was only one lineup."

A sad smile came across Calise. "That's all I got Lieutenant, all I got... "

Josh walked over and put out his hand. Calise raised his glass but did not try to shake Josh's hand.

Josh went to the door, "Thanks, Sarge. I appreciate your taking the time to see me. There is one more thing."

Calise, half listening, lost in the enigma of remembering and regret, looked up.

"Why would Fatso Bellofatto tell me to come see you?"

Calise eyes narrowed as he fixed Josh in a menacing glare. "You know what used to piss us off? The Rhode Island State Police." The words were deliberate and angry, if slurred.

Josh saw the alcohol fueled rage in Calise's bloodshot eyes.

"They'd come in and arrest a bunch of seventy-five-year-old men. Then claim they'd taken down a multimillion-dollar gambling operation. The lifeblood of organized crime my ass. Half the guys they arrested had holes in their pants. Then they'd leave the rest of the shit in the city for us to clean up," waving his hand around the room, "You know, like the gangs, drugs, shootings, robberies. It was all bullshit," slamming his glass on the table, rum splashing out.

He refilled the glass, tossing the now empty bottle into the trash.

Taking another long drink, his eyes bored into Josh. "Guys like Bellofatto cared more about the streets being safe then they did. He helped us out when we needed it. Never about his business, of course, but he heard things in places we couldn't go. I got to know the guy; I knew he was in prison when Grey was killed. I talked to him about it. He told me not to worry; the mulignan got what he deserved."

Looking to defuse the tension, Josh said, "I understand. The street isn't always black or white, is it? Thanks, Sarge," turning to the door.

"Wait a minute…"

Josh turned back.

Calise, his head down, appeared drained. "You got the case file?" he asked. "Our case file?"

Josh shook his head, "Not yet."

"Well, you'll find this out sooner or later…" Calise stood, walked past Josh, and went outside to the beach. Josh followed.

"This is why I live here, you know. This is my front window on the world," gesturing to the Gulf of Mexico, overlooking Sanibel Island.

Josh looked out at the water. It was a beautiful view.

"I was the one that grabbed him."

Josh turned and looked at Calise. "You were the arresting officer?"

"Yeah, working the east side near the Pawtucket line. We got the call for a suspicious auto. As we pulled up, we saw the guy dump the body in the river and run," Calise took another drink. "I went after him and caught him."

"You had him in view the whole time?"

46

Calise, his eyes red and brimming from the alcohol, looked at Josh. "That's what the report says."

"Is it what you say?" Josh asked.

"In the parlance of police work at the time, I observed the suspect run and apprehended him." A sad smile crossing Calise's face.

Josh waited a moment. "Who wrote the report?"

Calise, unsteady on his feet, tried to refocus his eyes on Josh. "It was a team effort. The arrest got me bumped to detectives," turning away. "Now that is all I got, Lieutenant. Take care," heading back to the trailer.

Josh watched him stagger away.

"Lieutenant," Calise said, over his shoulder, "don't bother trying to come back another time. When I said that's all I got, that is all I got. I'm done with this," disappearing inside, slamming the door behind him.

Josh turned to the beach and saw Keira walking toward him.

"How'd it go?"

"Not too bad, didn't give me much. Said we should check the lineup report. He made it sound like there was more than one report. And..."

Keira raised her eyebrows, "I thought there was only one lineup?"

"So did I."

"What else did he tell you?" Keira continued.

"He was the arresting officer. Said his report was a team effort. Someone coached him to make the arrest more solid. It got him transferred to detectives, a reward of sorts. They massaged the report to make it better."

"There's a shock," she answered.

"Let's take a walk," Josh said.

"Why, you are just full of surprises, aren't you Mr. Williams?"

Taking Keira's hand, they walked along the water's edge. After a mile, they came to a small bench near a beach access point. Josh pointed at the sign on the bench. "Who do you think Harry Gottlieb is?"

Keira smiled, "Says he's the Fort Myers Beach Director of Sunsets. Sounds like a great job."

They sat down, enjoying the warmth of the sun. Josh put his arm around her as she rested her head on his shoulder.

Josh remained quiet for some time, staring at the water. Keira looked up and said. "What's wrong? I can tell there's something bothering you."

Josh smiled, pulled her closer, his arm tightening around her. "It's nothing, just thinking."

Keira sat up, turning to face him, "You? Thinking? Now I know something is up," she laughed. "Okay, out with it. Or we spend the next five days sitting here until you talk."

Josh spoke, paused a moment, looking back out to the ocean. "It's nothing. Just bothered by the way things were back then. I wonder if it has changed all that much."

"Of course, it has changed," Keira said, taking both his hands in hers. "Your reopening this case shows it is different now. It's not perfect. They'll always be cops with attitudes, the sole arbiters of justice as they see it, willing to ignore the truth. But not you and not most of the people on the department."

She pulled Josh to his feet, "Come on, let's walk some more," wrapping her arm around his. "Listen to me. I know I am always ranting and raving about the injustices I see; but I know they are the exceptions to the rule. Doesn't make them any less evil, or me any less determined to bring them to light, but I realize they are not representative of most cops. Cops like you.

"Your willingness to search for the truth gives me hope. Things have changed. If there are people like you, Chris, Chief Brennan, and others it will continue to get better. I know it will."

"And you," Josh said, pulling her to him, kissing her, holding the embrace. "I may not always like what you do, but I always respect your courage and determination. I hate to admit this, but we need more people like you holding our feet to the fire."

Keira smiled, "Why, Mr. Williams I do believe you are trying to seduce me."

"Is it working?" Josh said, returning the look.

"Indeed it is, Mr. Williams. Indeed, it is."

"So, now what? Where would you like to go? I'll take you wherever you want," Josh said, kissing the top of her head.

"Why don't we just find a place to stay, lay on the beach, go out to dinner, and just forget about the rest of the world for a few days?"

"Sounds good to me," Josh answered. As they walked back, his thoughts turned to what Calise told him. *This will make some people unhappy.*

Returning to the rental, Josh opened the car door for Keira. A muffled, but distinct, noise caused them both to turn.

"What was that?" Keira asked.

"Fireworks," Josh answered. "You can buy them everywhere down here. I may get some and put one in Chris's coffee next time."

Chapter 10

Monday, August 31, 2009
East Providence Police Headquarters
East Providence, Rhode Island

Josh walked into the office, tanned and relaxed after his trip with Keira. As he sat at his desk, there was a knock on the door. Josh opened it.

Chief Brennan stood there, smiling.

Uh-oh.

"Good morning, Lieutenant. How are you this fine day? All tanned, I see."

"Good, Chief. Ah, how are you?"

"Well, funny you should ask, Lieutenant. I was just fine up to about ten minutes ago. Then my phone rang. Do you know who it was?"

Josh shook his head.

"It was my friend the Chief of Police in Providence. He was curious about something," Chief Brennan sat on Josh's desk, motioning for him to sit. "My friend the Chief wanted to know why one of my lieutenants was in Fort Myers Beach talking to a retired Providence sergeant? I had no idea. You know what, Lieutenant; I do not like having no idea."

"I can explain, boss."

"But wait," holding up his hand, "there's more," Brennan said. "What had the Chief pissed off is this retired sergeant, right after speaking to you, called his old department. He talked to some of his former colleagues, one of whom was my friend the Chief. Then do you know what he did?"

Josh shook his head.

"No? Well, let me enlighten you," Brennan said. "He shot himself in the head. Neighbors called the cops a few days later because of the smell."

Josh blanched, not wanting to believe what he just heard.

"I see I've got your attention," Brennan said. "Now, I'm ready to hear the details of your vacation exploits."

Josh closed his eyes. *Better go with the whole story and get it over with.*

After explaining the request from Vera and Chris, Josh waited for the reaction.

Brennan stood, shaking his head. "I should have known Hamlin would be mixed up in this," grabbing Josh's cell phone off the desk.

Hamlin answered on the first ring. "Hey, Josh. What's up?"

"Well, well, retired Lieutenant Hamlin, Chief Brennan here. I knew you might try to duck my calls, but never one from your favorite protégé. Please find your way to my office in the next 30 minutes. I need you and the cold case archaeologist here to explain what the hell you are doing, and why I should let it continue," staring at Josh as he spoke. "What? Fifteen minutes? Even better," putting the phone down, he walked to the door. "Fifteen minutes, my office. Think long and hard about this."

* * *

Josh met Hamlin as she came in the front door. "Calise shot himself after I spoke to him."

"What?" Chris said, "I thought you said he didn't have much?"

"He didn't. Just about the lineup. I was waiting for the Providence PD files, which we won't get now, before I did anything else."

Chris shook her head. "Brennan's pissed, huh?"

"A bit, he doesn't like surprises."

"Ah well, at least I already have my pension. You might have a problem, got any investments?" smiling at Josh.

The two walked into the reception area outside the Chief's office.

"Hi Donna, how are you?" Chris said.

"I am well, Chris. Nice to see you."

Chris saw the door to Brennan's private office was open; she couldn't resist. "Is the crotchety old bastard available, or is he napping again?"

The aide shook her head.

Brennan's voice boomed from inside the office. "Get your asses in here. I am not amused."

"His hearing is good, for an old guy," Chris smiled and walked into the office. Donna tried to stifle a laugh while Josh just shook his head, walking as if he was going to his execution.

"Please close the door, Lieutenant," Brennan said.

"Yes sir," Josh replied.

"Won't help, Williams, too late for that. Now sit, both of you, and tell me the whole story, and I mean the whole story."

"Don't we get coffee first?" Chris asked.

Brennan glared.

"Okay, coffee can wait," she smiled, dropping into a chair. "I'll sit and let Josh explain away."

Josh filled Brennan in on the history of the investigation. Starting with the reason for the trip to Fort Myers and the conversation with Calise. Brennan sat listening, showing no reaction.

When Josh finished, he looked to Chris to see if she had anything to add.

"I think that covers it, Chief," Chris said. "What's the problem?"

Brennan stared at her. "Where do I even begin?" he said. "First, there's the issue of an old case reopened on a request from an individual no longer active with the department. There's the fact I wasn't told of this by a Lieutenant in whom I thought I could place my full trust. There's the fact that this same Lieutenant misled me about the reason behind a request for an unscheduled vacation. There's the fact that I have the command staff of the Providence PD blaming us for one of their retired sergeants shooting himself. Give me time and I'll come up with some more."

"Chief," Chris said. "You always told me to follow the trail. No matter where it leads. And that is what I instilled in Josh," trying to gauge Brennan's reaction. "If there is something to this, and with Calise shooting himself I am willing to bet there is, we need to find out who and why. It's the least we can do."

Brennan turned to look at Josh.

"Look, Chief. The case was never closed by arrest or conviction, so I didn't have to reopen it..." Josh explained.

"Don't play semantics with me, Lieutenant. You know what I mean here. How did you find out about Calise?" Brennan said.

"I spoke to a few people about it and followed some leads." As soon as he said it, he knew he'd made a mistake.

"Who else did you speak with about this?" Brennan asked.

Josh looked at Chris, then back at Brennan. "Fatso Bellofatto."

Chris rolled her eyes.

Brennan stared at Josh for a long moment. "Lieutenant, please don't tell me a made member of organized crime knew we were looking into this matter before I did." Looking over at Chris, "Did I hear that wrong?"

"Turn up your hearing aid. That might help."

Brennan scowled, "I'll remember that when your license renewal is waiting on my signature."

Chris shrugged her shoulders.

"I told him it wasn't anything official. I said it was a personal..."

Brennan held up his hand. "Not what I want to hear, Lieutenant. Not what I want to hear." Standing up, Brennan walked to the window and looked out for several moments. "Look, I know I give you a lot of latitude in SIU. Some of this may be my fault. But this is not the way I want to find out."

"I am glad you accept some of the blame," Chris interjected, standing next to Josh.

Brennan glared at her.

She raised her hands and sat back down.

"It's clear you've stepped on somebody's toes. If there is nothing you've left out," Brennan sent questioning looks at Chris and Josh. "We might as well see where this goes."

"Look Chief," Josh added. "Nobody can read through the fog of police reports better than Keira. She has a knack for sensing problems. This one has big ones."

Brennan looked at Josh and Chris. "I remember the case as well, you know. I was around then."

Josh looked at Chris then back at Brennan. "You worked this?"

"I was working the night of the first rape. We spent a lot of time trying to find the guy. He seemed to vanish."

Brennan sat back in his chair. "You have to remember they were different times. Hell, we had one black guy on the job, Martin Soares.

"When Providence made the arrest, it took the heat off us. When the guy was killed in prison, we figured it was a good end to a bad situation."

Josh spoke up, "So, what do you think? Do we follow this or let it go?"

Brennan was quiet for a few moments. Looking at Josh, he said, "Follow it, but keep me in the loop. If you're going to piss off more people I want to know before the shit storm hits."

Josh smiled, "Thanks, Boss."

Brennan shook his head, "I may regret this next question, but will you be talking to anyone else I might be hearing from?"

"George Tucker and some retired troopers," Chris answered.

"Of course, why not a Supreme Court Justice and our friends from Scituate?" Brennan said.

"And we'd love to get a look at the Providence PD file," she added.

Brennan closed his eyes, rubbing his forehead.

"How about I let the Chief in Providence calm down for a few days; let them bury one of their own without my bothering them. Once that's over, I think I can get him to give me the file. He's a good guy and I think he'd like to know what happened to this one."

"Great," Chris said. "Now, how about you take me out for coffee?"

"If that will get you to shut up, fine. Let's go." Brennan replied.

Chapter 11

Thursday, September 3, 2009
1:00 PM
Office of the Chief Justice
Supreme Court of Rhode Island
Providence, Rhode Island

Three days after the meeting with Brennan, Chris met Josh on South Main Street in Providence.

"How do you want to play this?" Josh asked.

"I think we just lay it out. I worked with him a few times when he was a prosecutor. He's a straight shooter, almost to a fault. If he knows anything, he'll tell us. Although it will surprise me if he does. This is the shit he's been fighting his whole career. Can't imagine he'd involve himself in anything like this."

"I'll be happy with him recognizing the initials from the lineup. Then all we have to hope for is the guy is still alive," Josh said.

Walking into the main entrance, Chris went through the security screener. Josh flashed his credentials and the young Capitol police officer waved him through.

"Check her good. She looks rather unsavory," Josh said, as he waited for Chris to emerge from the metal detector.

The Capitol police officer smiled, "We've seen her here enough. She's okay," not realizing the link between them.

I must be getting old. They don't even remember Chris from the job. The times they are a 'changing.

The two walked over to the bank of elevators, Chris pushed the call button. Watching the clocklike display show the car descending from the fifth floor, they stepped back as the door opened.

Harrison 'Hawk' Bennett, Attorney-at-Law, stepped from the elevator.

"Of all the people in the world, it had to be you," Chris said.

"Will you look at this? Nice to see you, Lieutenant Williams. Not so much with you, Miss Hamlin. It is still Miss? Is that the proper term for a spinster like you?"

Bennett served as Josh's defense counsel in Federal court on a civil rights violation. Chris connected Josh with Bennett. The trial ended in Josh's acquittal.

"Are you surrendering her to the court for some atrocious act? Perhaps with a chipmunk or fowl?" Bennett asked.

"Something like that," Josh answered. "How are you Hawk?"

"I am well, my boy. I hate to admit this, but I believe I still owe you and your compatriot here dinner at the Capitol Grille. Let's do that soon, okay?"

Josh nodded, "How about next Wednesday? Keira and I go out to dinner on that night. Is she invited?"

"I see you've kept the relationship. Good for you. Not my preferred style, but if you're happy, I am happy." Hawk answered. "Of course, she's invited."

Turning to look at Chris, Bennett said, "I don't suppose you have anyone to bring, so you can be my date."

"I'd rather starve," Chris answered. "But, since I am now in a business which your practice could generate cases, I'll bring my two associates."

"This is growing rather expensive for me. Time to take my leave. 6:30 PM, Capitol Grille next Wednesday, reservations for six."

"Six?" Chris said. "I count five."

"Of course you do, I am surprised you can count at all. The new Mrs. Bennett will be there as well. You remember Candace, of course. She did the expose` on Collucci after the trial, albeit all for naught. The blind cattle that are the electorate of this state sent him to Washington anyway. See you then."

"Unbelievable," Chris said, as they watched Bennett head out the door.

* * *

Stepping into the elevator, Josh pushed the button for the eighth floor. This floor hosted the courtroom and chambers for the Rhode Island Supreme Court.

The doors opened, and they walked toward the office of the Presiding Justice. Entering the reception area, Judge Tucker's administrative aide greeted them

"Ms. Hamlin," the aide said, drawing out the name, "the Judge has a full schedule today. It would be more efficient if you explained the matter to me, so I can aid Judge Tucker in responding to your request."

"Yes, well that will not be possible, Ms. Atwell. Please inform the Judge of our arrival, we would appreciate it."

The aide waited a few moments, rose from her seat, walked to the inner office door, knocked lightly, and entered.

"Think she's trying to persuade the judge to let her handle this?" Josh asked.

"No doubt," Chris answered. "But Tucker wants to know what this is about. He'll see us, I am sure I piqued his curiosity."

Several more minutes passed before Ms. Atwell emerged from the office.

"Judge Tucker will see you now. Please be brief, we have a busy schedule to keep," Atwell said, standing guard at the door.

Chris smiled and walked into the office, Josh right behind, nodding at Ms. Atwell as he passed her.

Judge George Tucker was a physically diminutive character, but an intellectual giant. He had argued more cases before the United State Supreme Court than any other Rhode Island lawyer.

His true prominence came from his civil rights cases. He was the only Rhode Island Judge to receive Thurgood Marshall Award for Judicial Excellence.

This man took the words, 'All men are created equal, ' to heart.

Rising from his desk, he came around, extended his hand, "Chris, so nice to see you again."

"It's nice to see you also, your Honor," shaking the Judge's hand. "This is Lieutenant Josh Williams. He and I have worked together for many years."

Moving to face Josh, he took his hand. "Nice to meet you, Lieutenant."

"It's a pleasure to meet you as well, your Honor. We'll try not to take up too much of your time."

"I see Ms. Atwell has impressed the demands of my schedule on you. I had planned to read over briefs this afternoon, as I have been doing all day. This is a welcome break," the judge smiled. "Now, sit please," pointing to the conference table. "What can I do for you?"

Chris looked at Josh. "Why don't you explain things, Josh."

Josh gave the Judge the background of the case and the reason for their meeting. He left out the part about the retired Providence sergeant and Fatso Bellofatto.

The judge studied the two for a moment. "Sad to say, I am familiar with this case. I was the original special assistant AG assigned."

This caused Josh and Chris to exchange glances.

"Your friend Robert Collucci," nodding at Josh, "took the case over before the defendant died in prison. I was unable to pursue the matter at the time. There is not much more I can tell you."

Josh pulled the lineup report from the file and handed it to the Judge.

"Do you recognize those initials next to the space for the supervising prosecutor?"

Tucker looked at the document, the rage at his impotence flooding back. He put the document on the desk. "They appear to be my initials," folding his hands, "but they are a poor attempt to forge them."

* * *

"Well," Chris said as they left the courthouse, "that proved rather interesting, didn't it?"

"Forged initials aren't all that startling," Josh replied. "Most AG's I know have fixed documents. Somebody must have noticed them missing and added them in. I doubt the document would even get a second look in discovery."

Josh stopped a moment, looking back at the court. "Unless..."

"Unless what?"

"Unless he knows who forged them."

"Why wouldn't he tell us?" Chris asked.

"You heard what he said. He couldn't pursue the matter at the time," Josh said. "Maybe, he's hoping we will," looking at Chris. "It just seemed odd he'd remember the case so well from so long ago."

"Jeez, talk about conspiracy theory. I have known the judge for a long time. There's no reason to lie to us. I think he remembered the case because he couldn't do anything about it. Looks like we've got some traction on this one."

Josh headed to his car; Chris wanted to walk back to her office. On the drive back, he mulled things over.

Dead defendant, forged lineup reports, the cop who arrested Grey eating his gun, and Robert Collucci.

Josh needed no motivation for seeing this through, nothing more persuasive than Collucci's involvement.

Collucci's indictment and trial of Josh three years ago on the civil rights violations had not endeared him to Josh. He never thought he'd return the favor.

Now he had one. A good one.

* * *

"You want to interview who?" Chief Brennan asked, wide-eyed, incredulous.

"Collucci," Josh answered. "He was Deputy AG of the Criminal Division."

"Hamlin is right, I must need hearing aids. You can't mean United States Senator Robert Collucci," Brennan said. "Tell me the name is a coincidence."

"Nope, one and the same," Josh replied with a smile.

Brennan closed his eyes, massaged his forehead, opened them to look at Josh, and then continued rubbing. "Is this necessary?"

"Yup."

Brennan sat back in his chair. "Refresh my memory. This is to ease a daughter's memory of her dead father, correct?"

"Well," Josh answered, "it started out like that. But with what I've learned, we have to see this through. I'm not convinced Grey isn't the bad guy. But there is serious doubt."

Josh moved to the window, watching the passing traffic. "Look, Collucci is not on my favorites list. But this isn't about revenge," turning back to face Brennan. "I'm not gonna lie to you. I may enjoy the look in his eyes, assuming he meets with me, but I am just following the trail."

Brennan walked over to stand next to Josh. "Go talk to the son-of-a-bitch. I'd go with you if I could, but it would be too obvious."

"Obvious?" Josh asked.

Brennan smiled. "Obvious we were both taking pleasure jamming a hot poker up his ass."

Walking back to his desk, he reached into a file drawer. "I got something for you," throwing a large file on the desk.

Josh walked over, picked up the file, and looked inside. "How did you get this?"

"I told you, the Chief in Providence is a friend. We've known each other for years. Most are god guys who want to bury the past," Brennan said. "That's not to say they're thrilled with your activities at the moment. But they won't stand in our way."

Josh picked up the file and headed toward the door.

"How are you gonna handle Collucci?" Brennan asked.

Josh turned and smiled.

"Never mind," waving his hand at the door, "Never mind. Go."

Chapter 12

Monday, September 7, 2009
4:30 PM
Office of Senator Robert M. Collucci
Providence, Rhode Island

The sign on the building read, Senator Robert Michael Collucci: Office of Constituent Services.

Josh looked at Maggie Fleming and smiled. "So, what do you think he'll do when he sees me with you?"

Fleming laughed. "Shit himself, but smile as he looks for a way out."

Josh held the door for Maggie as they entered the building. Maggie went to the reception desk. A young college-aged intern smiled as she approached.

"My name is Margaret Fleming. We have a 4:30 appointment with the Senator." She didn't offer to introduce Josh.

The intern glanced at Josh, and then picked up the phone. After a brief conversation, she hung up.

Pointing to the door, the intern said, "The Senator is expecting you, please go right in."

"Thank you," Maggie said and the two walked to the office entrance. Pausing with her hand on the door, "Ready?"

"I am going to enjoy this," Josh smiled, as Maggie opened the door.

Collucci rose from his desk and glanced at his Chief of Staff.

"Margaret, good to see you," extending his hand to her, "and Lieutenant Williams, I must say this is a surprise," turning to shake Josh's hand.

Josh ignored the overture.

Turning back to Fleming, Collucci pointed to a man standing near private entrance, "This is Anthony Sorin, my Chief of Staff."

Fleming and Josh nodded at Sorin.

"How can I help you? You said this was of a confidential nature."

Fleming glanced at Josh, "Senator, I knew you'd be a bit put off by the Lieutenant's presence, but I assure you this is an important matter." Fleming eyed the Chief of Staff, "No offense intended, but we'd prefer to discuss this with you alone. The matter concerns an old case you once handled when you were with the AG's office."

Collucci smiled. "Well, let me disabuse you of any concern. Mr. Sorin has my full confidence. Anything we need to discuss, we can discuss with him present."

"Fine with us, Senator. I am going to let Lieutenant Williams take it from here. He is more familiar with the case."

Collucci turned to look at Josh. "If I may Lieutenant, before you start. I'm certain it is safe to assume I am not one of your favorites. Despite what you may think of me, I did what I believed to be necessary in the pursuit of justice. The jury spoke, and I accepted their judgment."

Josh nodded. "It's behind us now Senator. I am doing the same here, doing what I think necessary in the pursuit of the truth."

Collucci nodded. "Good, we understand each other. Please continue."

"Senator, back in 1972 you were the prosecutor of a rape and murder case. The defendant's name was Darnell Grey. Do you recall the matter?"

Collucci thought for a moment. "You'll have to excuse my memory. I was involved with most of the major cases. I'm sorry, but no I don't recall that defendant, what did you say the name was?"

"Grey." Josh answered. "Darnell Grey."

"Grey, Grey, hmm," Collucci repeated. "No, sorry Lieutenant. I don't recall the case." Rising from his seat to signal the end of the discussion.

"How many cases did you handle as primary prosecutor?" Josh asked, ignoring Collucci's actions.

"As a Deputy, my primary responsibility was to oversee the Criminal Division. I didn't get many chances to handle the cases in court."

Josh glanced at Fleming. "We spoke to Judge Tucker," Josh continued. "He recalled you telling him about taking over the case. Before the matter went to trial, the defendant was beaten to death in the prison," pausing for a moment. "Part of what we are trying to learn is how a defendant awaiting trial was placed in the general population."

Josh saw the change in Collucci's expression.

"Ah, now that you mention the incident at the prison, I do remember. I didn't recognize the name at first. As I recall, there were witnesses who identified the defendant. I believe the police caught him in the act dumping a body in the Seekonk River."

That's funny, from don't recall to total recall in thirty seconds.

"We've had the chance to review the Providence Police file," Josh said. "The officer never saw Grey at the site where the body went in the river. He found him a short distance away. There's some doubt about the officer arresting the right guy," fudging a bit on what the report said.

Collucci showed no reaction.

"Then there is this," handing Collucci a copy of the lineup report. "Do you recognize the initials?"

Collucci did a cursory look at the document and handed it back. "No, I do not. Why?"

"According to Judge Tucker, someone forged his initials on the lineup report. Were you present during the lineup?"

Collucci folded his arms across his chest. "I would have no way of recalling that. It took place a long time ago."

"Did you see this as a problem? Were you aware of an issue with the lineup?" Josh probed.

Collucci paused before replying. "With the defendant's death, I wouldn't have had any reason to pursue the matter. If the case had moved forward and there were problems, I would have dealt with them. This is a dead-end investigation, why continue?" Looking over at Fleming, "Why are you investigating history?"

Josh couldn't resist, "Like you've often said, Senator, justice for everyone."

Collucci turned back to face Josh, his expression dark.

"Lieutenant, I had my doubts about this little visit of yours from the moment I saw you. I am sure you'd like nothing better than to find a way for a little payback."

Looking at his Chief of Staff, Collucci pointed at the door. "Anthony, would you be so kind. Show our guests here the way out. This discussion is finished."

Josh and Fleming turned to leave.

As he reached the door, Josh turned back to face Collucci. "Senator, this discussion may be over, but our investigation is not. We do so appreciate your cooperation and concern over the death of an innocent black man. I'll be sure to note that in the final report, before we hand it out to the media."

Collucci glared at him. Sorin moved between them, blocking the Senator.

Josh stepped into Sorin's space, forcing him back. "As for you, errand boy, we'll find our own way out. Go stay with your master."

Sorin's expression never changed; he stepped to one side, watching them leave.

As the door closed behind them, Fleming laughed. "Well, at least we know we don't have to come back. He'll never take my call again."

On the other side of the door, Sorin stood at Collucci's desk. "Something our friends need to deal with?"

"Not at the moment," Collucci said. "I'll take care of any loose ends."

Sorin watched the Senator reach for the phone. I don't think so, Senator. We will do this our way.

Chapter 13

Tuesday, September 8, 2009
9:30AM
East Providence Police Headquarters
East Providence, Rhode Island

Josh received a copy of the Darnell Grey file from the Department of Corrections. He smuggled Chris into the Chief's conference room to help him review the information. Stained, mildew smelling, and incomplete, the documents were less than helpful. As they sorted through them, Josh's cell rang. "Lieutenant Williams."

"Lieutenant, Chief Brennan here, are you and former Lieutenant Hamlin making any progress?"

Josh knew better than to try to put anything past Brennan, "How do you know this? I thought you were hobnobbing with your brother wizards at the monthly Police Chief's pity party."

"Funny Lieutenant, most amusing," Brennan answered. "I wasn't sure, but I had my suspicions she'd weasel her way in. You just confirmed it."

Dammit, the bastard is freaking psychic.

"Lieutenant, I have a little tidbit for you. Seems at the time Grey was in the prison, the acting warden was a major from the State Police. He was there on a temporary basis while the state sought a permanent warden. It may explain the lapse in protocol. Of course, he has long since retired. His name is William Church. Rumor has it he is still alive and living in a nursing home in Burrillville."

"Thanks Chief, that's helpful."

"Lieutenant," Brennan added, "please do me a favor. If you decide to go talk to the major, make sure he lives longer than a few hours after you leave. I do not want them pissed at us also. Try to stay out of trouble Lieutenant," ending the call.

Josh explained what the Chief told him about the former warden. Chris held up a form from the pile. "There are notes in here from the Supervisory Corrections Officer the day Grey arrived. He listed Grey as a parole violator, which was not correct, committed to a six-month bid and ordered him sent to Medium Security."

Josh took the paper and looked at it.

67

"So, it was either an innocent error, or convenient excuse. Either way they covered their asses. Even if the guard is alive I doubt he'd recall it," Chris said.

"No shit," Josh replied. "Okay, look up where the nursing home is. We're gonna take a ride."

* * *

Josh walked back to his office. As he opened the door, Captain Charland appeared behind him. "Good morning, Captain. How can I help you?"

"Why were you in the Chief's private conference room?"

Josh continued into the SIU office. "Just placing some files in there as the Chief asked me to," trying to close the door, hoping the answer satisfied the Captain.

Charland blocked the door. "Lieutenant, as you know, in the Chief's absence, as the senior Captain, I am the acting Chief. You must clear any access to his office through me."

Josh started to answer when Chris came into the detective reception area. "Rubber Gun Charland, how are you Cap?"

Charland turned, saw her, and looked back at Josh. "Lieutenant, why is a civilian walking around this police department without an escort?"

Chris pushed past Charland and into the SIU office. "Now R G, if you insist on being a bastard about this I'll tell everybody about your little problem." Pointing her index finger in the air, smirking at Charland, and then drooping it down. "Remember? Half-mast and the moment past."

"Look Hamlin, you're no longer employed here. This is a violation of... "

Chris smiled at the Captain. "Okay, you asked for it. See Josh, one day old R G here and a former auxiliary officer engaged in some, ah, field exercises--." Josh pushed her further into the office.

Charland's face was crimson. "Chief Brennan will hear about this. Is that clear?"

Josh tried to hide a smile. "Sorry Cap, you know she's just kidding," closing the door.

Chris raised her voice, "So anyway, R G's knee keyed the mike and every radio in range got a blow-by-blow description of a... "

"Stop," Josh said, holding his hands up. "The son-of-a-bitch is always looking for a reason to screw with me and you have to go let him see you're in here. Why couldn't you just stay out of sight like I asked?"

Chris laughed, "Look Josh, old rubber gun got his name because he's crazy. Nobody listens to him. Well, that's not true. His political friends listen because he's their ear on the ground in here. Come on, you know this," taking a seat at Josh's desk. "He'll go back to his office, call one of his buddies, and whine about it. When I was here, he threatened me every other day and you know what? Nothing happened. He won't challenge Brennan. He knows Brennan's leaving next year and he's lining up support for the job."

"Christ," Josh said. "Can you imagine that nitwit as Chief? I'd have to go back to midnights. It'd be a nightmare working for the clown."

"Keep the faith my boy. That's a future problem. Let's see if we can find this major and go have a chat?"

* * *

Two hours later, armed with the address for the nursing home in Burrillville, they headed toward the small, rural town in northwestern Rhode Island.

As Josh and Chris pulled into the parking lot of the Country Meadow Nursing and Rehabilitation Center, it was just past 5:00 p.m. The sun was fading and the temperature cooling off. They parked the car and walked toward the entrance. Josh pointed across the street to the Country Meadow Heaven's Gates Cemetery. "I guess, if the rehabilitation doesn't work, it's a convenient next stop for the residents, don't you think?"

Chris shook her head.

"You might want to take a brochure there, old broad. They'll wheel you into a place like this soon enough."

Chris flipped Josh the bird, and then noticed the two nurses, escorting a patient in pajamas taking small baby steps, watching them. Dropping her hand, she opened the door.

"Great impression you made there on Nurses Ratchett and Kevorkian," Josh joked.

"If you don't shut up, you'll need their rehab services."

Throwing his hands up in mock surrender, they walked to the reception desk.

"How can I help you?" the receptionist, a scary looking septuagenarian said. She wore black bullseye mascara and an unnatural blond wig with the binding curled up. It looked like her skull was peeling.

"Hello there, my dear," Josh said. "My grandmother and I would like to see Mr. Church, if he's not busy."

Chris kicked Josh.

"Ouch," Josh flinched. Turning back to the receptionist he said, "You'll have to excuse her, spasms you know."

The receptionist nodded with sympathy and directed them to room forty-two. As they got to the door bearing the number 42, Josh said, "What do you know, the meaning of life," as he pointed at the number.

Chris looked confused.

"*Hitchhikers Guide to the Universe*. Answer to the meaning of life, 42. No? Haven't you read the book?"

"No," Chris answered.

"Jeez, you are getting senile. I gave it to you for your birthday, remember?"

"Oh, that science fiction nonsense. I gave it to Vera."

"I give up trying to give you some culture."

"How about we do what we came for and then you can tell me all about it."

Knocking on the door, Josh waited for a response. A moment later a tall, gaunt man came to the door, wearing a United States Marine Corps sweatshirt and holding a book in his hand. He looked at the two and asked, "Yes, can I help you?"

"Major Church, my name is Josh Williams. I am a Lieutenant with the East Providence Police Department. This is Chris Hamlin; she's a retired Lieutenant from there as well, now a private investigator."

"Well, nice to meet you. Are you related to Ed Williams from the State Police?" taking his measure of Josh.

"I am, sir. He was my father."

"Ah, good man, your father. How is he?" Church asked.

"Dead. He died several years ago. Cancer," Josh answered.

"Ah, sorry to hear that. I wish I had known. I went through a bad time a few years back. It must have been when I was in the hospital or I would have attended the funeral."

"I appreciate that. Can we go someplace private to talk?" Josh asked, as he saw the two other occupants of the room looking over Church's shoulder.

"Sure. We can go to the dining room," Church answered. "I'll buy the coffee," putting the book down on his bed and heading down the corridor.

The trio walked down the white-walled hallway. They maneuvered around wheelchairs and walkers occupied by other residents. They all watched them with varying degrees of interest, or perhaps consciousness. Several called out to Church, 'How are you, Major?' 'Nice to see you, Trooper.' It was obvious Church clung to his past with pride.

They all got coffee and sat at one of the dining room tables. Church said, "So what is this all about?"

Josh glanced at Chris then said, "Major, this concerns the time you served as acting warden at the ACI. There was an inmate named Darnell Grey. He was--"

"I know who he was," interrupting Josh, a noticeable change coming over his appearance. "He raped and killed a woman in Providence and raped several other women. White women. One of the victims was the daughter of a Trooper. Why are you looking into ancient history?"

Josh tried to soft-pedal the questions.

"I'm glad you recall it. We're trying to clear up some things. Since I am sure you recall he died in prison, the case is still open."

Josh watched Church for a reaction. The Major locked on Josh, narrowing his eyes, the muscles in his jaw flexing and tightening. "Do you recall if there was any issue raised about him being in the general population, since he was awaiting trial?"

Church shot a glance at Chris. Josh could see the tension rising. This was someone unaccustomed to having his actions questioned.

"Do you know anything about those times in the Corrections department? What the courts were doing to us?"

Josh shook his head.

"I didn't think so. Let me give you a brief history lesson." Church put his coffee cup down, leaning forward in his chair. "The Governor ordered us to move a bunch of mafia guys and gang members to out-of-state prisons. We needed to regain control. Up to that point, the inmates ran the place. The guards could not, or would not, do anything. It's why they brought in the State Police."

Reaching for his coffee, he took a sip. "Some goddamn..." Looking at Chris, "excuse my French."

"No problem," Chris smiled. "I say goddamn shit like that all the time."

Church raised his eyebrows, and then continued. "An ACLU lawyer went to Federal court. He convinced a judge to order the prisoners returned, because it was cruel and unusual punishment. This same goddamn judge used to be a prosecutor for Christ's sake. He put some of those guys in the damn prison. Then he orders us to bring 'em back. The place was a shit hole once again."

Josh said, "How does that explain an inmate awaiting trial being placed in the general population?"

"With the limited resources I had, and the courts tying my hands, we just brought them in and put them where we could. The guy was put in the general population because we had no other place else to put him."

"Come on Major," Chris said. "We're all big boys and girls here. You put him in the general population because you knew the inmates hated rapists. Who's gonna grieve a dead black rapist who targeted white women?"

Josh tried to get Chris's attention; she ignored him.

"Look, I don't give a shit if you did your fellow trooper a favor or not. For all we know, Grey did rape those women. We're just trying to find something to make his daughter feel better about her dad. If he was a shit bag, so be it. We just need to know the truth."

Church rose, towering over Chris. "I've said enough. You think whatever you want. I know what you're trying to do here. I am not going to help you. The guy was killed because of a liberal ass federal judge. I will tell you this though; none of us lost any sleep over the nig---," catching himself and taking deep breath, "over the guy's death." The major grabbed the coffee cups off the table, threw them in the trash, and said, "Find your own way out." He turned and walked away.

"I'll tell the nigger's daughter about your kind sympathy," Chris yelled, causing a few heads to turn and stare.

Josh stood, shaking his head. "Not helpful."

"Well, I thought that went well," Chris said. "He didn't say it in so many words, but they used the turmoil of the time to put the guy at risk. We won't get anything else from him. Is the victim he talked about, the trooper's daughter, still alive?"

"I don't know," Josh answered. "I suppose it is the next logical step. I'll check DMV records and see if we can find her."

The two headed toward the exit, just as they stepped outside a voice called out, "Lieutenant, could I have a moment please?"

Major Church stood on the steps. Next to him stood a short, black man wearing a Boston Red Sox sweatshirt.

Chris and Josh walked over.

"I want to apologize for my outburst. My friend and roommate Nate here," putting his hand on the shoulder of the black man, "reminded me how times have changed. To be honest with you, I never knew Grey was in the general population until they notified me he was dead," sitting down on the stairs. "You have to understand, I was in charge but not in control. There was rampant corruption with the guards; the inmates did as they pleased. The best I could find out, one of the guards and Al

Monson were cousins. If they did it, they hid their tracks well. No one wanted the truth, anyway. I'm sorry to say I didn't look harder," pausing a moment to look at his friend, he turned back at Josh. "You know who Monson is right?"

Josh nodded. "We were just going to see if we could find his daughter and talk to her."

Church looked at the ground, then back at Josh. "I'll save you the trouble. Sheila Monson killed herself two weeks after Grey died in prison. Al found her. It broke him. He died two years later from liver failure."

Chapter 14

September 11, 2009, 8:30 AM
East Providence Police Headquarters
East Providence, Rhode Island

Lieutenant Charles Akerley brought Keira from the scene into the interview room. "Would you like a coffee or something?"

"No thanks, Charley. Vodka maybe," Keira said, trying to smile. "I'll be fine."

"You sure? It's no problem. I can get you anything you want, vodka included," Akerley answered. Friends since childhood, Charlie Akerley and Josh were still close. "We're gonna find out what went on here, Keira. I promise. No one is going to get near you."

Tears formed in her eyes, she trembled, and then sobbed. Akerley put his arms around her. "I got you Keira, no worries."

Akerley sat with Keira, letting her cry out her emotions. As his anger rose, the rage consumed him. *When we find these bastards, I will kill them with my bare hands.*

Josh came in after an hour and sat next to his wife. "Thanks, Charlie." Akerley stood, kissed Keira on the top of her head, and patted Josh on the shoulder.

"You okay?" Akerley asked.

"Yeah, I'm good. Thanks for staying with her."

Akerley nodded, "No problem," leaning to whisper in Josh's ear. "When you find out who did this, I want a part in taking 'em out." He closed the door as left the room.

Keira looked up, wiping her eyes, taking a deep, shaky breath to calm herself. "What the hell was that all about, Josh? Were they after me, or you, or both of us? This is crazy."

"We don't know yet. One guy is dead. We think he's from Russia or somewhere. The other guy is a gang banger, MS-13. He's not talking, yet."

Keira looked at Josh. "Russia? How do...? What do you mean, not talking yet?"

"He's in the hospital. Sedated. Got a bunch of broken bones and a shit load of other injuries. We'll try talking to him as soon as we can."

"Does he have a lawyer?" Keira asked.

"A lawyer? Who cares if the piece of shit has a lawyer? If there hadn't been so many people around, I'd have shot the prick in the head right there."

Keira tried to smile. "Thanks for trying to be my knight in shining armor, but I'd prefer we follow the law," reaching out, pulling him close.

Tears welled up in his eyes. "I don't know what I'd do if anything happened to you," trying to control his emotions. "I would kill someone if they hurt you, I would without hesitation."

Keira hugged him. "Do this for me Josh. If you want to make me feel safe, follow the rules. It's what separates us from them. We play by the rules. You'll figure this out the right way. It's why I love you."

The door to the interview room opened and Chief Brennan started in. "Oops, sorry. I ah...," backing out the door.

"It's okay Chief, she's dressed now." Josh laughed. Keira smacked him on the side of the head.

Brennan poked his head back in. "Someday you're going to have to explain to me what the hell it is you see in him."

"I'm not sure I can, Chief, I'm not sure I can," she answered, smacking Josh again.

* * *

Once Keira finished giving her statement to the detectives, they brought her to Josh's office. Josh got her a cup of tea and sat with her.

"So, you want to go home or are you still going to the office?" Josh asked.

"Are you coming home with me?" she asked.

"I can't, I have to stay and work this. No way Brennan would let me leave."

"Okay then, if carrying on with your day is good enough for you, it works for me as well. I'll go to my office," Keira answered.

"How about you let me take you there? I had one of my guys drop your car off for the oil change. I'll take you to the office and when I pick you up we can stop and get your car on the way home."

Keira smiled, "I can take myself to work, Captain America. You don't have to protect me every moment."

"But--"

Keira held up her hand, "No buts, Josh. We'll meet at home after work and you can fill me in. I'll be fine."

The door to the office opened and Chief Brennan walked in. "The truck is out front, Keira. You sure I can't have someone take you to your office, or home?"

"Don't bother, Chief. I already tried talking her into it," Josh said.

Brennan took a seat next to Keira. "If it's any consolation, I don't think they were after you. Although based on your husband's work product, I can't imagine anyone wasting time trying to get him." He smiled, patting her on the shoulder.

Josh chuckled at the Chief's comments, then stopped when he caught the Chief's stare. His cell phone rang, interrupting the conversation.

"Hey, Chris, what's up? Oh yeah, of course you heard. I'll tell you the story when I see you. She's fine, sitting right here." Josh handed the phone to Keira.

"Hi, Chris, no I'm fine thanks. They have everything under control. Sure, stop by. I'll be at my office within the hour," handing the phone back to Josh. "Chris said she'd call you later."

Josh put the phone on his desk.

Brennan stood up, "Josh, can you come to the office for just a minute?" Turning to Keira, "I'll have him right back. You take care and call if there is anything I can do."

"Thanks Chief," Keira nodded and picked up her tea.

When Josh left the office, Keira rested arms on the desk trying to think. *What is going on here? They couldn't be after me; it must be Josh. Something the SIU is*--Josh's cell phone ringing interrupted her thoughts. After the ringing stopped, she turned the display to read the caller ID, *Doctor's Office.*

What the hell?

The door opened, and Josh came back in. Handing him the phone, Keira said, "You had a call, the display said doctor's office. What doctor, Josh?"

The look on his face said it all; he knew she knew.

"I was hoping to tell you this later. Once I had talked to the..." Josh said, sitting next to her.

Keira took his hand, "No time like the present, what's wrong?"

Josh fumbled with his phone, avoiding her eyes. "Remember around my birthday, when I had those headaches?"

"Yes, of course," Keira said.

"Well, I went to see Dr. Phillips. He ran some blood work, it was all negative for anything, told me it was stress related and I needed to learn to relax, get a hobby. If you remember, I took those five days and did some of the Long Trail in Vermont. You didn't want to go."

"I didn't want to sleep in the woods and the mud," Keira retorted. "You asked me to go to Vermont. I pictured a quaint Bed & Breakfast with long, pleasant walks through rolling hills. Not suck-stepping through mud, devoured by black flies." Keira pulled him closer to her. "Stop trying to change the subject. Why didn't you tell me about the doctor? And why are you getting calls from his office now?"

Josh tilted back in the chair, rubbing his hands together. "A couple of weeks ago, the headaches came back. I went to see Phillips again." Seeing the reaction on Keira's face, he bent toward her. "I didn't tell you because I didn't want you to worry."

Keira stared at him, "Josh there are no secrets here, remember? Let's not go down that road again. Anything that affects you, or me, we share, period."

Josh could see the disappointment in her eyes. *I am an idiot. I knew this would happen and I still tried to hide it. I am a goddamn moron.*

"So, what does the doctor say now?" Keira asked, her voice edgy, the tension rising, her eyes probing him.

Josh walked to his desk, opened his briefcase, and reached for his iPad. Holding it behind the briefcase, trying to cover his hiding spot, he withdrew the letter. He walked back and handed her the envelope. Sitting back down, arms on his knees, hands folded he watched as she read it.

She dropped the letter on the desk and looked into Josh's eyes. "You were just going to try to do this by yourself?"

"No, I mean yes, I mean…" Josh scrambled for the right words.

"Okay, Josh. I will tell you what happens now. You call the doctor's office, right now, with me here, and make an appointment. From now on we both go to see him, understood?" Her eyes began to well-up.

"I'm sorry, Keira. I just didn't want you to worry about this," Josh said, pulling her close.

She pushed him back, handing him the cell. "Nice try, not gonna work. Call, now."

Chapter 15

Three days after the incident, the bike driver had recovered enough for an interview. Between the interference of the lawyer and the natural lack of cooperation by gang members, they learned little.

The guy paid him in cash to give him a ride. No questions asked, no names offered. He had no idea the guy was armed.

The dead body proved just as uninformative, but much more intriguing.

No matches to the fingerprints in any database. The man carried no identification, and the body tattoos were a mix of Russian military and prison in nature.

The unknown caliber weapon also was interesting. The weapon had no serial numbers. They never existed. It was unique and unfamiliar.

The Bureau of Alcohol, Tobacco, and Firearms and the FBI asked about the weapon.

Josh had a good working relationship with ATF. He contacted the Special Agent-in-Charge of the Providence office, Monty Medeiros, for help.

The information stream went dry; three weeks passed.

* * *

Josh sat in the Chief's office for the weekly case status update.

"So, we have nothing? It's been almost a month," Brennan asked.

"Nope, still waiting on the Feds to get back to me."

Brennan picked up the phone, "Donna, get me the US Attorney's office in Providence please."

A moment past and the voice of the Chief's aide came over the line, "US Attorney on line one, Chief."

Brennan grabbed the phone, "Watch this," he said, smiling at Josh.

"Bill, how are you?" pausing for the reply. "Well, I need a favor. You are aware of the attempt on one of my officers. We have been waiting on information from ATF. Can you light a fire for me? The press is pushing me for information and I don't have anything."

Brennan smiled and covered the mouthpiece. "I bet we get an answer now," returning to the call.

"Great, thanks. See you next week at the Chief's meeting." Brennan hung up. "There you go, Lieutenant. I would expect a call from them today."

Two hours later, the phone rang in Josh's office, "SIU, Lieutenant Williams."

"Hey Josh," Medeiros said.

"Monty, what's up? Got something for me?"

"You gonna be around for a while? You've stirred some shit up with this one. Not to mention riling up the US Attorney."

"That was Brennan, he's not known for his patience. But I am here all day."

"We'll be right there," Medeiros replied.

"We?" Josh asked.

"Yup," Medeiros said, and hung up the phone.

A short time later, the receptionist called to let Josh know the federal agents were here. Josh went out to the lobby to get them.

"Lieutenant, this is Special Agent Brad Peterson from Homeland Security," Medeiros said.

"Pleasure to meet you Lieutenant," Peterson shook Josh's hand.

"Josh, please."

"Brad will do for me as well."

As they walked to the office, Chief Brennan came into the hallway. Josh introduced Peterson to Brennan and invited the Chief to come with them.

"I wouldn't miss this for the world," Brennan, gesturing for the agents to lead the way, followed them to the SIU.

* * *

The group walked into the office, Captain Charland, Services Division Commander, following behind.

"Can I help you Captain?" Josh asked.

"No, Lieutenant, you cannot. Chief Brennan issued an executive order that I am the supervisor dealing with all federal agencies. I am just following those orders."

Josh looked at Brennan.

"Captain," Brennan offered, "I meant for you to deal with them if I chose not to. I will handle this."

"Chief, shouldn't I be part of this? To maintain proper chain of command, should something arise?"

Josh turned away, hiding his smile.

Brennan walked over to the Charland. "Captain, while I appreciate your diligence, I believe Lieutenant Williams and I can deal with this matter. If something arises which requires your expertise, I'll be certain to let you know."

Charland nodded at the agents and looked back at the Chief. "Yes sir, Chief. I'll be in my office if you need me," doing a perfect about-face and walking out.

"The man means well," Brennan said. "But he's not what you would call operational material. He does do paperwork like no one else. God knows we need someone for that nonsense."

Josh sat down and motioned for everyone to grab a seat.

"Anybody want coffee before we start, I can call Captain Charland and ask him to get it," chuckling.

A slight grin emerged on Brennan's face. "You know, Lieutenant, I may decide to put your unit under the Captain's command. It might tame you a bit."

"Oh man, not that. Okay, I'll get coffee...anybody?"

Since no one else wanted coffee, Josh got one for himself.

Brennan watched with amusement as Josh went through his coffee ritual. Adding what seemed like a quart of cream and a pound of sugar to the enormous cup he kept on his desk. "Are you all comfortable now, Lieutenant? Is there anything else you need before we continue with work? You know, the stuff I am paying you to do?"

Josh shrugged his shoulders and sat at his desk. "Nope, I am good to go now, Chief. So, Monty, what does the ATF have for us today?"

Brennan shook his head.

Medeiros looked at Peterson, "Okay Brad, your show."

Peterson opened his briefcase and removed an evidence bag with the weapon from the incident on Route 44. Opening the bag, he withdrew the weapon and placed it on the desk.

"Notice anything unusual?" he asked.

Brennan picked up the weapon, "Other than I have never seen anything like it, no."

"Unless you had a friend in the Russian military, it is doubtful you'd ever see one of these." Taking the weapon from Brennan, Peterson said. "It's used by Russian Special Forces, known as Spetsnaz, but this one is unique. It's similar to the Serdyukov SPS 7.62 High Caliber weapon used by their special forces, but with some differences. "

Brennan raised his eyebrows and looked at Josh. "What kind of shit did you step in, Lieutenant?"

"Ya got me, boss."

Peterson put the weapon on the table. "This particular version is all composite material. There are no metal parts, even the ammunition is composite."

"Metal detectors wouldn't detect it?" Josh asked

"Nope, it might even slip by x-ray machines. The disassembled weapon consists of innocuous looking parts."

"Christ," Josh said.

Yup," Medeiros added, "even he'd have a hard time finding it."

"How'd the dead guy come up with a weapon like this?" Josh asked.

"The bigger question is why someone with this weapon targeting an East Providence Police Officer or his wife," Peterson added.

"I don't think my wife was the target," Josh replied.

"Well, we're not sure Josh," Peterson said. "She's involved with some high-profile appellate cases. We're going to need to do an in-depth interview with her."

Brennan chuckled.

"Did I say something funny, Chief?" Peterson asked.

"No, no. It's just, I know Keira and she won't respond well to an interrogation."

"When you interview her, I want to be there," Josh said.

"Fine," Peterson answered. "So long as we do the questioning."

Now it was Josh's turn to laugh. "Look, Brad. I know you have a big deal here with this weapon. However, you need to keep something in mind; my wife is a determined, smart, and forceful defense lawyer. She'll smell any attempt at an interrogation and jam it up your ass. All I am saying is ask nice, or you'll get nothing."

Peterson smiled, "Monty told me all about you and your wife. Look, I am on your side. I am inclined to agree you were the target and not your wife. The sooner we can eliminate her as the target the faster we can figure out why they were after you."

Josh nodded, "When you talk to her, tell her that. It will work better."

Peterson looked at Medeiros, "No time like the present for the rest of the bad news."

Medeiros nodded his head.

Peterson continued. "Okay, here's the rest of the story. From what we can find about the guy, he is former Russian military, Special Forces. The Russians are not enthusiastic about providing information. We do know many ex-Spetsnaz guys went to work for Russian organized crime. This guy surfaced in an investigation several years ago. The group operates out of New York with ties to DC, Boston, and Providence."

"Providence?" Brennan asked. "What the hell would Russians want in Providence?"

"Let me give you a brief history lesson about the Russian mob. First, they make the old Mafia types look like girl scouts. Second, they make money any way they can. Gambling, drugs, hijacking, stolen cars, land grabs, credit card fraud, extortion, protections rackets. You name it, they do it. They enforce their hold with sheer, unadulterated brutality."

Peterson let the words sink in.

"If your wife was not the target, then we need to figure out what you did to draw their attention."

Josh listened, then said, "All we have going in here is the usual nitwit drug dealers, a few gang related guys, but nothing of this level. I can't think of anything we're working that amounts to more than local stuff."

"Perhaps there is a link you haven't found. We'll need to review your current cases, as well as anything over the last few years. There is something here; we've just got to figure it out."

Chief Brennan rose from his chair. "Okay, we'll provide whatever you need." Turning to Josh, "Lieutenant, from this moment this is your top priority. If you need more help, I'll pull some people from detectives. You keep me informed. Am I clear?"

"Thanks Chief, I will."

Brennan turned to the federal agents, "If there is anything else you need, you just let the Lieutenant know and we'll find a way to get it."

Brennan shook the agents' hands and opened the door to leave. Captain Charland, sitting on the desk of the receptionist, tried to appear busy. "Is there something you need Chief?"

"No, Captain. I think we're all set." Shaking his head, Brennan returned to his office.

* * *

"I told you if you played nice, she'd cooperate." Josh said as he and Peterson left Keira's office, heading back to the station.

Peterson shook his head, "She is a piece of work. How the hell did you two ever meet, let alone marry?"

"Long story," Josh laughed. "Where do we go from here?"

"I reached out to the FBI Counterterrorism Center," Peterson said. "Maybe they have something new on the dead guy,"

"I may not have too many fans at FBI Headquarters," Josh said.

"Oh yeah, Monty told me the story," Peterson laughed. "I heard there was great merriment in FBI HQ with your little surrender party. Not to worry, these guys are some of the good ones. They hate it when US Attorneys misuse FBI resources. They want to help figure this out."

"Let's hope you're right," Josh said. "I have a feeling before this is over we might need their help."

Three years ago, Robert Collucci, then the US Attorney Rhode Island, indicted Josh. Collucci, driven by blind political ambition, forced the civil rights matter to a federal grand jury. He directed the FBI to make a big show arresting Josh, trying to inflict more trauma. Chris Hamlin, the Lieutenant in charge of SIU got word of the plan and arranged a nightmarish reception for the agents. When they came looking for Josh, the agents ended up in a giant shit show, orchestrated by Hamlin and carried out by members of the police department and many of Josh's friends. It was not something the agents would forget soon.

It proved embarrassing for Collucci. Not enough to derail his election to the Senate, but losing the case proved painful to his ego.

As they arrived back at the station, Josh saw the unmarked car in the front lot. Flashing back to his battle with the FBI Civil Rights Unit, he looked at Peterson.

"Friends of yours?"

"I hope so," Peterson answered, "I hope so."

Josh and Peterson went to the Chief's office. Captain Charland stood guarding the door to the inner office.

"Who's in there, Captain?" Josh asked.

Charland smirked. "That information is on a need to know basis."

The intercom on Donna's desk chimed in, "Is Lieutenant Williams here yet Donna?"

"Yes Chief, and Captain Charland as well," she replied.

The distinct sound of Chief Brennan groaning came over the speaker. "Ah, I see. Ah, oh hell. I'll be out in a minute."

Brennan came into the reception area, "Captain Charland, I am glad you are here," walking over to the Captain, bending down to whisper. "Would you compile a list of arrests by Lieutenant Williams and the SIU over the past three years? Please keep this confidential. Do the research yourself. Please do not involve any of the civilian records personnel."

Charland nodded, looked at Josh and the Homeland Security agent, and then left the office.

"That should keep him busy for a bit. Come on in gentlemen, you're gonna love this."

Josh and Peterson followed Brennan into the office. There were two others inside. Brennan introduced them as FBI Counterterrorism agent Zach Kennedy and US Deputy Attorney General Frank Lachance.

"Okay, now that we know one another, why don't you explain the nature of your visit," Brennan said.

Kennedy opened a briefcase and took out a small digital recorder. "What you are about to hear is not to leave this room, understood?"

Josh looked around the room and joined Brennan and Peterson in nodding agreement.

"The conversation I am going to play for you is from a court-authorized wiretap. The order came from the Foreign Intelligence Surveillance Court," Kennedy said. "This is serious stuff. We are monitoring an individual known to have connections to Chechnyan Terrorist organizations. I remind you, gentlemen, this is for background information only. We are here because Agent Peterson and the FBI Special Agent-in-Charge in Providence reached out for our help. He said we owed you one."

Lachance interjected, "I looked into the case against you, Lieutenant Williams. I wish I could say it never happened, but we know that's not possible. Let's just say once the Providence SAC explained the circumstances, I agreed we did owe you one."

"I appreciate it, sir," Josh replied.

"Frank, please Lieutenant. No need for formality."

Josh nodded.

Lachance looked at Kennedy and motioned for him to play the recording.

As the recording started, a voice came on speaking something other than English. The call was brief.

Kennedy explained. "What you heard was Russian. Here's a copy of the translation," placing a document on the desk.

Josh read the file.

Subject Shashenka Dmitriev, referred to as Sub SD
Unknown Caller referred to as Unsub Caller

Sub SD: "Yes."
Unsub Caller: "We need to meet, tonight."
Sub SD: "That is not possible."
Unsub Caller: "Make it possible."

Pause. Muffled background voices likely Russian.

Sub SD: "Tonight, 11 o'clock, same place as before."
Call ended

A second call followed, Kennedy explained, taking place three days after the first call. He put a second document on the table.

Unsub Caller: "You have the asset?"
Subject Shashenka Dmitriev (Subs): "Yes, where does it need to go?"

The next few words froze Josh's heart. He heard a description of his home address, his personal vehicle, and usual route in the morning to the station.

"What the hell?" Josh said.

Kennedy held up his hand, "Keep listening, there's more."

Unsub Caller: "Use someone local to drive him there. I want it done quickly. We don't need anyone looking into our agreement."
Sub SD: "I will see to it."
Call ended.

Josh slammed his hands on the table, glaring at Kennedy. "You guys knew this and didn't tell me they were coming. What the hell? Your idea for making amends is bullshit."

"Josh, listen to me for a minute," Kennedy said. "The caller never said what city or state. It was just an address. There were hundreds of similar addresses in the country. We had no idea which one."

Josh stood glaring at the agents. "Bullshit, same old fucking federal bullshit. What was so important you thought it okay to let them try to kill my wife?"

"Josh, listen to me. We looked at as many addresses as we could. This is a terrorist group we're looking at. We were focusing on high-level targets, something that would give them a splash in the news. These guys don't kill cops except as collateral damage."

Brennan spoke up. "Calm down, Josh. You're not a high-level target. You're not even a low-level target; except perhaps for Keira, when you wreck her car."

This caught Josh off-guard. He didn't realize Brennan knew about his wrecking Keira's car.

"Not much gets by me, son," Brennan said, catching the surprise in his eyes. "Sit down and listen to what else they have. These are good guys this time, trust me on this."

Josh walked back to his seat, "Sorry, I don't like it much when the job reaches my family."

"Understandable," Kennedy replied. "Let us explain something else and I believe you'll see this in a different light."

"Okay," Josh nodded, "I am all ears."

Kennedy stood and leaned against the wall. "After the first call, we weren't able to trace the caller. They use burner phones, one-time use, and they dump them. After the second call, we got lucky, or they got lazy. They made a second call with the burner phone, to a number we could trace."

Josh sat up. "Please tell me we know where this guy is now."

"The second call went to a woman, a working woman so to speak, in the DC area. We've had surveillance on the house since then. So far, it's been the usual collection of upstanding citizens. Lawyers, city councilmen, two or three Members of Congress, and an aide to a Senator. But nothing so far as we know connected to anything of significance."

Josh looked at Brennan, "Couldn't be, could it?"

Brennan chuckled. "This is Rhode Island, Josh, anything is possible."

Kennedy looked at the two, "Something you'd like to share?"

"The Senator's aide," Josh asked, "wouldn't happen to be the aide to Senator Robert Michael Collucci?"

Kennedy looked at Lachance, "Perhaps we all have something to share."

Josh explained the Grey investigation to Lachance and Kennedy. "I know I may have stepped on Collucci's dick with my little surprise visit but having me killed over it is a stretch. There must be something else here. Shit like this doesn't happen here. It's East Providence for Christ's sake, not Moscow."

"Obviously," Lachance answered. "Look, we took a chance bringing you guys into this. Now I think we may have a common interest in your matter. How about I have Zach provide you with any help we can offer and see if we can figure out Collucci's association with these guys?"

"We'll take all the help we can get," Brennan said. "I won't tolerate people trying to kill one of my cops, or their family, and I want the bastards who did this. We'll do whatever we have to do. You'll have our full cooperation."

Kennedy and Lachance shook hands all around and headed out. "We'll be in touch. Meanwhile, here's my private cell number." Lachance said, handing the cards to Josh and Chief Brennan. "You run into any roadblocks, you call me. Anytime."

After the Feds left, Josh, Brennan, and Peterson went into a side conference room. "Josh, I don't want to bring any more paranoia into this, but I want you to use this room to store any case information. I don't want any prying eyes seeing things and running to the press. There'll be rumors enough circulated by whoever saw the Feds here. Between that, and the little fiasco on Route 44, they'll be all over this shit."

Josh smiled, "Tell ''em they're trying to indict me again. The weak, lame, and lazy will believe it and it'll give them something to speculate about."

Brennan smiled, "A little disinformation campaign. I like it. Okay, I'll tell Charland to keep it confidential, which will guarantee every politician in the city finds out by the end of the day."

Chapter 16

April 8, 1972
Criminal Division
Attorney General's Office
Providence, RI

There is a hierarchy within the Rhode Island Department of the Attorney General. At the top is the Attorney General, an elected position. He or she appoints Deputy Attorneys General. They head the divisions, Criminal, Civil, Appellate, and others.

Next in line are the Assistant Attorneys General, career prosecutors with extensive experience. Usually, they rise from the ranks of the special assistants through talent, dedication, or just hanging around long enough. Last in line comes the Special Assistant Attorneys General. The AG appoints them, sometimes as political favors to campaign supporters or other influential people.

Cops, lawyers, and judges refer to the levels within the Attorney General's office as the AG, or the AG's office. A collective expression for all prosecutors. The abbreviation pronounced as were the A and G separate words.

The Criminal Division at the Attorney General's office held a weekly meeting to assign and discuss cases. As in most organizations, shit rolled downhill. The worst cases went to the newest Special Assistant AGs. They rarely, if ever, caught a good case, let alone one involving rape and homicide. They spend most of their time at arraignments, violation hearings, and bail hearings doing the unglamorous work of the office.

When the Deputy of the Criminal Division assigned the Darnell Grey case to George Tucker, the consensus was the case had problems. Big problems.

After the meeting, Tucker went to see the Deputy Attorney General, Robert Collucci.

Knocking on the office door, he poked his head in. "Can I talk to you for a minute, Bob?"

"Of course," motioning for him to enter. "Close the door will you, George?"

Tucker sat in the chair next to the window and waited several moments for Collucci to look at him.

"What can I do for you?" Collucci asked.

"Well, to be frank, why did I catch the Grey case? It's high profile. Is there something about it I need to know?"

Collucci paused a moment, then smiled. "You know, I've been watching your progress here. Your case preparation is thorough and comprehensive. You excel in the courtroom. I've heard many complaints from the defense side, which I take as a good sign." Rising from his chair, he came around to lean against the front of the desk, arms folded, looking at the young prosecutor.

"George, there comes a time when you have to move into the majors. Show us what you can do. This is your opportunity. From what I know of the case, it's solid. Witnesses, including cops, to his dumping the body. A solid lineup identification by one of the rape victims and some good circumstantial evidence to support the case. I see no problems." Waving his hand in the air, "That's not to say there won't be the usual issues, but nothing that can't be overcome."

Tucker listened, watching the animated Collucci's performance. *The guy is a real showman; you make a great speech, coach.*

"I understand you supervised the lineup?" Tucker asked.

Collucci paused a moment, returned to his desk, and looked at his appointment book. "I believe I did, I may have, sure. It will be in the file. I have a meeting in five minutes with the AG. Is there anything else?" dismissing Tucker by his inattention.

Tucker stood. "No. If I find any problems, I'll let you know. Do you happen to know who's representing him?"

"Public Defender, of course. Those bastards never have any money."

Tucker took offense at the patent implied racism. He wanted to say something, but knew it was useless. Now was not the time or the place.

Returning to his office, Tucker called and had the Grey file sent up. Resigned to the inevitability of the coming discussion, he called his wife, telling her he'd be home late.

They had their usual argument about the time he put in, not making enough money, not being home enough. He listened, phone held away from his ear, as he opened the file and promised to be home when he could.

After making a full pot of coffee, he settled in for a long night of reading about the evil men do to their fellow humans.

* * *

Tucker finished the file review around 11 pm. He filled two legal sized notepads with items he needed to address. One stood out from all the others. He needed to clarify this first.

The next morning, Tucker called the Providence PD Detective Division and spoke to Captain Gemma. Addressing his concerns to the captain, Tucker asked for the Gemma's help in resolving the conflict. Gemma assured him he would research the matter and get back to him soon.

Tucker hung up, closed the file, and put it on the cabinet in his office.

Later in the morning, on his return from court, Tucker found Detectives George Weslyan and Jimmy Calise in his office. More troubling was the fact they had the Grey file opened on his desk.

"What are you doing in here? Who let you in?" Tucker asked.

"Your boss did," Weslyan replied. "You called about a problem. Gemma sent us to fix it," smiling at Tucker. "We're fixing it."

Tucker moved toward the desk, trying to grab the file. Calise stepped in to block his path.

"Did you remove anything from that file?"

Weslyan sneered at him. "Look, Mr. Special Assistant AG. There was a mix-up in the report on the lineup. My fault, I started to type it out then got distracted. I made a mistake on it. The one that ended up in the file was the wrong one. I put the right one in there. This one," pulling a paper from his inside jacket pocket, "no longer exists. Understand?"

"No, I do not understand. If you made an error, it's no big deal. We can address it in discovery. But you cannot remove items from the file," Tucker argued.

"Well, too late. I already did. It shouldn't have been in there anyway. You just make sure the motherfucking stovepipe stays behind bars where he belongs. Don't let chicken shit procedures screw this up," Weslyan answered.

"What did you just say?" Tucker was angry; he hated this attitude of white superiority.

"Stovepipe, mulignan, whatever, I suppose you'd prefer black male?" the words spat at Tucker. "Just keep that 'boon in a cage where he belongs. Understand?" Turning to the other detective, "Let's go Jimmy, we're done here."

Tucker was shaking. Calming himself, he took the file and walked to Collucci's office. Collucci was not there. He wanted to go to the AG with this, but knew it was useless. He would have to wait for Collucci's return.

"Janice, would you please ask Mr. Collucci to call me as soon as he returns?" Pausing a moment, "Better than that, call me when he gets back, and I will come right over. Thank you."

He should have known better than to rely on Collucci's personal secretary.

He waited several hours for the call, unable to focus on anything else, his phone ringing just before the office closed.

"George Tucker," he answered.

"George, Bob Collucci. Sorry I missed you. I won't be available until later tomorrow morning. Is that okay?" he said, not waiting for the reply. "Come over to my office around noon. We'll go to lunch."

The dial tone bored a hole in Tucker's brain.

Son-of-a bitch, no good rotten son-of-a bitch.

* * *

At 11:45 AM, Tucker sat outside Collucci's office, drumming his hands on the case file and glaring at the secretary. He rehearsed in his mind what he would say, ending with his resignation if Collucci let this slide.

The door to the office opened. Collucci came out, followed by three other men. He stood at the door as they filed by. Tucker recognized Detective Weslyan from the incident in his office; he didn't know the other two. The group ignored Tucker, talking among themselves, as they left the office. As they left, Attorney General William Patterson came out and walked over to Tucker.

"George, right?" the perfect campaign smile anchored on his face. "I hear good things about you. Keep up the good work." Patting Tucker on the shoulder, he ambled past the secretary, and sauntered out the door.

"Come in George," Collucci said, still standing at the door into his office. "No interruptions Janice, none."

"Who was in the office with you and Patterson?" Tucker asked.

Collucci turned on Tucker, started to speak, then took a moment to calm himself. "Captain Anthony Gemma, retired State Police Lieutenant Alfred Monson, and Detective George Weslyan. We discussed some issues with the Grey case."

"Why wouldn't you include me? It is my case, is it not?" Tucker asked.

"Please sit down," Collucci motioned to a chair.

"I'll stand."

The rest of the discussion was brief but pointed. Collucci was a master at implied threats.

"Didn't you hear what I said?" Tucker questioned, his frustration boiling over. "They removed a document and put in a new one. For all we know, the whole file is fraudulent. Wesleyan's a bigoted bastard. All he cares is it's a black man they caught. If it's not the right one, it makes no difference to him."

Collucci sat with the fingertips of his hands pressed together, tapping the tip of his nose, looking past them as Tucker raged on.

"Enough," Collucci said. "I looked at the file, and the document they replaced. It was an oversight and nothing more. Weslyan told us he started the lineup report then got distracted. He didn't catch the time error. Look, it's no big deal. Discovery hasn't happened yet."

Picking up a folder and waving it in the air, "This is the reason we review files, to catch these errors before discovery," tossing the file on the desk. "I appreciate your concern. Patterson and I reviewed the file. We are satisfied we've met our obligations. The matter is closed."

Tucker understood politics better than most. He was a realist, and patient. *I may not do anything about this now… but someday.*

Returning to his office, he tossed his briefcase on the desk. Reaching into the bottom desk drawer, he withdrew a small file folder. Placing the file in his briefcase, he left for the day. *I'll put this in a place of safekeeping,* one day he would be able to do something about this.

* * *

April 15, 1972
Department of the Attorney General
Providence, Rhode Island

The phone rang on the Collucci's desk. Picking up the receiver, his irritation evident in his voice, he said, "Janice, I told you to hold all my calls."

"You might want to take this one," the secretary answered, "It's the warden from the ACI."

"Fine, put him through."

A moment later, Collucci spoke to the warden. "What the hell do you mean he's dead?" Collucci listened for several minutes. "How the hell does an inmate awaiting trial end up in the general population? A rapist and murderer for god's sake. What dumb son-of-a-bitch let that happen? What?" listening to the explanation. "Well isn't that convenient? You had better find a way to make this right. I don't care who gets burned over it," slamming the phone, breaking the receiver. "Janice," he yelled, "Get me another phone in here, now."

Jesus Christ, this just gets better and better.

Collucci took a moment to plan his course of action. *First, protect the office, the AG, and himself from the fallout, although not necessarily in that order. Then, make sure Tucker understands enough to let this go. That might not be so easy; I need leverage.*

Collucci left his office and walked down the hall to the main office of the Attorney General. It was an ornate but not large office. Dark, wooden paneled walls covered with bookshelves. The impressive centerpiece, a handmade mahogany desk, completed the setting. The office overlooked Dorrance Street with views toward the river.

Attorney General William Patterson, elected for his third consecutive term, was a cautious man. Collucci knew he would need to be diplomatic. Explaining the circumstances to the AG, he offered his suggestion and assurances. This could not affect Patterson's political position.

Satisfied the AG was onboard, he returned to his own office.

Picking up the now replaced phone, he called Tucker's extension.

"George, Bob Collucci. Do you have a moment for me?"

Five minutes later, Tucker was in the office.

"George, the AG and I were discussing forming a new unit within the Criminal Division. The focus would be on sensitive racial issues. We know you have strong feelings in this matter. We'd like to have you head the unit."

Tucker found himself puzzled, but pleased. He made no secret of his leanings in the civil rights area. He proposed something similar as soon as he started in the AG's office. Why now, he wondered. "I'd like that, Bob. As soon as I clear my calendar, I can get started."

"I've already handled it. I arranged to transfer your cases to some of the other assistants. I'll take the Grey case, which frees you up for this new project."

Tucker thought a moment, uncertain what was behind this surprise offer, then said, "Okay, where do I start?"

Collucci smiled. "Great. I'll arrange a meeting with Patterson, so we can plan this out. I'll let you know as soon as he is available." Coming around his desk, he shook Tucker's hand, "Thanks for taking this on. This is a high priority matter with this office and it will be a great opportunity for you."

As Tucker left the office, Collucci was back on the phone to Patterson. "Tucker bought into it. But we better move fast, before he finds out there's more to the story." After listening for the response, he said, "I'll be right there." *Now I have only to convince him it was his idea and hope Tucker doesn't hear about Grey until this is in the bag....*

* * *

"So, I guess that counts as a win," Special Assistant Attorney General Michael Webster said as he came into Tucker's office.

"Win?" Tucker replied. "What are you talking about?" opening a file folder on his desk.

"You haven't heard?" Webster asked. "The Grey case, your big claim to stardom? He's dead."

"Who's dead, Mike?" not looking up from the file.

"Darnell Grey, your Rape Homicide trial defendant, is dead. They beat him to death in the prison."

Tucker looked up, eyes narrowing, and looked at Webster. "What? When did this happen?"

"I don't know, this morning, last night?" Webster said, moving files to sit on a chair. "I was in a meeting with the AG. Collucci came in, asked us all to leave. I waited outside the office and overheard the conversation."

"Son-of-a-bitch," Tucker said. "The bastard knew it when he talked to me. Son-of-a-bitch," his face flushed, the veins in his neck pulsing with each shallow breath.

Regaining his self-control, Tucker told Webster the details of his conversation with Collucci. "I am going to resign. I can't believe this shit goes on here."

"What good will it do?" Webster argued. "Look, there's not much you can do to change this. You sure as shit can't do anything from outside the office. Resign and you gain nothing. Stay inside and maybe, just maybe, you can turn things around."

Tucker showed no reaction, spinning a pen in his fingers. "But I'm involved. I saw problems with the case. There are issues with the lineup. When Collucci put pressure on me, I just caved. He may not believe it, but I think the whole case is a big lie. Now he's trying to buy me off with this new job."

Webster put his hands on the desk, "So you saw problems with the case. Every case here has problems. Look, you didn't kill him. There may be issues, but from what I know, the guy was a brutal bastard. There was plenty of evidence against him."

Tucker looked at Webster, "I'm not so sure about it."

"You got another job you can go to? Isn't your wife pregnant? How you going to pay bills trying to start a practice? You know if you cross Collucci he will bury you. Listen keep your mouth shut and wait for the

98

opportunity to do something that will make a difference. You can't do that now and you sure as shit can't do it if you're unemployed."

Tucker looked out his window. "You're right, I guess. I don't have much choice, do I?"

Webster went to the door, looking back at Tucker. "Listen; meet me after work, my treat. You can tell me your plans for this new unit you're running."

Tucker smiled, "Okay, deal. Thanks, Mike," watching as the door closed.

I hope this is the right thing to do. I hope so...

SILENCE OF THE LIONS

Chapter 17

September 9, 2009, 11:30AM
Office of the Presiding Justice
Rhode Island Supreme Court
Providence, RI

Judge Tucker sat in his office reviewing Writs of Certiorari petitions submitted to the court.

His mind drifted back to 1972. He recalled sitting in his small office in the AG's office, contemplating his resignation. *A man died, and I did nothing. Now, perhaps I can make amends.*

Walking to a file cabinet in the office, he unlocked it and removed a file from the bottom drawer. Opening the faded manila folder, he removed two documents then returned the folder to the cabinet.

Placing them on his desk, he picked up the line to his aide. "Mrs. Atwell, would you please look up the address for the East Providence Police Department. Please prepare a large envelope addressed to Lieutenant Joshua Williams. Use my personal post office box for the return address and bring it to me as soon as you've had time to complete it. Thank you," ending the call.

Looking over the documents, the feeling of disappointment overcame him. *All these years and it isn't until now I find the courage to do something.*

There was a slight knock on the door and Mrs. Atwell entered carrying the yellow mailing envelope.

"Here it is, your Honor. Would you like me to mail it for you?" glancing at the files on the desk.

"Thank you, no, Mrs. Atwell. I will take care of it myself. I need to review a few things before I seal it." Waiting for Atwell to leave, Judge Tucker read over each piece of paper once more. He placed the two documents in the envelope, sealed it, and put it in his briefcase.

Picking up the extension again, he said, "Mrs. Atwell, would you place a call to Senator Collucci's office please? Ask the Senator if I might speak with him, thank you."

A short while later, Mrs. Atwell came into the office. "Senator Collucci is on the line for you, Judge, line 2."

"Thank you," lifting the phone and covering the mouthpiece, "That will be all for today, Mrs. Atwell. Why don't you go a little early? Get a head start on the traffic."

"Thank you, your Honor."

Tucker turned his attention to the call, "Senator, how are you?"

"Bob, please. No need for formality among old friends."

"Yes, well, I was wondering if we might meet Senator, sorry, Bob, just for a few moments?"

"I was planning on dinner at the Capital Grille this evening, perhaps we can meet for a drink before?"

"Great, I can be there around six. Does that work?" Tucker answered.

"Perfect. Looking forward to it," Collucci replied and hung up.

"So, what was that all about?" the Senator's aide asked.

"Not sure," Collucci said. "But coming on the heels of the little visit by Williams and Fleming I bet it's not a coincidence."

"How do you want to handle it?" Sorin said.

"I'll see what the good Judge has to say. If it's nothing, so be it. If not... well then we will deal with it." Collucci smiled.

"Our other friends are not happy with this sudden attention to us. They prefer you to remain under the radar."

Collucci looked at Sorin for a moment. "This is ancient history. It has no effect on them or me. You calm them down. I'll deal with the Judge. We don't need any more attention on Williams, or us."

* * *

Capital Grille
6:30 PM
September 9, 2009
Providence, Rhode Island

"This is rather nice of Hawk to take us all to dinner, don't you think?" Keira Williams said as she sat at the bar with Josh, Chris, Vera, and Maggie.

"Nice has nothing to do with it," Chris said. "He just wants to show off his latest wife."

"Do I detect jealousy here?" Josh laughed. "He did offer to make you his date, since he knew you'd have to rent one otherwise."

"Keira, would you mind if I beat your husband senseless?" Chris asked, leaning past Josh to look at Keira.

"He's already at that point," Keira answered. "Ignore him."

"Nice, my own wife."

A moment later Hawk arrived with the fourth Mrs. Bennett. "Ladies, Mr. Williams, I'd like to introduce you to my wife Candace," an ebullient smile crossing his face.

After the round of greetings and congratulations, the party moved to the private dining area. As they filled in around the table, Chris excused herself to go to the ladies' room. The other women accompanied her.

"What is it with the herd mentality of women and the bathroom?" Josh asked.

"One of the insoluble mysteries of life, my boy. Enjoy the quiet time. It gives one a chance to scan for targets of opportunity," smiling at the attractive waitress as she passed by.

"Aren't you a newlywed?" Josh asked.

"I also am a realist," Hawk replied. "My relationships follow a well-established, unalterable pattern. I have accepted my fate," turning to smile at the even prettier bartender working the private bar.

As the women rejoined the group Chris said, "Are you a believer in coincidences, Josh?"

"No, why?" he answered.

"Well, you'll never guess who's sitting at the bar."

Josh got up and walked to the door of the private dining area. Looking out toward the main bar, he saw nothing much. Then he spotted them, Judge Tucker and Senator Collucci, talking at the bar.

"Holy shit," Josh said as he sat back down. "That's no damn coincidence."

"What is so important that it draws the center of attention of this gathering away from me?" Hawk said.

"The Presiding Justice of the Rhode Island Supreme Court sitting at the bar talking to Senator Robert Collucci," Chris said.

"And this is noteworthy to you because?" Hawk asked.

Josh explained the Grey case, the attempt against Keira, and their interviews with Collucci and Tucker. Hawk's countenance grew dark.

"I do not doubt the depth of evil to which that son-of-a-bitch Collucci will stoop. But I am disheartened by Judge Tucker's association with him," Hawk said. "I have always held the judge in the highest regard. This is most troubling."

Josh listened to Hawk and said. "Tucker was a Special Assistant AG when Collucci was a Deputy. We know Collucci took the Grey case away from Tucker. We just don't know why."

"I still have some old contacts with people who were in the office then. As I told you, Bill Symonds and I worked there for a time in the appellate division. However, it was long after Collucci left. I may be able to get some inside info," Hawk offered.

"We should have thought to ask you in the first place," Chris added.

"Finally," Hawk said, "after all these years, she is coming to her senses," raising his glass in a toast to Chris.

Chapter 18

September 10, 2009
SIU
East Providence Police Headquarters
East Providence, RI

Josh sat at his desk looking over the files from Zach Kennedy. Josh could not think of any cases handled by SIU, or the whole department which would lead to someone trying to kill him. As he read the lines, nothing made sense.

"What are you reading, Lieutenant?" Detective Tommy Moore asked. Tommy was a recent transfer into SIU, aggressive, smart, and intuitive.

Josh looked up from reading, "Hey Tommy. Not much, just some stuff from the Chief."

Tommy grinned. "Oh, the super-secret-squirrel files from the Feds, eh?"

Josh glanced up and smiled. "Not too many secrets in this place, are there?"

"Nope. A couple of us were trying to recall the last time someone targeted an East Providence cop for murder. Someone other than a jealous husband or pissed off wife. We couldn't think of any. Not in the whole damn state."

Tommy walked over to Josh's desk. "Look, LT, someone tried to get you and almost took out your wife. It doesn't sit well with most of us. We want to help get the son-of-a-bitch."

Josh picked up the files, handing them to Tommy. "Look these over. Do not let the Feds know I showed them to you. I'm going to tell Brennan I included you. If you see something I missed, let me know," watching as Tommy took the files. "Wait, what do you mean most of us?"

Tommy returned to his desk, laughing. "Believe it or not LT, there are some cops here who don't like you. Maybe not enough to wish you dead, but they wouldn't mind seeing you step on your dick."

Josh shook his head as he picked up the phone and called Brennan. "Yeah, I know, but I'd like the second set of eyes on this. They'd never let me show Hamlin. Tommy's a smart guy. What's that? Okay. Will do. Thanks Chief."

Turning to Tommy, he said, "Brennan says keep your mouth shut about this or he'll transfer you to Records as a reports review bitch."

Tommy held up his hands, "Secret is safe with me, LT."

* * *

Tommy Moore spent the next few hours reading over the file and researching things online. "Hey LT," he said, "I got something you may want to look at."

Josh looked up from his coffee, motioning for Moore to continue.

"I checked some of the addresses they identified from numbers called on the gang banger's phone, right?"

"Yeah?"

"Most turned out to be the usual shit hole safe houses, heroin bagging operations I would assume. There are a few topless clubs requiring a personal follow-up; I will need some advanced funds from the city. Five hundred should do it in small bills," putting his hand out, smiling at Josh.

Josh shook his head.

"No? Okay, but it might be the key piece of..."

"Just tell me what you found. You're not getting five-hundred dollars in one-dollar bills, so move on."

"Okay, okay." Rolling his chair over to Josh's desk, he showed him a photo on his laptop. "This one I can't quite figure out."

"Where is that?"

"It's one of those office suite buildings. It's right at the bottom of Waterman Street in Providence, just before you get onto the Henderson Bridge. I got the picture from the tax assessor's database. Small businesses use shared administrative help and rent one or two-room offices. Doesn't make sense, MS-13 isn't the office type."

Moore now had Josh's interest. "So what else did you find?"

"Not much else. I can't see any connection to MS-13, Collucci, Russians, Klingons, Vulcans, or anyone else we know. It just stuck out as weird," shaking his head.

"How many offices are there?" Josh asked.

"About thirty."

"And the call just went to the main line?"

Tommy sorted through the call records. "The call went to the main trunk line, which is weird because each business has its own number. When a call comes into the operator, it displays which company the call is for and they answer for that business. No one calls the main trunk line, it's not publicized."

"Means the caller knew the number. Who owns the office building? Where would the main number ring?"

"Hang on a minute," Tommy said, bringing up the Excel spreadsheet on his computer. "The building is owned by Ashton Vision, LLC. They are a subsidiary of Burke, Cole, Silva, & Rego Management Consultants, LLC. The documents list Harriet Lane Enterprises as the main corporate entity. This last one is a Delaware corporation. Haven't had time to go further. We'll have to get phone records from the business to learn more."

"Chasing the corporate trail, always a great deal of fun. So, there must be something to this," looking at the call records. "The call to the main number was followed by two calls to disposable phones, and then another call to the main line. Had to be relaying information."

Josh studied the screen, looking for a pattern. "You're right; we need to get the call records from the main trunk number. Maybe it will be helpful," looking at Moore.

"Already working on it. I called Kristin Volpe. She said she'd let you know when the subpoena was ready. She sounded very excited by the prospect."

Josh broke eye contact on hearing Volpe's name. "Ah, good, that's good."

"There's something I should know about?" Moore asked, eyebrows rising.

"Let's just say I'd prefer you deal with her. We had an, ah, encounter and I don't want to repeat it."

Moore smiled. "An encounter? Is that what they call it now?"

Josh picked up his briefcase, holding it upright on his lap. "If you know what's good for you, you'll let this go. Deal with Volpe, I don't need any more complications in my life," dropping the case on his desk.

Moore laughed. "I will defend your honor and protect your chaste countenance, my Liege," bowing his head.

Josh flipped him the bird and went to get more coffee. *Just what I need, what was I thinking?*

* * *

Two days later, subpoena in hand, Josh and Tommy Moore met with Zach Kennedy. Josh decided Kennedy would be okay with Moore's inclusion in the investigation. His instincts about the agent were correct.

The three went to the corporate offices of Cox Cable to serve the subpoena. Cox was the service provider for the office building. As they entered the office building, a voice called out, "Well, will you look at this? See what happens when you leave the door unlocked."

Josh turned. He spotted retired State Police Lieutenant Danny Halloran.

"Danny, I didn't know you were here."

"Josh, how are you?" shaking Josh's hand, looking at the other two.

"Danny, this is Zach Kennedy from the FBI and Detective Tommy Moore from my department."

After the round of greetings, they went into Halloran's office. "So, what brings you here to my domain boys?"

Josh showed Halloran the subpoena. As he reviewed it, Halloran brought up a screen on his computer. He punched a few keys, "So, do you want me to print out all 6,589 pages? Or will a spreadsheet via email suffice?"

Josh reached into his pocket and withdrew a USB thumb drive. "How about we use this instead? I'm surprised they found a trooper who could use email, let alone a spreadsheet," smiling at Halloran.

"You know, they were going to offer Hamlin the job, but she still uses stone tablets," Halloran retorted.

Josh laughed, "You got that right. Technically illiterate that one."

Taking the USB drive, Halloran plugged the device in, downloading the file. "So, this must be something special for the FBI to grace our presence," smiling at Kennedy. "Related to the little incident on Route 44, I assume?"

Josh nodded, "Yeah, just trying to trace the guy's activities before he came after us."

"Well, if there's anything else you need, give me a call," Halloran walked them to the door. "Always willing to help. Say hi to Chris when you see her."

As they got into Josh's car, Tommy said, "And how long do you think it will be before he calls Scituate?"

"Who's Scituate?" Kennedy asked.

"State Police Headquarters," Josh answered, "Welcome to Rhode Island."

Kennedy shook his head, "So we can expect some parallel looks at this thing, I suppose. If FBI Headquarters hears about this, they'll pull me out of here."

"Not to worry. I have my own connections with Scituate; they'll let me know if someone takes an interest in this. Let's go look at the office building, maybe we'll see something."

"It must be the last brick building on the right, just before the bridge," Josh said, as they drove down Waterman Street.

Moore looked at his file. "Yup, that's it."

Josh pulled around the building and parked in the lot across the street. "Should we go inside?"

"How about I do it?" Kennedy said. "No one here knows me."

Kennedy walked to the main entrance and disappeared inside. He emerged a few moments later, returning to the car.

"Well, nothing obvious. I talked to the receptionist and told her I was looking for an office suite. She didn't know who owned the building or who to contact. She called the maintenance guy who, unbelievably, was much more informed. He gave me a number to call. I'll run it through our database when we get back to the office."

Driving back past the entrance, Josh pointed out the Waterman Grille. "Maybe we should conduct a little surveillance at the bar there. Convenient for those who work in the office suites. I'm willing to bet we get a few who go in there for drinks after work."

"I'm in," Moore replied. "Never let it be said I missed an opportunity to let the city pay my bar tab."

"There's a fucking shock," Josh answered. "How about you, Mr. Kennedy, can we persuade you to join us in the important mission?"

Kennedy smiled. "I suppose I should uphold the honor of the FBI and our commitment to investigative resiliency."

"What'd he say?" Moore asked.

"He's in," Josh chuckled. "You'll have to excuse him, Zach. He was a Jarhead. You have to use small words."

"This Jarhead is going to make you regret it, Air Force, bah. Nothing but glorified flight attendants taking the men to war," Moore replied.

Two hours later, the three sat at the bar in the Waterman Grille, overlooking the water. As they suspected, the place was crawling with office workers from the local businesses.

Josh had a deep conversation with a wish-I-still-was-a-thirty-something office manager. She proudly displayed her discount quality breast enhancements. Josh learned nothing. Moore, enraptured with a secretary as she complained about her lack of a love life, made no progress.

Kennedy spoke to a business owner. She provided information about rumors to the actual ownership of the building. Glancing around the room, whispering in her most conspiratorial voice, she said, "I hear the place is mopped up." Sipping her third Martini and nodding.

"You mean mobbed up, as in organized crime?" Kennedy asked, amused by the tone of her voice.

"Shh," she answered, glancing around again. "Yeah, mobbed, mopped, whatever. You gonna buy me another drink or what?"

After two hours of plying their investigative skills, they realized their efforts were futile. That and they ran out of money. Brennan authorized a $100 limit and they exceeded it.

* * *

The three gathered in the office the next morning.

"Well, as much as I enjoyed our surveillance operation yesterday," Zach Kennedy said. "I am sad to conclude, we didn't learn much."

"I disagree," Josh replied. "I did get an important piece of information, two as a matter of fact."

Zach and Tommy Moore glanced at each other, and then looked back at Josh.

"I got the name of the plastic surgeon who did my friend's implants. Son-of-a-bitch should have used a level. One was higher than the other and pointed around the corner," Josh said, laughing.

"You are a sick man," Tommy said.

Josh smiled. "Okay, listen. I did have time to think a bit about this. Maybe we're approaching this all wrong."

"What do ya' mean?" Zach said.

"Well, think about it. This shit all began when we started looking at the Grey case. We've gone through all our current and past SIU cases. There is nothing there. The Grey case is the one commonality."

Zach thought for a moment. "You may be on to something there. Pull the Providence PD file out. We must have missed something."

Josh sat back in his chair, going over in his mind the reports from all those years ago. His mind tried to focus on the reports, but it drifted elsewhere. *What have I stumbled onto? Shit like this doesn't happen here. What about Keira, what do I do for her? She'd never carry a gun. How do I protect her?*

While Zach and Moore reviewed the files, Josh called Joe McDaniel. Josh considered Joe McDaniel the best cop he'd ever worked with. When McDaniel retired, he took with him an irreplaceable amount of experience. Many cops still sought him out for advice.

"Hello," McDaniel answered.

"Hey Joe, Josh Williams."

"Ah, I was wondering when you were going to get around to talking to me. What took you so long?"

"You know what this is about?"

"I went to Jimmy Calise's wake and funeral. They brought him home from Florida for burial. Gotta tell ya' man, I got a fucking earful. You pissed off some people over there. Better find a way to make nice," McDaniel replied.

"Not sure if what we're doing is going to help," Josh said. "Can I stop by and talk to you?"

"Let's meet at Bovi's this afternoon. You can buy me a few beers and I'll calm the restless natives at Providence PD in exchange."

"Sounds good, see you there."

* * *

After hanging up with McDaniel, Josh logged into his computer to check his email. Then he searched for the Delaware Secretary of State Corporations Database.

"Hey," Zach said, turning his laptop to face Josh, "what's this look like to you?"

Josh looked at the screen. "What'd you find?"

"I was comparing calls from the main line at the office complex to every other number we have, looking for patterns or links. I found this match," tapping the screen.

Josh looked at the spreadsheet; Zach highlighted two inbound calls and one outbound call to the same number. "Okay, so whose number is it?"

"Maggie Fleming," Zach said.

Josh let out an involuntary laugh, "Yeah, right. Seriously, what'd you find?

"I am serious, Josh."

"Are you sure?"

"I checked it a couple of times. The calls are to and from her cell phone. I'd say that's a little suspicious," Zach answered, pointing again to the cells in the spreadsheet.

"There's no way," Josh insisted, disbelieving his own eyes.

"How well do you know her?" Zach asked.

Josh explained the covert help Fleming provided three years ago. "I mean, I don't know what would've happened if she hadn't tipped us to things. She resigned from the US Attorney's office because of what Collucci did. Took a lot of guts to do that," flopping back in his chair.

Staring at Zach, Josh struggled to get his mind around this. "What would she have to gain here? Why would she work with Chris? She would have no way of knowing any of their cases would get them access to SIU cases." Josh held up his hand, "And before you even think it, I know there is no way Chris is involved in any shit. What made you check her number?"

Zach looked at Josh. "Look, I am not trying to build the paranoia level any higher than it is, but I worked counterintelligence for a long time. They have all sorts of methods to infiltrate law enforcement agencies. Doveryai no Proveryai," Zach said in perfect Russian. "Trust but Verify. Remember that. I checked everyone's number. Yours, your wife's, Chris, Tommy's, Brennan's, everybody. We need to look at everybody."

Josh walked back to his desk. "I just can't see her involved in this. Not with Collucci, doesn't make sense. She wasn't even part of the original discussion about the Grey case. She went with me to see Collucci and played him well."

"Or played you," Zach answered.

"Bullshit, I think we settle this now," grabbing his portable radio from the charger. "Come on; let's go have a chat with Fleming."

"I'd suggest we wait. If it's nothing, there's no harm. If there is something to it, better we know, and she doesn't. Agreed?" Kennedy said.

Josh rubbed the back of his neck, he didn't feel comfortable about this, but it was the best course, for now.

Tommy Moore spoke up, "So are you guys all done with the scene from Russia with Love? Because, I think we have real police work to do rather than trying to act out bad spy movies."

Zach smiled and picked up the phone.

Josh plugged the radio back into the charger. He went back to researching the Delaware Corporations database. *Ah, Darnell what next? He thought. What next?*

Moore went back to his computer, but he couldn't help but wonder if being in a nice safe marked police car was better than this insanity.

Chapter 19

Josh pulled into the small parking area off Taunton Avenue in front of Bovi's Tavern. The bar is one of the best-known gathering places in the City of East Providence.

The usual after work crowd stood or sat in their accustomed positions. Joe McDaniel stood at the bar talking to Vinny the plumber and Reggie Stone.

When Stone spotted Josh, he came over, wrapped him in his huge arms, and kissed him on the cheek. "Josh, my brother from another mother. I missed you, man. Where you been at?"

Stone had been a roofer for as long as anyone could remember. Even now, he could walk up ladders carrying two bundles of shingles all day long. He was the guy wanted you on your side.

As a young officer, McDaniel had run-ins with Stone, yet the two had grown to be friends. As McDaniel always said, the one difference between the people driving the police car and those riding in the caged back seat, is the ones in the back got caught.

Josh stood next to McDaniel. "So, what words of wisdom do you have for me, Joe?"

McDaniel nodded toward Stone, "There's who you should talk to. He's related to Grey."

Josh looked at Stone. "For real, Reg?"

"Josh, my man, this is Rhode Island. We all related somehow, 'specially the brothers," flashing a wide grin.

Josh laughed. "I should know by now, if I want to find out anything about this city, ask McDaniel or Stone. You guys should be a road show." Flagging down the bartender Josh said," How about a round here?"

After the drinks arrived, Josh, Joe McDaniel, and Reggie gathered in a small circle.

"So, how do you know Darnell Grey?" Josh asked.

"Darnell is, or was, my cousin. He lived on Summit Street when we were kids, then his father died and his mother, she was from Providence, moved back to the south side. Wiggins Village."

Josh listened as Stone told the story of Grey being a standout athlete at Central High. "He had a shot at a scholarship at URI for basketball, but he couldn't afford to go. He was working full-time to help his mother out. They couldn't survive without the money. Of course, there was the little incident," smiling at McDaniel.

Joe McDaniel picked up the story. "Smiley here," tipping his glass at Stone, "and his cousin got the brilliant idea to grab a bunch of old copper from the Rocha warehouse, near Watchemoket Square. One of the owners complained, even though the place was abandoned. We went down there and spotted these two. I chased Darnell, Reggie here fell and old Fatty Sousa landed on him," chuckling at the memory. "Forty years on the job, Fatty never caught anyone except Reggie."

Reggie laughed. "Fat bastard damn near killed me. I weighed about 120 pounds then."

"That was a long time ago," McDaniel said, patting Stone on his gut.

"No shit," Stone laughed.

"Anyway, I was pretty fast back then," McDaniel continued. "Grey had forty pounds of copper on him and I couldn't even get close to him. Last I saw, he was over the Red Bridge and gone. The only reason we got him later was we knew he and Reggie here were inseparable."

Josh looked at McDaniel, "So what happened."

"After we charged the two of them, I found out about Grey's shot at a scholarship. I got the AG's office to file the charges," glancing at Stone. "All they had to do was stay out of trouble for six months. Or at least, not get caught."

Stone picked up the story. "After I recovered from being turned into a black pancake by Tubbo the Cop, Darnell and I just hung around together. Then he got drafted and went to Vietnam," Stone took a drink, eyes watering. "He came back a different man, Josh. He was always starting fights and getting locked up. After he got married, it got worse. Every time I saw him he was pissed off about something."

Stone motioned for another round of drinks. "I'll tell you this though; he never, ever hit a woman. His wife would nag his ass to death, but he never raised a hand to her. He'd leave and get into fights just to release the tension. But I know this for a fact; he didn't rape or kill nobody."

McDaniel looked at Josh, then said, "Reggie, tell him about talking to the cops."

Stone's eyes grew narrow and dark. "After I heard Darnell got arrested, I went to the station in East Providence to talk to the detectives. I told them Darnell and I was at my house all day when that first rape happened. He helped me do some work in the basement. Then, he and I, his wife and my girlfriend, had a cookout. A bunch of other people were there too. Darnell and his wife even stayed over that night. Cops wouldn't listen."

"Who'd you talk to, Reggie?" Josh asked.

"I didn't know his name, big, fat white guy. He said I was trying to cover for my cousin and he would arrest me for lying to the cops. You know what he said. Right to my face that fat piece of shit said, 'One nigger's word against a whole bunch of white people don't mean shit.' "

Stone shook his head, looking into his drink. "A couple of weeks later, Darnell's wife called and told us he was dead. Said he got killed in the prison. Shit never should have happened, Josh. 'S not right. He didn't do those things. His wife up and left town. We heard she was pregnant, but we never saw her again."

Josh looked at McDaniel.

"It was a different time then, Josh. The detective division was full of guys with a political hook, or they were drunks and they took them off the road. There were maybe five guys in the division who did all the work," McDaniel shook his head. "The Captain back then was an ex-Marine. Good guy. He used to say he was the highest paid babysitter in the city."

"Do you know who Reggie talked to?"

"Fat, white guy describes half the division. Not that it matters, nobody who worked detectives back then is still alive. Most of them never made it past two or three years after retiring."

"Looks like you're getting to be a fat white guy now McDaniel," Reggie chimed in.

Patting his own gut, McDaniel laughed. "Might be, but I'll never be as big a fat ass as you."

Stone winked at him and took a long drink. "So, tell me Josh. Why the sudden interest in this?"

Josh explained the story. He left out the details but told Reggie how they tried to kill Keira.

"No shit?" Stone said. "I find out who tried to hurt Keira, they won't live to see the next day. Soon as that girl comes to her senses and dumps you, she and I are riding off on my Harley. I'll show her some lovin' she'll never forget."

"She might take you up on it someday," Josh replied.

"Listen to me, Josh. You need something done about a problem, you talk to me." Patting Josh on the shoulder, tilting his head to McDaniel, "away from this dinosaur here."

"I will Reg, thanks," unsure how serious Reggie was.

"Can you get Darnell's daughter to come see me and my wife?" Reggie asked, with a slight tear in his eye.

"I don't see why not. She may not realize she has family here. I can have Vera Johnson arrange it. She's the girl's aunt. Well, sort of an adopted aunt."

"No shit, Vera? From the Library? What a small world," Reggie said.

"And how the hell do you know she worked in the library? I didn't think you could read," McDaniel joked.

"There's a lot of things you don't know about me, old man. A lot of things," nodding and draining the last of his drink. "Gotta run boys. I hope you find out who did those things back then. Clear my cousin's name. It would mean a lot to me, Josh."

Josh nodded, "I'll do what I can my friend, I'll do what I can."

Chapter 20

Tommy Moore came into the SIU office, catching the tail end of Josh's phone conversation.

"Thanks, Vera. Reggie and his wife will appreciate it. What's that? Yeah, I know. Small world. Okay, talk to you later."

"What was that about?" Tommy asked.

"Turns out Grey's daughter is related to Reggie Stone. Vera's gonna bring her over to meet Reggie and his wife."

Tommy smiled, "Well, at least one good thing came out this."

"Yup, now let's see what else we can do."

Tommy headed toward the reception area, "Going for coffee, want one?"

"Yeah great, thanks."

A few moments later, Tommy returned with the coffee and the morning mail.

"There's something for you, LT," handing Josh a large yellow envelope.

Josh looked it over. He didn't recognize the return address, just a post office box in Providence. Tearing open the flap, he pulled out two sheets of paper. "Holy shit, look at this."

Tommy came over to the desk.

Josh placed the pages next to each other on the desk. The heading on both were identical, Providence Police Department Lineup Report. Both forms were dated March 23, 1972. The time on one listed 21:00, 9:00 PM, in military format. The second listed 21:30, 9:30 PM.

On the first report, the order of names in the lineup had Darnell Grey in the first position. In the second report, he was in the third position. Both forms list Detective George Weslyan as the investigating officer. On the first report, next to the initials for the Supervising Assistant Attorney General were the letters RC. On the second report, it was evident someone erased the original initials and wrote GT.

"Grab our file, there's another copy of one of these in there. It's the one I showed Tucker when we spoke to him."

Tommy retrieved the file and found the report. Placing this copy next to the other two, they compared them.

Josh looked at Tommy. It was obvious the third report, the one from the Providence PD file was a poor copy of the one with the altered initials.

"Unbelievable, just freaking unbelievable."

Josh picked up the phone, "Donna, it's Josh, the Chief in?"

A few moments later, Josh placed the lineup reports on the Chief's desk.

"Where'd you get these?" Brennan asked.

"Came in the mail. P O Box for a return address. I'll bet they're from Tucker."

"Tucker?" Brennan said. "Why would he hold onto these for so long?"

"I don't know, but I am going to ask him."

"You sure they're from him? It wouldn't be helpful to accuse a State Supreme Court Justice of concealing evidence in a conspiracy without proof."

"Tommy's going to trace the P O Box, and then I'll go talk to Tucker. I'll be subtle," Josh replied.

"Subtle? There is nothing subtle about you, Lieutenant. At least try to be somewhat tactful. And," pointing his finger at Josh, "don't do anything stupid like arrest him for God's sake. Come back and talk to me first. Understood?"

Josh nodded. "If he did send it, and I am pretty sure he did, I bet he wants to talk to us." He explained to Brennan what they thought transpired with the Providence lineup.

"They did a second lineup and tried to alter the initials of the AG. We missed it in our file because the copy is so poor. I can see that. But why? I assume they fucked up when they left the first report in the file. That's evident. But why change the initials?" Brennan asked.

"A better question is who did it? Maybe the AG was aware of the two lineups and decided it would be better if he wasn't involved."

"Who is RC, anyway? Do you know?" Brennan asked.

Josh and Tommy broke into huge, shit-eating smiles.

Brennan looked at the detectives, back at the file, and then shook his head. "Oh, of course it is, and GT is George Tucker. What was I thinking holding out hope it was somebody other than them? So, explain this to me, again."

Josh pointed to the files. "The one on the left is the original. Just like Calise told me, there were two lineups. The one in the middle is the changed file with the same initials as the one on the left, RC. The one on the right is the one from the lineup they planned to use with the time changed and the altered initials, GT. Collucci must have smelled a rat and wanted to insulate himself from the fudged lineup report if things went south. If nobody noticed or--."

"Or if the guy got taken care of in the can. Case closed," Tommy interjected.

"Thanks Captain Obvious," Brennan replied. Turning to Josh, "Remind me again why I transferred him into SIU?"

"Nowhere else for him, too slow for anything complicated."

"Okay, okay. I was just thinking out loud," Tommy said.

"Stop it, son. You'll hurt yourself," Brennan added, patting Tommy on the back. "But we do face a rather frightening scenario. A United States Senator and a Justice of the Rhode Island Supreme Court complicit in murder. The murder of someone likely innocent of any crime. Perhaps, involved in framing him in the first place."

Josh shook his head. "I'd bet Tucker had nothing to do with it and Collucci's smarter than that. He didn't have to plan the murder, or even persuade someone to do it. The natural order of things in the prison has rapists just above child molesters. They are always held in protective custody. Take black defendant, white victims, and the racial conflicts of the era, hell, all they had to do is put the guy into the general population and let nature take its course." Josh picked up the file and looked at the original lineup report, "Collucci may have not had anything to do with the prison. Remember, one of our victims was a Trooper's daughter."

"Oh, I remember well the night it happened; I was working the next post. Once word got to Scituate... I didn't know there were that many troopers in the state. They were all over the place looking for the guy."

"Can't blame 'em for that. We'd have done the same thing. It's what happened after that worries me. Won't be winning any popularity contests with them either," Josh said.

Brennan looked at Josh for a moment. "You know, in the course of just a few short weeks you've managed to piss off Providence PD and a United States Senator. Now you might piss off the State Police and drag Judge Tucker into this. Are you sure this is worth it?"

Josh hesitated a moment. "Chief, I need to see where this goes. Keep in mind they came after me and almost killed Keira. I am going to find out who it was, wherever it goes."

Brennan's eyes narrowed, "How does this fit in with the damn 007 spy shit you brought on yourself?"

"All I know is when we started looking at this case, we made someone nervous. I don't think Collucci had anything to do with them going after Keira. But, I am willing to bet it is something, or somebody, he's involved with." Josh picked up the files, "That's why we keep looking at this case."

Brennan rubbed his chin, "Keep me in the loop before, and I mean before, any more shit hits the fan."

Josh and Tommy left the office.

"Tommy, trace the P. O. Box. I am going to go talk to Chris about her friend the Judge. See what she thinks. I'll meet you back here later. When Kennedy gets here, bring him up to speed on this."

* * *

Chris Hamlin drove down Metropolitan Park Drive. She pulled into Haines Park at the Barrington/East Providence city line. Spotting Josh's car near the boat ramp, she pulled up next to him.

Josh waited, arms folded, leaning on the hood of the unmarked unit.

"So, what's with all the secret-squirrel stuff?" Chris asked.

Josh stood and handed her a piece of paper. Chris looked it over.

"And this is important because?" looking up. "Wait a minute," looking back at the paper. "These calls are to Maggie's cell. What the hell is this Josh?"

"Those are call records from an office complex on Waterman Street. The number is a main trunk feed, not a published number, and she called it. Just before we met with Collucci...," looking out at the water. "The Feds didn't want me to say anything to her. But I had to tell you."

Chris smiled. "Ah, that explains the spy vs spy stuff. Okay, what do you think?"

"I don't know. My instinct says there's an explanation and to just ask her," Josh spun his car keys around his fingers. "This whole mess you got me into has taken on new dimensions. Chris, this is more than an old case. There are Russian mob guys with composite weapons, MS-13 gang bangers, shit that is not supposed to happen here."

"Russian mob guys?" Chris looked concerned. "Composite weapons? What are you talking about? Wasn't this a gang banger thing? Are you keeping shit from me?"

"Let's go get a coffee," Josh answered. "I have much more to tell you, my friend. Some of it I just found out. Most of which you will not believe. I am finding it hard to believe myself."

As they sat in the booth at the Kent Corners Dunkin' Donuts, Josh laid it out for Chris. The latest information on the attempt on Keira, the intelligence from the Feds, everything. Looking outside Josh said, "Speak of the devil, here's the hero himself," nodding his head toward the front parking lot.

Chubby White pulled into the lot. His shiny, repainted, and unblemished tow truck glistened in the morning sun.

Chubby came in and saw Josh and Chris. Walking over, he smiled. "Hey Lieutenant and used to be Lieutenant. How are you?"

"Great Chubby, thanks to you. Let me get you a coffee," Josh said.

"No, no, that's okay. I got a D&D gift card for $100 from the manager after he heard the story. I'm good."

"$100 gift card, that should last you, what, a day or so?" Chris joked.

"Well it would," Chubby answered, "but people keep buying my stuff for me, they recognize me from the news," rubbing his enormous gut. "But I am starting at the gym on Monday. I'll be ready for the agility test this time, Brennan said I have supervisor material in me," waddling over to the counter.

"Boy is determined, isn't he?" Chris said.

"And delusional, but I do owe him one. A big one," Josh replied, watching as Chubby picked out two dozen donuts.

"I saw his performance on the news," Chris chuckled. "They had to use a wide-angle lens to fit him and Brennan in at the same time."

Josh laughed, "I'll make sure I tell him you said that."

Chubby White came back over carrying his donut haul and a giant coffee. "You guys got a minute? I want to show you something on my truck."

Josh glanced at Chris, "Sure, Chubby. Lead on."

Chubby led them to the parking lot. Opening the driver's door, he gently loaded the pallet of pastry, closed the door, and motioned them over.

Painted on the side of the truck was an image of a motorcycle, body flying off, with circle around it and line through it.

"I saw it on the *History Channel*. Fighter pilots painted their planes when they shot someone down. Nice, huh?" beaming an infectious grin.

"Four more and you'll be an ace," Chris laughed.

"Let's not try too hard for that Chubby, okay?" Josh added.

Chubby laughed and climbed into the cab. Grabbing a donut with one hand, his coffee in the other, he pulled out of the lot.

"Steering with his knee I bet," Chris said, chuckling. "He is one happy man."

"Yes, he is," Josh agreed.

"Where do we go from here?"

"Like I said, my gut is telling me there's an explanation. I'd prefer to just ask her, but we need the federal resources on this. If they find out I went behind their backs, they'll pull out."

Chris thought a moment. "I'm not comfortable treating her like a suspect. I know there's an explanation. But, I suppose a few more days won't hurt."

"Give me some time to work on Kennedy. He's a good guy, not in the usual federal mold. I think I can convince him to let us talk to her. I'll call you in a few days. Meanwhile, if you decide to do anything else about the Grey case, keep in mind there is some serious shit going on here. We don't have any idea what it is."

Chris nodded, "Thanks, Dad. Not to worry. I can take care of myself," getting into her car.

Josh opened his door, "Hey," he yelled, motioning for Chris to open her window. "One more thing, I'm sure those copies of the original lineup reports came from Tucker. Should I go talk to him?"

Chris thought a moment. "Yeah, call him. I know there is no way he had anything to do with Grey ending up where he did. Tucker is too honest for any of it. I'd ask him. I am sure he had his reasons."

Josh watched her leave the lot. As he opened the door to his car, Chief Brennan pulled up next to him.

"Lieutenant, is it safe to assume this was just a friendly visit, nothing official like a briefing or anything?"

"Of course, Chief. I was just checking in with her."

"Make sure while you're checking in with her, the Feds don't find out. We need their help in this."

Watching Brennan drive away, Josh wondered how the man was always a step ahead of him.

* * *

Driving back from his meeting with Chris, Josh considered the risks. *Follow where this goes, whomever it involves, but at what cost? Someone came after me once; there's nothing to stop them from doing it again. What if they get to Keira because of something I do? I'd never forgive myself. I could just let it go. But, I can't. What are the chances we'll find anything to clear Grey's name anyway? The victims are dead, right? Wait a minute. Are they?*

Josh had his answer.

Pulling into the police station parking lot, Josh spotted Captain Charland walking out the back door. Charland saw Josh and headed toward him.

"Shit," Josh muttered. Grabbing his cell, he pretended to be on a call. Charland stood waiting at the side of the car, arms folded, tapping his foot.

Josh put the window down, tilting the phone away from his ear, "Hey Captain, this might take a while. The AG's office called me."

Charland smiled. "Fine, Lieutenant. I'll wait," turning and leaning on the hood.

Josh continued with his one-sided, imaginary conversation, hoping Charland would grow tired of waiting. No such luck. Putting the cell phone away, he got out of the car.

"What's up, Captain?"

"I've completed my review of your case files," a smirk growing on his face. "I've left a list of incomplete or incorrect files with the secretary. Please see that you resubmit them by Friday morning. I need to report the findings to the Chief. Is that clear, Lieutenant?"

"Friday?" Josh argued, "Captain, it's Wednesday. I do have current cases that need immediate attention. There's no way--"

"Lieutenant," Charland interrupted, raising his hand. "I am aware of what day it is. If cases aren't properly prepared, we lose them. These are just as important as anything you may be working on now. I trust you understand this is not a request. It is an order. See you follow it as such," turning and striding away.

Josh stood shaking his head. Grabbing his file from the car, he slammed the door and headed into the office.

Tommy was waiting for him, trying to conceal a smile.

"What the hell are you laughing at?" Josh asked, throwing the file on the desk.

"I was in the Detective Captain's office. He had some info on the stolen safe case from Amadeus Jewelry and wanted to run it by us. We saw the Charland encounter. It looked pleasant. Did you bond well?"

"Fuck you. That idiot wants me to fix cases from three years ago because they weren't organized to his standards." Grabbing the phone, dialing the Chief's office. "Did he, in his whole freaking career, ever arrest anybody? Mother--. Oops, sorry Donna. Is the Chief in? Great, I will be right over. What? Oh, okay."

Josh hung up, "Brennan's coming over here, wonder what that's about?"

"What do you think?" Tommy smiled.

"Charland talked to him first. Damn it. Brennan is gonna let him torture me forever isn't he?" Josh said, slumping into his chair.

The door opened, and Chief Brennan walked in.

"Good afternoon, sir. How are you this fine day? Might I get you a coffee?" Tommy grinned.

"No thank you," Brennan said, taking a seat at one of the empty desks. "I see you're training him in the same mold, aren't you, Lieutenant?"

"I know why you're here, I know. Captain Charland told me about the files. I'll get to them, I will," Josh said.

"Let me worry about Captain Charland. Something else occurred to me. We should locate the other victims. I was looking over our files and the statement from our other victim is missing, as is the original case report. I told Captain Charland to find the missing reports. That's what got him all excited. I don't know why I didn't think about this earlier."

Josh smiled. "Brilliant minds think alike, Boss. I thought of the same thing on the way over here. I was coming to tell you when Charland grabbed me in the lot. With all due respect, Chief, the guy is a pain in my ass. Was he ever a real cop? What does he have, like four hundred years on the job? Retire for Christ's sake."

Looking at Tommy, "Would you excuse the Lieutenant and I for a moment? Go enjoy your coffee," gesturing to the door, "somewhere else."

Tommy, bowing his head, slouched out the door, and left the office.

Brennan waited for the door to close, and then looked at Josh. "Let me tell you something, Josh. Something most people around here don't know. Charland was a cop in Boston for a few years. A group of radicals ambushed him and his partner back in the 70s. They shot Charland twice, his partner four times. Charland pulled the partner to safety, and then killed two of the bad guys."

Josh was stunned, not sure he was hearing this right.

"He left Boston PD because his wife was terrified he'd get killed. She was pregnant at the time. But he missed the job. He came here because his parents lived in the city. He was born here. He was a good street cop. As soon as he could, to keep his wife happy, he transferred into a records slot and made himself invaluable. Do not sell the guy short. I know he's a bit anal about things. I think it's how he copes with being inside."

"How is it no one knows this?" Josh asked.

"He never told anybody. I found out in a lecture I heard at the FBI Academy. It was about domestic terrorism and the old anti-war groups who turned to bombing and shooting at cops. The agent told the story of the Boston incident. When I spoke to Charland about it, he asked me to keep it to myself."

"Holy shit," Josh said.

"Look, he can be as big a pain in the ass for me as well as you, but he does his job right. If he had been in Records back then we wouldn't be hunting around for these files." Brennan rose and walked to the door. "I'll put him on looking for the old case records. If anyone can find them, he will. You just keep what I told you between us. Now go find those other victims."

Tommy came back into the office after seeing Brennan leave. "So, what's up? You in some shit?"

"Nope, Brennan's got it covered. He'll calm Charland down. We need to find the other victims in the rape cases."

Tommy walked to his desk. "I traced the P O Box listed on the return address from those lineup reports. Comes back to a company listed as JTS Management, LLC. The address listed is for a business that does corporation filings for other businesses. We can go talk to them, the office is downtown."

A short time later, Josh and Tommy walked into the offices of Corporate Services, Inc. on Washington Street in Providence. They spoke to the receptionist, she asked them to wait while she obtained the information for JTS Management.

"Here you go. The business is a property management firm. They list one company officer, a Ms. Jennifer Sorin, and an address of 141 Waterman Street, Suite 24, Providence, RI."

Josh looked at Tommy and back at the receptionist. "Did you say 141 Waterman Street?"

The woman looked at the screen again and nodded. "Yes, 141 Waterman Street, Suite 24. Will there be anything else?"

"Is there a phone number listed?" Tommy asked.

As she relayed the number, Tommy wrote it down. "Thanks. Can we get a copy of the file please?"

"Of course," printing out a copy and handing it to them.

"Thanks for your help." Josh said.

As they got in the car, Josh said, "I'll buy one coincidence with the gang banger calling, maybe even two with Fleming, but three connections to the same address? We gotta spend more time finding out who is behind that place." Josh pulled out of the lot, onto Washington Street, "And the name, Sorin, Sorin. I've heard it somewhere... Just can't put my finger on it."

Tommy nodded, "I am willing to bet this JTS Management is just a front for something, or somebody. When we get back, I'll do some more digging. See what I can find."

Josh nodded, already on the phone. "Zach, Josh Williams. You coming to my office today? Okay, cool. Got a few things to run by you. See you there." Putting the cell down, he said, "Kennedy's going to meet us there. Said he has some information as well."

Josh's cell phone rang. Looking at the caller ID Josh smiled, "Ah, my contact from the Golden Palace. Our friends in Scituate must have taken an interest." Answering the call, he said, "Hey, Jeff, what's up?"

Josh listened a moment and said, "Okay, thanks. I appreciate the heads up. Stop by Bovi's next time you're around, we usually go there on Fridays. Thanks again."

"So?" Tommy asked.

"Seems the powers that be detect a big case brewing and they want in, especially since we lit a fire under one of their retired Majors. I bet he tipped them off to the conversation we had. And, as we expected, Halloran called them as well."

"Jeez, they spend more time worrying about their damn reputation. If this were their case they'd be screaming if we tried to get involved."

"Not all of them, my friend. Most of 'em are good guys, there's a few with egos the size of the planet. You never know, they might be helpful," Josh said. "I'll give Brennan a call when we get back, he's got contacts everywhere."

Josh and Tommy grabbed lunch, and then made it back to the office. Tommy went to work on his computer, Josh called Brennan.

As Josh was making the call, Zach Kennedy came in the back door. "Hey boys, what's up?"

Josh motioned for him to wait a moment, "Hey Chief. Listen, I just got a call from Jeff Morris from the State Police. Seems we have sparked an interest with them. Yeah, yeah, I bet the Major called them. Can you see if you can work your magic?" listening for a moment. "Okay, great thanks."

Hanging up the phone, Josh said, "Brennan's gonna call the Colonel and see what he can do. My guess is we'll end up with a couple of troopers assigned. Hopefully, they'll be some of the good ones."

"What is it with Rhode Island?" Kennedy asked.

"Stick with us, Zach. You'll get used to it. We're the littlest state with the biggest egos. Not enough good cases to go around," Josh answered.

* * *

Friday morning, Josh walked into the SIU office. There was a knock on the door. Josh opened it and faced Captain Charland. The Captain, holding several file folders, smiled.

"Morning, Captain. Ah, I am sure you're here about those files."

"Yes, Lieutenant, I am. I must say I was--"

"Excuse me, sir. But I can explain," Josh interrupted.

Charland handed Josh the file folders. "No need, those files were to my satisfaction. As I tried to say, I found them completed and in the report review file for my approval."

No more surprised than I am. "Yes, well. I wanted to make sure they were, ah, complete."

Charland nodded. "Thank you for doing that, Lieutenant. I know you think those cases are less important than what you are working on, but they still need to be completed properly. Thank you for doing that." He handed Josh another set of folders. "These files are the ones that were missing from the cold case you've reopened. Chief Brennan asked me to locate them. It underscores my point of organization and thoroughness. If these files were properly stored, I wouldn't have to waste time looking for them."

Josh closed the door and sat at his desk. There was another knock on the door. Oh shit, he just realized I had no idea about those files. Opening the door, Tommy Moore and Kathy Lawrence, a records clerk, stood there smiling.

"You owe us lunch and then drinks after work," Tommy said.

"You two? You did the files?"

"Well, truth is it was Kathy who did the work. I just asked for help," Tommy answered.

Kathy smiled. "Doesn't have to be a big lunch, as long as it doesn't involve a drive-up window."

"Thanks, man. Thanks a lot. Anywhere you want to go, just name it. And after work, same thing."

"How about something simple, Gregg's restaurant works for me," Tommy said.

"Not you, smart-ass. She did the work. She gets an open bar; you get one beer. I shouldn't even do that since you let me hang out there knowing Charland would come looking for me."

"Nobody appreciates me around here," Tommy said, slumping into the chair at his desk.

Kathy laughed. "Josh, if my Captain comes looking for more stuff just let me know. I can handle him for you."

"I will, Kathy. Thanks again," watching as she left the office and headed back to the records division.

Josh opened the files from Captain Charland. Flipping through the documents, he found what he needed. "There were two victims in East

Providence, Sheila Monson and this one, Kathleen Lakeland, age 21 at the time. That would make her fifty-eight, right? Good chance she's still alive," Josh said.

"Where'd she live in the city?" Tommy asked.

"Village Green. My guess is she moved out of there after it happened." Josh answered. Picking up the phone, he called dispatch. "Hey, can you work your magic with the registry computer and see if you can find a Kathleen Lakeland. Hold on a minute," Josh shuffled some papers. "Her date of birth is March 15, 1951. There's a chance she married so you'll have to work the historical indexes for an old license number." Placing the file back on the desk, Josh laughed. "I know, I know. That's why I asked you to do it, thanks."

"Let me guess, Tanya, right?"

"The girl is a wizard with the Registry computer."

Twenty minutes later, the phone rang. Putting her on speakerphone, Josh had his answer.

"Hey Josh, Tanya. I found a driver's license number for Kathleen Lakeland; still listed under the same last name. She lives in the new condos off Veteran's Memorial Parkway, Unit 145. I could not find a telephone number, probably just a cell anyway. I looked at our files and we've never had any contact with her."

"Thanks, Tanya. You're the best."

"I know that," she replied, hanging up the phone.

"Let's take a ride and go see if we can talk to Kathleen," Josh said.

Leaving the lot, they headed onto Waterman Avenue, turning south onto Pawtucket Avenue.

"So, how do you want to approach this with her?" Tommy asked.

Josh turned east onto Warren Avenue. "I'll just lay it out for her. Let her know we are looking into this because the wrong guy got charged. See how she reacts."

Turning onto First Street, passing the Bridgeside Diner, Josh saw Chubby White coming out with a grocery-sized bag of food. Putting the window down, Josh yelled, "Hey Chubby, that part of your exercise program?"

Chubby smiled, waving with the bag in one hand, coffee in the other, and the last remains of a sandwich hanging from his mouth.

"The boy is so fat he didn't need to use the tow truck. He could've stopped that motorcycle with his ass," Josh said.

Heading south on the Parkway, they pulled into the old Getty fuel terminal. The area, once contaminated with toxic spills from years as a storage facility, was cleaned and reclaimed. A mixture of housing units turned the site into a pleasant neighborhood. Overlooking the bay, with a view of downtown Providence, it was one of the nicest locations in the city.

Driving down the hill, passing along the units closest to the water, they looked for number 145.

"There it is," Tommy said, pointing to the last unit on the waterside of the development. "Nice. She either married right, or made some good money doing something."

Josh pulled into the driveway behind a brand-new Audi with RI plates. "Let's just make sure," requesting a registration check on the plate.

A moment later, Tanya's voice came over the radio confirming the name and address. Adding, "I am never wrong," to the end of the broadcast. This caused a small eruption of bored cops, keying their radio mikes, and banging them on the dash or steering wheel. A police radio version of laughing at someone.

Josh and Tommy chuckled as they got out of the car.

Approaching the door, they saw a curtain pulled aside and a woman looking out.

"Someone's home," Tommy said, ringing the doorbell.

Several moments passed. The door opened, just a few inches. A woman looked out, the chain from the door lock blocking her face. "Yes?" she said.

"Ms. Lakeland?" holding up his badge and identification, "I am Lieutenant Josh Williams, and this is Detective Tommy Moore. Could we come in and speak with you?"

The woman hesitated a moment, closed the door enough to remove the chain lock, and then opened it. "Come in, please," holding the door as Josh and Tommy entered.

The woman passed by Josh and led them into a living room with a large window overlooking the bay. Tommy walked over to the window. "Wow, this is amazing. How long have you been living here?"

"I bought this pre-construction. I was one of the first to move in. It is a beautiful view," looking out the window. "But I am sure this visit is not about admiring my view. Can I ask why you're here?"

Tommy glanced at Josh.

"Ms. Lakeland we--"Josh began.

"Kathleen, please. Call me Kathleen."

"Kathleen, I know this may be hard for you, but we're here to talk about the, ah, incident back in 1972."

"You mean the rape, of course. You can call it what it is. I've learned to live with it."

"Yes, well. We wanted to ask you a few questions, if it's okay?" Josh explained the reason they had reopened the case.

"Have you learned the truth?" Lakeland asked.

"The truth?" Josh said. "What do you mean?"

Lakeland motioned for Josh and Tommy to sit. She walked to an overstuffed chair, sitting erect on the edge of the cushion, hands folded on her lap.

"Let me explain something to you. I did not get a good look at the man who raped me. I was in shock, stunned. He hit me on the side of the head as I was getting into my car after work. He choked me so hard I was not aware of what was happening."

Taking a deep breath, she looked at Josh. "About a week after this happened; two detectives came to my apartment. They showed me a photo of a black man and told me he was the one who raped me. They told me, mind you, they didn't ask me," studying the detectives' reactions.

"Did you recognize the man in the picture?" Josh asked.

"Yes, I did," she replied, causing Josh and Tommy to exchange glances.

"Was it the man who attacked you?" Josh asked.

"No, it was not," Lakeland answered. "Which is what I told the detectives. I recognized him from the Shell station where I stop for gas. I am from Barrington and attended Bay View Academy. I went to that gas station all the time. He wasn't the man who attacked me."

Tommy stood and walked to the window. Turning back to face Lakeland, "Did the detectives have you sign anything or take a statement?"

"No, and I couldn't understand why. They said I was too traumatized to identify him. But I know the man in the picture was not the one who attacked me. I never heard from them again. I read the story in the Providence Journal of the suspect in the rapes being killed in prison," glancing at Tommy. "I called the detectives to find out if it was the man who attacked me, they never called back."

"Kathleen was there anything about the man who attacked you that you remember about him? Something you're sure about."

"Yes, and I told the detectives this. He had a distinctive accent. My guess would be Caribbean or some such island dialect."

Josh glanced at Tommy shaking his head in disbelief. Reaching into his pocket, Josh pulled out a digital recorder.

"Kathleen, would you mind if we took a brief statement about the things you've told me? About the investigation and the incident?" Josh asked.

"No, of course not," she replied. "I've been waiting over thirty years for someone to ask me."

The statement took about twenty minutes.

Josh stood and walked over, extending his hand. "Thank you, Kathleen. I appreciate your speaking to us."

Lakeland stood and shook Josh's hand, turned to Tommy and did the same. "You're welcome. I hope it helps."

As they walked toward the front door, Josh glanced into a small side room, also overlooking the bay. There were several paintings in various stages of completion. "Are you an artist?"

"I am," Lakeland answered. "I was attending Rhode Island School of Design when it happened. I teach there now," running her hand alongside one of the paintings. "You know, I think the detectives back then thought I was some sort of hippie or something. I don't think they listened to anything I said."

Josh looked at Lakeland. "I am sorry for the way the detectives treated you, Kathleen. I hope we can find out the truth. When we do, I'll come back and tell you."

"It's not so much the way they treated me that bothers me. It was the person in the picture. He did not rape me, but those detectives decided he did. That's what haunts me, even after all this time. I should have gone to the police department and made them listen to me." Lakeland paused, studying Josh's face. "Can I ask you something?"

Josh nodded, "Of course."

"Was the man in the picture they showed me, the one killed in prison?"

Josh thought a moment. "I can't be certain, but I would think it was him."

Kathleen sighed. "I knew I should have gone to them and made them listen. It was an innocent man they arrested."

"None of this is on you, Kathleen. The cops didn't do their job. If they had, we might have found out who did this. But it's not your responsibility, it was theirs and they didn't do their job."

Kathleen stood at the door as they walked out. "Thank you for coming here. I hope you do find out the truth."

Josh and Tommy returned to the car and headed out. "Can you fucking believe that? No mention of any of this in the reports. No mention of the accent, her recognizing the guy from the Shell station, none of it. They just made up their minds this was the guy and let it go. I wonder if it had been a white guy if they'd been so adamant."

"Different times on the job back then, Tommy. I'd like to think things have changed, but I wonder sometimes."

"What's with the statement?" Tommy asked. "It's not like we're going to prosecute anyone over this history shit."

"Just in case," Josh replied. "Not sure what we're dealing with here but if anything were to happen to Kathleen we'd at least have this."

"Jesus, talk about paranoia?" Tommy replied. "Brennan's gonna love this story, isn't he?"

"There is another victim we need to try and speak with before we talk to Brennan. The first rape happened over near Brown. The victim is a Mary Ellen Lyons, she's fifty-seven now, 20 when it happened. I have an address on the East Side for her from the Providence PD file. She still lives in the same place," Josh said.

"Okay, LT. Let's go."

* * *

Heading down the Parkway onto 195 West, they took the Gano Street exit, heading over to the Wayland Square area. They drove past a large apartment building facing the Square on the corner of Wayland Avenue and South Angell Street.

Pulling into the lot of the Starbucks, Josh and Tommy headed over to the building entrance.

"Hey," a well-dressed Eastside trophy wife yelled from her SUV. "You can't park there, unless you're a customer of Starbucks."

Josh smiled, waving his badge and ID. "I buy enough coffee here to own the damn building, go park that tank somewhere else."

She was not intimidated. "I'll just leave it here, and then you'll have to wait for me to leave," blocking their car and getting out of her SUV.

Tommy smiled. "That would be one choice. Or, my preference would be to tow this thing out of here and arrest you for obstructing the State Police," dangling his handcuffs. "Your move," he added.

"Do you know who I am?" came the indignant reply, tapping her designer workout sneakers.

"Nope, don't know and don't care. But if you're having an identity crisis, I am sure a psych evaluation at Rhode Island Hospital would help you."

"Unbelievable," she said, climbing back up into the SUV and squealing out of the lot.

"The State Police?" Josh asked, arms wide apart.

"Always makes a better impression on these self-important nitwits. If she complains, we have plausible deniability," Tommy grinned.

"You have a bright future in community policing," Josh smiled.

"Why thank you, Lieutenant. I appreciate your confidence."

Approaching the front door, Josh rang the bell for unit 201.

"Yes?" a voice said over the intercom.

"Lieutenant Josh Williams and Detective Tommy Moore, East Providence Police. We're here to see Ms. Lyons," Josh answered.

"East Providence Police? Oh, okay. I'll buzz you in." The door buzzed a moment later.

As they walked up the stairs, a door opened and a woman appeared at the top landing. She looked younger than the one they were looking for, but there was a resemblance.

"Lieutenant Williams," Josh said, extending his ID for her to see, "this is Detective Moore."

"Dakota, Dakota Jones. Mary Lyons is my mother."

Following the young woman, they walked into the apartment. "How can I help you?" she asked.

"We'd like to speak with your mother if we could. It concerns something that happened a while ago. A long time ago," Josh answered.

"Well, I'm afraid that won't be possible. My mother is unable to speak. She suffered a stroke a few years ago. She is alert and aware, but she communicates by writing. She cannot speak at all."

A wheelchair with a gaunt looking woman rolled into the room. She was smiling and gesturing to a piece of paper. Dakota took the paper, read it, and handed it to Josh.

I may not speak, but I can hear, and write. Ask away Officer.

"As you've probably guessed, this is my mother, Mary Lyons."

"May I speak to you outside for a moment Dakota?"

The wheelchair bound woman reached up and grabbed Josh's hand. She gestured with her other, holding up one finger, then wrote.

The three stood watching.

If this is about what happened back in 1972, she knows all about it.

Josh looked at Dakota.

"My mother told me about it when I was going off to college. She wanted me to be aware of things. Believe me, other than her inability to speak, she is smart and capable."

Josh nodded. "Okay, I'll try to be brief."

Mary motioned for them to sit, pulled her chair over to face Josh, and held her pad and pen, ready to respond.

"Mary, were you ever shown a lineup or pictures to look at during the investigation?"

The woman looked down at the pad, wrote a few lines, and handed the pad to Josh.

A detective showed me a picture and asked if the man attacked me. I told him I could not be sure, but I did not think it was.

"Did you tell them anything else in way of identifying the man, anything you remembered?"

I gave them a written statement. I told them all I remembered.

Josh read the page and handed it to Tommy. He then returned it to the woman.

"The statement wasn't in the file, perhaps it got misplaced over the years. Do you recall anything about what you said which was specific to the man who attacked you?"

Again, she took to the pad with fury. This took a little longer.

I told them he spoke with a strange accent; I thought it was another language at first. Many years after it happened, my late husband and I went on a cruise. I heard the accent in the islands we visited, Caribbean Islands. I didn't know what it was until then.

Josh read it over, handing it again to Tommy.

"Mary, would you mind writing out a statement about the things we just discussed?" Josh asked. "I would appreciate it."

Mary smiled and took to her pen and pad. A short time later, she handed Josh a two-page statement in meticulous cursive style writing.

Josh read it over, "Thank you very much, Mary. You've been most helpful," rising from the seat.

Mary reached over, taking the pad from Tommy.

Do you know who did this? Was he ever caught? Turning the pad for Josh to read.

Josh looked at the daughter, then back at Mary. "No, I'm sorry. We believe the man they arrested was not the one who did it. They didn't do their job. I am sorry for that."

As they headed toward the door, Mary wheeled over and handed Josh the pad.

I am glad you came to talk. It's nice to know someone cares enough to try.

Josh smiled and shook Mary's hand. "Thank you, Mary. If I do find out anything I will let you know."

Standing in the door to the apartment, Dakota said. "You think they arrested an innocent man?"

"We're not sure. But it looks like that's what may have happened," Josh replied.

Dakota shook her head. "If you do find out, my mother would like to know. She is a remarkable woman, accomplished much in her life. She deserves to know the truth."

Josh nodded. "Dakota, when we find out the whole story I will come back. Thanks for letting us talk to her."

On the way to the car, Josh said, "Might as well take a swing by the office building on Waterman Street. We're right around the corner. Never know what you may find."

As they pulled out of the lot, a familiar SUV pulled in. Tommy said, "Crazy bitch must have waited for a spot, instead of walking. I guess the exercise ensemble was just for show." Putting his window down, he waved his handcuffs at the woman. "Just yell if you need these," he shouted.

"That is not helpful," Josh said, putting the window up, almost decapitating Moore.

Ducking back in the car, Tommy laughed. "When you get to the building, drive around to the back. Sometimes they mark parking spots for the business owners."

Josh drove down Waterman, pulling into the driveway and around to the back of the building. They came to an area boxed in by two sides of the L shaped building. Along the wall were several reserved parking signs for the businesses.

Parked in the spot for JTS Management was a new Mercedes with RI plates JTS 1.

"You are nowhere near as stupid as you look, Detective Moore."

"I'll take that as a compliment. Just to boost the paranoia level a bit, let's run the plate when we get back, rather than over the air," Tommy said.

"You know, I have to tell Brennan about this. He thinks you're just a Neanderthal. I'd say you're more likely the missing link between them and humans."

Tommy smiled, wrote down the plate, and pointed out of the lot. "Our job is done here. Drive me home, my good man."

***

Josh, Zach Kennedy, and Tommy Moore sat in the office reviewing the information gathered so far. The phone rang, and Tommy grabbed it.

"SIU, Detective Moore. Who's this?" smiling and putting the phone on speaker. "Chris Hamlin? A Lieutenant, you say, retired? Nope, don't remember you. Wait now, I know, the old broad. Swiss Cheeks, how are you?"

"You're gonna remember me real fast next time I see you," Chris Hamlin said, an edge to her voice.

"I'm so sorry," Tommy replied, winking at Kennedy and Josh. "From now on it will be Lieutenant Cheeks. That good enough for you, Grandma?" chuckling.

"Oh, real comedians aren't we? You're lucky I am not there, smart-ass. You'd be feeling the pain of this grandma."

"Hey Chris," Josh said. "You got something for us or are you just in a testy mood from the age-related hormonal changes?"

"I am not finished dealing with your snot-nosed errand boy yet, smart-ass. But you're next," Chris said.

"Why don't you get your caregiver to drive you here, wheel you in, and we'll see what happens. Don't forget your teeth and to put on your diaper," Tommy added.

"That's it. You wait right there. I am on the way."

The line went dead.

"Oh great," Josh said, "Now we gotta deal with her. Nice going, I hope you enjoy pain. She's going to kick your ass."

"What about you?" Tommy said.

"I'll lock myself in the safe, so she can't get to me," Josh answered.

"You guys have a weird way of dealing with each other. Isn't she the one who started this thing? She is a retired lieutenant, right?" Kennedy asked.

"Oh yeah," Josh answered. "But she deserves it. She was the biggest ball buster in the world when she worked here. Still is."

Twenty-minutes later, the receptionist called to let them know Hamlin was here.

"You go get her," Tommy said.

"No, Detective Moore, you started the war. You go get her," Josh ordered.

"Okay, but I am putting my vest on," laughing on the way out the door.

A few moments passed and there was a knock on the door. Josh opened it cautiously. Chris stood there smiling. Tommy was nowhere around.

"What did you do with my Detective?" Josh asked.

Chris pushed past, walked over to Josh's desk, and sat down. "How are you, Zach?"

Kennedy, amused by this, replied. "I am well. Is Detective Moore still alive?" he asked.

A moment later, there was a scream from the hallway. Josh walked out and saw the Chief's assistant standing outside the door of the ladies' room. Chief Brennan and Captain Charland joined the group.

"Hey Donna, what's wrong?" Josh asked.

Donna pointed, "Would you get him out of there, please."

Josh opened the door. A handcuffed Tommy Moore, pants pulled down to his knees, attached to the coat hook on the wall, looked out from the bathroom.

"What the--" Brennan said.

"Chris came by," Josh explained, "Tommy here issued a challenge."

"Would you get me down from here," Tommy pleaded. "I didn't want to hurt her, that's the only reason I'm here."

"Of course you didn't son," Brennan said. "Before you release him, have BCI come up and take some pictures. Post them in the roll call and locker rooms. They may prove useful in reminding Detective Moore, and others, to tread lightly with our retired sister in blue."

"Oh no, come on Chief, no pictures."

A few moments later the flash of BCI cameras, and several cell phones, were illuminating the scene.

When Josh returned to the office with Tommy, Hamlin smiled. "Now that we have re-established the proper balance and hierarchy, would you get me a coffee Detective Moore?"

"How about I..." then he laughed. "You have to show me that trick someday. I never saw it coming."

"Now, there's a good boy. Willing to concede to his superiors. Never mind the coffee, when you have time we can arrange some private lessons for you. I wouldn't want you to get beaten up by girls every day." Leaning forward in the chair, she looked at Josh. "So, what do we know now?"

Josh brought her up to speed on the records trace, phone numbers, and the interview with the two victims.

Kennedy interjected. "Josh, I think under the circumstances it is appropriate we bring her up to speed on the Fleming link."

This caught Josh off-guard. Kennedy caught the glance at Chris.

Kennedy laughed. "She already knows, doesn't she?" shaking his head. "I should have known better."

"Look, Zach. I'm sorry it's just--."

Kennedy held up his hands. "No need, Josh. I have had a few partners in my career I trust with my life. I understand." Looking at Chris, "With that said, I'd like to hear what you think about it."

"I'll tell you what I think. There is no fucking way she is involved. I know people, I can read bad guys. She's not one. There is an explanation and all we have to do is ask," Chris answered without hesitation.

Kennedy looked between Josh and Chris. "Okay, your call Josh. How do you want to do this?"

"Let's call her and get her over here," Josh answered.

Before he had spoken, Chris was on her cell. "Maggie, you busy? No? Good. Come on over to EPPD. Call when you get in the lot and I'll send out Detective Moore the doorman to escort you in," smiling as Tommy flipped her the bird.

While they waited for Fleming, Josh ran the license plate from the office building. "Holy shit," he said.

The other three looked at him.

"Anybody wanna take a guess who the plate comes back to?" Josh asked.

"Who?" Chris asked.

"RI registration JTS1 comes back to, wait for it, Jennifer Tucker Sorin."

"Holy shit indeed," Kennedy added.

"And Sorin, that name again. Where did I hear that name from?" Josh said. "I know it from somewhere."

Twenty minutes later, Chris's cell rang. "Okay, be right there," smiling at Tommy.

Tommy went to get Maggie Fleming. After introducing her to Kennedy, they brought her up to speed on things. "Now, my friend, here comes the dicey part. Do you recognize this number?" showing her the call records.

"Not off the top of my head, let me look at my contact list," taking out her phone and searching. "Wait, I called that number. It's the one Collucci's Chief of Staff gave me to reach him when I was trying to arrange the meeting with the Senator. And you guys...," looking around. "Holy shit, you guys must have thought.... Holy shit."

"Yeah, we got a lot of holy shits going on here," Josh said. "Who did you say gave you the number?"

"Collucci's assistant, Anthony Sorin."

There was a chorus of holy shits.

"You ain't gonna believe this one then," Josh added. He explained the connection to Tucker's daughter.

"So, let me get this straight. Senator Collucci's Chief of Staff, Anthony Sorin, married Jennifer Tucker, Supreme Court Chief Justice George Tucker's daughter. The bad guys called the same number I did, linking them, and me, to the office building where Tucker's daughter runs her business. And," pausing to think a moment, "Collucci and Tucker were involved in the Grey case from the beginning. Is that right?"

"Sums it up well," Josh replied.

"I am surprised you guys even talked to me about this. Apologies to Mr. Kennedy here, but I know the way the Feds think. It goes against their grain," Fleming said.

"No apology necessary. Having spent some time here now, I've learned a few things about cooperation that may not have occurred to me before. Their special investigative techniques are unmatched," Kennedy winked.

"They took you drinking, didn't they?" Chris asked.

"No. It was a well-orchestrated undercover intelligence gathering operation."

"Fed-speak for they went drinking," Fleming interjected.

Kennedy laughed. "Now the question is where do we go from here? This link to the Senator grows stronger and more ominous with each new piece of evidence. My bosses in DC are going to grow more interested in, and will want to assert more control over, this case."

"Not if we figure it out first," Josh said. "Maggie, when did Sorin give you the number?"

"When I was trying to arrange the meeting with Collucci, I called the main number for the Senator," Fleming answered. "It took me peeling through several layers of bureaucracy to finally get to his Chief of Staff. When I pointed this out to Sorin, he gave me this number to use. He said it would get right to him. I used that number to arrange the meeting."

"He either screwed up giving you the main line number or didn't realize it could be traced to the office complex. Then again, he had no reason to suspect you would," Josh said. "The issue is what is going on at this business and how involved is Collucci."

"Tommy, do you have anything else about those businesses?" Josh asked.

Moore wasn't listening, fumbling with his coffee cup, staring at his desk.

Josh looked at Zach, then back at Moore. "Hey, Tommy, you in there? Earth to Tommy," throwing a pen at Moore.

Moore looked up, startled, and realized everyone was watching him. "What? Oh, sorry. I was just thinking about... I mean. What did you say?"

"Do you have anything else about businesses at that location? Or about Jennifer Sorin?" Josh asked again.

"No, ah, not yet. I'll keep working on it," Moore answered. "I've got to run out for a bit, LT. If that's okay?" heading out the door, not waiting for the answer.

"What the hell was that all about?" Josh asked.

"Maybe I hit his head harder than I thought," Chris chuckled.

Chapter 21

Josh pulled up to the Benefit Street side of the courthouse and parked the car. Looking around, he spotted what he needed across the street. Walking over to the parked car, glancing around, he grabbed the parking ticket from under the windshield wiper. Walking back to his car, he put the parking ticket on his windshield. *Mission accomplished*, he chuckled to himself.

Walking up the stairs to the building, he passed through the security access point and walked over to the elevator. Getting off at the eighth floor, he approached Judge Tucker's administrative aide.

"Good day, Ms. Atwell. I hope you remember me, Lieutenant Williams from East Providence Police. I am here for my appointment with the Judge."

Atwell punched a few keys on her computer. "I am sorry, Lieutenant. I do not see it on the schedule. With whom did you make the appointment?"

"The Judge called me," Josh said, smiling at the assistant.

"That is strange," eyes narrowing, arms folded against her chest. "The Judge always has me schedule his appointments."

Josh shrugged his shoulders, "Well he called me, asked me to be here now. I am here. Could you check with him, please?"

Atwell slid back her chair, stood up and walked to the door, looked back at Josh, knocked, and went in, closing the door behind her.

Josh counted on the uncertainty and doubt he had unleashed on the assistant, and the curiosity of the Judge, to get him in.

Atwell came back, sat at the desk, and made a note in the computer. "The Judge will be with you in a moment. He said he must have forgotten to mention this to me. Please make it brief, Lieutenant."

Josh smiled and took a seat. He did not have to wait long. The door to the chambers opened and Judge Tucker came out, catching Atwell by surprise.

"Lieutenant Williams, good to see you."

"Your Honor, I would have been happy to bring the Lieutenant in," Atwell said.

"No need, Ms. Atwell. I thought the Lieutenant and I would go down to the coffee shop." Looking at Josh, "Shall we, Lieutenant?"

As they boarded the elevator, Tucker looked at Josh. "My assistant is never wrong, you know. Playing that little mind game will ruin her day. What was so important it was necessary to do that?"

"I got the documents you sent me," Josh said. "Thank you, but I have to ask. Why did you wait so long to bring these to light?"

Tucker watched the floor indicator, as it reached the ground floor he turned to Josh. "How about we take a walk outside, away from prying eyes and curious ears?"

Josh nodded, "Sure."

They left the building, crossing South Main Street to the walkway on the Woonasquatucket River. Standing at the railing, Tucker watched as two kayaks slid by. He leaned against the rail, folding his arms. "When you were a young patrolman, new on the job, did you see things that bothered you?"

Josh studied at the Judge and then stood next to him. "I did, a lot of things. Why?"

"What did you do about them?"

"Well, at the time, there wasn't much I could do. Police departments are hierarchical. There is a distinct pecking order," Josh said. "The Sergeants used to say we were lower than whale shit and that's on the bottom of the ocean. Rank and seniority were power."

"It is not all that much different in the AG's office. Brand new special assistants do what they are told, when they are told, as they are told." Tucker put his hands on the rail, "Much the same, it would seem, as a police department."

Josh nodded. "So, you waited, but why so long? Once you were out of there you could have brought this out. Might have derailed Collucci's career and that would not have broken my heart."

"No," Tucker smiled, "I imagine it wouldn't. The reality was I saw no benefit in bringing it to light. The defendant was dead; I never knew he had a family." Dropping his gaze to the ground, "Maybe if I had known?"

Josh turned to look at the river. "I suppose it would've been lost in the noise of other issues and accomplished nothing. Maybe this is the right time. It is helpful to me. Thanks for sending it."

"There's something else, Josh. Something I was vague about when I spoke with you and Chris," Tucker said, watching for Josh's reaction.

"What is it?"

"When I told you Collucci took over the case, I said shortly before Grey died," Tucker took a deep breath. "The truth is he took over the case the day Grey died. I found out just after he assigned me to a new project. It was all a sham to shut me up."

The Judge looked up at the sky, trying to regain control of his emotions.

"Judge it doesn't--" Josh offered.

Tucker interrupted him.

"It does matter," he said. "I let him manipulate me. I was a coward, afraid to do the right thing. I have regretted the decision my whole life."

"Judge, remember when you asked me about seeing things that were wrong but being unable to do something about it?" Josh said. "There's a difference between unwilling and unable. I understand the politics of the AG's office. Collucci would have bounced you out of there in a heartbeat."

Josh moved to stand in front of the Judge. "If you were fired from the AG's office, your career would likely have been very different. Keep that in mind."

The Judge perked up more. "You said Grey has a daughter?"

"He does. We're trying to find out the truth for her. It looks to me he is, or was, innocent."

"I would want that for my daughter."

Josh saw an opportunity here. "You have a daughter, your Honor? How old is she?"

Tucker came off the railing, facing Josh, eyes brightening. "I do, she's thirty-two. She was married. They are now divorced, unfortunately. She has a daughter as well, my granddaughter Kelsey, nine years old." His beaming smile and wistful eyes lit his face, changing the mood.

Josh thought a moment. How far should I go with this? A little nudge might tell us something. "Who was your daughter married to?"

"Anthony Sorin, Senator Collucci's Chief of Staff." The judge tried to gauge Josh's reaction. "Anthony was not..., let's just say he and I have different perspectives on things. He never sees his daughter. I have tried to tell him it is time you can never get back, but he is all about his career. He has taken good care of my daughter financially, though. Helped her develop a good business. For that, I am grateful."

"Collucci's Chief of Staff? Not someone I'm likely to associate with," Josh laughed.

"No, I would think not," Tucker replied. "Okay, so now you understand part of why I held on to the reports. Perhaps I was waiting for this opportunity. Do what you will with them. Don't worry about the fallout," taking a few steps toward the court before stopping. "Lieutenant, do you have children?"

"No, not yet, but we've talked about it."

Coming back to Josh, putting his hand on Josh's shoulder, he spoke in a soft, gentle tone. "Do yourself a favor. Have them, lots of them. Despite all the demands they can impose, it is one of life's greatest joys," he smiled. "I must be getting back. Next time, call Ms. Atwell first; she'll be fretting about this all day."

"Thank you, your Honor. I'll tell my wife I have a court order that she must endure many pregnancies."

Tucker laughed. "I am sure I'll hear about it next time she appears before me. Take care, Lieutenant," crossing back over South Main Street and disappearing into the courthouse.

Josh walked to his car. Driving through the East side of Providence, he turned onto Waterman Street. He took another ride by the office building. As he pulled into the lot, he saw a car bearing New York plates in the parking spot next to the one for JTS Management. The car looked out of place. Grabbing the camera he kept under the seat, he pulled into an open spot hoping to grab pictures of the occupants.

He did not have to wait long.

Two men and a woman came out of the building and approached the car. One man held the door for the woman as she got into the back seat. Josh shot a dozen quick images, then ducked as the car pulled out. He gave them time to get out of the lot, and then headed out, intending to return to the station. As he left the lot, he noticed another vehicle; the two occupants watched him pull out.

Turning toward the bridge, Josh saw the second car, a dark colored sedan, pull forward, and follow him. *Let's see how curious they are.* Just before he reached the point where Waterman Street and the bridge entrance diverged, he pulled to the side of the road.

Getting out of the car, he opened the hood, waiting for them to pass him. The car drove down Waterman Street, the passenger looking at Josh. As the vehicle passed the bridge entrance, it put him into a one-way section, near a small traffic circle. Josh closed the hood, jumped back in, and took off over the Henderson Bridge. The other driver had no choice but to drive around the traffic circle before he could get back to follow him.

Taking the first exit, he pulled a quick U-turn, and drove behind a commercial building. Two men working on a loading dock yelled as the car came speeding into the lot. Josh jumped out, waving his badge at the irate workers. He ran to the corner of the building in time to see the sedan coming down the off-ramp onto Massasoit Avenue, heading away from him. He could see the two occupants scanning the area, checking side streets.

Josh waited a few minutes, returned to his car, and then followed the sedan, once the hunted now the hunter. As he drove from Massasoit

Avenue onto Waterman Avenue, he passed the Red Bridge Cafe. Josh spotted a marked police unit, parked between the buildings, in the abandoned gas station lot next door. A favorite hiding spot of the uniform cops.

Pulling alongside the driver's window, a smiling, but unenthusiastic, Officer William Jones greeted him.

"Hey, Lieutenant, please don't tell me you need something. It's almost 2:15. All I have to do is avoid a call for the next hour and a half and I am out of here."

Jones represents a certain percentage of police officers known as PFLs, Patrolmen for Life. They strive for specific professional goals. Accumulate enough seniority to work the same shift, same post, every year, and operate under the radar. Handle calls as needed, avoid creating any problems, and get through each shift with minimal effort. Having the SIU Lieutenant pull up to you ninety minutes before the end of the shift was the worst possible scenario.

"All I need is for you to stop a car for me. I just need to know who's driving it," Josh replied. "I'll even tell dispatch I need you for the rest of the shift. Stop the car and you can maintain radio silence for the duration."

Jones sat back in his seat, putting his hands behind his head. "It is tempting. We've been getting a lot of last-minute bullshit and I have a bowling match at 4:15 today. Okay, deal. Hold on. No reports, right?"

Josh laughed, "Even if they shoot at us, no reports. How's that?"

"Okay," Jones answered, sitting up and adjusting his seat. "Wait a minute, shoot at us?"

"Just kidding. Dark colored sedan, two guys in it. My guess is they'll be back this way headed toward the Henderson."

As if that's all it took, the sedan drove down Waterman Avenue. The occupants oblivious to two police vehicles parked in the shadows between the buildings.

"I assume that's the one. I don't know it and I know all the locals," Jones said, pointing at the car as it passed by.

"Nothing gets by you does it, Jonesy?" Josh threw the car in reverse and backed out. Jones pulled out and caught up to the sedan.

Josh was on his cell phone to dispatch. "Tanya, send a marked unit to back up 207 on Massasoit, just off Waterman. He's out on a car stop for me." True to his word he added, "Also, put 207 out of service with me until end of shift. Thanks."

As Josh sat back in the seat, parked behind cars in the restaurant lot, he watched Jones approach the driver's side. The second marked unit arrived, and the officer took up a position at the rear passenger side. After a short conversation, Jones walked back to his car, waving off the other officer.

Josh stayed in the shadows and watched the sedan drive away. Once it disappeared, he walked over to talk to Jones; Josh waved at the second officer leaving the scene.

"Well?"

"Lieutenant, I want to thank you for covering me for the next hour. My bowling team will be most pleased I will not be detained at work," Jones said, leaning on the trunk of the police car.

"I can't tell you how thrilled I am, now who the hell were they?"

"Lieutenant, they were our cousins from the North, North Scituate to be precise. Landespolizei, the Rhode Island State Police."

"Of course they were," shaking his head. "Thanks, Jonesy. Enjoy the rest of the shift. I cleared it with dispatch."

Josh walked back to his car.

Jones returned to the cruiser, drove back to his nest between the buildings. He returned the seat to his resting position and ignored the radio. A happy man.

Josh grabbed for his cell, *I hope Brennan's connections can deal with this.*

* * *

Returning to the office, Josh filled in Kennedy and Moore on his talk with the Judge and the surveillance on Waterman Street. The got a giggle out of the guest appearance by the state police. "I called Brennan. He's gonna reach out to the Colonel. If he can't derail their curiosity, he'll ask for one of the troopers we've worked with on other cases. I should know something later today."

As the pictures downloaded from the camera, Josh ran the plate from the vehicle parked in the JTS Management spot. Looking at the information on the screen, he said, "Hey, Tommy, what was the name on that Delaware corporation you found?"

"Wait a minute. I got it right here," Moore's fingers flying over the keyboard. "Harriet Lane Enterprises, P.O. Box 465, Dover, Delaware. I can dig into it some more, why?"

"The car I spotted is listed to Harriet Lane Associates with a P.O. Box 487 in Delaware. No coincidence there. Do your magic and run that to ground. Get it all. If you need some intrastate subpoenas call--."

"I know, I know your favorite, Kristin Volpe," Moore interrupted. "I mean, ah, that is, or someone, anyone, else?"

Josh fixed Moore in his sights. "You handle it, whoever it is. Understand?"

Moore tried to contain the smile. Failing that, he ducked his head behind the computer.

Kennedy came over to Josh's desk. "Let me see the pictures you took."

Josh brought up the images. "It looked to me like the two guys were security of some sort. The woman was on a cell the whole time. They bracketed her as they walked out, heads on swivels, looking everywhere."

"Nothing familiar to me. How about we run them through our facial recognition database? Might get lucky," Kennedy suggested.

"I'll email them to you." A moment later, Josh said, "On the way. It will be interesting to see if you get a hit on them."

"Hey, listen to this," Moore interjected. "I did a Google search on Harriet Lane Enterprises and Harriet Lane Associates. Many stories on the business wires. They're buying up properties and businesses all over, quite a few of them here in Rhode Island. They are buying several companies which manage state lotteries and casino facilities." Tommy clicked through more search results. "Holy shit, listen to this one," Tommy said.

Kennedy and Josh looked at the excited detective.

"I just checked the LexisNexis search I've been running. Harriet Lane Enterprises acquired a fifty-five percent interest in Mohegan Sun. But here's the biggie, they just took over the parent corporation that owns Twin River," Tommy explained. "There must be some big money behind them."

"Twin River?" Kennedy asked.

"Twin River is a casino run by the state and a private entity in Lincoln, Rhode Island," Tommy said. "They had some big development plans in place for the site. The money involved must be huge."

"Wait a minute," Kennedy muttered, typing on his laptop keyboard. "Wait a minute, yeah here it is. Listen to this. It's an intelligence briefing from an informant in another Russian mob case. I sat in on the interview. These are my notes," he said, clicking through screens on the laptop. "He provided information they were using front companies to buy land located near ports."

Kennedy finished his coffee, putting the cup back on the desk. "We assumed they were looking for easy access to waterfront buildings for smuggling. However, suppose it is more sophisticated. Suppose the businesses themselves are fronts to launder money."

Josh and Moore followed along with the Kennedy's ramblings. "You mean use businesses with high cash flow to bury dirty money?" Josh asked

"Look, we know several things about the Russians. They've tried for years to gain control over political figures. It was inevitable they would get their hooks into someone. They use sophisticated methods of money laundering. There is no better cash flow than casinos and state lottery systems. Couple that with buying up waterfront locations. They pay premium prices as a legitimate way to induce the owners to sell. Failing that, they have other ways to encourage cooperation. It's perfect." Kennedy tapped his fingers on the desk, stroking his neck, "And it would explain the attempt on you, Josh. You're talking billions of dollars in revenues. There's a reason to kill."

Moore listened to Kennedy, and then asked. "I get the casino angle, easy to inject cash into the business, but I don't get the lottery. Isn't there more auditing controls over cash flow?"

Kennedy smiled. "Not if they control the controllers. Look, we know they have their hands in other businesses. If they control the Lottery, they control the audit trail." Kennedy stood and picked up a legal pad.

"If I print the tickets, distribute the tickets, collect the revenue from the tickets, and pay out the winnings on the tickets I can control the amounts reported. They eliminate the checks and balances by corrupting the process.

"So, you think this JTS Management is a front for them?" Moore asked

"No, too simple. They would never risk that level of their operations on an unaffiliated person. Either she's one of the cover companies, or they threatened her into complying." Kennedy scrolled through more screens on the computer.

"Tucker told me she was divorced but her husband set her up in the business," Josh said.

Kennedy looked up, smiling. "And her ex is the Chief of Staff of a sitting United States Senator. A Senator who sits on two of the most influential committees, Banking and Judiciary. If you can't control the Senator, you control the guy who does control the Senator. Or both."

"Will someone please tell me how we fell into this shit?" Moore said. "This is East Providence, not Leningrad."

"Think about it," Josh replied. "East Providence has one of the largest undeveloped waterfront areas on the East Coast. It has been sitting there, unused, for years. There is a deep-water port, access to railways, and a nearby airport, most of the necessary infrastructure. The politicians in the city never possessed the foresight to develop it." Josh turned to look at Kennedy, "We follow the money, right?"

"Well said, Deep Throat, well said. We look for recent land acquisitions, business transfers, or anything linked to the waterfront. Not just in East Providence, but throughout the area."

"Hey, I remember something…," Tommy said, shuffling through the piles of papers on his desk. "Take a look at this."

"And that is?" Josh asked.

"Application for Transfer of Liquor License. You know the old Oyster House Restaurant on Water Street; someone bought it and applied for the liquor license." Turning to Kennedy, "We get these all the time. Chief Brennan likes us to do the background. Perhaps we need to look into this one a bit deeper."

"Okay, here's what we need to do. Josh, you handle the local look at any land transactions along the East Providence waterfront. Don't limit it to just here, though. Look at anywhere along, what is it called?"

"Narragansett Bay?" Josh said.

"Yeah, that's it. Tommy, you check out the licensee applications. All of them. Dig deep on anyone you can find connected to them." Kennedy stood up, grabbing his cell phone off the desk, "I'm going to head down to DC. This will take some more resources, but I want to make sure we keep control of this here." Opening the door, he hesitated a moment. "One other thing, did you ever hear from Brennan about the State Police?"

"Brennan sent me a text. The troopers are sending two detectives, don't know who yet but I am sure Brennan worked his magic with the Colonel."

Chapter 22

Tommy Moore spent several hours plugging away online, digging into the myriad resources available. The license application was under the name of William A. Marshall, age 40 from Barrington, Rhode Island. He had no criminal record. Lived at the same address for 18 years and owned several restaurants in Boston, Providence, Worcester, and Newport.

The reviews of the restaurants were all excellent. They were several articles about Marshall in various culinary magazines and travel sites. His business reputation was spotless.

Yet, something about him bothered Moore. Something wasn't right; he just couldn't put his finger on it. Leaning back in the chair, he rubbed his eyes, exhaling.

Josh looked up from his desk, "Find something?"

Moore didn't answer.

"Hey, blockhead," Josh yelled. "You in there?"

Moore looked up, "What? Oh, sorry LT. Just looking into this license application shit. The guy is so clean it's scary. I bet he never had a pimple in his entire life. But...."

"But what?"

"I don't know, there's something. It just doesn't add up." Moore shook his head. "I just can't figure out what it is."

"So, tell me."

After detailing Marshall's business history, Moore put his feet up on his desk and sat back in his chair.

"How about prior businesses? Was he always in the restaurant business?" Josh asked.

Swinging his legs off the desk, Moore sat up. "Far as I can see, right out of school. Opened his first one at twenty-two years old. Been successful enough to buy his own plane. He has a pilot's license for single and multi-engine planes."

"Where does a twenty-two-year-old get the money to do that?" Josh asked.

The light went on in Moore's eyes. "Yeah, dammit. Where'd he get the money for that?"

"Check his educational background. Might be something there," Josh added, heading out for a meeting with Brennan. "I'll be back around five o'clock; we'll head over for a beer at Bovi's. Sound good to you?"

Moore was oblivious to the conversation, buried back in his computer. Josh smiled and left.

When Josh returned to the office four hours later, Moore was still engrossed in his research.

"Anything new?"

"Hang on LT; got a couple of things I am waiting for. I hit the jackpot with this one," Moore answered.

While he waited for Moore, Josh sat at his desk answering emails and catching up on routine matters.

"Son-of-a-bitch," Moore shouted. "Goddamn son-of-a-bitch," watching as several pages of documents came out of the printer.

"I take it you found something?" Josh asked.

"Wait until you hear this," grabbing pages from the printer. "Marshall went to Brown University. As we all know, a big money school, right? I used some of my contacts at the Brown police to dig into the finances. A trust fund paid for school, a big trust fund. Both his parents died when he was just a kid. After he graduated from Brown, he got control of the money. That explains the restaurants, sort of."

Rising from his chair, he walked to Josh's desk and stood against the wall. "Here's the thing. He majored in history. Wait for it, Russian History," waving the papers in the air. "He went to Russia several times on research projects."

"Don't tell me you think he got hooked up with the Russians then? Come on, Tommy."

"No, I don't. Let me finish. He graduates from Brown. Does he decide to chuck his Ivy League history degree to be a cook? Nope. He decides to open a restaurant so he and his best friend, and roommate, can hide their other sideline, cocaine."

"And you deduced this how?" Josh asked.

"Because my contact at Brown PD talked to his father, a retired Brown security guy. He remembered Marshall and his foreign roommate. Caught them a few times with coke, but the trustee paid off Brown with some extra donations to make it disappear. It all makes sense. The cocaine funded the restaurants. Marshall knew enough to hire good chefs and run a good operation, both the legitimate one and the not so legitimate one." Moore folded his arms, smiling.

"What does Russia have to do with any of this?"

"Ah, there's the rub, as some guy I can't remember says," Moore replied.

"Shakespeare." Brennan offered.

"Who? Oh, yeah," a grin creeping across Moore's face. "His foreign roommate," eyebrows bouncing up and down, "was Anthony Sorin."

"No shit?"

"And Mr. Sorin immigrated to the US from…" gesturing to Josh.

"Russia," Josh answered.

"We have a winner," Tommy laughed, pointing at Josh. "Tell us what he's won, Johnny,"

"Great work, Tommy. Wait until the Feds hear this one. How the hell did you find this out?" Josh said

"After I found out Sorin was Marshall's roommate, I called a friend at Immigration and Customs Enforcement. We served in the Marine Corps together. He tracked down the information about Sorin emigrating from Russia. When the family emigrated, they changed the name from Sorinkov to Sorin, sounds more American."

"Either way it was great work," Josh said. "Now all we gotta do is tie this to Collucci and my day will be perfect. Come on, I owe you a beer for all that hard work."

* * *

The next morning, Josh and Keira sat having coffee on their back deck. Josh threw the ball for Cassidy. The dog never tired of chasing and retrieving the ball.

"So, is there anything we can do for her?" Josh asked.

"You mean about the charges against her father?" Keira said. "Not much. I can file a motion to dismiss them. Get a judge to go along. A symbolic gesture at best. Other than that, nothing."

Josh grabbed the ball from Cassidy, faked a throw toward one side, and then threw the ball deep into the woods. "Can she sue the state? Or Collucci? Wrongful death or something? "

Keira shook her head. "Nope, the statute of limitations on wrongful death is three years. Collucci would be an agent of the state, indemnified by law unless you could prove a crime. I don't think you have enough. Trying to convince a court Collucci had anything to do with the prison murder case would never fly."

"So that's it?" Josh asked. "We can't do anything?"

Keira thought for a moment. "How about we do this? I'll file the motion to dismiss the charges and hold a press conference detailing the circumstances. Blast the shit out of Collucci. At least make him squirm a bit."

"Hmm, I like it," Josh smiled as Cassidy dropped the soggy, muddy ball into his lap. "Jeez, Cassidy put it on the deck, not me," tossing the ball once again.

"Your friend, Judge Tucker, might catch some shit over it," Keira said. "You willing to let that happen?"

"I think the Judge is hoping we do something with this. Otherwise why would he have sent those things to me?" Josh watched as Cassidy returned with the ball. "Let's go for it."

Cassidy ran up the stairs, dropping the ball at Josh's feet. "There you go. Good girl," Josh said, bending to pick the ball up.

Cassidy turned away, looking toward the woods, a low guttural growl coming from her.

Josh looked out toward the woods. "What is it girl? There a deer out there?" Cassidy continued to growl, sticking her head through the railings on the deck, her nose sniffing the air.

"What do you think it is?" Keira asked.

"Either a deer or coyote of something," Josh replied. "She doesn't like anything in her territory." Josh called the dog over. "It's okay, good girl. Keep them wild animals away."

Josh and Keira walked back in the house, calling Cassidy in and closing the sliders behind them. Cassidy sat at the door. Staring into the woods, she watched the shadow move away.

* * *

Josh headed downtown to meet with Chris and the others. Pulling up in front of the Packett Building, he walked into the lobby, taking the elevator to the third floor. Started in a one-room closet as an office, Alpha Babes Investigation had expanded to take over the entire third floor. Josh got off the elevator. Vera Johnson was sitting at the front desk.

"They got you on receptionist duty?" Josh asked.

"I like it out here, wide open. I can do my work without feeling cooped up. Nice view as well," pointing to the large window overlooking the South Main Street skyline.

"Are the other two evil ones in their caves?"

"Yes, they are. Anticipating an update on the Grey case which we hope will contain good news," Vera laughed.

"Indeed it does, my friend. Indeed, it does."

Vera put the phones on auto-answer and followed Josh into the conference room.

Maggie Fleming and Chris Hamlin came in with Vera's niece, Loren Grey.

"Hello Lieutenant Williams," Loren greeted him, "How are you?"

"I'm well, Loren. And you?"

"A little nervous, my aunt said you had some news for us."

"I do have some things to tell you," Josh said.

"By the way," Loren said, "thanks for getting me back in touch with Reggie and his wife. We have a lot of things to catch up on."

Josh nodded and smiled. "Glad to hear it. Okay, first the good stuff. Sort of," waiting as the group settled in around the conference table. "We've gathered a bunch of evidence that they framed your father for the crimes. The cops, the AG's office, and prison staff worked to put your father in the general prison population knowing they would kill him."

Loren sobbed, shaking her head. Vera put her arm around the young woman. "But why would they do that? Why?"

"Well, quite simply, because he was black and the victims were white," Josh said. "They wanted vengeance, not justice. They hid the truth to achieve their goal." Josh let the words sink in. "My wife, Keira, says we can file a motion to have the charges dismissed by the court. I know it's not much, more symbolic gesture than anything else. Nothing can bring him back, but we can try to restore his good name. And, she'll announce all this at a press conference. We can't do much more than make those responsible a bit uncomfortable, but at least it's something."

Josh put his hand on Loren's arm, "Your father was a soldier. Did you know that?"

Loren lifted her head, "No, I didn't know anything about him. My mother must have thought it would be too difficult for me to learn about him. I didn't find out about him until after she died. My aunt," reaching out and taking Vera's hand, "told me a lot of things she knew about him. I guess when it all happened my mother hadn't told most of her friends she was pregnant. I thought my step-dad was my real father."

Josh told her the story of the 1st Air Cavalry and the battle of the Ia Drang Valley in 1965 during the Vietnam War.

"Your father survived something which haunted him for his whole life. Like many soldiers, he was vilified when he returned from Vietnam. No one cared what happened to him. We cannot even guess how it affected his life. However, we do know this; he was innocent of those crimes. We can at least prove that. Keira has the motion ready to file," Josh looked around the room, and then said. "But, there is one thing I need from you."

"What?" Chris asked.

"Time," Josh answered, moving around the table. "We need time before we file the motion. In looking into this, we've stumbled upon a serious situation." Josh closed the door to the outer office. "What I am going to say has to remain among us. Agreed?" Watching as the women, looking at each other.

"Chris knows most of this," reaching for his coffee, he took a long sip. "Someone tried to kill me, and they almost killed Keira instead. She was driving my truck when they went after her. We were lucky, this time. We don't know if they'll try again. We do know this all began when I started poking around this case."

"I don't want anyone hurt over this," Loren said. "I'm happy with what you've found, just let it go."

"Hah," Chris laughed. "There's no way he's gonna let this go now. He's gonna follow this no matter what, aren't you, Ace? There's more to this he's not telling us."

Josh smiled, nodding his head. "Let's just say we found some new activity, involving some of the same people who framed your father. We may not be able to do anything about the past, but we may jam them up for the new stuff. I just need you to be patient. We're gonna use your father's case to push them some more. This time, we'll be ready for them."

Loren walked over to Josh and hugged him. "Thank you, thank you for doing this. I've waited this long for the truth; I can wait a little longer."

Vera took her niece back to the outer office, leaving Josh with Chris and Maggie.

"Okay, what's the rest of it?" Maggie asked. "Since I called one of the connected numbers, I think you owe us the full story."

Josh explained the connections between Tucker, his daughter, Sorin, the Russians, and the Senator.

Maggie and Chris listened, hanging on every word.

"You know, I always believed he was a son-of-a-bitch," Maggie said, "but this is even worse than I could imagine. If I was ever unsure about leaving the US Attorney's office, this eliminated all doubt."

Chris took a drink of coffee and added, "So, how we gonna nail this motherfucker?"

"Such eloquence," Josh answered, turning to Maggie, "I can see why you choose to associate with her."

"Just answer my question. How are we gonna do this?" Chris replied, her voice rising.

"First, there is no 'we' in this matter. I've already made the Feds nervous by bringing in Tommy. Kennedy suspects I've been keeping you in the loop. If his bosses find out I let you help, they'll pull him out."

Chris banged the desk. "Are you kidding me? Are you freaking kidding me? Now you're gonna play by the rules? What happened to you, Josh? Did Brennan cut off your balls?"

"Again, with the insightful discourse. Listen, you nasty old witch, and I mean that with all due respect to other witches, I said if they find out I am letting you help. We just have to be cautious, so they don't. Feel better now, or do I dump a bucket of water on you and melt you?"

Chris smiled and leaned back in her chair. "Well, now that we've settled that matter, tell me what we are gonna do."

* * *

Zach Kennedy pulled into the lot of the East Providence Police station on Waterman Avenue. He parked next to a dark colored Ford Taurus. *I wonder who's joining the party now.* There was no mistaking the car; it belonged to some law enforcement agency. He doubted an East Providence detective would park out here.

Walking into the lobby, he saw the two detectives standing at the window talking to the receptionist.

State Police, he guessed. He waited to see who came out to get them.

Josh poked his head out of the side door. "Well, will you look at this? The State Police are here. All hail the mighty State Police," bowing at the waist.

The two troopers turned and smiled. "Why is it whenever you guys step on your pecker, we have to come straighten it out?" Sergeant Joe Moreira replied.

"Because they cut yours off in the academy, so you have none to step on," Josh laughed, extending his hand to the sergeant. "And I see they really scraped the bottom of the barrel with your partner here. The bloodhounds were busy, I suppose, so they sent Donahue instead."

"Nice to see you too, Josh," Corporal Timmy Donahue smiled, taking Josh's hand. "Where's the crazy lady, did they finally commit her?"

"Retired," Josh answered, gesturing for them to come in. "She didn't want a party, just came in one day and pulled the pin."

"No shit," Donahue chuckled. "I would have loved to have seen that party."

Josh saw Kennedy hanging back, taking in the conversation.

"Hey, Zach, come on in. These are two of the dumbest troopers, and that's saying something, ever to wear those funny looking riding outfits.

164

If you haven't seen them, they look like a design by a blind French whore on LSD. Sergeant Joe Moreira and Corporal Tim Donahue."

"Nice to meet you guys. I take it you've worked with Lieutenant Williams before," Kennedy said, shaking hands with the troopers.

"Unfortunately," Donahue answered. "We all draw straws, losers have to come here."

"Ah, well. We all have our crosses to bear," Kennedy smiled.

They walked over to the SIU office. Moore looked up from his desk, "Jeez, we're gonna need a bigger office. How are you guys?"

After they settled in, Josh brought them up to speed on the case. Donahue shook his head. "You mean those bastards came after you and almost got Keira? That's not going to work with me. Going after my cousin means war."

Kennedy looked up, "Josh's wife is your cousin?"

Donahue laughed. "This is Rhode Island, bucko. We're all related somehow," a hint of the Irish brogue leaking through. "If someone goes after me cousin, they go after me."

"How would you feel if they had taken me out?" Josh said, folding his arms across his chest.

"I'd have been a source of comfort and support for me beloved cousin," Donahue smiled. "The woman must have been daft to marry you in the first place."

"Well, now that we've suffered through the family history lesson, let me tell you what else I have found," Moore said. Drawing their attention to his computer screen, Moore used the mouse to expand the view.

"You know how we identified the companies behind the business on Waterman, right?"

Josh nodded.

"Well, I did some more digging on those Delaware corporations. Our friend, William Marshall is an officer of Harriet Lane Associates. I then ran a comparison of all addresses we've found for any of the main players, Collucci, Sorin, Jen Tucker, and found this," pointing to the screen.

"What is that, Tommy?" Kennedy asked.

"I used Excel to build a linking chart cross-referencing the addresses, people, and businesses. Marshall and Sorin are on five different companies all with ties to Harriet Lane Enterprises. Jen Tucker is listed on the JTS Management corporate documents. Her prior driver's licenses, some old tax documents, and P.O. Boxes link her with two of the same addresses. I suspect this is from when she was married to Sorin. Collucci isn't listed on any of the corporate documents, business files, or anything else. The one link I can find is this," using a few mouse clicks and turning the screen so they could see.

Josh bent forward, getting a closer look.

"The registration information of the car you saw parked in the JTS slot on Waterman. The mailing address is a P.O. Box; the owner of the box is Anthony Sorin. A credit card listed to a PAC, which contributes heavily to Collucci, paid for the box. And there is more."

The investigators looked at each other. "Go on Tommy, you've got our attention." Josh said.

"One of the principals in the PAC is, Shashenka Dmitriev. A naturalized American citizen from?" pointing at Kennedy.

"Russia, with many business interests in the Ukraine. Like our dead shooter," Kennedy answered.

"Right," Tommy said. "There are a bunch of connections to Russia and the Ukraine, both businesses and individuals.

"What about the P.O. Box on the package the Judge sent, how's it tied in?" Josh asked.

"My guess is the Judge uses the P.O. Box courtesy of his daughter, unless?" Tommy replied.

"Unless what?" Donahue said.

"Unless the Judge is a little more involved in the whole thing. Having a friendly face on the Supreme Court can't hurt."

"I don't know, Tommy. I doubt he's involved," Josh said.

"Tommy, this is great work. How come you aren't with us on the State Police?" Donahue asked.

"I did the interview. When they asked if I knew both my parents and could spell, I said yes. Instant disqualification."

Donahue looked at Josh. "You train them well, don't you?"

Josh laughed, "I am so proud. Seriously, though, this is great work. Now what?"

Kennedy reached into his briefcase. "Well, I have a few things to add," handing out copies of several pictures. "These are the people Josh spotted coming from JTS Management. The two males are not in our system, they remain unidentified. The woman is a different matter. She is Alexandra Kosokov. She's the daughter of Shashenka Dmitriev and married to a known Russian mob leader, Motka Kosokov. She travels under a diplomatic passport. She is the Cultural Attaché at the Russian Embassy in New York, aka spy."

"All this talk of Russians makes me want vodka," Moreira interjected. "Maybe we need to do some field surveillance?"

Kennedy glanced at Josh, "Am I the only one unaware of this investigative technique?"

"I guess so," Josh smiled, turning his attention back to the photos. "So, I take it this Motka Kosokov is a real bad guy?"

"You could say that. We don't think he's in the country, but I wouldn't put it past him. He has traveled under diplomatic passports. The State Department is reluctant to release info absent firm proof of a crime. The relations with us and the Russians have improved a bit and they don't want to create problems."

"I'll say this one more time." Moore interrupted, rising from his desk. "How the hell did we get mixed up in this? Next we'll have poisoned tipped umbrellas issued to us."

"You know, Josh," Donahue added, "it is always an adventure when we come here to work with you East Providence guys."

Chapter 23

Tim Donahue, Joe Moreira, Zach Kennedy, Tommy Moore, Chief Brennan, and Josh gathered in the Chief's conference room. There was a single loud knock on the door and Captain Andrew McGurk, Rhode Island State Police, strode in.

The two State Police detectives came to attention. They presented picture-perfect hand salutes to the Captain. McGurk returned each one, individually, and then turned toward Tommy Moore. The Captain returned Moore's salute, then realized Moore was at attention with the back of his hand flat on his forehead, in a perfect Three Stooges salute.

Josh tried to hide his smile. McGurn glared, then walked to Chief Brennan and shook his hand.

"You'll have to forgive the comedian here, boy's not right in the head. How are you, Captain?"

"I am well, thank you Chief. The Colonel sent me here to be briefed on the investigation. Would someone fill me in on what you have so far?" Taking the seat next to Josh, he stuck out his hand, "Lieutenant Williams, right? I don't think we've met."

"No, sir, we haven't. I want to thank you for sending Tim and Joe to work this. We can use all the help we can get. I'm going to let Detective Moore fill you in." Leaning back to look behind McGurk at Tommy, eyebrows raised. "Tommy, will you please explain to the *Captain* what we have uncovered so far?"

"Sir yes Sir," Moore snapped, "I will be brief in briefing, so you'll be briefed briefly." Brennan dropped his head, trying to conceal a grin with a cough.

Josh shot Tommy daggers.

True to his word, Tommy gave a concise synopsis of the investigation. It seemed to satisfy the Captain. He thanked everyone for their work and left quickly.

When the door closed, the room broke into laughter.

Brennan tried to control himself, but even he laughed. "Moore, I shouldn't encourage this behavior, but Christ boy, that was funny. But, you should show some respect. I mean the guy is a Captain."

Tommy never changed his demeanor. "Look, we all know the guy just wanted to strut around and show us how important he is and that the Colonel is watching. Big deal. I briefed him. Although quite frankly, I think he's more of a thong wearing kind of guy."

Donahue burst out laughing, snorting his coffee. "Oh great, there's a fucking image I didn't need."

Josh took out a file from his briefcase. "Okay, now that we've finished dealing with the egos, can we decide what we're going to do next?"

"We need a way to smoke out the Russian connection to the Senator and his Chief of Staff. Collucci already created the legislation; it is pending before the Banking Committee. Since that's already in the works, there's not much we can do there. But," walking over to pour more coffee. "If we can show fraudulent land transactions, or get someone inside to talk to us, we may be able to create enough noise to derail the process," returning to his seat. "With the money involved, no doubt someone's getting paid off."

"Hey Joe," Donahue said. "Remember last year, the Governor had the Colonel withdraw us from the lottery oversight detail? Maybe there's a good place to start."

Moreira thought for a moment. "The State Police have always had responsibility for investigating backgrounds of potential lottery agents. We had two troopers assigned full-time to the detail. I can't remember when but at least a year ago, the Governor told the Colonel he no longer wanted troopers handling it. He argued they could do it more cost effectively with lottery personnel. The Colonel argued against it, citing all sorts of potential problems, but the decision stood. The Colonel had no choice but to reassign the troopers."

"You think this was part of their play? Get the State Police out of the way so they can better control who looks at what," Brennan asked.

"It all fits," Donahue replied. "We've always had a concern, without our oversight, Rhode Island politics would take hold. They would start handing out lottery licenses to the wrong people. Looks like it was even bigger than that. If they got control of the lottery, they could cook the books on revenue and skim millions off the top. It's a huge cash flow business."

"Or," Josh added, "they use the same mechanism to launder money. Nobody's gonna complain if the revenue rises. They kick in five or even ten percent of the dirty money on top of the legitimate state revenue. Everybody stays fat, dumb, and happy."

Tommy, busy clicking away on his laptop, oblivious to the conversation, made weird noises as he worked.

"Detective Moore," Brennan asked, "what is so interesting on that computer? Some game site I suppose."

Donahue added, "He's looking for his next online date, the only way the boy can get laid."

Moore smirked at Donahue, and then turned the screen for everyone to see. "I'll use simple language, so the troopers don't get confused. Since the Governor eliminated the State Police, lottery revenues have been rising. They are up twenty-two percent over the prior year."

"Holy shit," Josh exclaimed. "They've been doing this for a while. Everything else in the state's economy is going to shit."

"Twenty-two percent is a lot of money," Zach Kennedy chimed in. "If we assume for argument's sake just a quarter of the rise in revenue is dirty money," grabbing a pad and pen. "Let me do some quick math," writing furiously. "If they use just, say, five percent of the money to grow revenue, we're talking billions of dollars going through the system. They need a banking insider to do that. They need...," Kennedy threw the pen down. "They don't need a bank, they have all they want. Collucci sits on the damn Banking, Housing, and Urban Affairs Committee. They pass favorable legislation for the banking industry. In return, the banks provide the accounting expertise to hide the trail. There's a reason to kill somebody."

"But what the hell have I done to warrant their attention?" Josh asked.

"Collucci is their inside guy," Kennedy explained. "He goes, their system goes. They control him, and the Senate committee, through his Chief of Staff. Your little peek into his history might derail his re-election. If I remember right, he's maneuvering for the chair of the committee. He'll run the whole damn thing."

Kennedy sat back and looked at Brennan. "Chief, if we keep pushing this, they are going to come after him again," pointing at Josh. "With this kind of money at stake no one will be immune, Keira in particular. Anyone else involved is at risk as well."

Brennan looked at Josh. "We need to have a talk with Keira. I know you can't convince her to carry a gun, but we have to make sure she understands the severity of this."

"I'll talk to her. Maybe I could convince her to work from home for the next few weeks. Put someone in the house with her when I am not there."

* * *

"I don't care what you say, Josh. No one is holding me prisoner in my own house. I don't need a personal guard," Keira yelled, storming around the kitchen, slamming doors.

"You wouldn't be a prisoner, just in an environment we can control. Listen," Josh argued, "these guys are serious. This is huge money. Taking you out to get to me wouldn't faze them at all. It's safer this way."

"What about my cases? What about court? How am I supposed to do my job if I don't leave here?" she asked, hands on her hips, glaring.

"It won't be for long, just a few weeks. Can't you delay any motions or appearances for a little while? Or let someone else argue them?"

Keira stood staring at Josh, "Let me ask you something, are these threats gonna stop you from doing your job? Are you gonna stay here with me until this is over?" motioning for him to answer. "Well, are you?"

Josh was silent.

"I didn't think so," walking over and taking his hand. "Josh, I am not going to let them control my life. Not for one goddamn minute. I can take care of myself."

"But Keira, listen to me…"

Keira put her hand up. "Enough, I've listened. I know you are trying to protect me, but at what cost? They already came after me, or us. Whether I am here and you are out there, it doesn't matter. If that's what they are going to do, my being here won't change it," embracing her husband. "You can have someone assigned to go with me, but that is it. Nothing else."

"Will you at least carry my off-duty weapon?"

Keira looked into Josh's eyes, saw genuine fear. *Maybe I can at least do that.* "Tell you what, I'll carry the gun. If for nothing else than to get you to shut up."

Josh pulled her back to him and kissed her. "Great, I'll get Brennan to fast track the permit paperwork through the Mass State Police. Meanwhile, I'll get two detectives assigned to be with you."

Keira walked to the kitchen counter and sat on a stool. "All I had to do was not let you talk me into that first date and none of this would be happening to me," she smiled.

"Where would the fun be in that?" Josh answered, pouring her a cup of coffee, sitting next to her, and holding her hand.

There was a knock on the door, startling the two. Josh glanced at Keira and saw the apprehension in her eyes. Another knock, then the sound of a familiar voice, "Are you gonna open the goddamn door any time soon?" Chris Hamlin yelled.

Cassidy danced in front of the door, sniffing at the bottom, pacing back and forth in anticipation of the door opening. The dog loved company.

Josh opened the door and Chris came in. "Top of the morning to ya', bucko. Chris Hamlin, at your service," walking to the kitchen cabinet and getting a coffee cup. "Don't look so surprised, Brennan called me and told me the problem. I am here, problem solved. I'll stay with Keira, you go finish this."

Keira smiled, "Now I know I am in good hands," pouring Chris some coffee.

Cassidy jumped up, front paws in Chris's lap. "Everything is under control, Ace," scratching the dog's head. "You go catch the bad guys, Cassidy and I will take care of Keira. I'll stay with her until this is over."

* * *

Early the next morning, the investigative team gathered in the Chief's conference room. Josh brought them up to speed on the security arrangements for Keira courtesy of Chris Hamlin.

Donahue chuckled and said, "You're a brave man there, Lieutenant Williams."

Josh looked at Donahue, his eyes questioning him.

"There's no way I'd ever give my wife a gun," causing a round of laughter in the room. "One night I came home late after a, ah, surveillance if you know what I mean. My ex-wife was sitting in the dark. I could hear her spinning the cylinder, dropping bullets, and muttering, 'How do you load this goddamn thing?' I left." This caused another round of laughter.

Josh smiled at Donahue, "My wife wouldn't need a gun, and she'd stab me in my sleep if I fucked up."

"While I am sure we all appreciate the lesson in marital relations, can we move on?" Brennan interjected.

The group went over their options. There weren't many. Linking Collucci's actions in the Senate with the Russians and the dirty money would not be easy.

"What about the daughter?" Joe Moreira offered.

"You mean Tucker's daughter? Why her? She seems to play a very small part of this," Kennedy replied.

"Hear me out on this," Moreira said, rising from his seat. "She is set up in this business by Sorin. He's taking care of her financially; at least that's what she believes. However, we know the money comes from the bad guys. She has a daughter; she won't want to risk losing custody if she gets jammed up. Something happens, the Russians aren't going to save her. Sorin isn't going to save her. Daddy will not be able to. We can use this to gain her cooperation," looking at the group. "We professional investigators of the State Police call that," arms outstretched, "leverage."

"We in the FBI call that threats and extortion," Kennedy said, causing a new round of laughter. "I like it."

As the laughter died down, Josh looked around the room. "Anyone here got a problem with extortion?"

No one raised an objection.

Tommy Moore remained uncharacteristically silent.

Chapter 24

Anthony Sorin, checking the day's schedule for the Senator, located the one item that mattered. Reaching into the briefcase, he pulled out the position statement and supporting documents. I will need to review these with the Senator again. It is frustrating how slow the man is at embracing complex concepts. Perhaps, it is why he is so useful to us.

The phone rang, "Yes sir?"

"Good morning, Tony. I assume you're ready for the morning briefing?"

"Yes, Senator, I'll be right over."

Gathering his materials, Sorin headed to the Senator's office. As he walked down the windowed hallway in the McCormick Senate Office Building, his cell phone rang.

Glancing at the caller ID, he ducked into an alcove. "Yes?"

"All is good?" came the accented voice.

"Just going to review it with him now. We secured the supporting votes; the House group is onboard. We are ready on our end. Have you taken care of things on yours?"

"The funds are in the staging accounts. Once the vote is taken, the transfer through the usual channels will happen."

Sorin ended the call.

Senator Collucci's secretary was in her accustomed position, guarding access to the Senator.

"Good morning, Tony. Would you care for some coffee?"

"That would be great, Sandy. Please hold all calls; we've a lot to discuss this morning before the committee meeting." He handed the secretary a piece of paper. "I've made some changes to the schedule; we'll have to cancel a few appearances for today and tomorrow. Would you please handle those for me?"

"No problem, I'll get on this right away. Oh, by the way, the Senator received a call today from a Judge in Rhode Island. I have the name somewhere," shuffling through some papers.

"Judge Tucker?" Sorin asked.

"Yes, that's it. I have it here. He left a message on voice mail. Said it was important he speak to the Senator. Would you pass this on to him for me?"

"Of course," taking the note and walking toward the Senator's private office. "Oh, and Sandy, please delete the voice mail from the Judge. I'll make sure the Senator contacts him."

As he entered the office, he crumpled the note and stuck it in his pocket.

Collucci was on the phone as Sorin came in, motioning with his free hand for him to sit. "Yes, Senator, this is critical in several areas. Economic development and jobs." He covered the phone, "Senator Murray, wants me to support his construction bill. He says he'll support our motion."

"Our support margin is tenuous. I'd say agree," Sorin replied.

Returning to the call, Collucci became more animated. "Look, Senator. For too long Native Americans have been, to be blunt, screwed by the system. Oh sure, we gave them some casinos on tribal land but most of them are so far away from the main population centers they struggle to survive. Support my bill. It will create a partnership between government and the indigenous Native American tribes. The project in Rhode Island will serve as a model for the rest of the country."

Collucci listened a moment then said, "Okay, we are in agreement. You sign on in support of this legislation and I agree to support your bill. I will lobby for support from other members of the committee," pausing a moment. "Excellent, see you in the committee room. Thank you, Senator," hanging up the phone.

"Well, sounds like we've added to the margin," Sorin smiled.

"Indeed, we have. Now, what else do we need to do?"

A knock on the door interrupted the conversation. The secretary came in with coffee. "Will there be anything else, Senator?"

"No, that's all for now Sandy. Please hold all calls for the next hour. Thank you," watching as the woman left the office.

"Okay Tony. What else do you have for me?" Collucci put his hands behind his head and sat back in the chair.

"Tucker called," Sorin said. "It can't be anything good. We need to avoid any problems. We're too close to let this slip away."

Collucci's demeanor changed, "Tucker suffers from terminal conscience. He just cannot let the past go. Son-of-a-bitch has made a career out of playing up to the minority crowd out of a sense of guilt. Damn it, it's not as if he killed the black bastard himself. Pardon my political incorrectness," a smile creeping across his face.

"Senator, let me remind you our friends are anxious about this. They do not want any disruption of our arrangement. You need to deal with Tucker and dissuade him from creating any further problems."

Collucci put his fingertips together. "Perhaps it's time the Judge understands something. His interference can have a negative effect on his daughter. And, if that isn't enough motivation, the truth about his granddaughter."

Sorin smiled. "I'd like nothing more than to see that bitch suffer. What she did to me is unforgivable. If there was another way to manage the local aspect of this, I'd dump her and that annoying child of hers."

"Now, now Tony, is that anyway to speak of your flesh and blood, or your namesake? Once we finish with the land transfers we will sever the relationship."

Collucci watched as Sorin furrowed his brow.

"Careful, Senator, our friends have a huge stake in this venture. No one is indispensable. They decide who, or when, that might be, not you."

Collucci, ignoring the implied threat, turned his attention to the file on the desk. *When this is over, a new Chief of Staff is in order.*

* * *

A week after the Senate voted on the legislation, Collucci stood on the stairs in front of the Rhode Island State House. The Governor and elected officials from East Providence and Providence stood behind the Senator. The Sachems of the Narragansett and Wampanoag Tribes completed the list of VIPs.

Sorin motioned to the gathered media the Senator was ready to start. As Collucci waited for the crowd to quiet, he gave two thumbs up, pointed to various people in the crowd, and smiled for the cameras.

"Today," Collucci began, "we announce the dawn of a new era. A new chapter in the relationship between government and Native Americans," nodding to the two Sachems.

"The Comprehensive State and Native American Economic Development Partnership Act, a bill I wrote and sponsored, passed both houses of Congress. The President assured me he will sign the bill into law," pausing at the smattering of applause and nodding to the gathered dignitaries.

Turning back to face the cameras, Collucci continued, "Today, with the passage of my bill, we begin a new chapter in history."

More applause rose from the gathered crowd.

"We have the joint support of the Narragansett and Wampanoag tribes," pointing to the two Sachems.

"Through this cooperation, we begin the process of rectifying the injustices of the past." Collucci paused as the applause gained in intensity. "My legislation provides funds to acquire waterfront property in East Providence. We will link this with the reclaimed land from the Interstate 195 relocation project, creating a huge enterprise zone.

"The legislation funds an expanded deep-water port and railway links from downtown Providence to Boston and New York."

More applause from the crowd interrupted Collucci. He basked in the attention.

"But wait," he said, raising his hands, "there's more." His face broke into a huge smile as he watched the reaction of the crowd.

"The State of Rhode Island will move the headquarters of the Rhode Island Lottery onto the East Providence property. They will expand access to gaming activities controlled by Native Americans on tribal lands," causing another round of intense applause.

As the noise died down, Collucci looked around the crowd, allowing the anticipation to build. "But the keystone of the project is this," turning as his Chief of Staff removed a covering on a large design drawing. "The center piece of the project is the integration of the Twin River Casino and Newport Grand facility into one operation. The Native American tribes will operate the facility with state oversight. Upon completion, it will be the largest combined gaming facility in the western hemisphere."

The applause rose in intensity. Many of the assembled media struggled to maintain the sound levels of the live feed.

"With this consolidation, the people of Rhode Island and the Native American communities will reap enormous benefits. The projections for revenue potential are significant. This is an opportunity to reduce taxes and increase spending on important projects such as transportation infrastructure and schools. This is a momentous undertaking. I am proud to be the sponsor of this legislation and look forward to seeing its full implementation. Thank you," gesturing to the group surrounding him, "for making this possible."

Collucci walked around shaking hands and patting people on the back.

A few reporters shouted questions. "Senator, how will the selection of private companies be managed? What is the plan to deal with revenue lost to Lincoln and Newport? How much of the cost is the state responsible for?"

Collucci ignored the questions, waved at the crowd, and walked into the State House. The Governor and the others followed him in. Moving to a private reception, the group engaged in animated conversations on the announcement.

"Ladies and Gentlemen, if I could have your attention for a moment," Collucci said. Standing at the podium, he waited for the conversations to die down.

"This is a historic moment. By collaborating with our Native American brothers and sisters, we have the opportunity to right a terrible wrong. Not only will we open new avenues of economic growth, we also have the chance to share these opportunities in a most meaningful way. I want to thank all of you for your help. Without it, this day might never have happened." Reveling in the applause, Collucci stepped away from the podium.

"Senator, might I have a word?"

Collucci turned to the question, taken aback to see Judge Tucker standing there. Recovering his poise, he nodded. "Of course, my old friend, what can I do for you?"

Tucker looked around the room. "Perhaps we can go someplace private, after this little gathering?"

Collucci saw Sorin standing in the back of the room, watching them. "Let's go to my office on the third floor. I keep a small office here for my staff. Now's fine," pointing toward the exit, motioning for Sorin to come with them.

* * *

Collucci led the way to the office, followed by Tucker and Sorin. As they entered the room, Collucci told the on-duty staffer to leave. Collucci, rubbing his hands together, looked at Tucker. After the door closed, Collucci said, "What is it about you, George?" disgust in his voice. "Why can't you leave ancient history alone?"

"I do not care what you think. I did not come here to negotiate." The Judge's out-of-character, angry tone caught Collucci and Sorin by surprise. "I am here to tell you I am going forward with this. I prepared a document detailing all, and I do mean all, of the actions we took back then. I intend to deliver it to the media. With what I have learned over the past few days, I am ashamed of the way I behaved. An innocent man died because of us."

Collucci glanced at Sorin, who nodded. Collucci returned his attention to the Judge. "Time for a reality check here, your Honor. You release anything and all you do is ruin your career. Nothing in those files ties me to anything. You were the AG assigned, your initials are on the lineup, you indicted him, and you put him in the system. If that is what you want, go for it. Someone else will sit in your seat and your cozy little relationship with the minority community will suffer. Is that what you want for your friends of color?" The venom in the words shocked Tucker.

"Listen to me, Senator--"

"No, Judge, you listen to me," Sorin interrupted. "There's someone else you might want to consider in this matter."

"And who would that be?" Tucker asked.

Sorin shot a glance at Collucci and took two quick steps to stand in front of the Judge, drawing his attention. "Your daughter and precious little grandchild."

Tucker, surprised by the words, glared at his former son-in-law. "What do you mean? What do they have to do with this?"

"Much, my good Jurist, more than you realize. Seems your daughter was not satisfied with the amount of money I pay her in alimony and child support. She wanted more. The business of hers, I set that up. I arranged for her to meet a business associate. You will be happy to know your daughter has a good head for business. She owns, or thinks she owns, a good deal of the land for our new project. The truth is my organization owns it through a maze of cover corporations."

Watching the reaction on the Judge's face, he knew they had him.

"Some of those transactions have your name on it as well. It would be a terrible thing if you or little Ms. Jennifer were caught up in trading on inside information. Remember, yours was the deciding vote on the legality of re-zoning the affected property. Where would that leave your granddaughter?"

"My granddaughter?" Tucker shook with rage. "Kelsey's your daughter, Anthony. How could you do that to your own daughter?"

"Oh, yes. That is something else little Jennifer forgot to tell you. Remember that law student, that 'chorn' from South Africa? The one who stayed with you for a court apprenticeship about, let me see, 9 years and 9 months ago? Well, you'll be pleased to know, your granddaughter is a half-breed herself," Sorin spat the words at Tucker. "She's not my biological daughter."

Tucker blanched and collapsed into a chair, his mind reeling.

"How do you like that, Judge? You have been cozying up to those welfare-sucking scumbags all your life. Now you know your granddaughter might become one. You must be thrilled," Sorin laughed and leaned back against the wall. "All that remains now is for you to decide. Is the life of some long dead black piece of shit worth it? Your career in ruins, your daughter goes to jail, and your granddaughter ends up chased by lions in some godforsaken native village in Africa," Sorin pushed off the wall and whispered in Tucker's ear. "Remember this, you do anything to screw this up and I will turn over evidence to the Justice

Department that buries your daughter. Even if she avoided jail, Jennifer would end up losing her daughter."

Tucker tried to speak, but the words would not come. How had he not seen Sorin for what he was? His daughter said she loved him. How could she not know this side of him?

Sorin continued. "Here's another good incentive. My people have a great deal of money invested in this project. Do not anger them. You screw this up, and a lost daughter and ruined career will be the least of your worries."

Tucker stared into Sorin's malevolent eyes. The sound of a door opening drew his attention. He saw Collucci come back into the room. Tucker had not seen him leave. *Son-of-a-bitch.* He now realized Collucci had ducked out to avoid direct involvement.

"George, I apologize for stepping out," Collucci said, in a matter of fact tone. "I trust Anthony has resolved your concerns."

Tucker rose without saying a word, staggering to the door. Turning back, he started to speak.

Sorin held up his hand. "Don't say a thing, Judge. We will know what we need to do by your actions. Think long and hard about your choices," taking a couple of steps toward the Judge, backing him into the door. "Once set in motion, our decisions are irreversible."

Chapter 25

Josh and Joe Moreira sat in one car, watching the front entrance of the business, Tim Donahue and Tommy Moore covered the back lot. Over the past few weeks, they had monitored Sorin's activities, getting to know her habits and patterns. That's the thing about most people; they exhibit a consistent pattern of behavior. Follow someone for a week, and you can sum up their lives.

Today was a Thursday. She would leave the office between 5:10 and 5:20, drive to a nail salon in East Providence, then head to dinner with friends at Andrea's on Thayer Street. After dinner, she would drive to her father's house, pick up her daughter, and head home for the night.

True to form, they spotted her leaving the lot at 5:15. Donahue followed her onto the Henderson Bridge, off the Massasoit Avenue exit. He watched as she parked in front of the salon, and then went inside.

When she left today, her nails would be perfect, but no one at Andrea's would see them.

Jennifer Sorin left the salon at 6:00, made a U-turn on Waterman Avenue and headed back toward the bridge. The marked unit was waiting on Massasoit Avenue. The uniform officer stopped her and made a show of running her license and registration. He told her there was a problem with her license. She would have to come to the station to resolve it.

Placing her in the back of the cruiser, the officer also took possession of her cell phone. When he arrived at the station, he delivered her to Josh in the SIU office.

Josh offered her a seat. She declined. "Do you know who I am?" she said, arms folded, tapping her foot.

Josh just smiled, that didn't take long did it?

"Perhaps you know my father, Supreme Court Justice George Tucker?" drawing out her father's name and title.

Josh, raising his eyebrows and holding up his index finger, made a presentation of opening the door. A parade of serious looking men entered the room.

Sorin's eyes began to blink, her breathing growing rapid and shallow. Her heart raced.

Each man introduced himself and their organizations. Jennifer's face grew more and more pale. She collapsed into the chair. When FBI Agent Zach Kennedy finished his presentation, she appeared on the edge of vomiting; then she was over the edge.

Joe Moreira took her to the ladies' room.

"Where's, Tommy?" Josh asked.

"Don't know. Said he needed to check on some things and would be back later," Donahue answered.

When she returned from the ladies' room, Jennifer sat in the chair, trying to regain her composure. "I don't know what you expect from me. There isn't anything I know that will help you; I just run my business."

Donahue stood up, smiling as he walked past her, then opened the door, pointing. "Get the hell out. You want to take your chances out there, go for it. Who's gonna protect you? Your ex? Daddy? I don't fucking think so. You want your daughter visiting you in prison, or your grave, then get up and walk out. Otherwise, knock off the bullshit and listen to us. This is your one chance."

Jennifer sobbed. "I don't know anything about their business. I, I just manage properties."

Josh slid his chair closer, handing her a box of tissues. "Look, Jennifer. We know you got caught up in this. We know your ex-husband is in control. We just need you to tell us everything you do know, identify the properties, and anyone you know who's involved. No one will ever know you're working with us."

She let out a deep sigh, looking at the ceiling, trying to control the tears. "I knew this was going to happen, sooner or later. I just knew this was too easy. I wish I never married that asshole."

"We've all been down that road," Donahue muttered, causing muffled laughter.

"Jennifer," Josh said, "let's start from the beginning. Tell us how he started the business. Give us everything you know, and we'll get you out of here so you can go get your daughter."

Jennifer looked at Josh for a moment. "Can I call my friends and tell them I won't make it to dinner?"

Josh handed her cell phone to her.

Two hours later, they had enough investigative leads to keep them busy for a while. Donahue offered to bring her back to her car. Josh called him aside.

"I don't know, Timmy," Josh whispered. "You were kind of hard on her. She may prefer someone else to take her back."

"Nah, a little informant re-education program was all it was," Donahue said. "Having me go will keep her off balance; keep her a little on edge. We want to make sure she stays on the right side of this don't we?"

Josh thought a moment, "I suppose, but no hard ass stuff, okay? We don't want her breaking down in front of daddy and having him in the mix."

"I'll be the perfect gentleman."

"You've never been a gentleman in your entire life, perfect or otherwise. Just don't scare her any more than she already is, okay?"

"Got it," winking at Josh. "Come on, Ms. Sorin, I'll give you a ride back to your car."

Jennifer's eyes grew wide at the prospect. She looked around the room, eyes pleading for someone else.

"I don't bite," Donahue said.

"No worries, Jennifer. He's had his distemper shots," Moreira added. "He's somewhat housebroken as well."

Josh noticed the door to the office had opened and Tommy standing there. "I'll take her," Tommy offered, as if on cue. "I got this, LT."

Donahue shrugged and sat back down.

"Where have you been?" Josh asked.

"Had some things to deal with. No big deal, "Tommy answered. "Come on, Jen. I'll take you back to your car."

Josh looked at the other investigators.

Jennifer gathered herself together, following Tommy out of the office.

"Come on, Jen?" Donahue asked, once the door closed. "What the hell was that all about?"

Josh shrugged. "Sometimes Tommy shows he has a heart I guess."

* * *

They drove without speaking for a few moments.

"Did you tell them about me, Tommy?" Jennifer asked, breaking the silence.

Moore shook his head, looking straight ahead. "I didn't know it was you. Lots of people named Tucker."

"Oh, come on Tommy, you don't expect me to believe that do you?" Jennifer said, "The Lieutenant, what's his name?"

"Josh, Josh Williams," Tommy answered.

"Yeah, Josh. He told me you have been following me for weeks, investigating me even longer. I'm supposed to believe you didn't recognize me?"

Tommy glanced at her, and then said, "I wasn't sure until a few days ago. It doesn't matter."

"They don't know, I mean, about us? You're just going to make believe it didn't happen?" Jennifer asked. "Won't they wonder--"

Tommy cut her off. "There *is* no us, Jen. It was a long time ago. You made your choices. You are in some shit here. I don't think you realize how serious this is. That's what you should worry about."

Jennifer looked out the window, biting her bottom lip. "But when they find out, won't that be a problem? For you, I mean."

"Jen, there are things going on in this you aren't aware of. Big things. You may not be a bad person, as a matter of fact, I think you were doing what you thought was right for your daughter, but you are also not stupid. You knew something was going on and still you went along. And...," glancing over at her," and what happened between us in the past has to stay there. It has nothing to do with this."

Jennifer kept silent for the rest of the ride. As they pulled up behind her car, she turned to face him. "Tommy, I want to do the right thing. I knew nothing I was doing was illegal," choking back a sob. "I'll do whatever you say I have to do to help. You have to promise me you'll protect Kelsey," reaching out, taking his hand in hers. "Promise me," her eyes searching his face for answers.

Tommy, caught off-guard by the touch, felt his heart racing. The warmth of her hand brought the memories flooding back. He forced the thoughts from his mind.

"I, ah, of course we will. I, ah, we won't let anything happen to her," stealing a glance down at his hand, "or you."

She squeezed his hand tighter. "I want you to promise me, Tommy. I need to know she will be okay. I want you to promise me."

Tommy tried to avoid eye contact. He could feel his face reddening. "I won't let anything happen Jennifer, I promise. Besides, her father wouldn't let anyone hurt her," unable to avoid her eyes, seeing the reaction, "Or would he?"

Jennifer squeezed his hand once more and let go.

Tommy exhaled.

Turning her gaze out the window she said, "Anthony is not her father."

"Oh? Ah, well, I assumed... "

"It's a long story. No one knows, not even my father. I'd like to keep it that way." Her eyes met his as she searched for his reaction. "How do I get in touch with you?"

"Didn't Lieutenant Williams give you his number?"

"Yes, but I would feel more comfortable if I had yours."

Tommy took out his card, wrote his cell phone number on the back, and handed it to her. "You may want to just remember it, or hide it in your contact list, then lose the card."

She looked at the card and handed it back. "I'll remember it." A sad smile crossed her face as she opened the door. She looked back at him, "I remember everything, Tommy."

As he drove away, he glanced at her through his rear-view mirror. I always thought you'd stay in the past....

Tommy avoided the office, and the inevitable questions. He called into dispatch and had them tell Josh he was heading home. A moment later, his cell rang. He didn't recognize the number.

"See, I told you I remember everything," came the familiar voice, peeling away the years. "Thank you, Tommy."

Another call beeped through, EPPD SIU flashed on the caller ID.

He sent it to voice mail.

* * *

The next morning, Josh stood in the break room getting coffee. Chief Brennan came in looking for him. "Grab your coffee and come over to my office. Got something for you."

"Be there in a minute Chief," pouring the coffee into his mug.

In the conference room, he found Brennan, Kennedy, and Deputy US Attorney General Frank Lachance reviewing documents.

"Good morning, a little early for you federal types, no?" Josh joked.

"With good reason as you'll soon see," Lachance said, motioning Josh to sit next to him.

"What's up?" Josh said, sipping his coffee.

"As I told you in the past, what we show you here has to stay here," Lachance said, looking at Josh. "Sorry for the melodrama, but it is important."

"Of course, no problem," Josh answered.

Lachance took two of the documents, putting them in front of Josh to read. When he finished, Josh sat back. "Looks like we are onto something, aren't we? This is unbelievable."

"Well, believe it. We got confirmation of the currency transfers from a source in the Caymans. Your friends the Russians have been moving money, a lot of money, for quite some time. The new banking controls allow them to manipulate the reporting process. They will cover their tracks even better."

"So why the need to do anything here? Why come to Rhode Island?" Josh asked.

"That's what we've been trying to figure out and then Zach hit on the answer," Lachance replied.

Josh looked at Kennedy, "So, are you going to share, oh wise one?"

Kennedy laughed and said. "It's simple, if you think about it. The offshore banking process takes time and is expensive. The banks in the Caymans charge between twelve to fifteen percent to put the money into the legitimate banking system. Couple that with the fact the Russians can't blend in with the island crowd, like they can here.

"We know they've already acquired significant interest in two of the biggest casinos in the area. It all boils down to simple greed and need for control. They can do that here by controlling the accounting of the casino and lottery proceeds. If you consider their influence over Collucci it makes for an enticing scenario."

Josh sipped his coffee, looking over the documents again. "Do you think we can derail the plan with the things we've learned from Jennifer Sorin?"

"I think," Lachance answered, "if they find out we suspect anything it will just drive them to ground. They've done a good job of hiding the connection to Collucci. They will regroup and find some other willing Senator looking to bring money to his state. They'll find another venue." Opening his briefcase, Lachance flipped through it, withdrawing another file.

"But, if we remove the secrecy surrounding their control of the lottery, reveal the real reason behind the casino relocation to the property they acquired, then link it all together in an understandable story, we just might create enough of a problem for them. Knowing we know may be enough to stop it, but I would prefer to lock a few up. Look at this," handing Josh the file.

Josh looked it over, and then slid it to Brennan. As he read it, the Chief's eyes grew wide and he slid it back to Josh.

"What about keeping this information source quiet?" Josh asked.

"We'll be in the background. You guys take the lead. I'll get you more information like this," motioning to the file Josh held, "to make a solid case to the public. In the meantime, our ears on them will be working overtime as they try to compensate. I don't know if we can tie Collucci in with them, he has done a good job of insulating himself, but we may derail his appointment as Chairman. That, in and of itself, will kill him."

"Not if I get to the motherfucker first," Josh said, not meaning for anyone to hear.

Lachance looked at him. "I'll pretend I didn't hear that."

Josh smiled and shrugged his shoulders. "I meant figuratively."

Brennan spoke up, "There must be something more we can do to Collucci. Ways to jam it up his ass, and I mean literally."

Lachance couldn't help but laugh at the Chief's remarks. "I'll leave it in your hands, Chief. I am sure you'll find some way to achieve your goal," closing his briefcase and putting on his jacket.

"Here," Josh said, handing him the file, "you don't want this leave this laying around."

Lachance, smiling, ignored the gesture. "I'll be in touch. Do whatever you see fit."

Josh and Kennedy headed back to the SIU; Tommy and the troopers were waiting.

"So?" Tommy asked. "What new national secrets are you privy to?"

Kennedy looked to Josh. "Have at it Ace, I am sure Lachance expects us to include these guys in the loop."

Josh filled the group in on the latest intelligence on the Russians. He explained Kennedy's analysis of the move to a local operation in Rhode Island. "And then there is this," holding up the file Lachance left behind.

"And that is?" Tommy asked.

"Banking transactions, money transfers, bearer bond purchases by Harriet Lane Enterprises, a list of payments to various local, state, and federal politicians, and..." pausing for the effect, "surveillance photos of Anthony Sorin meeting with the guy who tried to kill Keira."

"No shit?" Donahue said. "When do we go get the bastard?"

"Lachance left it to us," Josh answered. "Gave us the file to do what we like. Since we cannot use it in court, I'm not sure what we do. I am open to suggestions on where we go from here."

"Simple," Tommy said. "The pen is mightier than the sword, right?"

"What the hell are you talking about, Tommy?" Josh asked.

"Let's go back to the beginning, to what started this in the first place, Darnell Grey. We started looking and it made them nervous. Not because they give a shit about what happened. They care because any attention to them, even from a decades old case, is bad. So, we use our friends in the Fourth Estate," Moore said.

"Who?" Donahue asked, "What estate?"

Tommy turned to smile at the troopers. "I should have known, since it involved reading, it would confuse my friends here from the State Police."

Donahue flipped him the bird.

"The press is the Fourth Estate," he explained. "We feed the story of the miscarriage of justice to certain friends in the media. We show them the surveillance information and banking transactions. The investigative guys love this stuff. Give them a Senator or two they can fry, and it will put them in a feeding frenzy. They do not have to play by the same rules we do, and they have absolute protection of their sources. We let them interview Grey's daughter and the trio from Alpha Babes Investigations. The Feds can scream and yell about unauthorized disclosures of intelligence information. Play it up for the media as they do so well. Won't matter. Media shit storm to follow."

Donahue stood up, causing Tommy's eyes to widen. "Calm down there boy. I can handle your juvenile sense of humor, and I've seen the picture of you handcuffed in the ladies' room. I must admit, though, it is a brilliant idea. What was the name of the journalist who did the story on the Department of Transportation guys sleeping in their trucks?"

"Candace Ferguson," Josh replied.

"Yeah, that's her," Donahue nodded.

"Her name is Candace Bennett now. She married Hawk Bennett, the lawyer who represented me in the civil rights trial. She still uses Ferguson in her reporting job, though. She will eat this up. She wrote a scorching expose' of Collucci's tenure as the US Attorney, almost cost him the election. I'll have Chris call her and set it up," Josh said, dialing the phone.

The troopers, and Tommy, stood to leave the office.

Josh put his hand over the phone. "Hang on a minute, Tommy. I need to talk to you."

Donahue raised his eyebrows at Moreira.

Tommy hesitated, started to speak, and then resigned to the inevitability of the coming conversation. He slumped into the chair at his desk.

* * *

"So?" Josh said, hanging up the phone and leaning back in his seat. "Something you want to share?"

"What?" Tommy said, fumbling with a pen.

"You want to explain yesterday? You disappear once we get Sorin in here and are MIA while we interview her. Then, you ride in like a knight in shining armor and take her away," Josh said.

"I just thought it best if one of us wasn't involved in the interview. Sort of stay neutral," Tommy offered.

"Neutral? Are you kidding me?" Josh said, moving around to lean on the desk, staring at Tommy. "You gotta do better than that. Right after you take her out of here, you go on radio silence, won't answer your phone. Come on, Tommy. What the hell is going on?"

Tommy looked back at Josh, then down at his desk. "It's nothing, LT. I thought it'd be best not to be in the interview with her."

Josh went back to his desk, "You and Jennifer Tucker attending Providence College at the same time has nothing to do with this?"

Moore's eyes gave him away. "You knew?"

"Tommy, I read her file. The one you helped put together. I saw she graduated from PC. So, did you. You're about the same age as her. I am a goddamn Lieutenant, you know. I do have some investigative skills," slamming his hands on his desk. "You should have said something to me. I was hoping you would. Now...."

Tommy looked up, "Now? What do you mean, now?"

Josh looked back at him, "Now I don't know. We need someone to go undercover with her. I wanted to use you. The feds won't let Zach do it and the troopers aren't right for it. But now, I don't know if I can rely on you."

"Look, LT," Tommy said. "I knew her in college. We went out for a while. She broke it off when she met Sorin. I didn't know who it was at the time, just an older guy with money, but that was it. I moved on, she moved on." Moore put his head in his hands, massaging his forehead. "I know I should have said something, but I don't want my personal life to be part of this job, so I didn't. I'm sorry."

"Listen," Josh said. "I try to keep my personal life personal too, but it didn't happen in this case did it? This job affects your personal life, no matter how hard you try to stop it. I need you to be upfront with me. Always. Can't be any secrets here, okay?"

"Okay," Tommy said, "sorry I fucked up."

"Alright, it's done. Go ahead and do whatever it is you were heading out to do. I've got some calls to make."

"Well, in the interest of my new policy of full disclosure, I wasn't going to do anything. I was trying to avoid the conversation we just had for as long as I could," Tommy smiled and opened his laptop.

Chapter 26

At 9:00 AM, Candace Ferguson arrived at the offices of Alpha Babes Investigations.

Vera Johnson brought her and the camera operator into the conference room and made the introductions.

Josh stood at the back of the room, out of camera view.

Candace began by having Loren Grey tell the story of her father. Loren held a picture of her father in his Army uniform just before he went to Vietnam. The camera went between Loren's face and the image of the father as she told the story.

Next up, was Chris Hamlin. She explained their investigation into Grey and discovering the forged lineup report. She named Collucci as the AG assigned to the case. She talked about the discussion with Major Church and his recollection of the conditions in the prison. She also got in that one victim was the daughter of a Rhode Island State trooper.

Josh thought, the State Police and Providence may not be too happy with opening this old wound, but we can do nothing about it.

Ferguson ended the interview. The camera operator took a few shots of the Alpha Babes Investigations logo and Chris, Maggie, and Vera sitting with Loren at the conference table.

"I want to thank you for bringing this to me. We'll be doing some more digging to add corroboration then run with the story in a few days, a week at most."

"You can thank Josh. It was his idea," Chris replied, pointing to Josh.

Candace came over to Josh. "Is there some official involvement in this investigation?"

Josh nodded. "Let's just say given as the matter was never resolved, it is still an open case. We are looking into some things that remain under investigation. That's all I can say now."

"Is Senator Collucci a target of this investigation?" Ferguson asked, the camera operator now recording the unplanned interview.

"We would like to interview anyone involved in the matter. Senator Collucci was the AG assigned to the case. At some point, yes, we will try to interview him."

"Have you contacted his office? Is he cooperating?" Ferguson persisted.

"We have been in contact and the Senator has been cooperative so far." Josh moved to get behind the camera operator, preventing him from taking any more video.

Ferguson smiled, "Come on, Josh. Here's a chance to take a few shots at Collucci."

"No thanks, I'll let you do that. I am just here for background. No more questions," walking toward Chris's office, he motioned for Candace to follow him. As they got inside the office, he blocked the camera operator from entering. "This is not something for the camera to see," he said, closing the door.

* * *

Candace watched while Josh opened his briefcase. "The microphone is off, right?" Josh asked.

"Yes, of course. Why the sudden secrecy, Josh? I thought the point was to air this for the world?" she asked.

"There's more to it. You'll have to do some digging before you run this part of the story. This isn't going to be a single report on the news. Once you read this," handing her a file, "you'll understand."

Candace leaned against the desk and flipped through the file. Her eyes grew wider with each turn of the page. Glancing at Josh, then back at the file, she asked, "Where did you get this?"

Josh smiled.

"I know, I know, stupid question. I hoped you would elaborate. I am not sure how we can corroborate this. I mean, wow. There is some serious stuff here."

"The trips to the various islands should be easy," Josh said. "The dumb bastard made a show out of doing research for his new banking legislation. He went to the Caymans and to the Isle of Man, another favorite for money laundering. That should be in the record. About the other stuff, you'll find a way I am sure."

"What if we can't? Is there a contact you have to get more information? Someone else we can talk to?" she asked.

"Tell you what, you start looking into this. If you need something, call me. I'll see if I can get more, okay?"

"Okay, that would be helpful," she replied.

"And Candace," Josh said, his eyes betraying concern, "these are serious people. The fewer who know about you looking into this, the better. If what we have uncovered so far is correct, you are talking billions of dollars. They won't take kindly to the interruption."

Candace smiled, "Thanks for the warning; I can take care of myself. This won't be the first corrupt bastard we've gone after."

Josh shook his head, "Don't underestimate them, Candace. This is on a completely different level. I have one more story for you. You have to assure me you will keep this to yourself, for now at least. This is not for publication; it's so you know how serious this is. Okay?"

Candace nodded.

Josh knew he had her attention now. He told her about the incident with Keira and the motorcycle. She listened, trying to control her reaction, but Josh could see the effect on her.

"Just be careful, okay?" he said.

"I will," Candace answered. "Thanks for the information."

She left the office, gathered up her camera operator and equipment, and headed out.

Returning to the conference room, Josh sat next to Loren. "Okay, here's what's going to happen now. Keira will file the motion to dismiss the charges in court and have the results of our investigation read into the record. It's symbolic, I know, but it will also add fuel to the fire. We can get things into the record which might otherwise not be there," watching the reaction from the group. "Then, we wait until Candace's story breaks. She'll let me know a day or so ahead of the broadcast date."

"And in the meantime," Maggie spoke up, "What do we do?"

Josh smiled. "Our ace researcher," pointing at the former librarian turned Sherlock Holmes, "uncovered a fortuitous piece of her family history. Vera, through the generosity of her father, is the unwitting owner of a strategic piece of property, right in the middle of their development plans, overlooked by our adversaries."

"And you, oh former assistant US Attorney, are going to represent her in negotiations. So, polish up your property law skills."

Chapter 27

Josh and Maggie sat outside the office of East Providence City Manager Paul Wilson. As they waited for their scheduled meeting, the city's finance director, Jean Teixeira, came in.

"Lieutenant Williams, how are you?"

"Fine, Jean, and you?"

"I'm good. To what do we owe the pleasure of this meeting?"

"Jean, this is Margaret Fleming. She's the one for whom I arranged the meeting."

"Nice to meet you, Ms. Fleming," extending her hand.

"Maggie, please," Fleming replied, shaking her hand.

"Well, then call me Jean and we can all be friends," Teixeira smiled, "I'll go in and see if Paul is ready for us."

Josh waited for the door to close. "Okay, here's what's going to happen. Paul is a good guy, trying to do the right thing for the city. He's going to be pissed if he thinks our little maneuver here will disrupt the development on the waterfront."

"We're going to do that, no?" Maggie asked.

"We're going to put a wrench into the plan, not disrupt it. Once the Russians find out what we've done, they'll try to find a way to fix it. It will force them to do something. I suspect they'll use Jennifer Sorin," Josh folded his arms. "When they make their move, we'll be able to see who's behind this. And use it to unravel the whole thing."

Maggie, looking at her notes, said, "So it will derail the project. If I know politicians, they'll try everything to prevent us from doing that."

"All we need is for them to believe we can do this, by the time they figure out a way to prevent it, we'll have what we need."

Maggie shook her head and laughed, "You missed your calling, Josh. You are Machiavellian in that brain of yours. You should run for office. You'd fit right in." Smiling, "Well, except for the conscience, that's a big liability." She looked over as the door to the City Manager's office opened.

"Lieutenant, how are you?" City Manager Paul Wilson asked, as he came striding out the door. "What is this important business we so urgently have to discuss?"

"Good morning, Paul. This is Margaret Fleming, Attorney-at-Law. She was once an Assistant United States attorney," Josh replied by way of introduction.

"Ms. Fleming, Paul Wilson," Wilson extended his hand.

"Maggie, please,"

'"Well then, Paul for me as well. Unless there is a reason I have to adopt a more adversarial attitude," arching his eyebrows. "Why don't we join Jean in my office and see what havoc Lieutenant Williams is trying to create."

* * *

"Are you freaking serious?" The veins in Wilson's neck throbbed and bulged. "I manage to get some serious waterfront development started and you're here to tell me it is dead in the water," slamming his hands on his desk. "You give me one good reason I should let this happen, one good goddamn reason."

"We're not saying it is dead in the water. It's a matter of an opportunity. One that was available to anyone who took the time to research it. My client wants to follow the provisions of the city charter and protect her interest," Fleming answered.

Wilson glared at Fleming, and then looked at Josh, "And what does this have to do with the Police Department, Lieutenant. Why is the city paying you to be here? Is Brennan aware of this, this, this extortion?" folding his arms and leaning back in the chair. "That's what this is, extortion. Well, boys and girls it is not going to work. Jean, go find the city solicitor. Find a way. We'll end this nonsense now."

Texeira rose from her seat, an uncomfortable look on her face, and fled the office.

When the door closed, Wilson smiled. "This had better be worth it, Josh," leaning forward and putting his arms on the desk, eyes wide. "If it does screw up this project, I'll find a way to have a lieutenant at the sewer treatment plant on the midnight to eight shift. Understand?"

Maggie looked back and forth between the two men, "You planned this little escapade? The whole thing was a setup?"

Josh laughed, "Not a setup, more a disinformation campaign. Your new friend, Jean Texeira, is the sister-in-law of the head of the City Council. They have ambitions to replace Paul. She'll run around to all the politicians spreading the news of our little play here."

Wilson laughed, "I bet she's already buying new curtains to redecorate this office. Now, onto the gory details, tell me what this sudden discovery involves and what we're going to do about it."

Fleming laid out the information discovered by Vera Johnson.

Almost forty years ago, Vera Johnson's grandfather deeded a right of way to a small parcel of land for the city to use. East Providence used the deeded right of way to build the city's animal control shelter.

City records show the property as a Water Street address on the right of way deeded by the old gentleman. This was inaccurate. Prior title searches missed it because of the incorrect address.

Johnson's grandfather ran a boat service on the waterfront and used the property for extra storage. His wife, a longtime supporter of the animal shelter, wanted the city to build a new one. She convinced her husband to deed the right of way and grant the city access to the little used property.

In the early 80's, the city built a new police station and moved the animal control shelter to city property on Commercial Way. They abandoned the deeded property.

The land remained unused.

During the intervening years, the city never moved to annex the property. Under the terms of the right of way deed, if the city abandoned the property it would nullify the right of way. It would then revert to the original owner. Vera Johnson inherited the property from her father and her son ran his own boat storage business there. They paid taxes on the property, which included the long-forgotten right of way.

Johnson now owned the property that stood directly in the path of the access road to the waterfront development project.

The phone rang on Wilson's desk. "Yes? Hmm, as we suspected. Remind me to keep a closer eye on our friend the Captain there. Thank you Chief. What?" listening for a moment, "Of course, I'll give the Lieutenant the message," hanging up the phone. "The Chief said the line activity is up. I suppose that means something to you?"

Josh leaned forward, arms extended, palms up, "It means it is already working."

Wilson walked from the desk and poured himself more coffee. "Brennan also said Captain Charland just hosted an impromptu meeting of politicians. The coup d'état has begun. Just as you said it would, Lieutenant."

Josh pointed at the City Manager. "Like Brennan always says, keep your friends close, your enemies closer, and everyone under surveillance."

Chapter 28

"What does that mean?" the Russian accented voice asked.

"It means a minor delay. It is a minor issue. We will negotiate a more than generous price and continue with the project," Sorin answered.

There was a delay in the response. "Fix this," the angered tone rising, "or we will fix it our way. Understood, Mr. Sorin?"

"Of course, I will take care of it."

"Mr. Sorin, it has been some time since you've been in Russia, no?"

Sorin did not respond.

"If you fail us, you will be seeing the motherland again. However, it will not be a pleasant trip for you, or your entire family. I hope, for their sake and yours, you do understand."

The call ended.

Sorin walked down to the Senator's office. Entering without knocking, he announced, "We need to talk. Now."

The Senator, looking up from his desk, saw the fear in Sorin's eyes. "What is it now, Anthony?"

"Not here, we need to go for a ride."

The surveillance team watched as the two men left the building, heading toward the Senator's car. As the two men arrived at the vehicle, the preemptive idea Josh had paid off.

Collucci got on his cell, made a quick call, and then walked to Sorin's vehicle. The flat tire on the Senator's car served its purpose.

Getting a court-ordered electronic surveillance warrant for a Senator's aide was one thing. Getting an order for a United States Senator was near impossible and dangerous. No telling what hidden ambitions sat on the bench of the United States District Court of Rhode Island.

"Senator, there is an issue with certain rights of way which pose a problem to the project moving forward."

"Anthony, this is important to many, many people. What is the issue?" Collucci replied, keeping his plausible deniability options wide open.

"There is a small parcel of land blocking the development. It is an overlooked right of way abandoned by the City of East Providence. The project backers want this matter resolved. They have emphasized the urgency behind the timetable. They are adamant in this."

"Well then, find the owner and negotiate. Make it irresistible for them to sell. If that fails, we can approach the city for an Eminent Domain proceeding."

Sorin thought for a moment. "Senator, you're missing the point. Why is it this problem surfacing now? Think, Robert. This is not a coincidence. I think we have a bigger problem. I may regret my association with

Jennifer, but she is not a stupid woman. She either held back the info as leverage or…." Sorin watched to see if the Senator caught on.

"Or somebody created this problem," Collucci said. "Williams. Damn him. He used his contacts within the city to falsify the records."

"I suspect as much," Sorin said. "We may have to resort to more direct measures to deal with this."

Collucci looked out the window. "Talk to your ex-wife. Let them know, we know. Then find a way to fix it."

After driving around Providence during the conversation, Sorin dropped off Collucci. He then headed toward the East side of Providence.

* * *

"Delta 1, Delta 5," the surveillance team leader radioed. "Subject headed your way, they bought the story. Sort of."

"Delta 5, got it. We are waiting for him with eyes and ears on the office," Josh replied.

Josh radioed to his other team members, "Okay, boys and girls. Sorin is on his way. Time for some fun." Tommy jumped out of the car and headed inside.

He fumbled with the tie as he walked into Jennifer's office, uncomfortable in the suit.

Jennifer came over and straightened his tie. "You look fine, stop fidgeting. You're making me nervous."

"Sorry, not used to wearing one of these, I try to avoid them."

"So, did you tell Williams?"

Tommy looked at Jennifer, "He knows we went to school together, went out a few times. That's it. He doesn't need to know anything else."

Jennifer frowned, "This will come out, Tommy. They will find out you are a cop. They'll do anything they can to make you look bad. You need to let Lieutenant Williams know the whole story."

"There's nothing else to say," Tommy argued. "It was a long time ago. Past history. What can they do with it? Besides, how is he gonna find out I'm a cop? This will never come out."

"He will find out, Tommy, "Jen said. "I know him all too well. He will stop at nothing. Anthony did not get to where he is by leaving loose ends. Once they find out you are a cop, they look into your background. They will do anything to discredit you. If they can't find something, they'll create it."

"Williams won't care. He knows me, trusts me. It won't make any difference," Tommy answered, turning away.

"Tommy," Jennifer pleaded, "Put yourself in his place. What would you think? We were engaged, Tommy. That's more than a casual romance. I never thought any of this would come out and look where I am. When this is over, I'll either be dead or in jail."

Tommy spun around, "You're not going to jail and nobody, I mean nobody, is going to get near you or Kelsey. Understand?"

Tommy's cell chirped. Looking at the display he smiled, "Sorin's almost here. Show time."

Tommy went to the desk, turned on and checked the concealed cameras and microphones. Jennifer went to her desk and brought up an Excel spreadsheet with property listings. Business as usual

"Delta 5, just coming down Waterman," Josh radioed.

"Delta 1, got him. Delta 5 continue over the Henderson and go grab another car."

"Delta 5, Delta 1, Where the hell am I supposed to get another car, this is East Providence not some goddamn TV show," Josh laughed.

"Delta 1 Delta 5, go to your back lot, I had some extra vehicles brought over," Zach Kennedy replied. "I knew you poor locals wouldn't have any spares."

"Can we keep 'em when this is over?" Josh asked.

"No, and I have a list to verify I get them all back, Delta 1 out."

Josh headed back to the PD. *Nice working with the Feds sometimes; hope one is a convertible....*

Sorin pulled into the back lot.

"Delta 3, subject entering the back door."

"Just how you troopers like it," Josh radioed as he drove back to the surveillance operation. "Reminds you of sleeping in the barracks, doesn't it?"

"Delta 3, Delta 5 remind me of that in person, smart-ass," Donahue answered.

The sound of a wet kiss came over the radio.

"Delta 1, could we be serious for just a few minutes?" Kennedy asked.

"Where's the fun in that?" Josh answered.

"Delta 2, video and audio is up. Live from inside, Sorin just walked into the office."

Anthony Sorin walked into Jennifer's office and eyed Tommy. Jennifer came around her desk, "Anthony, I didn't expect you. This is Tom Meadows; he and I have formed a new partnership. We're looking into abandoned properties with historical tax credits available. There is great market potential."

Tommy, aka Tom Meadows, stood and shook Sorin's hand. "Nice to meet you, Anthony."

Sorin returned the handshake, "Yes, well it is my pleasure. Jennifer, can we discuss our current project? A small issue has been brought to my attention," glancing back at Tommy.

"Of course. Tom is up to speed on the project in East Providence. He was most helpful in furthering many of the property acquisitions there," Jennifer answered.

"Really?" his eyebrows arched, "Why is it this is the first I've heard of Mr., ah, Meadows is it? Or his contribution," watching Jennifer, his eyes narrowing.

Jennifer looked at Sorin, "We agreed I would have full control on this end. I found Tom's experience with these matters most helpful. We have worked on other projects together. I decided to take advantage of those skills. I recently convinced him to join my firm. There was no need for me to clear it with you," staring Sorin down. "What is this new issue? I am sure we," nodding at Tommy, "can deal with it."

This seemed to placate Sorin. He took a seat, withdrew a file from his briefcase, and placed it on her desk.

"There is a small piece of property, overlooked in your original work, which requires your attention." He pointed to the file. "I find it troubling you missed this. Seems odd this problem arises now. How did that happen, Jennifer?"

Jennifer took the file, looked it over, and pushed it back to Sorin. "These are old files we are dealing with. The process of digitizing the files is not 100% accurate. It may be simple as that."

Sorin looked at Jennifer, then at Tommy. "What do you say, Mr. Meadows? Do you think this is just an oversight? Dissuade me from my feeling this is incompetence by this company of yours."

Tommy walked over and looked through the file. "A deeded right of way for a narrow piece of property dating from the 1950s, not surprising it didn't show up in a title search. Most of the property involved here sat undeveloped for years. There was no reason for anyone to notice the error. Once we contact the owner, I have no doubt we can arrange a sale and transfer."

"That's your problem," Sorin answered, closing his briefcase. "If you and your partner here are as good as you claim, I trust you'll resolve this quickly," rising from his seat. "I hope you appreciate the urgency in this. The investors have many options available to them. You wouldn't want to miss out on the contract bonuses," opening the door, turning back to look at the two. "Or face the consequences." Nodding his head, "Mr. Meadows," and left the office.

Tommy waited a moment to insure Sorin was out of earshot, "Well, he seems pleasant enough. I can see why you married him," turning off the surveillance cameras.

Jennifer shot him a glare as she turned to the computer.

"Remember, we swept the place for bugs, it's safe to talk, but I would bet they track your email and online activity."

"Okay then," Jennifer answered. "Let me give them something to look at," returning her attention to the computer.

Leaving her to her research, Tommy called Josh on the cell. "So where is our friend now?"

"He's sitting in his car, parked across the street. My guess is he's going to see if you go anywhere, or if someone shows up here."

"Okay," Tommy said, "Jen is going through the motions of researching the property online. We'll do that for a bit, then head to East Providence City Hall."

"Okay, cool. I'll let you know if Sorin moves or gets company," ending the call.

* * *

Sorin sat in his vehicle and considered this unexpected personnel addition and the land issues. He lived by the Russian expression, Doveryai, no Proveryai. Trust, but Verify. Reaching for his cell phone, he called a number. "I need you to do some research for me. A Tom or Thomas Meadows, about thirty, thirty-two or so, from Rhode Island I would guess. Find out everything for me and do it right away," ending the connection.

"Delta 1, subject just called the main trunk line number at the office building. Looking to find out about our undercover guy. It would seem we have another associate in the building. I'll call the AUSA in Providence. We need to get up on that phone ASAP," Kennedy said.

A few moments later Kennedy radioed, "Delta 1, US Attorney's office is working on it. Delta 3, do you think one of you could reach out to the retired trooper at Cox and get a quick look at any outbound calls from that number today?"

"Delta 3, I'm on it. I'll call Danny right now," Donahue said.

* * *

206

As soon as Sorin left the office, Jennifer was on the computer going through the motions of discovering what they already knew. She made a production out of tracing the incorrect addresses and information relating to the right of way. Printing out all the documents and storing them on her backup system. She now had no doubt Sorin monitored all the office activity. She hoped her activities cemented the story in his mind.

"Okay, now what?" she asked.

"We take a ride to City Hall and get copies of the original deed, tax payments. Make a big production out of it."

"Cool, I'll get my jacket."

As they walked to the car, Tommy spotted Sorin parked across the street. Not too good at surveillance are you, Ivan? You Russian prick.

"Our friend is watching us," he told Jennifer as he opened the door to the car for her.

She looked. He touched her shoulder, "No, no we're just a couple of dumb property managers, remember? Just act normal."

Once they were both in the car Jennifer said, "Anthony never did that."

"Did what?"

"Never opened a car door for me. It's nice of you. I miss that," Jen answered.

"Oh that," Tommy chuckled. "Force of habit. My grandparents raised me after my mother and father died. My grandfather was a bit of a traditionalist. He drilled those habits into me. To this day, I cannot sit if there is a woman standing. Just can't do it."

Jennifer's eyes grew wide, "I never knew about your parents. Why didn't you ever tell me?"

A sad smile crossed Tommy's face. "By the time I got to college, both of my parents and grandparents were dead as well. There wasn't any point. It wasn't something I talked about to anyone."

Jennifer smiled and took his hand, "You are a man of mystery, Mr. Moore. I always wondered why you never talked about your family."

As Tommy drove out of the parking lot, Jen glanced toward Sorin. She felt her heart race and a tightness in her chest. This nightmare was real now. Still holding Tommy's hand, she said, "You sure nobody will get to Kelsey, right?"

Tommy felt the warmth, and tension, in her hand. "I'm sure," yet unsure why he let his hand linger in hers. He was certain Sorin was watching them, taking it in, as they spoke.

An hour later, as they left City Hall with the documents, Tommy called Josh. "Hey, LT, where's our friend now?"

"He followed you to City Hall then went back to his office," Josh answered. "He made a shit load of calls, so we have plenty of new things to work on."

"Great, I'll take Jen back to the office. Want me to come in?"

"No, let's stick to the script. Go to the office and pretend to work, which shouldn't be hard for you, then go to the undercover apartment. You're gonna have to stay undercover for the next few days, until this breaks."

"Well then, we property managers like to unwind with a cocktail and dinner after a long day. I will be exercising the undercover business credit card provided by the FBI."

Josh laughed, "You do that, just don't do too much damage to the national debt."

Tommy hung up and looked at Jennifer. "Want to go to dinner and drinks on the government? Get some of your tax dollars back?"

Jennifer looked confused.

"Part of our cover, remember?"

"Oh sure, of course. Let me call my father and check in with him. He and my daughter should be at his condo in Aruba by now, and then I am all yours."

Alarm bells rang in Tommy's head, silenced by other, more powerful, physiological manifestations.

Tommy took out a disposable phone and handed it to her. "Use this whenever you want to call Kelsey. They won't be able to trace the calls. They may know about the condo, but there'll be some doubt whether they went there."

While Jennifer made the call, Tommy drove to The Federal Tap House on Atwells Avenue in the Federal Hill section of Providence.

"Have you been here before?" Jennifer asked, handing the phone back to Tommy.

"No, but one of my friends told me about it and I figured the name would add some irony, Federal Tap, get it?"

"I do indeed. Umm," leaning in and whispering, "what do I call you?"

"Call me Tom, or Tommy, it will sound natural. This is Rhode Island-someone in here might know us from PC."

"What if somebody recognizes you from the police department?"

"Well, I'm not from Rhode Island, been out of school awhile, and up until a year ago I was working nights. I didn't go out much. We'll just hope for the best."

Tommy asked for a table in the back and sat so he could watch the door. After looking over the menu, they settled on appetizers and a bottle of wine. Once the wine was open, Tommy relaxed.

"Can I ask you something?"

"Let me guess, why did I marry him?" sipping her wine.

"Guilty," Tommy shrugged. "I mean, it's just...."

"What can I say? I met Anthony while I was in Washington doing the internship with Senator Strain. You went off to hike the Appalachian Trail or something," looking into her glass. "We saw each other a few times, worked on a few projects together. After you and I fell apart...I don't know... he was around...."

She held out her glass for more wine. "When you told me you were heading off to OCS at Quantico with the Marine Corps, I thought you wanted to get away from me." Pausing and glancing up as the server delivered the first dishes.

Tommy just sat there, leaning on his elbow, hand covering his mouth, listening.

"It was nice at first, with Anthony I mean," Jen waited for the server to leave. "We didn't even get married for the first few years...."

"I didn't mean to raise bad memories. I was just curious why someone would let you go," Tommy said, finishing his wine and refilling the glasses.

"You did," she said, eyes brimming.

"I got sent to Iraq. I didn't have a choice. The Marine Corps is like that, you know, they don't give you options. I told you that the day I left. I said I'd be back. You didn't wait," he answered. "What about your daughter?" trying to change the subject.

Jennifer started to say something, let out a sigh, and then just sat looking at him.

"Jen, what's wrong? What is it?"

"I knew from the beginning Kelsey wasn't Anthony's child. I let him believe she was that's the kind of person I am. When I found out that's when he left."

Tommy watched as Jen took a long sip of wine, looking into her glass, lost in the dark memories of the past. Let it go for now, Tommy, let it go.

The rest of the dinner taken up with small talk about the different paths of their lives. When they were through, they had invested two hours and three bottles of wine in their efforts.

As they walked to the car, a voice called out, "Jen?" causing them both to turn toward the sound. Jen lost her balance and reached out for Tommy's hand. He put his arm around her, steadying her.

"Jen? I thought it was you." A woman walked over to them, smiling at the pair.

"Hi, Karen, how are you?" Jennifer asked.

"Not as good as you," giving Tommy the once over. "I see you're having some fun tonight, good for you. And this is?"

Jennifer looked at Tommy, then back at her friend, "this is a friend of mine, Tom Meadows. He's my new partner in the property management company," turning to Tommy. "Tom, this is Karen Reynolds. She has an office in the same building."

Tommy reached out his hand, "Nice to meet you, Karen."

"Nice to meet you as well, Tom. Well, I will let you two carry on. Give me a call sometime, Jen," tilting her head and casting a side glance at Tommy. "You can give me all the details about this one. Nice to meet you, Tom," smiling as she turned and walked off.

Tommy watched the woman cross Atwells Avenue, getting into car parked across the street. "Is she going to be a problem?"

"Not if you want Anthony to know we were out together. I bet she's calling him now," Jennifer answered, smiling. "She had a thing for him. I think they had an affair after he left me, while she was still married."

"Well then, at least it will make our association more realistic and believable to him."

They both stood and watched as the car pulled into traffic. As the woman drove past, Jennifer reached over and kissed Tommy. Taking him in a long embrace, she whispered, "Now I am sure she'll call him."

Tommy smiled and kissed her back, the flood of memories filling his thoughts.

Chapter 29

The sunlight leaked through the curtains, waking Tommy from his sleep. As he tried to focus on the clock, he smelled coffee.

Jennifer walked into the bedroom, wearing Tommy's unbuttoned shirt, carrying two cups. "Cream and sugar, right?"

Tommy pushed himself up against the headboard, still groggy. "Uh, yeah, thanks, I ah... " smiling and trying to act nonchalant.

"Ah yes, those first uncomfortable moments," Jen chuckled. "You realize you started yesterday with your chastity intact and woke up the next day without it. Don't worry; I may have had something to do with it."

"What, no, no I mean I, we both..."

"Yes, we did," leaning over and kissing him, "several times if I recall and I do believe we owe the backyard neighbor an apology." Handing him the coffee, she slid in next to him.

"Oh, holy shit," was all he could say.

His cell rang. Glancing at the caller ID, he mouthed the words, "It's Josh."

"Well, best not use video calling to answer it. I'll be quiet," draping her arm across his chest, nuzzling against him, "unlike last night."

"Good, um, good morning, LT," Tommy answered, trying to sound innocent.

"Yes, Detective Moore, I bet it is. Why is it you are not at the briefing this morning?" Josh asked.

"Ah, I, ah, I thought I was to stay undercover," Tommy fumbled in response. "Isn't that what you said?"

"Well, be that as it may, please find your way down to Haines Park so we can discuss our next moves. Call Jennifer, tell her you have some project work to do."

Good, at least he doesn't know she's here. "Okay, will do LT-- Hey," Tommy shouted, reacting to Jennifer's intimate touch.

"Hey what, Tommy?" Josh said. "Stop screwing around and get down here."

If you only knew, LT, if you only knew.

"Okay, on my way. I'll let Jen know I'll be in later," hanging up the phone. "Duty calls, got to go meet Josh. This is official notice to inform you, I'll be in later," trying to slide out of the bed.

Jen smiled, pulling him back. "Well, since you said you'd be in later," moving on top of him, sliding out of his shirt, her erect nipples signaling her arousal. "Let's let you in now and you can be a little late to your briefing."

* * *

Moore flew down Veteran's Memorial Parkway hoping the time-to-make-the-donuts twins were not running radar. The two officers bore a remarkable resemblance to the baker in the Dunkin' Donuts commercials.

The father of one was mail carrier. His job offered many opportunities to distribute his genetic code to lonely women, raising suspicions of the source of their remarkable similarities.

As Moore drove over the hill near the first overlook, there they were. Fortunately, they had two cars stopped and were focused on writing summonses. Moore flashed by and beeped the horn, flipping them off as he passed them.

They did not look up.

Lazy bastards. If somebody flipped me off, I'd be on their ass in a heartbeat.

Moore continued onto Pawtucket Avenue, heading toward the Looff Carousel, the centerpiece of the former Crescent Park, a once thriving amusement park. The historic carousel, one of a handful still functioning in the country, restored to its former glory by community involvement. It stood at the intersection of Crescent View Avenue and Bullocks Point Avenue.

Tommy turned onto Crescent View Avenue. He drove past the housing development built on part of the former amusement park land. He wondered what idiot thought it was a good idea to combine elderly housing with the mentally challenged. People trying to live out their remaining years surrounded by people who believe they are from another planet is not a good mix.

The uniform guys called it Thorazine Manor, since half the residents took anti-psychotic drugs.

He turned onto Metropolitan Park Drive, following the road to the city line with Barrington, and pulled into Haines Park.

Josh, Zach Kennedy, and the two troopers were waiting.

"Nice of you to make it," Josh said.

"Hey, you told me to stay in undercover mode. I did. I slept in."

"Anything else?" Josh asked.

Moore looked up, the iron taste of the adrenaline rushing through his body flooded his senses. "Nope. I am here, ready for the briefing."

Josh shook his head. Moore smiled at the two troopers. "See, none of that saluting nonsense you guys go through. Us real cops just get to work."

"A little discipline might do you some good," Donahue countered.

"Jahwohl, Mein Kapitan," saluting Donahue with his middle finger and goose-stepping around the car.

"Don't waste your time, Tim. He's not even housebroken," Josh said, motioning with his index finger for Moore to come over to the front of the car.

"Okay, here's the latest..."

After detailing Sorin's calls and conversations, Josh said, "So, in a nutshell this is the story. He is trying to find out more about you. He doesn't quite trust her, doesn't trust this unexpected addition to the staff, and suspects I created the issue with the property."

"Do you think the profile the Feds created for him will hold up?" Donahue asked, looking at Kennedy.

"As long as they just use standard law enforcement sources, DMV, driver licenses, educational background checks, it should. We assume they have somebody, a cop or someone working in a PD, they can use."

"And if they dig deeper?" Moore asked.

"You are screwed," Kennedy said. "The FBI usually take months to set up a phony background for their undercovers, here we did it in a week."

"If we push hard enough we just may be able to force Sorin's hand before they find out you aren't what you appear," Josh added.

"You mean he's not a moron?" Donahue laughed.

"Bet it took all day and night for you to come up with that one, didn't it?" Moore said.

"Nope, first five minutes in the station and I figured you out."

Josh laughed, "Okay, now that you've practiced your comedy routine, we need to make sure we keep Tommy covered; no lapses in the surveillance. We know what they are capable of and don't want them to get an opportunity; if they find out he's a cop."

Donahue nodded, "Let's get the new tracking device the Feds were telling us about. Have him carry it." Blowing a kiss at Moore, "I wouldn't want to lose you, sweetheart."

Moore smiled. "I didn't know you cared, you big handsome bitch. Okay, sounds good. I had better head to the office. When you get the equipment, call me and we'll arrange a meeting," Moore said. Certain the tracking device was not such a good idea.

Chapter 30

"Mr. Chairman, Senator Collucci is on line one for you," the administrative aide said over the intercom.

"Thank you, Denise," Clevon Castillo, acting Chairman of the Federal Communications Commission replied. Unexpected calls from Senators are never a good thing.

Castillo reached over, picked up the phone, and pushed the button for line one.

"Good morning, Senator. To what do I owe the pleasure of this call?"

"Good morning, Clevon. I hope you are settling into your new office," Collucci replied.

"Well, I am not so sure I should unpack yet," Castillo said. "The confirmation hearing isn't until next week, lots of things can happen."

Collucci let the words hang in the air for a moment, "Well from what I gather, your friends on the Hill have done a good job of gathering support. I have no doubt it will be the right outcome."

Castillo wondered about the Senator's phrasing, not a rousing show of support. "It may be presumptuous of me, but I hope I can count on your vote, Senator."

"Of course, Clevon, I see no major obstacles to your appointment. You have my full support," Collucci answered.

"If I may, Senator, you said no major obstacles. Are you aware of any obstacles or issues? If you have some questions, I'd be happy to address them."

"No, no. Nothing specific except, well, there is some concern the FCC is moving too fast on the ZMI merger with ANM. Those opposed to your appointment may raise this as an example of politics entering into the process. The merger of two of the largest media companies in the world could be of concern to some."

Castillo could feel his anger rising, fighting to lash out. *This pompous, self-important....*

"Your previous job as legal counsel for ZMI became a point of contention in your nomination hearing," Collucci explained. "Perhaps a delay of the process, more a deferral until after the confirmation, is appropriate."

Clevon Castillo was an ambitious, yet cautious man. A two-term Congressman from Massachusetts, he was an early supporter of the President. He resigned his seat to manage the Presidential campaign fundraising organization. Surviving the firestorms of the President's first term in office as an envoy to the Middle East, he garnered much praise and admiration for his diplomatic skills. He'd learned the art of persuasion, threats coupled with concessions, from the best.

When the President was re-elected, Castillo approached him for a new position. The President offered him the position of Secretary of State. He declined. He preferred one with influence yet offering a measure of security and anonymity. He set his sights on the FCC, hoping to hide there for a few years and turn it into a nice, private sector offer when his term ended. Gaining allies and support for his own run for the Presidency was his long-term goal.

"Senator, both the House and Senate committees vetted the ZMI merger. They dealt with any issues or concerns," Castillo argued. "If I canceled a hearing scheduled for tomorrow, wouldn't that appear as political maneuvering?"

"I suppose, but I am concerned about discussions I have had with a number of other Senators. Those that, I should point out, have indicated their support for your confirmation. Hang on a moment," Collucci said. "Ah, would you excuse me, Clevon? Someone just walked into my office and I need to deal with an issue. I'll call you right back." Collucci hung up, not waiting for the response.

Sorin sat in a chair facing the Senator, "You seemed to get the point across, no?"

"I'll let him think about it for an hour or so. By the time I call back, I have no doubt he will already have delayed the approval hearing," Collucci said. "Once I confirm he has, we'll have a chat with our friends at ANM and persuade them to kill the story."

"This had better work, Senator. Our friends will not let all their work go for naught," Sorin said, adjusting his cuffs, concern in his eyes.

The look was contagious. "It will work," Collucci said, tapping his fingers on the desk. "Castillo is ambitious, but smart. He'll see it as beneficial to keep us happy."

Two hours later, Collucci called the FCC acting Chairman back.

"Clevon, I apologize for the delay. Senator Harrison, you recall him I am sure, one of your critical supporters. He needed me to co-sponsor some last-minute legislation. I apologize again."

"That's fine, Senator. I understand you have many things pressing on your time," Castillo answered.

"Now, where were we? Ah yes, discussing the delay in the ZMI Media merger. Have you had time to consider our concerns?" Collucci asked.

"I have, Senator. I spoke to my legal counsel and he agreed a short deferral may well be in the best interests of all parties," Castillo said. "My press secretary is preparing a briefing and I have spoken to the heads of both media companies explaining the delay. I told them I had concerns over political appearances in the midst of the nomination hearing. I assured them the process was not derailed, just delayed."

"Excellent," Collucci said. "Your sensitivity to these matters reinforces in my mind your qualifications for this position. I am sure this will go far to insure adequate support for your nomination. Thank you Clevon, or should I say, Mr. Chairman? Take care and we will speak soon."

Collucci ended the call, and then pushed the intercom button. "Would you find Anthony for me and tell him I need him in my office as soon as possible, thank you."

Sorin arrived moments later, "Well?"

"Done, he delayed the hearing. Arrange a meeting with our friends at ZMI, I want to make sure they know what I am capable of with just a phone call," Collucci said.

Sorin's eyes narrowed, "Be cautious in dealing with Dmitriev. He may appreciate your influence, but he will value it as he sees fit, not as you would like. You and I are important to this. Nevertheless, should it suit their needs, they will replace us. Be cautious, Senator. It is best to keep them as supporters, not adversaries."

"Of course," Collucci said. "I just want them to see me as a valuable partner. One they should protect."

Sorin watched the Senator pack up his briefcase. "Don't you have another aspect to deal with?" he said.

"Yes, I do as a matter of fact," Collucci said. "I have one more call to make," pushing the intercom button. "Would you please get Maurio Bartoletti from ANM Media on the phone for me, thank you."

"How are you going to handle him?" Sorin asked.

"It's simple. Bartoletti wants this merger to go through. It is his ticket to the good life, cashing in on his work at ANM. I will show him the risk running the story poses to the merger. Getting him to pull it will be the best solution. He will do it. Mark my words," Collucci said, a smile crossing his lips.

The voice over the intercom interrupted, "Mr. Bartoletti on line one for you, Senator."

Collucci grabbed the line, putting the call on speaker. "Maurio, how are you my friend?"

"Not happy at the moment, Senator. It would seem the FCC has put a hold on our petition for merger with ZMI. Do you know anything about it?" Bartoletti asked.

"Well, I must say it is a surprise to me. I was under the impression it was moving along well. I spoke to the acting Chairman earlier today. He never mentioned it," Collucci said.

Son-of-a-bitch, goddamn son-of-a-bitch. "What can I do for you, Senator?" his voice coarse and curt.

"Maurio, do you recall the story we discussed? The one you spoke with me about, this nonsense over an old criminal case in which I had little involvement?"

"I do, Senator. One of our affiliate stations was running something. Why do you ask?"

"Well, Maurio, one of the concerns of the Senate is too much consolidation within the media," Collucci said.

"Go on, Senator. I am listening," Bartoletti said.

"Given these sensitivities, don't you see the risk a controversial story, such as the one by your affiliate station, poses? I have no issue with their right to run the story, but there needs to be fair and balanced reporting. Some of my colleagues may see this story as illustrative of a lack of diversification among the media as a real problem. Do you see where this is leading?" Collucci said.

"I do indeed," Bartoletti replied, his response angry, but controlled. "What would assuage these fears, Senator?"

"An opportunity to present a different side, my side, and show these allegations to be frivolous. Given adequate time, I can get your reporters access to information they may find illuminating." Collucci paused a moment, letting the seed take root. "But as I said, Maurio, it will take some time to arrange."

There was no immediate response. Collucci could make out muffled, angry voices in the background.

"Senator, what say I do this? I will call the local station manager. See if he is willing to defer the story, pending this new information. I am making no promises here. We pride ourselves on the independence of our affiliate stations. I am sure the manager will appreciate your--" catching himself, "or rather, our concerns. I am certain he will take the opportunity to check these other sources. Would that address your concerns?" Bartoletti asked.

Collucci smiled, nodding at Sorin. "Maurio, don't misunderstand me. I am not in the least worried about this so-called expose`. It is baseless and unsubstantiated political slander. I have dealt with bad press before; this is nothing new. I am trying to give you an opportunity to avoid jeopardizing the process. I will call the Chairman back and see if I can clear up the issue before the FCC."

"I will make some calls, Senator. I am sure I can handle this to your satisfaction."

"Thank you, Maurio. It is always a pleasure to talk to you my friend." Collucci hung up. "Well?" he asked, rubbing his hands together.

Sorin nodded. "He got the message. I'll know soon enough if they kill the story."

"Okay," Collucci said, rising from his chair. "I am off to a meeting with the Banking subcommittee, time to push the Chairman out, and put me in. I take it you had things delivered to the appropriate people?"

"Done," Sorin said. "I will make the arrangements for us to meet with our friends later this evening. Call me when you finish."

Returning to his own office, Sorin took out one of the disposable phones. Dialing a number from memory, he waited for the call to go through.

"Da?" a voice answered.

"It's me. Have him call back, this number," Sorin hung up.

A moment later, the disposable phone rang.

"We need to arrange a meeting. Tonight," Sorin said.

"Come to the club on Wisconsin Avenue near the Embassy, 9:00 o'clock. Take the usual precautions." The call ended.

A moment later, Sorin received another call on the disposable. "Yes?" he answered.

"Can we rely on this solution?" the accented voice said.

"I am not sure, Shashenka. I believe they will kill the story. I will know soon. Whether it is permanent or not remains a mystery," Sorin replied.

"The Senator is coming with you tonight, is he not?"

"Yes, he wanted to meet you."

"Excellent, I will impress upon him the urgency of this matter. Perhaps, educate him about our level of determination. He needs to realize our success in paramount, not his. His usefulness to us depends on it. I look forward to our meeting."

Sorin stood up, dropped the phone on the floor, and crushed it. Taking the pieces, he disposed of them in several trash containers on the way to his car.

Chapter 31

Vera, Maggie, and Loren gathered around the television in the conference room. Promotions about an important investigative report ran every few minutes along the bottom of the screen. They were planning to air it on this evening's nightly news.

Chris and Keira arrived, carrying several boxes of Chinese food and some drinks. As they set the food down on the conference, the phone rang.

Vera answered the phone, "Alpha Babes Investigations."

"Hey Vera, Josh. Is Chris there with you?"

"Yup. Hang on a minute," motioning for Chris to take the phone. "It's Josh."

"Hey, Josh. What's up?" Chris said.

"I'm not on speaker, right? No one can hear this but you?" Josh asked.

Chris could not stop herself and glanced around the room. Maggie caught the look and raised her eyebrows at Vera.

"Nope," Chris said. "What's going on?"

"The State Police are sending a protective detail to your office," Josh said. "Somebody at the TV station tipped Sorin to the subject of the impending story. He made some calls to certain cell numbers of suspected MS-13 gang members. Nothing specific, just arranging a meeting. We just want to be cautious. They're sending one to the TV station as well, for Candace."

"I see," Chris said, nodding her head, trying to control her reaction. "Okay, thanks. I'll take care of it."

"Good, the troopers will stay out of sight for the most part," added Josh. "The bad guys may assume we're listening. We don't want to confirm it for them though. The troopers are just a precaution. Now I gotta call Hawk and hope he doesn't decide to go to war over this."

"Well, good luck with that. I will handle it here. Thanks," ending the call.

The three other women looked at Chris, waiting for an explanation. "What are you looking at?" Chris said.

"Chris, we are ace investigators here, remember?" Maggie said. "I know the look on your face, so out with it. What's going on?"

"Nothing, it's nothing. Josh wanted to know if I was going to be here. That's all," Chris lied. "He said he was sending some troopers over to talk to me about an old case of mine."

Vera stood up, walked over, smiled at Chris, and then slapped her on the back of the head.

"Ooww, hey, what the--" Chris said, rubbing her head.

"Girl, you know you can't lie to me. When you gonna get it through that thick skull of yours?"

Maggie and Loren were chuckling.

"Okay, okay. Go sit down and I'll tell you. Jeesh, that hurt," massaging her head. "Josh called to tell me the State Police are sending some troopers here." Chris held up her hands as Vera rose from her seat. "Listen, he's sending troopers here as a precaution. There have not been any direct threats, but Josh found out the bad guys know about Candace's investigative report."

"See, I knew something like this would happen," Loren said. "I wish Josh would let this go. I'm happy with what you found out for me. I don't want anyone hurt over this."

Chris sat next to Loren, taking her hand. "Listen, I don't know everything Josh is working on in this case, but I do know it's much bigger than you think. Even if they wanted to, they could not stop this. Once the whole story comes out, you'll understand. Until then, one of us will be with you all the time," Chris said, looking at Vera and Maggie nodding in agreement. "No one's going to get anywhere near you."

The TV screen showed the opening news segment, the teaser for the investigative report no longer running.

Good evening and welcome to the 6 o'clock News you can trust...

They watched the first few opening stories and then the broadcast turned to sports.

No story.

"Why'd they pull the story?" Maggie asked.

"Don't know," Chris answered. "We'll have to wait to talk to Josh."

There was a loud knock on the door, startling the group. Chris looked at the others. She motioned for Maggie to get the door. As Maggie opened the door, Chris slid her hand into her top desk drawer.

Standing in the doorway, were two of the biggest men they had ever seen.

"Let me guess, State Police?" Chris said, closing the drawer.

"Yes ma'am, I am Detective Dussault and this is Detective Cunningham. I take it you were expecting us?"

"Yup," Chris answered. "Come on in, I'll put on some coffee. Make yourselves comfortable," although Chris doubted they would even fit in the chairs.

* * *

After the call to Chris, Josh looked through his contact list for Harrison 'Hawk' Bennett.

Bennett, one of the premier defense lawyers in New England, was not one to trifle with. A former Green Beret, he served three tours of duty in Viet Nam and had a slew of medals for bravery in combat to show for it. He kept himself in amazing physical condition.

His appearance and demeanor could be deceiving, as Josh learned the hard way several times. To tell Bennett there may be a credible threat against his wife, and convince him to take no action, would not be easy.

Josh took a deep breath, hesitated over the call contact button, and then put the phone back in his pocket. He decided this was a message best delivered in person.

"Hey Zach," Josh called to Kennedy, "feel like taking a ride? Meet a living Rhode Island legend?"

"Sure," Kennedy answered, the confusion evident on his face. "I didn't realize you knew any legends."

"Wait 'til you meet this guy," Josh said, "then you'll understand."

Josh and Zach left the station, heading to downtown Providence. Finding a rare open parking spot on South Main Street, Josh grabbed it. "Hope you don't mind walking a bit. We'll never find parking near his office."

Kennedy shook his head, "No problem for me. I like walking."

The pair headed toward the financial district of the city. Providence being on the small side calling it a district was a stretch. A block maybe, or perhaps a square, but district was a clear exaggeration.

They walked toward the building housing Bennett's office. Kennedy pointed at the large head protruding from the front of the structure. "What the hell is that?"

"That, my friend, is the Turk's Head on what is the Turk's Head building for obvious reasons," Josh said. Kennedy studied the large, turban-wearing, mustachioed figure. "Makes for a perfect landmark reference, you can't miss it."

"I should say not," Kennedy agreed.

Taking the elevator to the seventh floor, Kennedy followed Josh down the narrow hall. This ended at a door bearing a hawk etched in the glass and no other identifying information.

"Rather subtle, don't you think?" Josh said, turning the handle.

Kennedy just smiled and nodded.

Entering the office, they encountered the latest in Hawk's rotating stock of administrative assistants. Josh was somewhat disappointed this one resembled none of the others. No breast augmentations, or other cosmetic improvements, in evidence.

"Good afternoon, gentlemen. How can I help you?" the woman said, with remarkable poise and professionalism.

"Good afternoon, ah, Samantha," Josh said, glancing at the nameplate, "Is Mr. Bennett available?"

"And you gentlemen are?" she asked.

"Lieutenant Josh Williams, East Providence Police and FBI Special Agent Zach Kennedy," Josh answered.

"Please have a seat and I will be right back."

Josh sat in one of the two chairs looking around the office, surprised by the change. The organized bookcase, neat files, the office tidy; the transformation was remarkable.

"Mr. Bennett will see you now, gentlemen. Right this way," Samantha gestured to the back office.

Josh smiled as he passed Samantha, watching as she returned to her desk.

"Josh, what a pleasant surprise," Harrison 'Hawk' Bennett said, shaking Josh's hand. "And this must be Special Agent Kennedy," turning to face Zach. "The FBI in my office is not usually a welcome occurrence, but I trust the Lieutenant's judgment." Reaching out, he shook the agent's hand.

"Pleasure to meet you, Mr. Bennett," Kennedy said. As they shook hands, the strength of the grip surprised Kennedy. Bennett, slight of build, wore a rumpled sweater over a shirt and tie. He resembled a professor of philosophy, not a former Green Beret.

"Hawk, please. All my friends call me Hawk."

"You'll have to explain how you got the nickname," Kennedy said.

"I was hoping to explain it to you myself," Josh interjected. "But the new receptionist didn't fit the normal mold. What is up with that, Hawk? I was looking forward to the reaction of agent Kennedy. Imagine my disappointment. Your receptionist is literate and competent, with no signs of plastic surgery or body enhancements. What gives?"

"Yes, well... you see, it is Candace's doing," Hawk grumbled, folding his arms and sitting on the corner of his desk. "Damn woman has taken over my office staff, she's managing my practice. The woman controls everything."

"Perhaps she was a bit more aware of your behavior pattern before she married you. She won't let you replace her, will she?" Josh chuckled. "I think you may have met your match in her; no wife number five for you, in this lifetime anyway."

Hawk smiled, gesturing for them to sit. "Aside from poking fun at my domestication, what brings the East Providence Police, along with the FBI, to my office?"

"Well, as a matter of fact it does concern your wife. Some issues with a story we fed her," Josh said.

"She's told me about it; getting a little payback on our friend Collucci, I see. Good for you," Hawk said, "couldn't happen to a better guy."

"That is a bonus to the whole thing, but it's not why we're here," Josh replied. "I can't tell you how, but I can tell you we have good information your wife may be at risk for doing this story."

Josh watched Hawk's expression change, the muscles in his face tightened. His eyes narrowed. He faced Josh. "Go on," Hawk said.

"There's a security detail of troopers at the station now. They will stay with her until this is over. I wanted to tell you myself, so you knew how serious we're taking the threats," Josh said, glancing at Kennedy.

Hawk rose from his desk and paced the room, arms locked behind him. "When I was on my second tour in Nam, they sent us to a small village in the highlands. They wanted us to protect a village chief from the Viet Cong. We stayed with the man for a month. Then, new orders came down from Saigon, and they pulled us out." Hawk stopped pacing, studying the Viet Cong flag displayed on the wall with bullet holes evident in the cloth.

"Do you know what happened?" Hawk asked, "I mean, to the man, after we left."

Josh shook his head.

"The VC came two days after we were gone. Killed the man and his entire family. Do you know why?"

"War, things happen?" Kennedy asked.

"True, but this had to do with the incredible patience of the Viet Cong. They knew we'd lose interest. Eventually, we would leave. So, what happens when you leave, Josh? What happens then?" Hawk asked.

"We're gonna close them all down, lock 'em up. That's what will happen," Josh said.

"Josh," Hawk said, turning to face him. "Candace told me about the story, the whole story. She showed me the documents you gave her. These are serious people. You will not get them all. You will not get most of them. You'll get a few and then what?" Hawk, arms folded, rocking back and forth on his heels, looked for their reaction.

Josh looked at Kennedy, then back at Hawk. "I don't know. I suppose you're right."

"Look," Hawk said, "Once I found out about the people behind the story, I took my own security measures. I appreciate the troopers being there, but they have different rules of engagement. Under my rules, we do not worry about grand juries, prosecutors or, with all due respect to Mr. Kennedy here, the FBI. I will protect Candace. Use those troopers somewhere else for someone also at risk, like Keira."

Josh shook his head, "I knew you'd never let us do this. I got Keira covered. Believe it or not, she agreed to carry a gun."

"Not a smart move my boy. Never, ever arm your wife," Hawk laughed. "You let me worry about Candace. Get the story out there and burn that son-of-a-bitch Collucci. Speaking of which, shouldn't the first part be on soon? Tonight, I believe." As the words came out, his cell phone rang.

"We were just talking about you, Candace. Oh, with Josh Williams and my new friend Zach Kennedy from the FBI. What's that? What do you mean pulled it? Hold on a minute, let me put this on speaker phone so they can hear this."

Hawk hit the speaker button and put the phone on his desk. "Go ahead, we're all listening," Hawk said.

"Hi Josh," Candace's voice filled the room, "the station pulled the story. They said on advice of counsel. They want us to get more information. This is bullshit, the station manager is hiding, and I can't get a direct answer from the producers."

"Do you think they're just nervous because it's Collucci or is there more to it?" Josh asked.

"I don't know. We had a ton of discussions about this. We knew there would be political pressure, but no one ever said we wouldn't run with it. We already had the station lawyers sign off on it. I don't know what to think," Candace said.

"Alright, see what else you can find out. If you can't find the station manager, we will. I'll call you later," Josh looked as Hawk reached for the phone. "Hang on; your husband has some more words of wisdom." Hawk took the phone off speaker.

"Hey, listen. This is just a delay. If they don't run it, I will find someone who will. When you find your wimp of a station manager, tell him what I said." Hawk listened for a moment. "I know, I know. Let them stay with you for now. It'll make them feel better," Hawk laughed. "Okay, but don't let them touch it, bye."

Josh looked at him, his brow furrowed. "Don't let who touch what?" he asked.

"Your friends, the state police. When they got there and explained their purpose, Candace told them she didn't need them. She showed them the Glock 30-S.45 caliber she carries and the Saiga shotgun in her car. It's Russian made, semi-automatic. I got her a customized thirty round drum magazine for it. I rigged a mount for it behind the passenger seat. Concealed of course, with a thumbprint encoded lock release."

"I thought you said it was a bad idea to arm your wife?"

"No, I said it was a bad idea to arm your wife, mine is sane."

"Good point," Josh said.

"Where do you get a thirty-round mag for a Saiga shotgun, in this country? Legally, I mean," Kennedy asked.

Hawk shook his head, glancing at Josh. "See, the Feds just can't help being anal. Well, Agent Kennedy, my wife and I both have Federal Firearm Licenses." Hawk's stare did not betray affection for the question. "If you'd like to make an issue about it, feel free."

Kennedy turned up his hands, "Oh, hell no. I have no problem with it. I meant I wanted to know so I could get one for my Saiga."

Hawk laughed. "A Fed with a personality and sense of humor. Will wonders never cease?" Hawk reached into his desk drawer, withdrew something, and flipped it to Kennedy. "Compliments of a friend in Special Forces. All perfectly legit."

'Ah, thanks," Kennedy said, turning to Josh. "You were right about this guy, definite legend material."

Josh rose from the seat, shook Hawk's hand, and shepherded Kennedy toward to door. "Let's get out of here before he shows us the Claymore mines he's planning on deploying around his house."

As he got to the door, Kennedy turned back to look at Hawk shaking his head. First, side to side denying the statement, then up and down with a grin growing wider and wider.

Chapter 32

Josh and Zach walked back to the car on South Main Street. On the way by, they stopped in to check on things at Alpha Babes Investigations.

Chris was entertaining Keira and the troopers with war stories. Vera and Maggie were out picking up some takeout. Loren was captivated listening to Chris, amazed at how little she knew about the police. The stories Chris told unveiled a never-before-imagined world.

Josh and Zach came in. Josh kissed his wife, and then introduced her to Zach Kennedy.

"Nice to meet you, Keira," Zach said. "Your husband is quite the guy."

"Is that a nice way of saying he's crazy?" Keira smiled. "You must be a little crazy yourself; Josh hasn't had the best of experiences with some of your FBI colleagues."

Zach chuckled, "I know, I heard. But we're not all like that."

Keira nodded, "Well, I hope you can help them figure this out quickly. As much as I love Chris, I hate having a babysitter."

Josh filled them in on the conversation with Hawk and the station pulling the story.

"We're not going to just let it happen, are we?" Chris said.

"What do you think? Josh replied. "Zach and I are on the way to deal with it. I'll call you later; go tell `em more made up stories."

Kissing his wife once more, Josh and Zach left the office.

Back in the car, Zach asked, "Okay, now what?"

"We go find the station manager and have a little chat. I have an idea where he'll be," Josh answered. Pulling a quick turn across South Main Street, driving between the buildings, he headed to the highway on-ramp.

"And where do you suspect we'll find this station manager?" Zack asked, as they drove across the Washington Bridge.

"Just before my trial, a couple of the reporters from the same station Candace works for decided to follow me around. I spotted them right away. With the help of a couple of my brethren, we had some meaningful dialog with the reporters," Josh replied. "They filed a complaint about it."

"Yeah? And I should tell you I don't want to know any more than that," Zach said, "but I won't."

"A couple of days later, Chris and I were on a stakeout at Village Green Apartments. Lo and behold, here comes the station manager. He pulled into the parking spot right next to the surveillance van. Moments later, one of the female evening news anchors arrived. She greeted the station manager with great enthusiasm. We thought her tongue was going for the record in his throat," Josh smiled.

"Needless to say, compromising pictures and video ensued as they went inside. A short time later, something we pointed out to him in a later discussion, they left the apartment. We shot some more pictures. A bit of research found the apartment listed to station manager's brother. He happened to be on deployment with the United States Air Force," Josh said.

"Let me guess, they dropped the complaint?" Zach said, chuckling.

"I believe they decided it was just a misunderstanding," Josh said. "But here's the best part, he still uses the apartment. I bet he's hiding there."

Several minutes later, they arrived at the entrance to Village Green Apartments. The complex is just off Pawtucket Avenue, near Bay View Academy. Josh drove down to the last driveway and pulled in.

He and Zach got out of the car; Kennedy glanced around, checking cars and windows. They went to the door.

"Now what?" Zach said, "I don't think he'll buzz us in."

"Probably not," Josh answered. "Watch this. Joe McDaniel showed me this trick." Josh took out his keys, holding them in his left hand. With his right hand and shoulder, he pushed against the panel with the buttons for the various units, forcing it up. As the bottom of the panel cleared the frame, he stuck the key under and pried it up, revealing the wiring underneath. Taking the key, he placed it against two of the adjoining wires and the door lock buzzed.

"Grab the door," Josh said.

Zach shook his head and opened the door as Josh replaced the panel.

"Piece of cake," Josh smiled, walking inside. "Stick with me, I'll teach you all sorts of tricks."

"My first burglary, Deputy Attorney General Lachance will be so proud," Zach said, as he followed Josh inside.

"Don't worry, Hawk will get us off with an insanity defense," Josh snickered.

Walking up the stairs, he pointed to the last unit.

Zach looked at Josh, "We're not breaking in the door, are we?"

"Nah, I'll just knock. He'll think it's one of his neighbors," Josh said, banging on the door and holding his hand over the peephole.

There was the sound of movement inside, then a male voice. "Yes, what is it?"

"Hi, I think I backed into your car. Black BMW with Rhode Island plates?" Josh answered.

The door swung open.

"Hi there, Jim," Josh said, pushing past the man. "We need to talk."

* * *

Josh dropped down onto one of the living room chairs, feet dangling over the arm. "Jim, we have a problem. More to the point, we have a problem with you."

Jim Collins held the station manager's position for the past eight years. He was articulate, experienced, and not one subject to intimidation. Collins kept looking from Josh to Zach and back.

"Who's this?" he asked, pointing at Kennedy.

"Unimportant at the moment," Josh answered. He could see the tension level in Kennedy's face decrease. "Tell me why you killed the story."

"On the advice of counsel, but I didn't kill the story; they wanted more corroboration. That's all," Collins answered, glancing at Kennedy.

"Bullshit," Josh said. "Now I want the truth about this. Otherwise, I will be corroborating your use of this little hideaway with Mrs. Collins. How is she and the, what is it, five or six little Collins children? You'd have to get a second or third job for that child support payment."

Collins face blanched, he paced the room. "It can't come from me. I need this job. Come on, Josh. We've always been helpful with you guys. I know, I know we had that little misunderstanding--"

"See," Josh interrupted him, looking at Kennedy. "I told you it was just a misunderstanding."

Kennedy rolled his eyes and pretended to look out the window.

"That's all very nice, Jim. Look, I want to know who killed it and why. We never had this conversation. After this, we're even," Josh said.

Collins looked back and forth between Kennedy and Josh. "Okay, it came from our headquarters in Atlanta. The main corporation that owns us, along with several hundred other stations. They are in merger discussions with another media conglomerate; negotiations which are not yet public."

"So why would they care about this story?" Josh asked.

"Because this other conglomerate is ZMI Media, right?" Kennedy asked.

Collins eyes grew wide, "How would you know?"

"You might find yourself surprised by the things I know, Mr. Collins," Kennedy said. "We have what we need, Josh. Let's go."

"We do?" Josh asked, looking confused.

"Yes," Kennedy said, eyes widening, "we do," stretching out the words.

"Okay then, we got what we need," Josh said. "Thanks, Jim. Say hi to Natalie and all the little Collinses."

"We're even now, right?" Collins asked.

"Of course, I didn't have anything anyway. I was just guessing," Josh smiled. "Of course, now I do. Funny how that works. Let me ask you something, Jim. If we come to you with more corroboration, will you run the story or you gonna run scared over this?"

Collins thought for a moment. "I went along with pulling it because I knew there'd be a shit storm over it. Some of the information sources are a bit questionable?" looking at Kennedy. "Get me something confirming those wire transfers and I'll run it no matter what."

"We'll go one better than that, Mr. Collins," Kennedy said. "Give us a few days," Kennedy's eyes narrowed as he looked at Collins, "then I will hold you to your end of the bargain. Understood?"

Collins swallowed hard. Josh tried to contain his surprise.

Kennedy opened the door and walked out, Josh followed.

"That went well, didn't it?" Josh asked, as they drove out of the parking lot. "You gonna tell me what we learned? Because I have no idea."

"First of all, let me thank you for my first successful experience with breaking and entering with extortion thrown in as a bonus. I am sure it will add some sparkle to my bureau resume," Kennedy said.

"Not to worry," Josh replied. "By the time this is over, you'll be the director of the FBI."

"I'll be happy if I am not in prison and still have a job," Kennedy said. "This has been quite the ride."

Josh chuckled, "You seemed to have a natural talent for the implied threat from what I saw back there."

"I am learning from the master," Kennedy said, bowing his head.

Josh laughed, "Thanks, I'll take that as a compliment. Are you going to tell me what we learned anytime soon? Because this half of we still has no idea."

"As soon as we get back to your office, I have some work to do. Then, I'll show you," Kennedy said. "I need to bring up some intelligence files to explain the story."

Chapter 33

Zach Kennedy spent the next few days working away on his laptop. When he wasn't online, he was contacting sources within the intelligence community.

Wednesday morning, Josh walked into the office with Donahue and Moreira. Kennedy was already there.

"Thank you, Director. I appreciate your understanding," Kennedy said, hanging up his cell phone.

"Who was that?" Josh asked.

"Director of National Intelligence," Kennedy answered. "I needed his permission to talk to you guys about this."

Josh exchanged looks with the rest of the group. "Talk to us about what?" he asked. "Are you finally going to tell me what we learned from Collins?"

Zach leaned back, putting his hands behind his head. "Okay, boys, you cops are pretty smart. Of course, then there's Detective Moore, the proof of an exception to every rule," laughing as Tommy flipped him off. "I'm serious, if you were the Russian mob, what would offer you influence over the highest levels of government?"

"A judge?" Donahue offered.

"The Attorney General?" Joe Moreira suggested.

Josh just sat shaking his head, "No idea."

"Gotta think bigger, boys. Tommy," Zack asked, "your thoughts, if there are any?"

Moore studied his pen for a moment, and then the light came on. "The media, of course. The goddamn media. Whoever controls the press controls the news. Publicity drives politics. Reporters have access to everyone. Good press, lots of votes, bad press, lots of votes for the other guy. If you control the stories which are broadcast, you can manipulate public opinion; blind the public to the truth."

"Gentlemen, Tommy here has figured out the rest of the story," Kennedy said, turning the laptop for them to see. "The part we've been missing. The banking legislation, land grabs, money-laundering organization, front businesses is one part. Controlling what would be the largest media outlet in the United States is the other. Control the news and you contain any bad press."

"So how are they going to do that?" Josh asked.

Tapping his laptop screen, Kennedy said, "This is an intel report we got several years ago. It is from a source in the Syrian intelligence agency. He told us the Russians were infiltrating Al Jazeera, trying to take control of the media service. Nobody put much credibility in it."

He clicked through a couple more screens. "A year or so later, we got another report, this one from the French. They had information about a Russian mogul purchasing a majority ownership of a large French media outlet. Using a series of front companies, they were trying to exert control over the media. Two senior executives of a French newspaper turned up dead days after they ran a story about the Russian involvement. We started to pay attention." Kennedy punched a few keys, and a picture came up on the screen.

"Who's he?" Tommy asked.

"Shashenka Dmitriev," Kennedy answered.

"Oh, of course," Tommy added, looking at Josh. "Why couldn't you piss off the Irish mob, LT? It would be much easier if Danny Morrison wanted to kill you," Tommy paused a moment, studying the image. "Wait a minute, isn't he the guy I found who--"

"Yes, it is," Kennedy interrupted. "Our computer research genius found Dmitriev listed as a PAC board member. He also linked him to Harriet Lane Enterprises. Turns out the French intelligence report was on the money about the guy being Russian, they just didn't have the whole story. The guy was born in Russia, but he is now a naturalized American. Shashenka Dmitriev is the money behind the media merger. His organization owns the French media company and controls ZMI Media. I bet he shut the story down."

"ZMI Media is Russian?" Tommy asked. "How can they buy an American company?"

Kennedy turned the laptop around and clicked through more pages. "Dmitriev is a naturalized American citizen. He can do anything he likes, within the law. ZMI is a shorten version of *Novyny Zasoby Masovoyi Informatsiy*, a Ukrainian expression for news media. ZMI Media is a multi-national company with holdings all over the world. We know Dmitriev has connections to Russian organized crime group Solntsevskaya Bratva. He made billions from oil and natural gas production. He also was a member of the KGB, with Vladimir Putin."

"How the hell does a former KGB agent, with ties to organized crime, become an American citizen?" Tim Donahue asked.

Kennedy just looked at him. "You have to ask?" hands held wide apart.

"Money, of course, it's always about the money," Donahue answered, shaking his head.

"To make a long story short," Kennedy explained, "once Dmitriev became a US citizen it limited our ability to track him. If he was a foreign national, we have great latitude under FISA-"

"Under what?" Tommy asked. "Too goddamn many acronyms working with you guys. What is FISA?"

"Foreign Intelligence Surveillance Act," Josh answered. "It established a court, the Foreign Intelligence Surveillance Court. They review requests for electronic surveillance orders targeting terrorism and national security."

"Excellent, Lieutenant Williams," Kennedy said. "I am impressed."

Josh looked around the room, shrugging his shoulders. "I'd say we have enough to persuade our friend, Mr. Collins, to run the story now. Show him the link between the front companies we found, ZMI Media, and the money movement. What do you think, Zach?"

"I agree," pointing at Josh, "but when you say persuade, it sounds more like a threat rather than convincing him we have what he asked for. Makes me nervous," Kennedy chuckled.

"Must be from working with the FBI," Josh said. "You guys are a bad influence. Let's go talk to Brennan; I haven't brought him up to speed lately. Then we'll call Candace, fill her in, and arrange to meet with Collins as soon as we can."

"Before we do that," Tommy said. "Why don't we arrange for Jen and me to meet with Sorin one more time? Maybe get something useful on the phone or from the bug in his car. Tie in Collucci a little tighter."

"I don't know," Josh said. "What do you think, Zach?"

"Might be a good idea," Kennedy agreed. "Collucci has some plausible deniability here. If we can get him in a conversation with Sorin discussing these things, it may be enough to indict him."

Josh thought for a moment, "Okay, Tommy. Call Jennifer and set up a meeting. We'll hold off on talking to Collins until we see how it goes."

Tommy was already on the phone. "Jen, it's me. Yeah listen. I need you to do something. Use the phone in the office and call Anthony. Arrange another meeting. Tell him I asked to speak with him about our options with the property."

"What if he wants to know what the problem is?" Jen asked.

"Tell him you're not sure. Just say I called you to arrange the meeting and leave it at that. Hang on a minute."

Josh was waving at him, trying to get his attention.

Tommy put the phone down, "what's up, LT?"

"Line recorder is ready. Tell her to make the call," Josh said.

"Okay," Tommy answered, turning back to the phone conversation. "Jen, we're ready. Make the call. I'll head over there after it's over."

A moment later, the alert tone on the recording devices indicated an outgoing call. The digital display showed Sorin's cell phone.

After two rings, Sorin answered.

"Yes, Jennifer. What is it now?"

"Hello Anthony, I am well. Thanks for asking," Jennifer snapped. "I thought you'd like to have an update on the property situation here. Can we meet in the next day or so?"

"Isn't this something we can discuss over the phone? Why is a meeting necessary?" Sorin asked.

"If you like, but Tom asked me to call you and arrange a meeting. He said there are some options and wanted to discuss them with you. If you'd rather not, I'll tell him."

Sounds of muffled voices in the background came over the line. Sorin came back on. "The Senator and I will not be back in Rhode Island until next Thursday. We will meet Friday morning 9:00 AM your office. That's the best I can do." The call ended.

Tommy looked at Josh, "Such a pleasant guy. When we do get to arrest him, I hope he puts up a fight. There is nothing I'd enjoy more than knocking out a pussy like him."

Josh chuckled, "Just make sure he throws the first punch."

"He can throw the first two or three. I'll throw the last one," Moore smiled, banging his fist into his hand.

Chapter 34

October 2, 2009
Hart Senate Office Building
Washington, DC

Sorin watched from across the street as Collucci paced back and forth in front of the building. *Let him learn patience; might do him some good.*

"Take your time getting to him," Sorin said, finally ordering the driver to move. The driver nodded, ignoring several opportunities before entering the flow of traffic. Amused, Sorin watched the anxious Senator searching for the car.

Collucci opened the back door himself, motioning for the driver to stay in the car. "Nice of you to show up," he snarled. Tossing his briefcase onto the seat and climbing in.

"Traffic was difficult," Sorin replied, gazing out the other window. "Did your meeting go as planned?"

"Of course, it did," Collucci replied, "The Chairman will resign by month's end and the vote taken to replace him with me a day or so later. Did you have any doubt?"

Sorin ignored the question. "I received a call from Jennifer a few moments ago. They have an issue with the land problem in East Providence. She and her partner, Mr. Meadows, would like to meet with me."

"So, meet with them. Get this resolved. The sooner the better," Collucci said. "We need to move forward on this."

Sorin wasn't listening, lost in his thoughts. *I must learn more about this Mr. Meadows.* Reaching for his cell phone, he dialed a number.

"Have you learned anything about the name I gave you?" Sorin asked, listening to the response. "I need you to dig deeper. I want to know everything you can find about him. Call me as soon as you learn anything."

Collucci stopped flipping through his email; eyebrows raised, he held a questioning look at Sorin. "Is there a problem?"

"I don't know. It's just a feeling I have. No matter, I will deal with it," Sorin answered.

"See that you do," Collucci said, returning to his messages.

After a circuitous route through the city, they arrived at a nondescript brown stone building. The driver came around to open the door.

"Stay nearby," Collucci ordered. "As soon as we finish here I want you ready to pick us up. Understood?"

The driver, glancing at Sorin, nodded. "I'll be right here."

Sorin and Collucci climbed the few stairs to the entrance. As they reached the top step, the door opened. Shashenka Dmitriev stood in the shadows, just inside. "Come in, my friends, come in. I have been looking forward to this meeting."

* * *

"May I offer you gentlemen a drink?" Dmitriev said, directing them to chairs next to the fireplace.

"Scotch for me. Neat. Single malt if you have it," Collucci answered, taking in the ornate surroundings. "So, what is this place?"

"It is private," Dmitriev snapped in return, turning back to face Sorin. "Anthony?"

"Vodka," Sorin answered, taking a seat near the fire.

Dmitriev nodded to the waiter. The drinks arrived within the minute. "That will be all for now," Dmitriev said, dismissing the server. "See we are not disturbed."

"Da," replied the man, backing out and closing the double pocket doors.

Dmitriev waited for the doors to close, and then turned to Sorin. "I trust you took normal precautions before coming here?"

Sorin nodded. Collucci took in the exchange, raising a questioning look at Sorin.

"Good, good," turning his attention to the Senator. "Mr. Sorin tells me there is a problem with some property in Rhode Island. I trust the issue is in hand?"

Collucci smiled, "Mr. Dmitriev--"

"Shasha, please, we are among friends here. My friends call me Shasha." Dmitriev smiled, placing the tips of his fingers together and looking over the top at Collucci. "For as long as they remain my friends."

"Shasha," Collucci said, "we have the property issue under control. If we cannot get them to sell, we can move in the court to take it by eminent domain."

"I do not understand these niceties of the American system. Is this not a beneficial project to the area? Will it not help a significant number of people? How is it one person can obstruct what is good for the many?"

Collucci smiled, "Shasha, my good friend. If we are going to do business here, and grow that business, you have to learn to use the system in place. Trying to run roughshod over a minor problem will always create more problems." Tipping his glass to Sorin, "Anthony and I are more than capable of resolving this and moving the project ahead."

Taking a long sip of his drink, Collucci smiled. "I am sure you are aware of how I dealt with the little issue with the local news. It is a good example of why I am valuable to your organization."

Dmitriev smiled. "Speaking of running, as you say, roughshod over a minor problem, I am well aware of your inept little demonstration of power and influence," the rage in his voice rising. "Your little delay of the merger vote costs my organization millions of dollars a day. Your approach was amateurish, motivated by self-preservation, and ill-advised."

Collucci sat back in his chair, stunned. Looking at Sorin, he saw a grin crossing his face. "Shasha I think--."

"Enough," Dmitriev said, banging his fist on the table. "I want to make something clear; having your assistance in this project is helpful, but not invaluable. I am certain it is not worth the cost you have forced my group to absorb. You will take no further action on your own without clearing it through me. And you will do this through Anthony," pointing to the now grinning Sorin. "Is any of this unclear to you?"

"Anthony?" Collucci said, leaning forward in his chair. "You expect me to clear things through my assistant? I don't think so," shaking his head. "He works for me, not the other way around. I will do what I want, when I want. I am a United States Senator, an influential one, Shasha. You do not tell me what to do," slamming his drink on the table, the contents splashing over his hands.

Dmitriev placed the tips of his finger on his nose, "Pozhaluysta, ostav'te nas."

Sorin rose, without speaking, and left the room.

Collucci watched Sorin leave, and then turned back to Dmitriev. "I am not intimidated, by you or anyone else. Do not make that mistake my friend," trying to match Dmitriev's stare.

"Senator," Dmitriev smiled, "I am a patient man. I have worked myself into the position I occupy *by* being patient. However, along with patience, one needs the intelligence to know when and how to act. You possess none of these qualities."

Dmitriev leaned in, a finger pointed at Collucci. "You are a self-important, self-centered, egotistical little man. You have pretentious aspirations to which you lack the proper skill set." The words stung Collucci. "I will say this once, Senator. You will do what I say, or you will find yourself, as we say in Russia," leaning back and smiling, "prekrashchayetsya."

"What does that mean?" Collucci asked, less sure of his position.

Dmitriev smiled, "Terminated."

Collucci felt his face redden. A door opened, and Anthony Sorin returned to the room.

"The Senator and I have reached an agreement, Anthony. He has shown wisdom by agreeing to follow my advice. Please see that he remembers this."

Collucci rose to his feet, trying to regain his composure. "Sha--"

Dmitriev raised his hand, "From now on, Senator, when you address me please feel free to call me Mr. Dmitriev." Turning his back to Collucci, he nodded at Sorin, and walked out of the room.

Collucci looked at Sorin.

"I tried to warn you," Anthony said, shaking his head. "Having him unsure of your usefulness is not helpful. Let's go."

"He just threatened me? He cannot threaten a United State Senator. I can--"

"Robert," Sorin said, staring down Collucci's attempt at bravado. "Shashenka Dmitriev does not threaten anyone. He tells people what he will do, and then he does it. If you know what is good for you, for us, you will remember that. Now let's get out of here before he reconsiders his decision."

Chapter 35

On Monday morning, Tommy Moore walked into the office on Waterman Street. As he entered through the rear door, he saw Karen, the woman he and Jen spoke with after dinner a few nights ago.

"Good morning, Karen. How are you?" Tommy said.

"Tom, right? Jen's friend?" Karen smiled, "I am well, how are you?"

"Great. "Looks to be a beautiful day today, doesn't it?" Tommy said.

"It does, doesn't it?" Karen said. "I hope I get to enjoy some of it, not spend the whole day stuck in the office."

"So, what is your business, Karen?" Tommy asked. "Jen told me you had an office here, but she didn't say what it is you do. Just curious, you're not the competition, are you?"

"Not at all," Karen laughed in answer, moving to stand next to Tom. "I was just running over to the cafe next door for coffee. Care to join me? I'd be happy to tell you all about my business. Perhaps we can exchange some ideas."

Tommy glanced at his watch, "Ah, sure. I would love to. Jen and I have a meeting but it's not until later this morning. I was just going to do paperwork anyway," pointing to the door. "Lead on."

Settling into a table by the window, overlooking the Seekonk River, the two sipped their coffee.

"So, out with it., are you a spy? What are you?" Tommy asked, trying to charm the woman.

"You are an insistent one, aren't you?" Karen replied. "Nothing so exciting. I run a pre-employment verification service. We do background checks, drug screenings, license and educational verifications, that sort of thing."

"How's the business doing, I mean, if you don't mind me asking?" Tommy said, the information setting off alarms in his mind.

"No, of course not. I love talking about my business. I am doing well. I just signed a long-term contract with two nationwide companies. They are in the midst of huge hiring increases," Karen said, taking a drink of coffee. "There is no such thing as too much business. But I am struggling with the decision to hire someone to help with the increased volume. So, I guess you'd say I'm doing well."

"So, how does one go about doing background checks? Is it just a Google search? Or is there more to it?" Tommy asked, leaning forward arms on the table, hands around the coffee cup.

"No, it's a lot more than that. I subscribe to some information services. Depending on the nature of the job, there are certain things we can and cannot check. It's not exciting, but I enjoy it and it pays the bills as they say."

"How'd you pick this business?" Tommy probed. "I mean, it's not something I knew even existed as a separate business. I thought companies did their own backgrounds."

"Interesting story," Karen said. "After I graduated from Fordham, I wanted to be an FBI agent." Seeing the reaction in Tommy's eyes, she laughed. "Didn't work out for me. I made it through the FBI Academy, and then got hurt in a car accident. It affected the nerves in my wrist. Couldn't fire a weapon to qualify anymore."

"You were an agent?" Tommy said, the incredulity evident in his voice.

"You never know who might be a government agent," Karen said, winking and smiling at him.

You can say that again. "So, what happened? Was the accident while you were on the job?" Tommy asked.

"No, it happened on my way home from a brief vacation. I was an agent for two weeks," Karen said, staring out the window. "Ah well, the past as they say is in the past. I did make some connections at the academy, got a job working in Washington at one of the think tanks doing research. I always knew my way around computers. There's a lot of litigation around hiring practices, something I learned from an old boyfriend who was a lawyer, and it seemed like a good idea."

"Sounds like a brilliant idea to me," Tommy said.

"I got lucky," Karen said, finishing the last of the coffee. "With Brad's help, his name was Brad," her tone caustic, "I got introduced to some personnel managers. I made a pitch to do the backgrounds quicker, better, and more cost-effectively. The rest, as they say, is history."

"So, what happened to Brad?" Tommy asked.

"Another funny story," a sad smile crossed her face, "I had just started my subscription to LexisNexis and some other background services. They let you do unlimited searches to show the power of their databases as an introduction. I ran Brad. Turns out he was married to a Naval Officer. She was on assignment overseas."

"Oops. I'm sorry," Tommy said by way of apology, "didn't mean to raise bad memories."

Karen smiled. "No worries. It all worked out in the end."

She stood up, grabbing her cup, reaching for his. "You done?" she asked.

"Yup," Tommy said.

Karen grabbed his cup and tossed them in the trash. "Gotta head back; it was nice talking with you. If, in your property management world, you come upon a need to do a background on anyone, just ask. I'll be happy to help if I can," she smiled.

"I'll keep it in mind," Tommy said. As he stood to leave, his cell phone rang. Looking at the display he said, "Gotta take this; let's do this again sometime." As he answered the phone, he watched her leave the cafe.

"What's up LT?" Tommy asked.

"Where are you?" Josh asked.

"At the office on Waterman, just had an interesting conversation with a woman who works in the same building. Long story how I met her. I may have found Sorin's other connection in the building."

"Not the one with the crooked tits, is it?" Josh said, laughing.

"No," Tommy answered.

"Okay then, what do you want to do with that piece of info?" Josh asked.

"Let me run a few things by Jennifer," Tommy replied, "she knows her better than me. She thinks this woman had an affair with Sorin. Maybe we can use it to smoke her out and see if she is the insider."

Tommy headed back across the street, walking to the back of the building. As he approached the door, he spotted a van parked across the street. It was a surveillance vehicle; Tommy got on his cell and called Josh.

"Hey, got a problem. There's a van parked across the street. I'd bet you it's a surveillance van. Maybe we can get our friends from the State Police to do a little intervention?"

"No problem," Josh said. "I am with Tim Donahue now. I'll have him take care of it."

Ten minutes later, two marked State Police cars pulled up to the van. Tommy watched them extract two males from inside the vehicle. The troopers spent a few minutes talking to the men, and then released them. A moment later, Tommy's phone rang.

"Tommy Meadows, Genius speaking. How can I help you?" he answered.

"Genius?" Donahue said, "I doubt it. In this case, you were right. The van is DEA. They caught wind of the MS-13 connection to the building and decided to go fishing and see what they could find. We've dissuaded them from continuing."

"You dissuaded them?" Tommy said. "And how do the state police dissuade the DEA?"

"We have our methods," Donahue answered. "They won't be back."

* * *

Tommy walked into the office; Jennifer was back at her desk.

"Did you enjoy your coffee with Karen?" she asked with slight edge to her voice.

"Is that jealousy I detect? A bit juvenile don't you think?"

Jennifer scowled, "I was just curious," turning back to her computer. "Never mind, it doesn't matter."

Tommy walked over and put his arms around her. She tried to struggle away from him, and then gave in to him.

"Calm down, crazy woman. It was just a professional conversation. We think she may work for Sorin, feeding him information. I have an idea and I need your help."

Jennifer turned to face him. "I'm sorry. I know we just kind of fell back together here," looking into Tommy's eyes, "If we're even together at all."

"Jen, we're back together. I am glad this happened. But we're still in the middle of this and there's a lot that can go wrong. We have to be careful. Tell me about Karen and Anthony. How did you find out they had an affair?"

Jen explained the history behind her moving her office to this building. "It was Anthony's idea to move here," she explained. "Once I had my office set up, I noticed Anthony stopping by Karen's office a couple of times. The first time I saw them together, I knew something was going on. I just knew."

"Did he know her before you met her?" Tommy asked.

"I assume so," she answered. "She was here before me. I guess that's how they met."

"No, you got it wrong," Tommy said. "I bet he put you in here, so she could keep an eye on you. She seems to pay a lot of attention to you. It's no coincidence; she's here to track your activities for Sorin."

"What do we do?"

"I am going to ask her to do something in confidence. See what she does with it. We'll have to add her to the people monitor."

"What are you going to ask her to do?" Jen eyes widened.

"I am going to have her do a background on Anthony Sorin. If she's working for him, she'll alert him right away," Tommy said. "It will be

248

interesting to see what she comes up with." Tommy took out his cell and made a call.

* * *

The next morning, Tommy came into the office with Jennifer. As they walked in, Tommy went to the window overlooking the back lot.

"Okay, here's what I need you to do," Tommy said. "When Karen pulls in, you head out the back door so you run into her. Tell her you are going to a meeting or something. Once you leave, I'll go over to her office and ask her to run the background in confidence."

"What if she refuses or makes up some excuse not to do it?" Jen asked.

"It won't matter. Either way she reaches out to Sorin if she's working for him. It will confirm our suspicions," Tommy answered, sliding the blinds back and looking out the window. "Okay, she just pulled in. Show time; go do your thing then head to the apartment. After I talk to her, I'll meet you there."

"Why the apartment?" Jen asked.

Tommy just smiled.

"Oh my, during the day?" Jen laughed, a slight blush to her face.

"Yes, Jen, during the day and night and in-between, now go," Tommy said. "I'll be there soon."

Jennifer left the office and met Karen as she came in the back door.

"You're off early, where you headed?" Karen asked.

"Got a meeting downtown," Jen answered. "Some new property came on the market and I need to take a look at it. How are you?"

"Oh fine, late start today for me. New client coming in later. Where's Tom, not going with you?" Karen asked, looking around.

"No, he has some things to do in the office, contracts to review, that sort of thing. Business is growing faster than we can handle," Jen said. "See you later, maybe we can get together for a drink soon?"

"I'd like that, see ya."

Karen headed into her office. A short time later, there was a knock on her door. Opening it, she seemed surprised to see Tommy standing there.

"Hey Tommy, what's up?"

"Hi Karen, can I come in for a moment?" Tommy said.

"Of course, come on in. What can I do for you?"

"Karen," Tommy said, a hint of seriousness to his voice. "I have a favor to ask. I also need to know you can keep this confidential, just between us. Can you do that?"

Karen looked at Tommy for a moment, "I can keep things confidential as long as it's legal. It is legal, correct?"

Tommy glanced around, adding to the tension. "Let me explain, I had a previous partnership in this business. It did not end well. Now understand, I have no issues with Jennifer. She is all I could hope for in this industry. It's her ex-husband, Anthony Sorin. He's what I am concerned about."

Karen moved around in the chair, unable to get comfortable, folding her arms around herself. "Anthony? Why are you concerned with Anthony? From what I know of him, he has been good to Jennifer, I mean, considering the circumstances."

"Let's just say I'd like to know more about him. Is it something you can do? Something you would do? I am prepared to pay whatever your fees are for an in-depth background." Tommy watched for her reaction.

"Well, under the circumstances I can do a bit of checking into his background. Past affiliations, employment, those sorts of things. I don't think I can justify a credit background, not enough financial risk or ties for that. But I can make sure he's not an alien invader." Karen smiled, trying to lessen her tension.

"That would be great. And this stays between us, right? I don't want Jennifer to know about it. She seems to walk on eggshells whenever he's around."

"Of course, I can keep this between us. It's a reasonable request. Your business relationship is quite significant, so it falls under due diligence," Karen said.

"Great, what do you need, fee wise, to get started?" Tommy asked.

Karen thought for a moment. "How about you let me see what I can find with the database inquiries. I should be able to get most of what you want without incurring any costs. How's that sound?"

Tommy stood up and turned to leave, "Sounds great. If you do need any money though please let me know, okay?"

"Of course," Karen replied.

"Thanks. I appreciate your understanding in this," Tommy headed back out of the office.

Karen watched Tommy leave. She reached for her cell, dialing a number from memory.

"Yes, what is it?" Anthony Sorin asked.

"Someone is asking questions about you," Karen answered. "He's hired me to do a background check."

"Who?"

"Tommy Meadows, Jennifer's new partner."

"Well, then by all means follow the request. Make it thorough and believable," Sorin replied. "We need to step up our inquiry into Mr. Meadows. I want to know everything you can find on him, use all your contacts." The call ended.

Karen sat at her desk for a moment. An idea formed in her head. Something Tommy said while they were having coffee struck a chord. Perhaps she had been going about this all wrong, making the wrong assumptions.

Reaching for her laptop, she logged into a specific website and began a search. Guessing Tommy to be early to mid-thirties, she limited her search to a five-year period. Downloading the information into a spreadsheet, she isolated likely candidates.

Eighty-five names on the list matched her criteria. Filtering those by location, she narrowed to search to Rhode Island and Massachusetts.

This narrowed the list to fifteen. She ran a Google image query using the fifteen names, adding three other specific search terms.

Within seconds, she had her answer. On her screen, smiling with a sense of accomplishment was an image of Mr. Meadows. His real name was Thomas Moore. The image is from his graduation from the FBI National Academy session in 2007.

A few more quick searches and she knew all she needed about Mr. Moore.

Reaching for her phone, she hit redial.

"Yes?"

"We have a problem," Karen said. "Mr. Meadows is in reality Detective Thomas Moore, Special Investigations Unit, East Providence Police Department."

"How'd you find this out?" Sorin asked.

"We had coffee the other day. I told him about my background with the FBI and he said something which jumped out at me."

"Which was?" Sorin asked.

"When I told him about the accident, he asked if it happened while I was 'on the job'. It's something a cop would say. Not 'at work' or 'while you were working'. 'On the job,' "Karen explained. "That gave me an idea."

"How do you get from there to finding out he's a cop?" Sorin asked.

"It was easy. I had assumed Meadows, or Moore, was a businessperson. I decided to approach it from the idea of his being law enforcement. One thing I learned in the FBI Academy is undercover officers need to keep their stories straight. While changing the last name was a given, they often use their own first name for simplicity"

"This is good, Karen," Sorin said. "But why look at local cops; it could have been one of thousands of FBI agents?"

"You told me the local yokels at East Providence PD started the initial investigation," Karen explained. "I decided to see if I could find someone matching the description with a local connection. Many local departments send officers to the FBI National Academy. In today's connected world, everyone posts images on social media. As soon as I saw the image, I knew I had him."

"Excellent work, now you need to get rid of any evidence of your inquiries," Sorin instructed. "You can handle that, no?"

Karen's fingers went over the keyboard several times. "Done," she said. "I used an anonymizer and IP spoofing to do the searches. I'll destroy the laptop as well. I will add the cost to your fee, of course."

"You do that, Karen. You do that," Sorin said. "I'll be in touch, send the bill through the usual channels. Great work, thank you."

Sorin thought for a long moment. Karen has proven most useful in this, but she represents a loose end. There can be none of those. Reaching for a disposable phone, he placed a call.

* * *

"Did we get that?" Kennedy asked Tim Donahue, via the secure radio link.

"Yes, we did," Donahue said, explaining what they had just monitored. "Better get Tommy and Josh on the phone and let them know what's happened."

A moment later, Josh came in to the SIU office.

"What's up? We get anything?" Josh asked.

"Oh yeah," Donahue said. "She figured out who Tommy is and told Sorin. Maybe we need to pull him out before anything else happens."

Josh was on his cell phone calling Tommy.

"Hey Lieutenant, what's going on?" Tommy said.

"Our friends know about you," Josh replied. "Soon as you left, she called Sorin. A few computer searches later, she figured out who you are. It's time for the spy to come in from the cold."

"Why don't we let it play out a little more," Tommy argued. "We suspected she would call him. She's not the killer type. We'll just be more cautious. I think we let this continue at least until the story breaks, couple of days at best."

Josh paused for a moment. "Okay, but let's assume they will start to follow you. We'll have to cover the UC apartment and make sure we choreograph your movements. We can keep an eye on you and identify any surveillance. Go find Jennifer and meet us at Haines Park. Call me when you're on the way."

"You got it, LT. I'll go find Jen and head down there. Give me an hour or two, she went downtown to a meeting," Tommy lied. "I'll meet her somewhere and bring her." Tommy hung up.

"So?" Jennifer asked.

"Our good friend Karen is the other link in the office. Soon as I left she called Sorin and told him about my request," Tommy hesitated a moment. "But there's another problem. She knows I'm a cop."

"What?" Jennifer said, as panic spread across her face. "How did she find that out?"

"We've underestimated her abilities in doing background checks," Tommy answered. "She did some advanced Google searches, applied a little logic, and found my picture from the FBI National Academy. Once she had the name, the rest was easy."

Jennifer hands trembled. Tommy reached over, cupping her hands in his. "Don't worry; this will go on a few more days at most. We're gonna add some more surveillance and make sure they can't get near us."

"What about Kelsey and my father?" Jennifer sobbed. "Anthony will assume I was the one who went to the cops in the first place. He'll go after my father, I just know he will."

Tommy pulled her close, stroking the back of her head. "The FBI already has a team on them in Aruba. They're bringing them home. They'll be fine. Besides, going after them doesn't make any sense. It's...."

"It's what?" Jen asked, searching his eyes.

"Nothing, it's nothing. We're going to be fine." Tommy hugged her again. "We won't be coming here together anymore though, too risky."

Jen sat up, pulling herself away from Tommy. "So now what do we do?"

"For now, we just hunker down and ride it out," Tommy said. "Get dressed. We have to go meet with Josh and the others. As much as I'd like to drive around in the car with you dressed as is, it might raise some suspicions."

Jen gave him a weak smile, kissed his hands, and gathered her clothes.

* * *

Josh and the investigative team sat in the far corner lot of Haines Park, waiting for Tommy and Jennifer. Josh took out his cell phone. "I think I had better call Hawk. Let him know the threat level is up a bit," dialing the number. "Maybe I can defer his declaring war."

Kennedy chuckled, "Good luck, I'm just glad he's on our side."

A moment later, Hawk answered.

"Lieutenant Williams, what can I do for you?"

"Ah, listen Hawk. There's been a change in status with the case," Josh said. "Our adversary has found out about Tommy being a cop. Sorin has been making calls all day on a variety of phones reaching out to some rather unpleasant people. There's nothing definite but might be worth bumping up your security arrangements. You sure you want to handle this alone? I've got plenty of manpower."

"While I appreciate your offer, Josh, I've already adjusted for the worst-case scenario. Candace tells me the first report is on for tomorrow night. Things should get interesting then. Thanks for the call. Talk to you later." The call ended.

"So?" Kennedy said.

"Yeah, so?" asked Donahue.

"I don't know," Josh said. "Maybe I shouldn't have called him. Hawk does not react- he prefers to be pro-active. I hope he leaves this alone, but I doubt he will. He might just solve the problem for us."

"Hey," Donahue said, "if he finds a way to terminate these bastards with extreme prejudice, I'm good with it."

"You and me both," Kennedy added. "Just don't mention it to the Deputy US Attorney, if he asks."

* * *

After Hawk ended the call with Josh, he considered his options. If there was one thing he learned in Vietnam it was this, when someone is trying the kill you, there is no such thing as overreacting.

He thumbed through his contacts and placed another call.

"Hawk, my old friend, usually it is me calling you. To what do I owe this surprise?" the voice on the line said.

254

"I may need some of your specialized services. Someone is trying to make things personal with my wife and some friends of mine. I won't let that happen."

"Whatever you need. When should we meet?"

"As soon as possible, is the restaurant still open for lunch?" Hawk asked.

"Of course. 1:00 tomorrow okay?"

"See you there."

* * *

Josh spotted Tommy's car and flashed the headlights at him.

Tommy and Jennifer got out of the car and climbed into the surveillance van.

"So, how are you doing?" Josh asked her, as she squeezed between Donahue and Kennedy.

"Nervous," Jennifer said. "Tommy told me they know he's a cop. I'm worried about my daughter and father."

Kennedy spoke up. "I just got a text message from the FBI team with them. They landed a few minutes ago at North Central state airport in Lincoln. They're taking them to a safe house until this is over."

"Okay," Tommy said, "how do you want to deal with Karen?"

"I'm open to suggestions," Josh answered.

"Here's what I think," Tommy said. "I'll go to the office. Make sure Karen knows I am there. If she doesn't come right over, it will give me an excuse to call and ask how she's making out on the background. I'll tell her Jennifer had to go to a meeting in Baltimore with another client and will be away for a few days. Give them some doubt about where she is."

"I don't know, Tommy," Josh said. "It leaves you too exposed in there."

"She's never seen me," Donahue offered. "Let me go in there with him. Even if she assumes I am a cop, with two of us it poses a bigger problem for them."

"I like it, "Tommy said. "I can hide behind his fat ass if they start shooting, fucking thing would stop a missile."

Donahue flipped him the bird. "I can take care of little Miss Tommy over here while we see what she does. Even if they were going to go after him, they wouldn't do it there. Too many things can go wrong. They'll look for somewhere isolated."

Josh caught an exchange of looks between Tommy and Jennifer. *I knew it, damn it, I knew it.*

"Okay," Josh decided. "Tommy you go to the office. Tim you go right behind him, meet in the parking lot as if it were pre-arranged. I'll have another team head over there before you."

"What about me?" Jennifer asked.

"How about we take you to meet with your daughter? I'm sure she'd be happy to see you," Josh said.

"I'd like that. Thank you," Jennifer replied.

"Okay, Joe and I will take Jennifer to the safe house," Josh said. "Meanwhile, you guys work out a cover story for Tim to be in the office. As soon as we get back, we'll have you guys head there."

* * *

They drove to the safe house. The secluded cabin, on Waterman Lake in the village of Chepachet, was ideal for this purpose. There were no paved roads. Access was a dirt trail, difficult, if not impossible, to find unless someone pointed it out.

The cabin sat high on a piece of land, jutting out into the lake. A narrow path led down to the lake through the cliff controlled by a wrought iron gated access. Angled razor ribbon, concealed by the bushes, made climbing difficult, if not impossible. The edge of the steep cliff covered with thick, impenetrable briar bushes. With its panoramic views of the lake, it was impossible for anyone to approach the house from the water.

For extra measure, the state police brought two of their German Shepherds. The dogs had free roam of the peninsula. They offered a measure of intimidation to anyone curious enough to approach through the woods.

As they approached the house, the dogs went on alert. They barked and yelped, circling to contain the intruders.

Joe Moreira stepped in front. "Colonel, Major, Heir. Platz," commanding the dogs in perfect German.

The response was instantaneous. Retreating behind Moreira, they sat down without breaking eye contact with the two unfamiliar faces.

"Friendly I hope?" Josh smiled, matching the watchful stare of the dogs.

"Unless I tell 'em not to be," Moreira smiled. "I may have a little fun with that smart-ass friend of yours, the defective Detective Moore. But for now, they are harmless."

Turning to the dogs, he said, "So ist brav, frei." The two dogs ran to Jennifer and rolled on their backs, begging her to scratch them.

"They are dogs of culture and refinement," Moreira laughed. "They know who to go to."

Jennifer bent down and rubbed their bellies. The dogs squirmed in delight.

"Come on inside," Moreira motioned to the front door. As soon as the words were out of his mouth, the two dogs made a beeline for the cabin. Moreira yelled, "Nein, stey," the German commands halting the dogs in their tracks. "Back to work. You can come in later."

The shepherds sulked on the porch, watching as the trio went inside.

As they came in the front door, Kelsey ran up and hugged her mother. "Hi, Mom. Did you meet Colonel and Major? They are really cool dogs. Can we get one?"

Jennifer scooped her into her arms, "Oh honey, I don't know. I am not sure we have room for that kind of dog. Maybe a smaller one? Let's wait and see."

"Grandpa said we can move into his house. It's much bigger. He said he's lonely and would love to have us come live with him and we can get a dog and they can sleep in my room and Grandpa says he wants us to. Didn't you grandpa?" finally taking a breath and smiling at the judge.

"I may have mentioned it," he said, shrugging his shoulders. "But that's up to your mother. For now, let's enjoy playing with Colonel and Major."

The sound of whining came from behind the door. Moreira opened it. The two shepherds stood side-by-side, right at the threshold, anxiety on their faces, waiting for the invitation.

"They must have been listening and heard their names," Moreira laughed. "Okay, hier," calling them in. "Five minutes, then back to work."

The dogs ran in, tails wagging, and surrounded Kelsey and Jennifer. Alternating between lying on their backs and running around the mother and daughter, the dogs reveled in the attention. Kelsey laughed at the dogs' antics in trying to outdo each other.

Judge Tucker motioned with his head for them to step outside. After the door closed, he looked at Josh. "Lieutenant, first let me thank you for looking out for my family," putting his hands on Josh's shoulders. "It is much appreciated."

"You're welcome, your Honor," Josh said. "The more I've learned the more I've come to realize Jennifer, and your granddaughter, are as much victims here as anyone else. We'll make sure nothing happens to them."

"Yes, well Jennifer may have some explaining to do with her involvement," Judge Tucker said. "She is a bright woman, she must've suspected something. That is for another discussion. For now, I need you to deliver something for me." He handed Josh a large envelope.

"What's this?" Josh asked.

"It is a detailed, sworn affidavit about my involvement in the Grey case," the Judge explained. "I have included, to the best of my recollection, the events that transpired ending with Grey in the prison system. I think it may be useful in corroborating the information in the news broadcast. And there's this," handing Josh a smaller envelope.

Josh gave the Judge a quizzical look.

"My resignation," the Judge said, gazing out into the woods. "I cannot in good conscience continue to sit on the bench in light of the things I did or failed to do. Please see that Judge Michael Campbell receives this."

"Judge, no. I can't deliver this. It won't change anything," Josh argued. "You're the kind of person we need on the bench. Please reconsider. We may need a sympathetic ear in the court until this is resolved."

Tucker glanced at the envelope in Josh's outstretched hand. Reaching for it, he said, "I will hold onto this, for now. I will not make any promises, but I will give it more thought. Thank you, Josh."

"Josh, I know about a million prosecutors that would want your head for that," Moreira said, chuckling, trying to lighten the moment.

Tucker laughed. "I am afraid the Sergeant is right on that one, Josh. If some of my brethren at the bar knew you held my resignation in your hands, and returned it, I dare say your life would be in jeopardy."

"Won't be the first time," Josh said. "Let's go back in and see what havoc the dogs have wrought."

Chapter 36

Tommy drove to the office, parking in the rear of the building. As he got out of the car, he spotted Karen looking out the window watching him. She waved, and he returned the gesture. She motioned for him to come to her office.

He grabbed his briefcase, trying to delay until Donahue arrived. *Where the hell is he?*

Tommy started toward the door.

Donahue drove into the lot and beeped at him. Tommy waited for Donahue to park, glancing to see if Karen was still watching.

"Hey Tim," Tommy said. "Come on into the office," shaking Donahue's hand, putting on a little show for Karen.

Tommy let Donahue into Jennifer's office. "I'll be right back, got to stop at the office down the hall," he said, if someone was listening.

Karen was waiting at the door for him.

"I see you have someone in the office," she said. "This can wait."

"Do you have something for me about Anthony?"

"You sure you have time?" Karen asked. "Is Jennifer back in the office with the client?"

"No, she flew down to Baltimore," Tommy said. "We got a lead on some properties just on the market and decided to expand the scope our operations. The guy in the office is a friend of mine from college. He is considering joining the group if we open another office out-of-state. He had some calls to make, so now is good."

Karen smiled and returned to her desk. She logged into the computer, brought up a spreadsheet, and scrolled through the file.

"Well, the good news is Anthony seems to be quite successful as the Senator's aide. I can't find any adverse information on him," Karen said. "I'm not supposed to do this, but I took a brief glance at his financials. Nothing alarming, no bankruptcies, excellent credit, nothing to concern oneself with."

"You think he's on the up and up? Just not the friendliest of personalities?" Tommy asked.

Karen laughed. "I know he can be a bit abrupt, but as far as his background there's nothing alarming. His connections in DC make it worth tolerating the abrasive personality in exchange for the business he brings in."

Tommy sat for a moment, watching Karen scroll through more screens. "What do I owe you?" he said.

"Nothing," she replied. "I was able to do this all through sites where I have unlimited access. No extra charges accrued."

"I appreciate this, Karen. Are you sure I can't compensate you for your time?" Tommy asked.

"You buy the coffee next time," Karen said. "How's that?"

"Deal," Tommy said. "Thanks again."

Returning to Jennifer's office, he found Tim on the phone.

"Who you talking to?" Tommy asked.

Donahue held up his hand for Tommy to wait.

"Really," Donahue said into the phone, grabbing a notepad and pen. "Tell me again what she said. Lovely, thanks. I'll be sharing that with him momentarily." Donahue hung up and wrote a few more lines.

"So?" Tommy asked, hands outstretched, palms up.

"The surveillance team updating me on your friend Karen," Donahue said. "Seems as soon as you left the office she called Sorin and filled him in."

"What did she tell him?" Tommy asked.

A broad smile crossed Donahue's face. "I have it here," Donahue said, waving the paper. "I wrote it down, so I could do it proper justice."

"Tim, what the fuck are you talking about?" Tommy said, his frustration growing.

"Ahem, ahem," Donahue cleared his throat. "She said, and I quote, 'I just talked to the blockhead Moore. He bought the story. East Providence PD must have some real morons. He is supposed to be a detective. He's not bright enough to be a school crossing guard."

"That fucking bitch," Tommy said. "I should go over there and slap that fake smile right off her face."

"Tommy," Donahue said, his smile growing wider, "is that anyway to talk about someone who is such an intuitive appraiser of her fellow humans."

Tommy laughed. "We'll see how intuitive she is once I lock her ass up."

* * *

Josh and Zach walked into the lobby of the news station. Approaching the receptionist, Josh showed his badge and ID. "We're here to see Mr. Collins. I'm Lieutenant Williams, East Providence Police."

"Just a moment, I'll see if Mr. Collins is available," the receptionist said, smiling at Josh.

"I bet he will be when you tell him who it is," Josh smiled back.

A moment later the receptionist said, "Mr. Collins will be right down. He wanted to know if you would like coffee, tea, or water. I'd be happy to get that for you."

"You know, that would be nice, if it's not too much trouble?" Josh answered. "Coffee for me, cream and sugar. Zach?"

"I'll have coffee as well, the same way."

"I'll be right back," she said, heading off to get the coffees.

Jim Collins appeared in the lobby wearing a dark colored suit, maroon tie, and a headset with microphone boom around his neck.

"Lieutenant Williams, what a surprise," he said, shaking Josh's hand. "I see you have your secret partner with you, Special Agent Zach Kennedy of the FBI," enjoying the look of surprise in Kennedy's eyes.

"We are not without our own resources," Collins smiled, shaking Kennedy's hand.

"I am sure you are not," Kennedy said. Leaning closer and whispering in Collins's ear, "But I caution you about what you do with the information, Mr. Collins." Squeezing the hand until Collins pulled away.

Rubbing his hand, Collins said, "Now that the pleasantries are over, let's go to my conference room."

Josh looked toward the missing receptionist.

"Not to worry," Collins said. "She'll bring the coffee," gesturing toward the door, "The conference room is this way."

As they settled in around the table, the coffees arrived. "Will there be anything else, Gentlemen?"

"No, thank you Yvonne that will be all. Would you call Candace Ferguson and have her come to the conference room, please?" Collins said.

"Of course, I'll get her right away," closing the door behind her.

"Okay," Collins said, looking around the room. "Before Candace gets here, let's leave out any discussions of our earlier meeting. Leave it that you decided to speak to us in light of new developments and want to provide some more information. Agreed?"

Josh nodded. Kennedy just ignored the remarks, sorting through some documents in his briefcase.

"Mr. Kennedy?" Collins asked, "Are we in agreement?"

Kennedy looked up, "I'm sorry, Mr. Collins is it? I am terrible with names, particularly when I have just met someone. I apologize, what was the question?"

Josh tried to conceal his smile but failed. Collins just sat in silence, looking at Kennedy.

The door opened, breaking the quiet, and Candace came into the room. Collins motioned for her to sit down, "Candace, I assume you know these gentlemen."

"I do indeed. How are you?" Candace said.

"Well, we were just getting acquainted with Mr. Collins, Jim I believe," Kennedy said. "Just a couple of new friends."

The smile on Josh's face grew wider and he looked away for a moment, scratching the back of his head. "When we heard the story got pulled," Josh said. "We wanted to find out why and let you know we've found some more information. That's the reason for our visit."

Candace looked at Collins, "Jim will have to address the reason behind the story getting tanked. I was under the impression it was ready to go. Jim, you want to answer that?"

Collins cleared his throat and put his arms on the table, hands folded. "I held the story based on a request," making the quote sign with his hands, "from corporate. Maurio Bartoletti himself, our CEO, called me and asked me to hold the story."

"Did he say why?" Josh asked.

"Not in so many words. But it was clear it had to do with the pending merger," Collins answered.

"Merger, what merger?" Josh replied, feigning ignorance.

"ANM Media, our parent company, and ZMI News Media are in the midst of negotiations. There is a petition pending before the FCC to approve this merger. Once the vote happens, the process can move forward. Without it," Collins explained, "it is dead in the water."

"What does that have to do with this story? There's no relation to your company," Josh asked, glancing at Kennedy.

"I have no idea, but it was obvious to me he was getting pressure from someone with a great deal of influence," Collins said. "Your guess is as good as mine who it was."

Josh looked at Kennedy. Kennedy gave him a slight nod.

"Jim, Candace," Josh said, "what I am going to share with you will corroborate the story. You have to assure me you will not reveal the source of this information, agreed?"

Collins glanced at Candace, and then faced Josh. "I am sure I don't have to explain the protections of the First Amendment to you, but I do answer to my corporate office. They may ask where we got the information."

"Then you tell them it came from me. No one else but me," Josh said. "Make sure you understand this before we go any further."

Collins nodded.

"I believed what we had was more than enough," Candace said, shooting a glance at Collins. "But if you have something even bigger we need to move fast before they try to stop it, again."

Josh opened a folder and took out a picture, "Do either of you know this man?"

Collins slid the picture over, looked at it, and then passed it Candace. "I don't know him."

Candace looked it over, "No, me either. Who is he?"

"That, my friends, is your new CEO. Shashenka Dmitriev, current CEO of ZMI News," Josh said, seeing the reaction by Collins.

"You knew? You knew all about the merger. What is this about? What's going on here you're not telling us?" Collins asked, glancing back and forth between Kennedy and Josh.

"Dmitriev is a naturalized American citizen," Kennedy explained. "He was born in Russia, served in the KGB with Vladimir Putin, and made billions of dollars in gas and oil production."

Collins face blanched.

"That's right Mr. Collins, your company is about to become part of a multi-national conglomerate. One controlled by Russian organized crime," Kennedy said. "The early stuff we fed you might have derailed that, but now? Well, now we need to step up the pressure a bit. So, what's it going to be? You gonna show some spine and run with this, or you gonna just hide and hope it goes away?"

Once Collins regained his composure, Josh laid out the interconnections between the Russians, Sorin, and Collucci. He detailed the links between the companies involved in the waterfront projects, the infiltration of the lottery and casinos, and the Cayman Island money laundering.

By the time he finished, Collins appeared stunned by it all.

"I bet if we looked hard enough at this, we'd find Collucci using his influence to squash the story. We know he knows about it. This has his fingerprints all over it. Is that enough for you to move forward on this, Jim?" Josh asked. "Because if not, I'll find someone who will."

Collins looked at Josh, "I think, Lieutenant Williams, I have an obligation to do so. If just half of what you say is true, this is the biggest story of governmental corruption since Watergate."

Josh smiled at Collins, "I have one more thing for you," handing Collins the affidavit from Tucker.

Collins read over the ten-page document. "Holy shit, this is unbelievable. Where'd you get this?" Collins asked, sliding the document to Candace.

"I do not normally reveal sources, but in this case I'll make an exception," Josh said. "The judge gave it to me. Told me to deliver it to whomever I thought could use it. He gave his permission for you to use as you see fit."

Collins took out a notepad and wrote something, "Candace, call this number. Have them meet us at the downtown studio. We're going to redo the original production, add in as much of this new information as we can, and get it on the air tomorrow. We'll do a two-part expose', start with the Grey case and the affidavit from the Judge. Then, do the real damage with the second part when the interest in it is at a peak."

Candace questioned him with her look.

"We can't risk using our production staff. Someone will tip headquarters if we start working on this again," Collins explained. "We're going to use some URI Harrington School Communication students to do the production. They've been working with our equipment for some time now. They can handle this. Once the story breaks, no one will be able to stop it."

Collins rose from his seat and walked to stand next to Kennedy.

Kennedy stood, one hand leaning on the table.

"Mr. Kennedy," Collins said. "I owe you an apology. I hoped my little surprise might annoy or intimidate you. It was childish on my part. I appreciate you bringing this to us."

"Jim, you just make this as good as you can. I'll be happy with that," Kennedy answered, closing his briefcase and hanging the strap over his shoulder.

Candace, Kennedy, and Josh walked out of the office. Candace motioned for them to follow her into a small, backup studio. "Well we got his attention," she said. "How did you convince Tucker to give you the affidavit? It's gold for these kinds of stories."

"I didn't," Josh said. "We brought Jennifer to see him and her daughter. We have them in a safe location. Tucker just gave it to me."

"Can I ask you something, if it's not too much trouble?" Kennedy said, causing Candace and Josh to look at him.

"Ah, sure. What?" Candace said.

"Can I see it?" Kennedy smiled.

Josh looked at Candace then back at Kennedy, "See what?" Josh asked.

"She knows," Kennedy said. "Her husband and I discussed it."

Candace chuckled, "Okay, hang on." Disappearing for a moment, she returned and said, "Follow me."

The trio walked out to the back lot. Josh spotted the two troopers assigned to the station security detail parked in the lot and waved at them.

Candace opened her car, reached behind the passenger seat, and put the weapon on the front seat, "Don't hurt yourself." She stepped back as Kennedy sat in the car.

Josh watched while Kennedy examined the Saiga shotgun and the barrel magazine. "Oh man, I've got to get one of these," Kennedy said, admiring the weapon.

"Boys and their toys," Candace chuckled. "Would you like to handle it as well, Lieutenant?"

Josh laughed, backing away, hands up. "Nope, I'm good. Not a big gun nut like my friend here."

* * *

The group gathered in the Chief's conference room, awaiting the start of the 6 PM news. Josh, Tommy Moore, Jennifer Sorin, and Judge Tucker sat at the table. Tim Donahue, Joe Moreira, and Zach Kennedy stood behind them.

Just outside the office, Donna, the Chief's aide, entertained Kelsey Tucker. "You sure you don't mind doing this Donna?" Brennan asked.

"Not at all, working here I have a lot of experience babysitting."

"Good point," Brennan chuckled, leading the way to the conference room, accompanied by Chris, Maggie, Keira, and Loren Grey.

Josh and Tommy got up to let the others have a seat. "Well, aren't you the gentleman?" Chris said, sitting in Tommy's seat.

"Didn't want you to faint from having to stand, old lady," Moore replied.

"Chief, do you have the pictures of my friend here trussed up in the ladies' room handy by any chance?" Chris said.

"Okay, okay. Sorry," Moore said, moving to lean against the wall.

"If I'd have known that's all it took to get you under control I'd have had Hamlin do that years ago," Brennan said.

The opening music for the news broadcast started. Josh hit the remote to turn up the sound....

Tonight, an I-Team exclusive. An investigation into a tragic injustice and corruption in some of the highest offices of government. That comes up following today's headlines....

Josh muted the sound. "Well, this should be interesting. Zach, anything new out of DC on Sorin or Collucci?"

Kennedy smiled, "The usual political doublespeak from Collucci. His office sent out a press release trying to get out in front of it, calling it a politically motivated attack. Sorin has been MIA since the story teasers started. He's gone missing off the grid."

"What do you think that means?" Josh asked.

"Either the Russians see him as a liability and moved to minimize the damage, or he is orchestrating some response. In any case, I'd say our friend Collucci has some big problems."

"It's back on," Chris said, grabbing the remote and turning it up.

…I-Team investigative journalist, Candace Ferguson, has the exclusive story. Candace, what have you uncovered?

The camera view changed to a live feed of Candace standing in front of the Superior Court building on South Main Street.

Thank you, Mark. The I-Team has learned of a terrible injustice leading to the death of an innocent man in state custody while awaiting trial….

The camera changed to a view of Darnell Grey in his Army Ranger uniform. Over the next 60 seconds, Candace detailed the botched investigation leading to Grey's arrest, his placement in the general population, and his murder in prison.

She did a remarkable job of winnowing down the investigation into sound bites and images. Senator Collucci's involvement was the focal point of the story, the affidavit from Judge Tucker cementing Collucci's participation. The interview with Loren Grey and Alpha Babes Investigations played a prominent part in the story.

The scene switched back to Candace, the Superior court in the background.

Keira Williams, the Attorney representing Loren Grey, told us she intends to file a motion in court to dismiss the charges against Darnell Grey. She acknowledges this is a merely symbolic gesture. Ms. Williams also said they are exploring the possibility of a civil law suit because of Grey's death while in state custody."

Thank you, Candace for that story. Has Senator Collucci responded to this at all?

We have contacted Senator Collucci for his response to these allegations. So far, there has been nothing from his office other than a short press release. We have been unable to speak to the Senator.

Thank you again, Candace. Now, time for today's forecast…

Josh flicked the TV off. "What do you think?"

"I think we made our point, did some damage to Collucci. Now, seeing how he reacts will be most interesting," Brennan said. "When will the next story break?"

"Candace said they're going to try to interview Collucci," Josh said. "She thinks his ego won't let him hide for long. She's hoping to lure him into a studio interview, and then ambush him with the new allegations."

"Let's hope the national media notices this and runs with it," Kennedy added.

Tommy picked up his coffee and headed to the door. "I did notice one big thing the national media couldn't miss," he said, drawing everyone's attention. Satisfied he had a captive audience, he smiled. "They say the camera adds ten pounds. I can tell you that's not the case." Pointing at Chris, "Seeing that view of her fat ass added at least twenty or more."

The room broke into laughter.

Chris started around the table after him; Josh tried to slow her down.

Brennan said, "Let her go, Josh. Boy is a glutton for punishment, sooner or later he'll learn."

A few moments later, talking over the yelling and screaming coming from the hallway, Brennan said, "Sounds like he's learning another lesson as we speak," bringing the room to a new level of laughter.

Chapter 37

Sorin sat in the Senator's office fielding phone calls from other Senators, trying to control the damage. Collucci came in, looking exhausted. "Where have you been?" he said, glaring at Sorin.

Sorin held up his hand for Collucci to wait, "I'll have to call you back, Senator. Yes, yes, I know. This is all politics. Nothing has changed. The Senator appreciates your support. Thank you," ending the call.

"So, what the hell just happened, Robert?" Sorin asked.

"Those pieces of shit Williams and Tucker did this. I wish that fucking nigger did have a gun back then and killed Williams before Williams killed him. He'd be a forgotten dead cop, instead of a pain in my ass."

All five lines in the Senator's office were ringing, "Go out there and tell the damn secretary to put the phones on night service. I am not talking to anybody right now," Collucci said.

Sorin left the office and returned a moment later, the lights on the phone lines continued flashing, but the ringing had stopped.

"What are you going to do, Senator? You have any ideas?" Sorin asked.

"Nothing, we do nothing. We let it blow over as it always does. This is all sound and fury; there is no truth here. Nothing linking me. We'll do a longer press release tomorrow. Let's get out of here and go find somewhere they don't know me. Get a drink and forget about this for a while, "Collucci said.

The two left the Senator's office. Looking out the front door, they saw the media horde lying in wait.

"Where's yours parked?" Collucci asked.

"Inside parking garage."

"Great, we'll take yours."

A few moments later, Sorin drove out of the lot heading away from the crowd.

"We still have problems, you know. The second part of the story, remember? We don't have a clue what is in it. If it mentions our friends, we have a bigger problem. One which a press conference won't solve," Sorin said.

"There is no way they have anything about it. How could they?" Collucci asked.

Sorin shook his head. "Because one of our property managers has an undercover cop working in her office, perhaps? Why else would he be there?"

Collucci laughed aloud. "Anthony, you're not from Rhode Island so you wouldn't understand. It is small, unsophisticated, and simple minded. This mindset infects those who make up the police departments. The East

Providence Police do not have the intelligence to figure out what we have done. They thought they could catch me boo-hooing the poor dead innocent black guy I sent to the can. Dumb-asses."

"What about the Feds?" Sorin asked. "If they get involved, that's a whole different animal."

"I have my resources within the FBI. There's nothing going on. If they had an open case, I would know. Now find me a quiet bar to have a drink. I need to think for a bit," Collucci said.

The two FBI agents in the surveillance van smiled.

"I can't wait to play the 'dumb local cop' line for Josh and Tommy. I cannot wait," one of the agents chuckled.

* * *

Sorin's cell phone rang, "Yes?"

"I am with the Senator, can't this wait? Okay, I understand, of course."

Sorin hung up and turned the car around, "Change of plan, Dmitriev wants to meet. Where do you want me to drop you off?"

"Doesn't the almighty one want to meet with both of us?" Collucci asked, the veins in his neck throbbing.

"No," Sorin snapped. "Now where do you want to go, or do I just drop you back at the lot to talk to the media? Your call."

"Take me home; drop me off on the back street. I can get in without anyone knowing I'm there," Collucci said, resigned to his status. "I'll stay there for a while."

As they pulled onto the street behind Collucci's home, Sorin cautioned him. "Do not do anything until you hear from me."

Collucci ignored him, opening the door. Sorin grabbed his arm. Collucci glared. "I am serious, Robert. You heard Dmitriev. Do nothing without me."

Collucci snarled at him, "Don't push this too hard, Anthony. I am not afraid of you or him," slamming the door as he walked away.

After dropping Collucci off, Sorin drove to the downtown area, parked the car and hailed a cab. He directed the driver to an address on Embassy Row.

He hailed a second cab, taking this to a small, unremarkable building behind the United State Supreme Court. As the cab drove off, a black limo arrived. Sorin got in.

"Anthony, how are you?" Dmitriev said. "Would you care for some vodka?"

"Definitely Shasha," he said, a tentative look on his face, "I am still extended this privilege, no?"

"Of course, my friend, no worries as these Americans say," handing Sorin a glass. "But with the Senator, my patience grows thin. Are you sure he is worth this effort?"

"As Chairman of the Banking Committee, his assistance will be most beneficial. Assuming he survives this controversy," Sorin said, sipping the drink.

"And if not?" Dmitriev asked.

"Then we would have to reevaluate his usefulness," Sorin answered. "It has taken a considerable effort to get to this point. I believe this will pass. American politics are fickle. Today it's Collucci, tomorrow someone else."

Sorin smiled, "Speaking of which, don't we have some images we can leak of some other Congressmen? If I know you, Shasha, you've got a treasure trove of useful information." Raising his glass in toast.

"That is one possibility, my friend. But under the circumstances I do not think it would be sufficient," offering to refill Sorin's glass. Sorin accepted the vodka and settled back into the seat, studying Dmitriev.

"In light of this, Anton Antonevich," he used the Russian term of endearment, "I have decided to do some traditional Russian intervention. We cannot afford to lose Mr. Collucci at this point. It may change in the future, but for now we must move to protect him as one of our valuable assets."

Dmitriev reached into his jacket pocket, took out a notepad, wrote something, and then handed it to Sorin.

"I understand you will be returning to Rhode Island soon. Call that number," pointing at the note, "arrange to meet with our friends. They will need guidance in locating the targets and determining their vulnerabilities."

"Targets? What targets?" Sorin asked.

Dmitriev looked at Sorin, his eyes looking for any doubt or resistance. "The police officers and the Judge responsible for this news story. I want them eliminated."

"But Shasha, if we--"

Dmitriev cut him off. "This is not open to further discussion. Once they understand the risks they incur, they will think twice before interfering with our goals."

"What about the last time?" Sorin asked. "It seemed to steel their resolve, not lessen it."

"Last time was an amateurish attempt," Dmitriev said. "My men are not amateurs." As these words came out, his eyes burned with an anger unfamiliar to Sorin. "Do as I ask, and we will move on."

Sorin nodded, folded the paper, and put it in his pocket.

Dmitriev saw the concern on Sorin's face. "Not to worry, Anthony. They will make it look like a hit by some street gang members or a botched robbery. One of those commonplace occurrences that plague this country. There will be nothing to link it to us."

Sorin nodded. "I will see to it, Shasha."

"I know you will, Anton Antonevich, of that I am certain."

Chapter 38

Sorin and Collucci waited in the Senator's congressional office for their driver to arrive. The news story had run its course, overtaken by the passage of time and other news.

"Are you sure this is a good idea?" Sorin asked. "No one cares about it anymore, let it go."

"Anthony, how long have you and I worked together?" Collucci said. "Did you think I would let a little political ambush of a news report intimidate me? Call that reporter, arrange the interview."

"Dmitriev told you everything needed to be cleared through me. Remember?"

"He isn't running my goddamn campaign. I do that," Collucci slammed his hands on the desk. "You are my Chief of Staff, not his. I need to continue in this position if I am to be useful. Is that not true? I know how to do damage control. That is my bailiwick. If you want to tell him what I am doing, go right ahead. However, I am doing this with you, or without you. Makes no difference to me."

As Sorin reached for his cell phone, Collucci grabbed his arm. "Tell them the interview will be in my office tomorrow 2:00. Not open for any discussions. Are we clear?"

Sorin nodded.

"And it's just the reporter and the cameraman. No one else," Collucci added, looking over as the door to the office opened.

"Senator, the car is here. The driver said there are several reporters waiting outside also. Do you want him to go around to the private parking garage entrance?" The aide asked.

Collucci smiled, "Of course not, Yvonne. The media has a job to do. I have a responsibility to be available. Tell the driver to stay where he is. We'll be down."

After the door closed, Collucci sat back in his chair. "Make the call, Anthony. Take your time in the conversation. There's no need to rush," Collucci said, folding his hands behind his head. "I will give our friends in the media their chance at asking questions, but I will make them wait a bit for the opportunity."

While Sorin arranged for the interview, Collucci reviewed his notes. They may think they have wounded me, but it would be a mistake. Two can play at the innuendo game and I have had a lot more practice.

"All set," Sorin said, putting his phone back in his pocket. "2:00 pm our office in Providence."

Collucci nodded without looking up. "Okay, let's go," he said, closing his briefcase. "Time to show these bastards how to play the character assassination game."

Striding out the front of the building, Collucci smiled as the media surrounded him.

"Senator Collucci, how do you respond to the allegations you framed an innocent man?"

"Senator, is it true you concealed evidence in the Grey case?"

"Senator, do you take responsibility for the death of Darnell Grey?"

Collucci handed his briefcase to the driver, motioned for Sorin to get in the car, and then turned to face the cameras.

"Ladies and Gentlemen. I do not understand the basis of these questions. What I saw on television the other day was nothing more than a politically motivated attack. An attack on the integrity of the criminal justice system and my character. In my over 40 years of service to this country, I have never violated an oath of office."

Collucci turned to get in the car.

The reporters continued to shout questions.

Collucci looked back, holding up his hands. "Just so you'll all have this clear. This reporter, Candace Ferguson, breaks a story based on alleged information from a liberal civil rights attorney married to a defendant I once prosecuted for shooting an unarmed black man. This same reporter is married to the defense lawyer who represented the officer," shaking his head, "if that is not a sordid little mess, I don't know what is. Look into their motivations. Therein lies a story," Collucci opened the car door.

"Instead of standing here shouting questions based on lies and innuendos, why don't you act like reporters and look into *those* facts."

Collucci climbed into the car, slammed the door, and ordered the driver to head to the airport.

* * *

Candace Ferguson knocked on the station manager's door. Collins looked up and saw her through the side panel glass. He motioned for her to come in.

"Good morning, what's up?" he asked.

"You are not going to believe the phone call I just received," Candace said.

Collins sat back in his chair, "Do I have to guess, or will you be telling me anytime soon?"

"Anthony Sorin," Candace replied.

"Who?"

"Anthony Sorin, Collucci's Chief of Staff. He called and arranged a personal interview with Collucci tomorrow afternoon, 2:00 PM in the Senator's office."

Collins leaned forward, "Are you serious? I cannot believe... no wait; we're talking about Collucci here. His ego is bigger than anyone I have ever met and believe me I have met some major egomaniacs. Tell me the conversation."

"Well," Candace began, "there wasn't much to it. Sorin called and asked if I would hear the Senator's side of the story. He told me the Senator would meet with me at his office for an interview. I was to come alone with just the camera operator. No one else and....."

"And what?" Collins asked.

"And we could do whatever we want during and after the interview, but there was to be no publicity about it beforehand."

"Do you think he suspects there's a second story coming about him?" Collins asked.

"I don't know what to think. He may be trying to contain the damage, or fishing to see what else we may have. Either way this is great for us. He said I could ask him anything. So, I'll ask. On camera," Candace said. "I should call Josh and tell him."

"No, do not call anyone about this. This is our story. We decide what we want to do with it. This is not a police matter," Collins said, looking at Candace to see her reaction.

Candace gave Collins a withering look, "Don't you think we owe him at least a heads up about this? We would not have this story without him. There may be some things he can feed me to ask Collucci," Candace argued.

"Candace, look. We don't work for them. We're not a tool for the police. We are not here to help them do something they cannot do under the law. I appreciate the fact they brought this to us, but they did it because they could not do what we can. If they could have accomplished their purpose without us, they would have," Collins said. "This stays in house, understand?"

Candace nodded and left the office. The reason you did anything, Mr. Collins, is Josh and the FBI pushed you. Okay, can't tell Josh, he didn't say I couldn't tell someone to tell Josh. She called Hawk.

* * *

The American Airlines flight from Ronald Reagan airport to Providence took just under an hour. Collucci and Sorin boarded as part of the pre-board group. They sat in the first row. While many of those boarding the plane recognized the Senator, no one said anything to him.

As the aircraft taxied to the gate, Sorin took out his cell and placed a call to the limo driver.

"Are things in place?" he asked.

"All set, Mr. Sorin. The media is here, near baggage claim. I spoke to the American Airlines station manager. She was most accommodating. As soon as the door opens, she will meet us in the jetway and escort us through the security area. The airport police will be there as well to provide security. They've arranged for me to be waiting at the airport corporation secure parking area."

"Excellent, thank you." Sorin put the phone away. "The local station manager will take us out through the secure area. The media is in the baggage claim area. We'll avoid them and be gone before they even realize it."

Collucci nodded. "Should be a rather interesting few days, don't you think?"

Sorin tried to smile. "I hope this is the right thing to do. You may be setting yourself up for bigger problems."

Collucci patted him on the shoulder. "Nonsense, Anthony. I live for this stuff. This will all blow over and we'll move ahead with things. Trust me on this; I know what I am doing. You just make sure our support for the Chairmanship stays firm. Some of those Senators sway with the slightest breeze. Keep the pressure on them."

The plane came to a stop, seat belt light went off, and the door opened.

A slight woman in her mid-forties stepped aboard. "Senator? Barbara Johnson, I'm the American Airlines station manager," extending her hand. "If you'll follow me gentlemen, I'll get you out of here."

Collucci shook her hand, grabbed his briefcase, and followed her. As they left the jetway, she directed them toward an alarmed door. Two airport police officers stood to either side of the door. She swiped her card, entered a code, and opened the door.

As one officer held the door, she directed the Senator and Sorin out the door and down the stairs. Weaving through corridors beneath the terminal, they came to a gated area facing a secured parking lot.

Once again, she swiped the card and entered the code. The gate opened.

"Thank you so much, Ms. Johnson. You've been most helpful," Collucci said, walking through the open gate. Sorin shook her hand and followed the Senator. Their driver waited by the car, doors opened.

As the car drove off, Collucci waved at the woman and the two police officers. They returned the wave.

One officer looked over at his compatriot, "They all think they're so damn special, don't they? Wonder if he would feel the same if we told him this is the way they take out the garbage as well."

The others laughed.

As the car left the parking lot, Sorin placed a call to the number Dmitriev had given him.

"Yes, Mr. Sorin, I've been expecting your call. When can we meet?"

"This afternoon. Name the location," Sorin replied.

Collucci raised his eyebrows as he listened to Sorin, waving his hand to get his attention he said, "I am not meeting anyone today."

Sorin ignored him.

"I will be at Waterplace Park, the benches near the mall. Please come alone." The call ended.

"Anthony, I am not meeting--"

"Stop," Sorin snapped. "The meeting is not of concern to you."

The tone caught Collucci by surprise. "Is this something from my ex-friend Shasha, I suppose?"

Sorin turned in the seat, facing Collucci. He pushed the button for the privacy screen between the back seat and the driver and waited for it to close.

"Mr. Dmitriev is not happy with you at the moment. You would do well to keep that in mind, Robert. Do not delude yourself with your belief in your power or position. If you are as smart as you think you are, you will resolve this problem. You need to focus. All that matters is that you take over the Chairmanship and continue to make yourself useful. If you fail ... well let's just say it would be in your best interest not to."

Collucci looked at his assistant; he started to speak then thought better of it. We will see who is capable of what, my friend. We will see.

Chapter 39

Josh's cell phone rang. Looking at the caller ID, he saw it was Hawk Bennett, "Hawk, what can I do for you? You haven't terminated someone with extreme prejudice, have you?"

Kennedy looked up from his laptop when he heard the name. Donahue and Moreira also showed interest.

"Not yet, but I do have some news," Hawk answered. "It would seem your two best friends in the world Misters Collucci and Sorin are coming back to Rhode Island soon."

"Hawk, come on. The whole world knows," Josh said. "Collucci's travels are well documented, particularly in light of the sudden media interest. We're watching every move. Tell me something I don't know."

"Well then, my omniscient police officer friend, do you know what Mr. Collucci will be doing tomorrow afternoon at 2:00 PM?"

"Resigning?" Josh asked.

The other investigators were even more attentive.

"We couldn't be so lucky," Hawk answered. "No, it's much more intriguing. He will be participating in a one-on-one interview with my wife. What say you to that?"

"When did you find out? Why didn't Candace call me?" Josh asked.

"It would seem the station manager, Mr. Collins, no longer feels any obligation to include you in the inner circle. He directed Candace not to call you," Hawk said. "He neglected to tell her not to talk to me about it nor does he have any control over what I might do with this information."

"Wow, thanks Hawk. I'd like to talk to her before the interview. Think we can arrange it?" Josh asked.

"I will see to it, expect a call soon. Take care," Hawk hung up.

Josh looked up to see three faces staring at him.

"So?" Kennedy said, "What the hell was that about. Is Collucci resigning?"

Josh laughed, "Nope, next best thing though. He's going to let Candace have a one-on-one interview. Tomorrow."

"No shit?" Donahue said. "He has no idea the nightmare he's about to walk into, does he?"

"So, what do we do?" Kennedy asked.

"Hawk's going to arrange for me to speak to Candace. The station manager told her not to call us."

"He what?" Kennedy said, "That little fucking weasel turd slimy no balls piece of crap."

"Whoa there, Mr. FBI," Josh said. "Is that appropriate language for a federal agent?"

Donahue and Moreira laughed. Kennedy smiled, "I just can't believe that slimeball wouldn't even extend us the courtesy of a call. Next time, I am going to break his damn hand."

"Somebody write that down. I may need it next time some FBI agent wants to talk to me about a brutality complaint," Donahue chuckled.

Josh's cell phone rang, the caller ID blocked. "Hello," Josh answered.

"Hey Josh, it's Candace."

"Well, that was quick. Where are you?"

"In my car, using one of Hawk's special phones. He told you about Collucci right? Can you believe it?"

"Hawk did fill me in," Josh said. "I can't say I'm surprised. I assumed he would try to find a way to fight back. So, how are you going to handle him?"

"That's what I wanted to run by you," Candace said.

"Hold on, I'm gonna put the phone on speaker so we can all discuss this," Josh said, motioning for the others to gather round the desk. "Okay, Candace. We're all listening," Josh said

"Hi, guys. Anyway, what I was saying is I will lead in with the Grey case. I'll let him air his explanations and excuses, then ask about the affiliation with the Russians. How far can I go with this? I don't want to force them to react violently in light of the threats they've already made."

"Candace, it's Zach Kennedy, as long as you don't mention the source of the information I'm comfortable with you using anything you have. We'll be keeping a close watch on things from now on. Once this breaks, they'll regroup and try to find a way to contain the problem or throw Collucci to the wolves and find another Senator. They'll protect themselves and hang him out to dry."

"How about I do this, after we discuss the Grey case I'll ask him if he thinks this will have any effect on his waterfront project. Let him take the conversation in that direction. Once he begins discussing it, I'll ask about the business fronts and the Russian links. Sound good?" Candace said.

Josh spoke up, "I think that's a smart way to approach him. I know he said to come there alone, and I doubt his friends would risk doing anything, but just out of a sense of precaution, we'll be in the area. Although, I will assume your husband will have his own arrangements."

"I am sure he will," Candace chuckled. "Okay, thanks guys. I have a bunch of things to review and preparations to make. Talk to you soon."

Josh canceled the speaker function, and then looked around. "So, what do you think? Will this be enough to bring down this whole thing?"

Zach Kennedy stood up and walked over to pour coffee. "If the Russians see him as a liability they will not leave him out there. Now, before anyone goes ballistic on me, hear me out." Kennedy looked at the three men watching him.

"I realize the guy is a scumbag piece of shit, but he is a sitting United States Senator. It is likely they will kill Collucci and Sorin, if for no other reason than to show others the risk in failure."

"I don' think I am going to like where this is going, am I Zach?" Josh said.

Kennedy smiled, "Probably not. The Justice Department would not be pleased if we did nothing while a foreign organized crime group assassinates a sitting US Senator, no matter how much of a son-of-a-bitch he is."

"Are you fucking kidding me?" Donahue chimed in. "You want us to protect the asshole?"

"In a manner of speaking," Kennedy said. "I think we should try and turn him. Convince him to cooperate."

"I can't believe what I am hearing," Donahue said, turning to his partner. "Joe, can you believe this? Now we're gonna try to work with this asshole. Unbelievable."

Joe Moreira shook his head, "I hate to admit it, but it does make sense. He's an arrogant bastard, doesn't realize the shit he's stepped in. But, it is worth a shot. Hell, Tim, we used to warn mob guys all the time when we had info they were gonna get whacked. We turned a few guys and got some good information. I don't like it much, but I think we need to give it a shot."

Kennedy looked at Josh, "Well?"

Josh rolled a pen repeatedly in his fingers. "You know, I knew I would regret letting them talk me into working with the damn FBI," smiling at Kennedy, "but you're right. We should at least give it a shot."

Donahue rolled his chair back, put his feet on desk, and folded his arms. "I vote to let them whack the son-of-a-bitch. It will serve him right. Aren't we forgetting they tried to kill Keira? Isn't this the same case?"

"Oh, we're not forgetting that, Tim. We're not forgetting any of it," Josh said. "But I think it's s worth a shot just for the look on his face when I tell him what we have. Hell, he may shit the bed right there."

Laughter filled the room. The door opened, and Chief Brennan walked in.

"Did I miss the joke?" He asked.

"Nope," Donahue said, pointing. "Tommy's still here."

Tommy flipped him off.

Brennan sat on the edge of the desk while Josh filled him in on the developments.

"And you think this is the way to go?" Brennan asked, looking around the room.

"Well, everybody but Donahue. He thinks we should help the Russians kill him," Josh joked.

"No, I don't," Donahue said, slamming his hands on the desk. "I think we should let the Russians kill him, and then we kill the Russians," as a smile crossed his face.

Brennan smiled, "I can appreciate that. So, when will this great conversation take place?"

"After the interview," Josh said. "Once Candace leaves, we'll go talk to Collucci. Meanwhile, we'll run full-time surveillance on Sorin. He showed back up in Rhode Island with the Senator; we thought they may have liquidated him."

"Liquidated?" Brennan said, "What are we cold war spies now or have you been playing Moore's video games?"

"I just like the word," Josh laughed. "I think from now on I will make it a practice of liquidating my enemies. I like how it rolls off the tongue."

"Chief," Donahue said, "this boy needs help. Serious help. How is it he managed to fool my cousin into marrying him?"

"That's a question we all struggle with I'm afraid," Brennan answered.

* * *

The surveillance team sat parked across from the Senator's office. Shortly after 3:00 pm, Sorin left the office, walking toward City Hall.

"Where do you think he's going?" Josh asked.

"Not sure," Donahue answered, "his cell phone hasn't been active. I'd bet he's using burner phones. Call Zach; tell him we need more bodies down here. Whatever he's up to, we need to stay with him."

While Josh made the call, Donahue got out of the van to follow Sorin. They walked through Kennedy Plaza, down to the Biltmore.

Sorin went in the front door of the hotel and waited just inside, watching the street.

Donahue realized Sorin was trying to spot any surveillance. *I don't think so. Been doing this a long time.* Donahue sat on the steps of the City Hall, eating the sandwich he'd brought with him. The angle of the sun illuminated the Biltmore entrance, silhouetting Sorin in the light.

Satisfied he was alone; Sorin came back out the door heading toward to Providence Place mall.

Donahue's cell rang, "Yup."

"Tim, Zach. Got three more agents available, where are you?"

"Heading toward the mall, we're just going through the lot near the Capital Grille. He's wearing--"

"We got it, Josh sent us a picture. I'll wait over near the GTECH building with one of the other agents. The other two will get closer to the mall. If he's meeting someone he'll want a crowd to get lost in."

Walking through the lot of the Capital Grille, Sorin took Memorial Boulevard to Waterplace Park. He followed the river, crossing over the pedestrian bridge into the park.

"He's headed into the park," Donahue said into his cell.

"I got him," Zach replied. "There's a guy sitting on the bench along the water, dark jacket, baseball hat. See him?"

"Yup,"

"He's been looking around, looks like he's waiting for someone. Sorin's heading right toward him. Hold on a minute, I am gonna conference in the other agents."

A moment later, Kennedy said, "Okay, we have a guy at Cafe Nuovo and one at the bridge crossing the river just west of them. Where's Josh?"

"Hang on," Donahue said, calling Josh and adding him into the call.

"Where are you now Josh?"

"I am parked near Jackie's Galaxy, got a perfect shot of them with the surveillance cameras."

Sorin approached the bench, shook the man's hand, and then sat down.

"You have a job for me?"

"I do," Sorin answered, reaching into his pocket and handing the man an envelope.

"When does this need to be done?"

"The addresses, notes of places frequented, all you need to be successful is there." Sorin rose from the bench. "Do this as soon as you can."

Sorin walked away, stopped, and turned back to the man. "When you go after the police officer named Meadows, if there is a woman with him, kill her also."

The man studied Sorin, "It is not part of the contract," he said.

"Do it for as a favor for me," Sorin replied, walking away.

* * *

Josh shot off images and video of the meeting, focusing on the faces. As Sorin left, Josh said," So now what, do we let this guy go?"

"I don't think so," Donahue said. "We have no idea who he is, where he's from, nothing. We can contain this here. I say we snatch him and squeeze him."

"Zach?" Josh asked, "What do you think?"

"I may regret this, but I think Tim is right. We need to grab this guy. Okay, we all stay with him. Soon as Sorin is away from the area, Tim and I will approach the guy. Is he moving yet?"

"Nope, just sitting there watching the river," Josh answered.

Sorin crossed back over Memorial Boulevard and disappeared behind the Capital Grille building. The team waited another minute, and then moved in.

Donahue walked along the path, staying behind the man's field of vision. Kennedy approached from the opposite direction. The man eyed Kennedy, remaining on the bench, focusing on the agent.

As Kennedy got within 10 yards, the man reached into his jacket. Donahue spotted the movement. He cleared the distance to the man, blindsiding him, grabbing him around the neck. Lifting him from the bench, he slammed him into the ground. Kennedy heard the man's wrist fracture, yet he continued to struggle.

Kennedy threw his weight on top of the guy. Josh arrived with the others and got the man in handcuffs, hustling him to the van. Kennedy showed Josh the Glock handgun he pulled from the guy's shoulder holster.

"Where to?" Kennedy asked. "We gotta get out of here. We're drawing a crowd," motioning to people gathering and watching.

"Let's take him to EPPD," Josh said. "Keep him there for a while until we decide what to do with him."

Donahue looked at Kennedy. The agent nodded. As they drove to police department headquarters, Josh searched the man more thoroughly.

Kennedy called the US Attorney's office, requesting a detainer.

"Will you look at this? Son-of-a-bitch had two guns," Josh said, holding up another unique Russian weapon. He grabbed the man by the throat, "I've seen one of these before, asshole. Someone used one to try and kill my wife."

The man's face reddened, his airway restricted, yet he maintained the blank look, ignoring Josh.

"You know where that asshole is? Huh?" Josh said, banging the man's head against the wall of the van. "He's dead. Which is what you're going to be if you don't start talking."

"Josh," Kennedy said, pulling him away from the man, "Josh, look at this."

Kennedy held the envelope Sorin had given the man, he handed Josh a piece of paper. Attached to the paper was a photo. Josh grabbed it from Kennedy as he continued to glare at the man.

Kennedy made a movement with his head; Donahue looked confused then realized what Kennedy wanted him to do. He moved between the man and Josh.

Josh glanced down at the paper; he felt the blood drain from his face. He was looking at a picture of himself and Keira playing with Cassidy in their backyard. The paper listed their vehicles, their home and work addresses, the name of their dog, everything someone would need to get to them.

As Josh looked up from the paper, Kennedy moved to grab him. "Josh, we need him alive. This would not be helpful. We stopped them; it won't do any good here if we lose him."

Josh tried to get around Kennedy, Donahue held him back. "Josh, knock it off. Think what Keira would want."

Josh sat back, glaring at the man. Kennedy handed him more documents. These contained pictures and details of Tommy Moore, Judge Tucker and Karen Reynolds.

Josh tried to absorb it all. Someone was trying to kill him, Keira, Tommy, and anyone else who is in the way. How can this be?

How can this be?

As they pulled into the restricted area of the station, a uniform officer directed them to a garage door at the rear of the building. Known as the sallyport, it provided a controlled way to bring prisoners into the station.

They hustled the prisoner out of the van, bringing him into the cellblock area. Josh had called ahead, and East Providence Rescue was waiting for them.

"And what do we have here?" Paul Carson, one of the rescue firefighters, asked.

Josh pulled him aside, "Paul, I have to ask you a favor. This has to be off the books for now. Do your best to patch him up, but he can't leave here for a while."

Carson and his brother, Mike, had been working as a team on rescue for years. They were two of the most respected firefighters. Josh was counting on their experience, and their trust, in going along with his request.

Paul smiled, "Let me look him over. Tell you what I think," patting Josh on the back. "Mike's out at the truck, go tell him the story while I'll see what I can do here."

Josh nodded and walked out the door to the rescue. Donahue and Kennedy stayed with the guy while Carson examined him. Josh explained things to Mike and the two came back into the cellblock area.

"So, what we got, Pauly?" Mike Carson asked, dropping more equipment on the floor.

"Well, not too bad," Carson smiled, "I've seen a lot worse in this place."

Josh chuckled, "Just tell me what we have and what you can do, smart-ass."

"Okay, let's see. We got a broken wrist, some scratches and contusions around the throat. I'd say a potential broken rib, severe bruise at least." Carson reached into his bag. "I can put this inflatable air splint on the wrist. The ribs are more of a problem, so you need to immobilize him. If they are broken, there's a potential for any movement to puncture a lung." Carson slid the splint over the wrist and inflated it.

"I assume you don't want him to puncture his lung?" Carson asked.

"Well," Donahue said, "not right away."

The two rescue guys chuckled.

"In that case, you have to limit his movements," Mike Carson said. "Just keep him still and he should be fine. I could give him some pain medication, but we'd have to document it. I assume that is not something we want to do?"

Josh shook his head, "Okay, thanks. We'll take it from here. How you gonna write up the run?"

"How about I put one of the prisoners fell down the stairs?" Carson laughed. "No one will pay attention to that."

"Is everybody who works for this city a comedian?" Donahue asked.

"Pretty much," Josh said. Turning back to the rescue brothers, "Thanks guys. When this is all over I owe you some drinks and the rest of the story at Bovi's."

The two firefighters returned to the rescue.

"Did you notice the guy never talked," Paul said. "He never said a word. The guy did not even flinch when I probed his chest. It had to hurt."

Mike smiled, "You never know what waits for you in a police cellblock."

Paul thought for a moment, "I don't know, something was different about this one. When I examined him, I noticed several scars. If I had to guess I say they were bullet and knife wounds," looking for his brother's reaction.

"Bullet wounds?" Mike asked.

"Yep, no doubt in my mind," Paul said. "I don't know who that guy is, but he's been shot and stabbed more than once."

"Did you tell them?" Mike asked.

"I pointed them out," Paul said. "The big guy, I think he's a trooper, saw them but didn't say anything."

"Okay then," Mike said. "Whatever the guy is, I hope they don't let him go."

After the rescue guys left, Josh brought the prisoner up to the juvenile cellblock in detectives. "We can keep him in here away from prying eyes."

As the words were coming out of his mouth, Captain Charland walked into the office.

"Why is there an adult prisoner in the juvenile detention cell, Lieutenant?" Charland asked. "You know this is a violation of protocol."

"Captain, there is a need for this man to--." Josh stopped in mid-sentence as he saw the grin come over Charland's face.

"Is there something I'm missing, Captain?" Josh asked.

Charland smiled, "Just having a little fun at your expense, Lieutenant. You have to learn to lighten up. Brennan informed me there are special circumstances in play." Charland patted Josh on the shoulder and continued on to the Detective Captain's office.

Josh stood there, watching Charland walk away. He looked at Donahue, "What the fuck was that?"

"Seems like a nice guy to me," Donahue said. "Maybe you just need to give him a chance."

"You have no idea," Josh said. "Okay, let's go talk to Brennan. Find Kennedy, maybe he found a way for us to hold this guy for a while without arraigning him in court."

Chapter 40

Kennedy came back into the SIU office, "Where's our friend?"

"I got him in the Juvenile detention cell," Josh said, turning his laptop to face Kennedy. On the screen was a camera view of the man. He sat in the corner of the room, staring at the camera.

"Has he said anything?" Kennedy asked.

"Nope," Josh said, "not a goddamn word."

"Really?" Kennedy replied. "I spoke to Justice. We can hold the guy on the weapons charge and violations of the Terrorism Act for 24 hours. Then we have to charge him."

"Let me talk to him for a minute," Donahue said. "I have some cousins that were IRA. Maybe we can bond."

Josh laughed, "He already has a broken wrist and fractured ribs from your last chat. We don't need him to talk anyway. I have an idea." Josh grabbed his camera and motioned for them to follow him.

Josh led them into the juvenile office. Handing Donahue the camera, he opened the cell door, motioning for the prisoner to come out.

The man looked at Josh for a moment, stood, and then came out of the cell. Josh pointed for him to stand against the wall. The man moved to the wall, turned, and faced Josh.

"Ready?" Josh asked.

"Ready for what?" Donahue replied.

"A picture with my friend here," Josh said, standing next to the man and putting his arm around him.

The man tried to pull away. Josh grabbed the splint on the broken wrist and pulled him back. The man grimaced, and then resumed the stoic look.

Donahue shot off a few frames, nodded to Josh, and showed the images to Kennedy while Josh put the man back in the cell.

As they returned to the SIU office, Josh took the memory card out, plugged it into his laptop, and brought up the pictures. Selecting two, he sent them to the printer. He then added some pictures from the surveillance of the meeting and printed those.

"And these are for what, your scrapbook?" Donahue asked.

"Nope," Josh smiled. "When we go talk to Collucci tomorrow, I have no doubt Mr. Sorin will be there. These are a bit of leverage."

Kennedy's cell phone rang. He spoke for a moment, and then held the cell out from his ear. "The US Marshals are here for our friend. Where do I send them?"

"Have them drive around back," Josh said, "I'll go out and bring them in."

Twenty minutes later, with the prisoner in the custody of the US Marshals, Josh called Tommy.

"Tommy, where are you right now?"

"At the office with Jennifer," Tommy said. "I was just going to call you. Sorin called Jen, he wants to meet now, instead of tomorrow. He said something has come up."

"Yeah, you could say that," Josh said. "When is he going to be there?"

"He said within the hour," Tommy replied. "She just got off the phone with him."

"Okay, we're on the way," Josh said. "Whatever you do, don't agree to go anywhere with him or leave the office. I'll explain later." Josh hung up and said, "Okay, we gotta go. Sorin's on his way to meet with Tommy and Jennifer. We need to get there, now." Grabbing his portable radio, he led the group out to the surveillance vehicles.

* * *

It took just fifteen minutes for the surveillance team to set up on the office, but it seemed longer. Josh worried Sorin might try to act on his own. He didn't want to put Tommy on edge by giving him too much information, but he needed to make sure he was aware things had changed.

Josh called Tommy's cell. "Hey, LT, you guys set up?"

"All set," Josh tried to control the tension in his voice. "Listen to me, Tommy. We've had some developments that may change things a bit. Sorin reached out to some bad people. These guys may try to go after us. Us as in you and me. However, they would not let someone else being there stop them. You understand?"

"I got it," Tommy said, the tone now serious and somber. "I doubt he'll do anything here, it's too public. But if he even flinches the wrong way, I'll light his ass up."

"That's my boy," Josh said. "Okay, there are four of us out here. We'll be monitoring everything he says. First sign of things going south, and we'll be crashing the door."

"L T," Tommy said, "if things go south, by the time you crash the door he'll have already bled out."

Josh smiled, "Let's hope it doesn't come to that. Assuming all goes well, call me after he leaves. We will bring you guys in. None of this will be necessary after tomorrow."

Tommy noticed Jennifer had been listening to the conversation.

"Something I should know?" she asked.

Tommy walked over to her and took her in his arms, kissing her on the top of her head. "Nothing, it's nothing. We're just covering all possibilities. Sorin doesn't have the balls to do anything and even if he did, it wouldn't be here."

Jennifer snuggled closer to Tommy. "When this is over, can we go away somewhere? Where it's just you and me?"

"You got it," Tommy said, kissing her on the lips. "Wherever you want to go, we'll go. I promise."

Tommy's cell chirped with a text message. Jennifer looked up into his eyes.

"It's Josh, Sorin's here. They spotted him as he pulled in."

Jennifer turned to go to her desk; Tommy pulled her back to him. "No one is going to hurt you, Jen. Not ever, I won't let anything happen."

She smiled, touched his cheek, and walked to her desk.

"Methinks, there be hormones afoot in the office," Donahue said, as they sat in the surveillance van. "I wish I hadn't heard that. He must have forgotten about the mikes being live."

"I hope it doesn't get out of hand," Josh said.

Sorin parked out front and walked into the main lobby. Ignoring the receptionist, he went to Karen's office, glancing around making sure no one saw him enter.

Karen looked up from her desk, "Anthony," she said, her eyes widened as she realized he had been standing there. "This is a surprise."

"I have some business to attend to with Jennifer," Sorin said. "I was wondering if you might be available for dinner tomorrow night. I think it time we discussed some new opportunities."

Karen hesitated a moment, "That, ah, that would be lovely. Where should we meet?"

Sorin glanced at his watch, "I'm running a bit late here. How about I call you tomorrow afternoon and we'll arrange things then?"

"Sounds perfect," Karen said, smiling at Sorin. "I'll look forward to hearing from you."

"Great, talk to you then," Sorin said, walking back out the door. As he stood in the hallway, he pulled out one of the disposable phones, sending a quick text.

"Where the hell is he," Josh asked. "He went inside ten minutes ago."

"I wonder if he stopped to see the other one, what's her name, Karen Reynolds?" Donahue said. "What the hell is that buzzing noise, is your cell going off?" looking around the van.

Josh shrugged, continuing to listen for any signs of Sorin getting to Jennifer's office.

"Who the hell does this belong to?" Donahue said, holding up a vibrating cell phone.

"I don't know," Josh said, taking the phone. "It's not one of ours." Then the light went on. "It must have come from the guy we grabbed. When we tossed him in here, it must have fallen out of his pocket. I knew it was weird he didn't have one on him."

Josh looked at the display. *KR, tomorrow 9:00 PM, call me before.*

"What does that mean?" Donahue asked.

"Not sure, but it's obvious he's telling him to do something tomorrow at 9:00." Josh picked up his own cell and called Kennedy, reading him the text.

"What do you think?" Josh asked.

"Not sure, but I wonder?" Kennedy said.

"Wonder what?"

"I bet KR is Karen Reynolds. She was one of the named targets. Maybe he's made arrangement for her to be somewhere at that time?" Kennedy speculated.

"Do we respond to the text?" Josh asked.

"I'd say no," Kennedy said. "If they have a pre-arranged code we'd tip them to their guy is in custody. It's more likely there wouldn't be a response to limit potential for any interception of the messages."

"He's in the office," Donahue interrupted, putting on a set of headphones.

"Gotta go, Sorin's inside," ending the call. Josh put on his own headset.

* * *

Sorin barged into the office. He shot a glance at Tommy, and then moved toward Jennifer. Placing both hands on her desk, "So what are these so-called issues you need to discuss, Jennifer?" he demanded. "This is pretty clear cut. Either you have the land, or you do not. Which is it?"

Tommy explained, "Anthony, the reason I wanted--"

Sorin held up one hand without looking at Tommy. "I am asking the person whom I hired for this task. I am not interested in talking to her errand boy," turning his head to face Tommy. "When I want you to speak, I will ask you the question. Until then, be quiet."

He returned his attention to Jennifer. "Now, what is the damn problem?" slamming his hands on the desk, causing Jennifer to jump. "Do you have the land or not?"

Tommy moved toward Sorin, but Jennifer's look told him to stay where he was. "Anthony, we have settled the land problem. If you had bothered to return one of my calls, I would have told you."

Sorin glanced between the two, folding his arms. "Why didn't you tell me when I called?"

"I tried. You wouldn't listen. So, I am telling you now. We have the property title. You can thank Tommy for that. He was the one who negotiated with the owner. She was resistant to selling."

Sorin looked at Tommy. "I am glad to see someone in this office can follow simple instructions." He walked toward the door. "Please send all the necessary documents to the attorneys at Harriet Lane Corporation."

"You're welcome," Tommy said, smiling as Sorin face him.

"Mr. Meadows, you should be cautious in your flippant attitude. I made this business thrive. I can change that, if it suits me," slamming the door as he left.

"I am going to break his jaw when this is over," Tommy said, gritting his teeth and driving his fist into his hand. "Then I am going to hurt him."

Tommy grabbed his cell and called Josh. "The motherfucker is gone. He is a real son-of-a-bitch."

"I know," Josh said, "we heard. Such violent tendencies, Tommy, I may have to send you to *Be Nice School* for remedial training.

"I am sure that will help," Tommy said.

"Let's wait a half hour or so, then you guys head out to the Lincoln Mall off Route 146. I'll have the state police meet you and take Jen up to the safe house until this is over. Once they pick her up, you come back here."

"You got it, LT," Tommy said, clicking off his cell.

Jen came over to his desk and sat on the edge. "Now what?"

"Now I take you to stay with your daughter and father," Tommy smiled. "This will all be over in a couple of days. We'll just keep you guys safe and sound while we roll this up."

"I won't see you?" Jen asked. "Do we have to leave right away?"

"Josh and the rest of them headed back to the station. He said he had some things he needed to fill me in on. Soon as I drop you off, I am going to head to the station- why?"

Jen walked to the office door, locking it, then turned back to face Tommy. As she walked toward him, she slowly unbuttoned her blouse, removing it and tossing it aside.

Tommy pushed himself up from the chair and walked toward her. Reaching around, he undid her bra. As it fell to the floor, Jen undid his pants.

Tommy reached under her skirt, sliding her panties down. Then stopped and looked around.

"What's wrong?" Jennifer whispered in his ear.

"I gotta turn off the recording devices," he said, trying to walk as his pants fell to the ground.

"Good idea," she giggled, following close behind him as she slid out of the rest of her clothes.

* * *

Two hours later, Tommy pulled into the parking lot of the police station. Chief Brennan was just getting into his car.

"Chief," Tommy nodded.

"What is this? We have a Detective Moore sighting," Brennan said. "Can I believe my eyes? Nice of you to stop by."

"Well you know how it is, Chief," Tommy smiled, "The demands of working undercover."

"I do so hope you'll be able to resume your normal duties with us little people when this is over. We are still paying you; it would be nice to get a return on that investment."

"To be honest with you, I am looking forward to it," Tommy confided. "Don't get me wrong, I like some of it. But this is not something I want to make a career of. I like things the way they were."

"You and me both, son, you and me both," Brennan said, firing up a cigar and getting in his car.

Tommy walked into the SIU office.

"Glad you could join us," Kennedy said.

"Where's Josh?" Tommy asked.

"Back in a minute, had to bring something over to the Detective Captain's office," Donahue said.

The door opened, and Josh walked in. "Well, well," Josh said, "he found his way home. Did you get lost?"

"No," Moore shook his head. "I did what you said. We waited a bit, and then I took Jen up to the mall and met the troopers."

Josh stood with his hands on his hips, looking at Tommy. "Hey Tim," he said. "You worked the road in uniform, right? How long does it take to drive from the office on Waterman to Lincoln and back here?"

"30 minutes tops," Donahue said. "What'd you do with the rest of the time, Tommy boy? You haven't been playing hide the shillelagh with the Judge's daughter have you now?"

"Fuck you, Donahue," Tommy said. "It's none of your damn business what I do," glaring at the trooper.

"Okay, okay. Just a little joke, Tommy. Calm down," Josh said.

"Yeah, a wee little joke of a shillelagh," Donahue said, holding his index and thumb an inch apart. "Come on now, Tommy boy. You have been busting my ass since we got involved in this mess. You gotta expect a little payback."

Tommy laughed, "I suppose I brought it on myself, didn't I? It's just you pretty boy troopers make such easy targets."

"There's the spirit, lad. A little joke among friends," Donahue said, smiling at Moore. "A tiny little joke," ducking as Moore threw a pen at him.

"Okay, now that we've settled that, we've got some things to show you Tommy," Josh said. He handed him the documents from the guy at Waterplace Park.

"Holy shit," Tommy said, flipping through the documents. "Where'd you get this?"

Josh filled him in on the Sorin surveillance, the arrest in the park, and recovering the weapon and documents.

"You think he would've shot Zach?" Tommy asked.

"My guess would be yes," Zach said. "I could see it in his eyes. If Tim hadn't got to him in time, I am sure he'd have pulled the trigger."

"And Sorin set this up?" Tommy said, shaking his head. "That motherfucker deserves to die. I hope he reaches for a weapon when we grab him. I want to empty a magazine right in his goddamn face."

"Okay then," Josh said, "Now that we all understand how bad Tommy wants to shoot this son-of-a-bitch, we need to move on."

Chapter 41

Candace Ferguson and her camera operator pulled up to the front of the Senator's office. There were no other media present.

A recent release of photos of the ultra-conservative darling of the Christian right Congressman from Texas cavorting in a hot tub with two naked women and what appeared to be cocaine on his nose turned the media focus elsewhere.

The short-term prurient interest of the public redirected from Collucci to someone else for the time being.

Unloading the equipment, they headed inside.

Sorin was waiting for them as they entered the office. He led them to a small conference room. While the camera operator set up, Candace tried to ask Sorin a few questions.

"Mr. Sorin, does the Senator deny his involvement in the Grey case? We've seen documents related to the case and the Senator's name is on many of them."

"Ms. Ferguson," Sorin replied, "I'll let the Senator address this himself. Let me remind you, as Deputy Attorney General the Senator's name would appear on thousands of documents relating to criminal cases. Not to mention appeals and a host of other matters related to his job as head of the Criminal Division.

"To surmise some improper actions on the Senator's part, based on names in a document, is reprehensible. The Senator arranged this interview to address these issues. I will let him answer those questions. I am just giving you my opinion of this poor excuse for journalism." Sorin turned and left the room.

Candace and the camera operator exchanged glances. "Well," Candace said, "I guess we know where Mr. Sorin stands on this, don't we?"

The camera operator chuckled, fine-tuned the camera lighting, and nodded he was ready.

Candace placed the microphone on the table and waited for the Senator. "Want to bet how long he makes us wait?" she asked.

"Ten minutes," the camera operator said, without hesitation.

"Fifteen," she replied.

Fifteen minutes later, almost to the second, the Senator came into the conference room.

"Ms. Ferguson," Collucci said, reaching to shake her hand. "I apologize for keeping you waiting. I had a last-minute conference call with the members of the Banking subcommittee that was unavoidable."

"That's fine, Senator. Perfectly understandable," Candace said. "Shall we get started?"

"Please," Collucci said, motioning for them to sit. "As my assistant told you when he arranged this interview, I want to address this issue with facts, not innuendo."

Candace smiled, "Okay, Senator, then let's get right to the heart of the matter. Were you involved in the Grey case?"

"Yes, I was, in my capacity as the head of the Criminal Division, of course. As the Deputy in charge of the Criminal Division for the Attorney General, I was involved in all cases in some way, shape, or form."

"But in this particular case," Candace asked, "the records bear out you had direct involvement. Judge Tucker, in his affidavit, was specific about it. Are you denying this?"

Collucci paused for a moment, smiling for the camera. "I am glad you brought up the Judge's affidavit. I would like to address that. Judge Tucker was a Special Assistant Attorney General back then; he worked for me as a junior prosecutor. He showed great potential. I saw a raw talent in his courtroom demeanor and legal thinking.

"I decided to assign him the Grey case based on these signs of his legal talents. Sometimes, we are all guilty of errors of judgment. In this case, Tucker was in over his head. Let me say for the record, I take full responsibility for that. Certain other prosecutors brought these issues to my attention. I found that Tucker had not done a full review of the police files. I learned he had permitted a detective to replace a report in the file with one changed by the investigators. All matters which gave me grave concern."

"Senator, are you saying Judge Tucker tampered with a criminal case file?" Candace asked.

"No, no. Not at all," Collucci said. "What I am saying is that Tucker's inexperience caused him to make certain incorrect decisions. While not wrong in any legal or technical sense, they were against the Attorney General's policy. The process for handling of criminal cases was specific; in the Grey case, Judge Tucker did not follow policy."

"So, what did you do in the Grey case? Did you take the case over?"

"What I did was reassign the case. I informed Tucker I would assume temporary responsibility for the matter. This was for the purposes of continuity. It was a mere formality insuring someone maintained responsibility for the file. My intention was to assign the case to a more experienced, seasoned prosecutor. Unfortunately, before that could happen, Mr. Grey died in prison."

"Did you investigate the circumstances of his death, his murder?" Candace asked.

"The Attorney General and I met with the State Police. It is the normal practice for the State Police to investigate criminal matters arising from the prison. They investigated. Based on that investigation, we tried and convicted two inmates for Grey's death."

"Senator, did you conduct an internal probe? One targeting the original arrest of Grey and the potential tampering with the lineup?"

Collucci placed his fingertips together, tapping his chin. "Ms. Ferguson, the Attorney General's office does not have the resources to verify every single file submitted by the police. We rely on the internal controls within police departments to insure cases contain all evidence and reports."

Candace wrote notes then said, "So in this case, nothing happened once Grey died. Is that accurate? Your office conducted no further investigation. You did nothing to make sure Grey was in fact responsible for the crimes with which he was charged?"

"Ms. Ferguson, once Mr. Grey died in prison there was no compelling reason to investigate anything other than those responsible for his death. I would like to say we tried to do more, but that is the problem with hindsight. We did what we had a responsibility to do at the time. Nothing more and nothing less,"

Collucci paused for a moment. "For Judge Tucker to submit this affidavit as a way of assuaging his conscience for his failures, and then try to shift the blame onto others, is shameful. He should resign from the bench, as he no longer holds our respect. He has done a great disservice to the court and the people of Rhode Island."

Candace glanced at Sorin leaning against the wall, and then looked at her notes. "Senator, I have some questions on another matter."

"Please, Ms. Ferguson, that's why we are here." Collucci smiled for the camera, "Ask away."

"Do you think this matter will disrupt you plans for the waterfront in Rhode Island?"

"Not at all," Collucci said. "Let me make something clear, I have no plans for the waterfront. I wrote and sponsored the legislation to permit the project to go forward. The development is all in the hands of private companies."

Candace reached for a document in her folder, looked it over for a moment. She caught the glance between Collucci and Sorin. She had their interest now.

"Are you familiar with the group, Solntsevskaya Bratva?"

Candace caught Sorin's movement out of the corner of her eye.

Sorin came over and whispered into Collucci's ear.

"Perhaps Mr. Sorin would like to answer the question since he has ties to some of their members in the US?" Candace probed.

Collucci leaned forward, hands folded in front of his mouth.

"Ms. Ferguson, I have no idea what it is you're getting at with these questions, and I resent any implications."

Candace smiled, "Well, Senator, perhaps you can explain this. Are you aware of a company called Harriet Lane Enterprises? It is a Delaware corporation which has contributed significant amounts of money to a Super PAC which indirectly supports your campaigns?"

"There are many organizations that support me, Ms. Ferguson. These are all legitimate groups subject to intense oversight by the Federal Election Commission. Is there something else you wish to ask, or is this just more media innuendo?"

Candace handed Collucci the document.

Collucci looked it over, and then showed it to Sorin.

"Senator, as you can see, Shashenka Dmitriev controls Harriet Lane Enterprises. According to the Justice Department, Dmitriev has ties to Solntsevskaya Bratva. The company is also involved in the Rhode Island waterfront project as well as the Lottery relocation matter. Were you not aware of this, Senator?"

"Ms. Ferguson," Collucci said, his voice slow and deliberate, "I extended this invitation to address inaccuracies in your reporting. I see you have decided to persist with these baseless accusations against innocent individuals and legitimate American businesses. Many of them support this critical project in Rhode Island. I will not sit here and let you denigrate the good work these people have done. This interview is over," Collucci stormed out of the room.

"Mr. Sorin, might I have a word?" Candace asked.

Sorin just smiled, shook his head, and left.

"Guess not," Candace said. "Let's get back to the studio; we gotta edit this stuff into the story."

* * *

Josh, Zach, Tim Donahue, and Tommy sat in the surveillance van. They watched as Candace and the camera operator loaded up their equipment. Josh took out his cell and called her.

"Candace, Josh. How'd it go?"

302

"Let's say he was true to form. He blamed everything on Tucker, but with enough wiggle room to give him some plausible deniability," Candace said.

"And the other stuff?" Josh asked.

"That was priceless," Candace said. "If the camera wasn't there, he would have physically thrown me out. Sorin played cool, didn't show much emotion. But I know we rattled them."

"Good to hear," Josh said. "When will the story air?"

"We're headed back to do the editing and add this stuff in. If all goes well, we'll be ready for tomorrow night."

"Great, talk to you later. Thanks for your help," Josh said.

Josh filled the rest in on the interview. "Shall we go complete the Senator's day?"

"I cannot wait," Tommy said.

"Not you big fella," Josh said. "You and your new best friend Trooper Donahue are the backup squad. You stay here in case something unanticipated happens."

"Are you--" Tommy argued.

Josh cut him off. "Not open for discussion. We want to antagonize them into reacting, not kill them."

Donahue put his arm around Tommy. "Cheer up, Bucko. You get to spend time with me, listening to my war stories of the State Police."

"Great, do I get to hear both of them?" Tommy said.

"Over and over, my boy. Over and over."

Josh looked at Zach, "I think these two need to be alone. Let's go."

Zach watched as Donahue tried to kiss Tommy on the lips, "Come here you big handsome stud," Donahue said.

Moore pushed him off, "I'm gonna have to get shots now you bastard. Where's my gun?"

Zach shook his head and climbed out of the van. "You sure they'll be okay in there?"

"They'll be fine," Josh said. "There's a case of beer on ice in the cooler. Donahue will find it, and all will be right with the world."

"You guys do have a different way of doing things. I never knew what I was missing."

The two walked in the front door of the office. Collucci and Sorin were standing just inside. When Collucci saw Josh, he blanched.

"Don't worry, Senator, not here to arrest you. Not yet anyway," Josh said. "Of course, I can't speak for my friend here from the FBI. Are you here to arrest them, Agent Kennedy?"

"That remains uncertain at this point," Kennedy answered.

"What do you want Williams? I don't have time for this nonsense," Collucci said.

"Just a moment of your time, Senator," Josh said. "And yours as well, Mr. Sorin."

The two glared at Josh, "Make this quick," Collucci sneered. "I have a meeting to get to."

Josh reached into his pocket and took out the printed pictures. He lay them out on the table, watching for a reaction.

"What are these?" Collucci asked.

"They are pictures of your assistant here meeting with a Russian contract killer. See where he hands him the envelope?" Josh said, pointing to one photo. "We got the guy in custody. He's quite talkative. See, here I am with him in the police station."

Josh grabbed Sorin by the arm, "Come on, and take a look. Remember giving him this?"

Sorin pulled away, "Senator, there is no reason to listen to this nonsense. We should leave."

Collucci looked at Sorin and then at Josh. "So, Anthony met with the man. What is the significance?"

Josh walked to Collucci backing him into the wall. Sorin started to intervene and Kennedy pushed him away.

"I'll tell you what the significance is, Senator." The anger rose in Josh's voice. "Your assistant here met with that man to arrange for him to kill me, my wife, and some good friends of mine."

"That's ridiculous," Collucci said, pushing off the wall.

Josh grabbed him by the throat and slammed him back. "No Senator, it's not ridiculous it's a fact," pushing him away and turning to Sorin. "And you, you motherfucking low-life piece of fucking shit. You went after me once, almost killed my wife," pushing Sorin into the wall. "Didn't think we'd find out, did you?"

"I am a United States Senator, you cannot come in here and assault me and my chief of staff," Collucci yelled. "Sir, if you are an FBI agent I suggest you arrest this man for assaulting me. If you don't, you'll soon find yourself out of a job."

Kennedy just grinned, "Sorry Senator, I haven't seen any assault."

Sorin took the Senator's arm and led him toward the back room. "Let's go, Senator."

"Hey Anthony, you slimy little cocksucker," Josh said, causing Sorin to turn back to face him.

The blood drained from Sorin's face. Collucci let out a panicked, "Oh my god." The two men froze with fear.

Josh stood facing Sorin, holding the weapon seized from the man in the park. "Wouldn't it be ironic if I used the gun you intended to kill me on you, Mr. Sorin?"

The front part of Sorin's crotch darkened, the stain spreading, widening down both legs.

Josh pointed the weapon at the stain in Sorin's pants. "Looks like you may have to change before the meeting there, Anthony."

Josh gathered up the papers and headed out the door, followed by Kennedy.

"I might have missed something in the briefing," Kennedy said. "But I thought the purpose was to gain their cooperation?"

"They were never going to cooperate," Josh said. "They're more afraid of the Russians than they are of us," Josh said. "They'll regroup, salvage what they can, and try to explain this away. Collucci is so arrogant there is no way he'd have it any other way."

Kennedy shook his head.

"Besides, there is no way I was letting them get in the van," Josh said.

"Why not?" Kennedy asked.

"The pussy pissed himself. He ain't getting in my nice surveillance van with wet pants," Josh smiled.

"A point of order there, Lieutenant Williams," Kennedy said. "This is an FBI surveillance van and I have to give it back,"

Josh just smiled.

Kennedy opened the door to the back of the van. Donahue and Tommy Moore were sitting next to the camera monitors surrounded by empty bottles of Becks beer.

"Back so soon?" Tommy laughed. "Grab a beer; I think there's some left."

"Some left?" Josh said, climbing in behind Kennedy. "I put a case in there."

"Really?" Donahue chuckled. "They must have been small ones," tapping his bottle against Tommy's.

Josh shook his head, "Did you hear anything from Moreira? Has Sorin made any calls?"

"Oh yeah," Donahue said, "He wants you to call him about it. Sounds important."

"You guys are morons. Move over so I can get up front, "Josh said.

"I'll drive," Tommy said.

"I don't think so," Kennedy said. "I'll drive; you guys enjoy your beers."

Kennedy climbed over Donahue and into the driver's seat. Josh slid into the front passenger side and took out his phone.

"Joe, Josh. Any activity?"

Joe Moreira replied, "Oh yeah. Sorin called Dmitriev and told him about the conversation you had. Dmitriev was not pleased. Told Sorin he'd get back to them. I'd say they're in some serious shit with him."

"Great, hopefully by throwing them off balance they'll do something stupid," Josh said. "Did you hear from the team on Dmitriev?"

"Yup, he's at the private club in DC and two other rather interesting people showed up," Moreira replied.

"Who?" Josh asked.

"Maurio Bartoletti and someone they didn't recognize," Moreira said. "They're emailing the images."

"Okay," Josh said. "We'll sit here for a bit. See if anything develops. Let me know if you hear anything."

Kennedy looked at Josh, "What'd they have?"

"Not much yet. Bartoletti met with Dmitriev at the private club in DC. He showed up with someone they couldn't identify. They're sending pictures." Josh took out his laptop and logged into the secure email connection. Turning the screen to show Kennedy, he said, "Here, take a look."

Kennedy looked at the dark images, "Can't see his face. I'll send them to our image lab; maybe they can enhance them. Give me the laptop for a minute."

Kennedy forwarded the message then took out his cell, handing the laptop back to Josh.

"Zach Kennedy, ID 24 Alpha 1Bravo X-ray Alpha Delta. I sent two images to you under a different email account. See it?" Kennedy asked. "Great, see what you can do to enhance them and send them back to the same account. Call me when you've sent them. Thanks."

"Hey Josh," Donahue said, slurring in his speech. "When are we gonna get super-secret-squirrel codes like them? We need them right away."

"Yeah," Tommy added. "Alpha Bravo Shithead 1 Delta emergency. I need another beer."

"Roger wilco," Donahue replied, grabbing two more beers out of the cooler. "Problem solved. The code we troopers live by, proper planning prevents poor performance."

The two back seat riders laughing at their own humor.

Kennedy smiled at them, "I think we've created a dangerous combination with those two."

"I have no doubt," Josh replied.

"I gotta pee," Tommy said, looking around the van.

"Not in here you don't," Kennedy said. "Get out and go find someplace outside."

"I'll just go in one of the empties," Tommy said, kneeling and reaching for his fly.

"No," Kennedy yelled. "You'll piss all over the damn place. Get out."

"Don't worry," Donahue grinned. "I have it on good information that old needle dick here will fit inside the bottle. No worries about errant spray."

Moore struggled to maintain his balance as he flipped Donahue the bird and tried to hold onto the bottle.

"Jesus Christ," Josh said. "Tommy, get the hell out."

Moore smiled at Josh, and then hobbled toward the door. Donahue opened the side door and Moore slid out. Looking around, he spotted a large tree surrounded by bushes, deciding this was the perfect spot.

"What the hell is he doing?" Kennedy said, pointing at Tommy.

Josh looked and realized Tommy didn't see the RIPTA bus stop crowded with people.

"Oh boy, too late," Josh said as Tommy engaged in the urgent activities. People pointed and laughed.

"Hope no one calls Providence PD," Josh said.

Tommy returned from his mission. "That went well."

"You think so, huh?" Josh said. "Didn't notice the old ladies waiting for the bus that you flashed?"

"They couldn't see anything anyway," Donahue chuckled. "They couldn't see it if they were standing next him," laughing once more at his own humor.

"Time to reload," Tommy said, grabbing his beer. "I'm happy now."

An hour later, Kennedy's phone rang. "What do you have for me? Okay, got it. No, makes sense, thanks."

"What's up?" Josh asked.

"They're sending back the images," Kennedy said. "They couldn't do much to enhance them, too low a resolution. Check your email, they should be there."

Josh fired up the laptop again. "Yeah, didn't help much," showing Kennedy the screen.

Kennedy nodded. "Ah well."

Josh examined the pictures again, "Still, there's something familiar about him. I think I've seen him somewhere before. No matter, we got what we need right here," closing the laptop and propping his feet up on the dash.

Josh's cell rang again. "Hey Joe, what's up? No shit, okay cool thanks." Turning to face Kennedy, he said, "That was Joe Moreira, Sorin just got a call back from Dmitriev. He told Sorin he has a solution to the problem."

"If Collucci's smart he shouldn't even consider going along with it. Russian solutions to problems are usually not gentle," Kennedy said.

"I doubt they do anything so dramatic," Josh said. "They'll go dark for a while to see if things blow over. They may release a few more photos of Congressmen or Senators to draw attention elsewhere."

"Do we stay on them, or call it day?" Kennedy asked.

Tommy and Donahue chanted, "Call it a day, call it a day," from the back.

"The idiots have it," Josh answered. "Let's go."

Kennedy started the van and headed back to EPPD Headquarters. "What say we drop these two at home?"

"Good idea," Josh said. "Tim, where do you live?"

"Oh, it's a ways from here my friend, out in Burrillville."

"He can stay at my place," Tommy said. "Drop us off at Bovi's, we can walk from there."

"I don't think you can walk in there," Josh said. "You sure about this?"

Tommy nodded, Donahue agreed.

A short time later, the van pulled up in front of Bovi's Tavern. "Come on roomie, couple more drinks, we'll grab a pizza, and head home."

"Don't be thinking you can get me drunk and take advantage of me," Donahue said as he climbed out of the van. "I do have morals."

"You're already drunk," Tommy said.

"Oh yeah," Donahue agreed. "Good point."

The bartender was smoking a cigarette just outside the entrance. She looked at Josh as he leaned out the passenger side window, smiling.

"You're not leaving them here with me, are you?" she said, sizing up the two.

"They're all yours," Josh laughed as they drove away.

Tommy put his arm around her, "Oh come on now Karen, you know you love me," dragging her into the bar.

* * *

Collucci sat in the office, shuffling papers on his desk. Sorin walked in wearing a new set of clothes.

"What the hell was he talking about, Anthony?" Collucci asked. "Who was the guy you met with?"

Sorin stared at Collucci, deciding how much to tell him. "I warned you not to take Dmitriev lightly. He decided to do things his way. I delivered a message for him, that's it. I had no idea what it was."

"But the guy had a weapon," Collucci said, fists clinched together banging the desk. "If this hits the media…."

"It doesn't matter," Sorin replied. "They can't prove anything. If they could, they would have arrested me. They have nothing; this is just a poor attempt to intimidate us. It will pass."

"I hope so," Collucci said. "The vote for the Chairmanship is Tuesday. We do not need any problems."

Sorin's phone rang. "Yes?" The conversation was brief.

"Who was it?" Collucci asked.

"Dmitriev again," Sorin said. "He wants us in Washington, tomorrow morning, at 8:00."

"Tomorrow? We just got back here. There aren't any flights to get us there by that time."

Sorin looked at the Senator. "Mr. Dmitriev places a higher value on you than I realized. He's sending his private jet for us. It will be at the airport in an hour."

A wide grin crossed Collucci's face. "See, Anthony, I told you they need us."

I am doubtful this is to save you, Senator. He has his reasons I suppose. I will make sure we follow through in dealing with this Lieutenant Williams. I will not let that go.

Sorin picked up the office phone and called for a driver. *One other lose end to deal with, dialing a second number.*

"Karen, it's Anthony. Do you have anything important planned over the next few days?"

"No, why?" Karen replied.

"We have a business opportunity in Washington I'd like you to work with me on," Sorin explained. "Pack a bag for a few days in DC. We'll be by to pick you up in twenty minutes."

"Ah, okay. Kind of sudden isn't it?" Karen asked.

"It's the way things are, when an opportunity presents itself you have to act. Talk to you in a bit," ending the call.

Chapter 42

Saturday morning, Josh met Zach Kennedy for breakfast at Ceba's Diner on Taunton Avenue.

"Hear anything from our two friends?" Kennedy asked.

"Oh yeah," Josh smiled. "Up until about 12:30am they kept sending me text messages with pictures of various body parts. My wife wanted to kill them. I called the station and had one of the sergeants go there and drag them out."

"That must have been pleasant," Kennedy said.

"I sent Gabe Armstrong," Josh said. "He's got a lot of experience in these matters."

"With you guys, I am not surprised," Kennedy laughed. "Want to guess where our other friends are?"

"No idea," Josh said.

"Back in DC," Kennedy said. "Sorin got another call from Dmitriev after we left. They flew on Dmitriev's jet back to DC. And, there was a woman with them."

"A woman? Any idea who?" Josh asked.

"Take a look," Kennedy said, handing Josh his cell phone.

"Karen Reynolds," Josh said, handing the phone back.

"Yup, a little more involved than we thought perhaps," Kennedy replied. "So, what's next?"

"I talked to Candace about this last night," Josh said. "With all the footage from Collucci they decided to make it a longer segment. It will be on Monday night. Until then, we just maintain things the way they are. As long as they're in DC, we can take it easy over the weekend. Unless things change."

"Sounds good to me," Kennedy said, finishing his food and sliding the dish away. "I'll call Deputy Lachance and fill him in. The guy from the park is on a federal detainer, he's not going anywhere. The Marshals took him to the Wyatt Federal Detention Center. Put him in lock down to keep him away from the other inmates until we decide what to do with him."

"Does he have a lawyer?" Josh asked.

"No," Kennedy said, "and I found that a little weird. Usually they're standing in line to represent these guys. He declined court appointed counsel. Who knows?" shrugging his shoulders. Finishing the last of his coffee, he reached for his wallet.

"I got it. It's on me," Josh said. "Least I can do."

"Thanks, so I guess I'll see you Monday morning. Take care. If anything comes up, I'll call you."

* * *

Monday morning the investigators gathered in the SIU office. Josh was on the phone to the AG's office lining up some time before the grand jury. Zach Kennedy was busy fielding inquiries from other FBI field offices.

Kennedy hung up the phone. "Looks like the guy we grabbed at the park was rather busy."

"How so?" Donahue asked.

"I sent his photo and information about the weapon out to the other intelligence offices," Kennedy said. "Four of them have active cases involving someone fitting his description and the same type weapon."

"Any matches on the ballistics?" Tommy Moore said, jumping into the conversation.

"Nope," Kennedy shook his head. "That's the problem. With the composite weapon, they dispose of the barrel after firing just a few rounds. It makes ballistic matches impossible."

"What about ejection marks?" Tommy asked.

"They didn't recover any casings," Kennedy answered. "They either retrieved them all or used an ejection port collector to prevent leaving anything behind. Either way, there's nothing to compare it to."

Josh got off the phone and said, "Just talked to Candace. They're running the story tonight. They are getting some heat from the corporate offices again, wanting them to hold the story for a few days. Candace thinks it's because the vote on the Chairmanship of the Banking Committee is Tuesday."

"Who's the pressure coming from?" Kennedy asked.

"All she said was the station manager told her to run with the story and not to worry about the consequences," Josh said. "Of course, he then left the station and they haven't seen him since."

"I bet we know where he is," Kennedy smiled.

Josh laughed, "No doubt, Mr. Kennedy. But no need to pay him a visit, yet anyway." Josh reached over and flipped on the TV. The morning news was just ending. The camera focused on the morning anchor...

...As part of the I-Team exclusive report, our investigative journalist has uncovered more shocking revelations and evidence of corruption in government. Tune in tonight for Candace Ferguson's one-on-one interview with Senator Collucci and continuing coverage of this developing story. Tonight, on the 6:00 news....

"I bet they'll be running it all day," Tommy said.

"Good," Donahue added. "I hope the son-of-a-bitch is shitting himself in DC."

The door opened, and Chief Brennan came in. "Morning boys, I see we've been busy ruining our friend the Senator's day."

"Morning Chief," Josh replied, "just following the trail."

"Yes, I am sure you are," Brennan said. "Josh, you and I need to be at the AG's office this morning at 10:00. The AG wants a briefing on what we have and what we're going to do with it."

"Why the sudden interest?" Josh asked.

Brennan smiled, "You know sometimes your naiveté is staggering."

"What?" Josh said, hands outstretched palms up.

"What?" Brennan said, "I bet even Detective Moore can figure this out."

"Already did, El Jefe. Way ahead of you." Tommy smiled.

"Please," Brennan said, "educate the Lieutenant here, would you?"

"I'd be happy to," Tommy said, rising from his seat. "I'll keep it simple so even Donahue will understand." Smiling as the trooper flipped him off.

"Okay boys, it goes like this," Tommy explained. "Collucci is one of the two Senators from RI. He is a Republican. The other Senator, William Strain, is a Democrat. Collucci is in trouble, big trouble and it is about to get bigger. Depending on how bad he suffers from this story, he may resign. He could be indicted. Either way, there is an opening for someone to finish his term. The Governor, whom we all know owes his election to the support from the Attorney General, appoints that someone. A Democratic AG, a Democratic Governor, and a chance to change the majority party in the Senate. See the picture?"

"That's good, son. I am impressed," Brennan said. "So now you understand. We are to meet with the AG, fill him in on the case. Then he can call the Governor and start the process to replace Collucci. You know, just another day of open government here in Rhode Island."

"I hate this shit," Josh said.

"You think that's bad," Donahue added, "wait until the Colonel leaves next year. The maneuvering for that job is sickening. There'll be a train of wannbes up there kissing the Governor's ass."

"Kind of how you got your job, right Chief?" Tommy joked.

Brennan turned to face Tommy, a grin crossing his face. "Ah yes, the subtle humor you're so famous for. Perhaps a little stint as School Resource officer at the high school might temper that."

"You wouldn't do that, would you?" Tommy asked.

"I don't know," Brennan replied. "I'll have to ask the politicians on the City Council for their guidance," walking to the door. "I'll keep my options open, for now," leaving the office.

With a look of panic in eyes, Tommy asked, "Lieutenant, tell me he wouldn't do that. Would he?"

"He might. Just for the sheer entertainment value," Josh said. "But I doubt it. Wouldn't want you near all those innocent children."

Tommy tried to smile, but the concern still showed. "I gotta learn to keep my mouth shut."

9:30 came around and Josh's phone rang. "Hi Donna, what's up?"

"The Chief said to meet him at his car in five minutes," Donna said.

"I was hoping he would forget," Josh said.

"He didn't," Donna replied. "He's heading out there now, better get going."

Brennan and Josh drove to the AG's office on South Main Street. As they came in the front door, Kristin Volpe was talking to the receptionist. She looked up and spotted Josh.

"Well, will you look at this? He's alive. Cancel that missing person broadcast," she said, walking over to stand in front of Josh. "Don't you ever return calls?" she smiled.

"Hi, Kristin, do you know Chief Brennan?" Josh fumbled with the words.

Brennan raised an eyebrow at Josh.

"I do, we've met before," she answered. "How are you Chief?"

"I am well, Kristin. We are here to see your boss. I had to drag Lieutenant Williams kicking and screaming down here."

"Doesn't surprise me," Kristin said. "For some reason he's developed an aversion to this place, or maybe it's me?" taking Josh's arm under the elbow. "No matter, he's my prisoner now. Come on, off to the torture chamber. I'll take you there."

"Will you be joining us?" Brennan asked.

"I will," Kristin said. "The AG wants me to handle any criminal cases which come out of this investigation. Great news, wouldn't you say Josh?"

"Yeah, that's ah, good. Glad to hear it," Josh replied without much enthusiasm.

"I see us spending a lot of time together." Kristin grinned, "Won't that be fun?"

Brennan watched Josh's reaction. As they got to the conference room, Kristin said, "Would anyone like coffee, I'll have it brought to us."

"I'd love some, black for me," Brennan said.

"Ah, sure, I'll have--"

"Cream and sugar, I remember," Kristin interrupted. "Be right back."

As she left the room, Brennan looked at Josh. "She seems pleased to see you here, Lieutenant." His eyes narrowed, "Whatever the reason may be, don't let it get out of hand."

"Chief it's--"

"All I'm going to say about it," Brennan said, holding up his hands.

The dog and pony show with the AG took about an hour. The AG thanked them for their time. He told them Kristin Volpe was the contact should they need anything from his office and left the room.

"So, how long until he starts the play for Collucci's seat?" Josh asked.

Kristin smiled, "I see we've been keeping up on inside politics. He is a good guy, Josh. He knows the AG's office is not a good platform for future political aspirations. If he gets appointed to the Senate seat, it makes running for a full term much easier."

"Does that mean you're running for something?" Brennan asked.

Kristin paused for a moment. "I'd be lying to you if I said I hadn't considered it. But that's way down the road. We'll see. I'll decide when the time comes."

Josh stood and looked at Brennan. "Ready, Chief? I've gotta get back. We've got tons of things to deal with before tonight."

"All set," Brennan said. "Thanks, Kristin. Nice to see you again. Looking forward to seeing how this case plays out."

"You're welcome, Chief," Kristin replied. "Josh, I'll be by the station later this afternoon. I will need you to bring me up to speed on all the details, so we can decide how to proceed. I've set aside time in the Grand Jury on Wednesday if we need it."

"Okay, I should be there most of the day," Josh answered.

Kristin looked at Brennan.

"I'll make sure the Lieutenant is available when you get there, Kristin. Not to worry," Brennan offered.

"Thanks, Chief. Maybe you should lock him in the cellblock," she chuckled.

"Don't think I haven't considered it," Brennan said. "Sometimes I think we'd all be better off if I did that once in a while." Brennan shook her hand and they followed her out of the office.

* * *

Brennan and Josh returned to the station. As they walked in the front door, Josh's cell chirped. Looking at the display he read, Kristin Volpe, AG's Office. *On the way, Josh. You can run, but you can't hide*, followed by the smile symbol.

Brennan looked over his shoulder. "Son, listen to a guy who has been down that road. Whatever she thinks, you gotta set her straight or you'll be dividing your pension with an ex-wife and that ain't cheap. Of course, that's assuming Keira doesn't kill you."

"Thanks, Chief. I'll try to keep that in mind," Josh said, deleting the text without replying.

Josh walked into the SIU office. "Tommy, come here. I need you to do me a favor."

'What's up, LT?"

"Kristin Volpe is on her way here," Josh said. "I need you to--"

"Got it. You want to be alone," Tommy said. "No problem, we'll go take a ride for a while. Give you time."

"Not funny, Tommy," Josh said. "I just need you to stay here, in the office, while she's here. Okay? Can you do that?"

"You got it, LT. No problem," Tommy smiled. "I'll protect you from the evil AG."

"Thanks," Josh said.

Twenty minutes later, Kristin walked into the SIU. Josh introduced her to Zach Kennedy. She knew the two troopers and Tommy from other cases.

Josh and Zach took turns detailing the case. Kennedy said the Justice Department would leave the criminal case to the state, unless something dramatic changed.

After the briefing, Kristin closed her briefcase and stood to leave. "Okay, let's plan on Josh and Tommy testifying before the Grand Jury on Wednesday. We'll leave it an open-ended case for now; just get the foundation set for the indictments. I think we look to indict Sorin and the guy in the park on conspiracy to commit murder, weapons violations, and anything else I can think of. With Collucci, I gotta do some more research. Sound good?"

"Sounds good to me," Tommy said. "Want me to walk you out?"

"No, that's okay," she said, glancing at Josh. "I can find my way. Call me if anything changes." Kristin opened the door and left the room.

"Well," Tommy said. "That was painless."

"I heard that," came the voice from outside the closed door.

"Oops," Tommy cringed.

Donahue started to say something.

"Don't," Josh said, holding up his hand. "Just let it go."

Donahue turned to his computer. "I was just going to say how nice she looked. She seemed to be radiant, didn't she?" A smile growing on his face, "I wonder why?" Bringing another burst of laughter.

Josh returned to his desk, buried his head in his hands; resigned to the inescapable fact that he had a problem. A self-inflicted problem.

Chapter 43

At 5:00, Brennan called the SIU office. "Were you planning on refreshments for tonight's entertainment?"

"Not sure what you mean, Chief. Refreshments?" Josh replied.

"Order some pizzas; have them brought to my conference room. I will take care of the rest. Didn't Hamlin teach you the fine art of command?"

"Apparently not," Josh said, hanging up.

"Tommy, Chief wants us to order pizza for the news cast. Can you take care of it?"

"How much can I spend?" Tommy asked.

"I don't know, get enough for everybody. Just take care of it for me," Josh said.

"Consider it done," Tommy replied, picking up the phone.

At 5:45 PM, the group gathered in the conference room.

The chief's aide, Donna, came into the room. "Where would you like me to have them put the pizzas?"

"How about on the shelf over there?" the Chief said.

"Not enough room," Donna replied, arms folded and a grin crossing her face.

"Not enough room?" Brennan said. "How many pizzas did you order, Josh?"

"Ah, I put Tommy in charge, Chief. You'll have to ask him."

At that moment, Tommy came into the office. "Hey there, boys. What's up?"

"How many pizzas did you order?" Brennan asked.

"The LT told me get enough for everyone," Tommy answered. "I figured one per person, so I ordered thirty to make sure."

"Thirty?" both the Chief and Josh said in remarkable unison.

"Yeah, all the uniforms working, the dispatchers, night detectives, plus everyone here. You did say get enough for everybody." Tommy said. "Oh, and here's the bill. I put it on my credit card and tipped him well, so I'd appreciate a quick turnaround on the check to cover it."

"Unbelievable," Brennan said. "But then again, your heart was in the right spot. Give me the bill; I'll get it covered for you."

The parade of delivery drivers carried in the pizzas, scattering them on all the available surfaces. Tommy called over to the Officer-in-Charge and had him work out a rotation to bring the road cops in. Josh delivered several pizzas to dispatch and put twenty in the Patrol break room.

"Okay," Brennan said. "Now that Tommy has done his best to improve morale, lock the door. I have a special surprise, my own version of a morale booster."

"Oh goody," Tommy said. "I love surprises."

Brennan started to reply, then just groaned and shook his head. Waiting for Josh to lock the door, he removed a large cooler from behind the closet door.

"Here you go, Gentlemen, and of course you as well, Donna. Compliments of your favorite Chief of Police. He opened the cooler, revealing beer, wine, and a bottle of Single Malt scotch.

Tommy reached for the Scotch. Brennan snatched it away from him.

"You're not old enough to appreciate this," Brennan said. "Maybe someday, if you ever grow up. Which is unlikely."

Moore smiled and grabbed a beer. "I was going to pour it for you, Chief."

Brennan chuckled, "An answer for everything, don't you? An answer for everything," tipping his glass to the smiling detective.

"Jeez, Tommy, how many anchovy pizzas did you get?" Donahue asked.

"Just five, because it ain't pizza without anchovies," grabbing two slices with the salty fish and finding a seat at the table.

"It's on," Josh said, turning up the volume.

Tonight, an I-Team exclusive. Last week our I-Team investigators revealed shocking allegations of wrongdoing in US Senator Robert Collucci. Tonight, our I-Team has uncovered new allegations and we have an exclusive interview with the Senator you will only see here. That report, when we return...

Josh muted the sound. "I'll bet this gets Collucci's attention."

"He's a resilient bastard," Brennan said. "I'll give him that. Remember the story Candace broke after your trial. Son-of-a-bitch survived it and managed to get elected. Don't count him out yet."

"It's back on," Tommy said, through a mouthful of food. Pointing his beer at the screen.

Brennan looked at the detective.

"Wha?" Tommy mumbled, chewing away.

...here's I-Team reporter Candace Ferguson with the report.

Candace this all started with the story you broke last week. What else have you uncovered?

Tom, we broke the story of Senator Collucci's involvement in Darnell Grey, a case of an innocent man dying in state custody. The Senator agreed to an interview with us just a few days ago.

The screen changed to the Senator's office. *Several excerpts from the interview ran, highlighted by Collucci's angry exit from the interview after the questions about the Russians.*

Sources in the Justice Department confirmed the links between Shashenka Dmitriev and known members of Russian organized crime. The I-Team has learned Dmitriev is the CEO of ZMI Media, which is in the midst of merging with this station's parent company.

Sources also confirm that Senator Collucci put pressure on the Chairman of the FCC to slow the decision on the merger to prevent our bringing you this story.

Our investigation has also uncovered large contributions funneled to the Senator's campaign fund through shell companies controlled by Dmitriev.

The screen changed to an image of Dmitriev.

Shashenka Dmitriev, shown here, refused our request for an interview. Sources close to the investigation tell us authorities recently took an individual into custody in possession of a high caliber composite weapon used by Russian Special Forces. This man had a list of home addresses and personal vehicles belonging to some of the local police officers involved in this investigation. Candace Ferguson, I-Team investigations.

Thank you, Candace, for that troubling report. Do you expect more to come of this?

We know a statewide grand jury is looking into this and Federal authorities are working with the state and local police.

The screen switched back to the news anchor desk. Josh muted the sound.

Holding up his glass of wine he said, "Here's to the demise of Robert M. Collucci. Couldn't happen to a better guy."

"So, do you think Sorin did the original hit on you? The one that almost got Keira?" Tommy asked.

"I am not sure we'll ever find out. I doubt he'd have the balls to do it on his own; someone either arranged it for him or put him up to it. Either way we're gonna indict the son-of-a-bitch tomorrow and then I get to lock his ass up."

"We get to lock his ass up," Tommy said. "I want a piece of that prick also."

"Zach, did you give her the info on the guy in the park?" Josh asked. "Because I didn't."

"Let's just say I told someone in federal court the story knowing it would get out," Zach replied. "A little fuel to the fire." Raising his glass.

Chapter 44

Sorin jumped when the phone rang. "Yes?"

"I am not pleased with the news from Rhode Island," Dmitriev said. "I need to reevaluate our association with the Senator."

"This can be contained," Sorin argued, drawing Collucci's attention. "Once the initial reaction fades we can move ahead. Things are too far along for anything to prevent it from going forward."

"When is the vote on the committee?" Dmitriev asked.

"Tomorrow afternoon," Sorin replied.

"After the vote, come to my office," Dmitriev ordered. "Bring the Senator and Ms. Reynolds; perhaps she can be of some use in finding dirt on this holier than thou Lieutenant Williams." The call ended.

"What'd he want?" Collucci asked.

"He wants to see us after the vote tomorrow," Sorin explained. "I suggest we get on the phone and do damage control. Make sure the votes are still there."

"They'll be there," Collucci said. "I have enough on all those bastards to insure it."

"We should make the calls anyway," Sorin said. "If for no other reason than to remind them of that."

The two spent the next few hours talking to the other members of the Banking Committee, shoring up their support. They monitored CNN, Fox, and the other networks for any serious reaction.

So far, the story remained local, with only a mention on the national services. The other Senator of Rhode Island took to the floor of the Senate and called for Collucci to resign. He took up twenty minutes of a C-Span broadcast, speaking to an empty Senate floor.

* * *

The schedule called for the vote on the Chairmanship at 11:00 AM. Collucci convinced his colleagues to move the time up to 9:00 AM to avoid the media throng. As he arrived at the committee hearing room, the Senator from Texas, Wyatt Santangelo approached him.

"Senator," Santangelo said, "might I have a moment of your time?"

"Of course, my friend. Of course," Collucci replied, putting his arm around the Senator.

"I think it may be in the best interest of all concerned if you withdraw your name from consideration," Santangelo said.

Collucci could feel the rage welling up inside him. "Withdraw, are you serious? Based on a falsified news report with unnamed sources and statements from a disgraced judge? I have no intention of withdrawing."

"Bob listen to me," Santangelo said. "You no longer have the votes. I do not care what any of them told you, I know what's going to happen. One of them will abstain, someone will be absent, and the vote will fail to get the needed majority. If you withdraw, you will have an opportunity to come back. Make a statement you want to fight these allegations and are doing it for the sake of the committee's work. If you lose the vote, you'll never get another chance."

Collucci glared at Santangelo, "You listen to me, Senator. If you think I'll just go away after all I have done to put myself in this position, you are mistaken. If they go against me, they do it at their own peril. I am a man of my word, you tell them. What I said I will do, I will do."

Santangelo weighed his words. "Bob, I am a man of my word as well. I do not take to threats well, either. I don't know what you have over anyone else, but you have nothing on me. I supported you in the past, I supported you for this position, but in light of what has come out, I cannot vote for you. I'm sorry it's come to this, but I will not support you for the chairmanship." Santangelo turned and walked away.

"Problem?" Sorin asked.

"We'll see," Collucci said. "We'll see what happens when he's forced to really choose."

The vote tied at 4 to 4. Three of the Senators Collucci counted on for support did not show up. Collucci argued to defer the vote, but his request failed.

Sitting in his Senate office, Collucci fumed. "I cannot believe that local yokel Williams fucked up three years of work. If it's the last thing I do, I will pay that son-of-a-bitch back."

Sorin made a pretense of listening to the Senator, but his thoughts were elsewhere. *Best-case scenario, Dmitriev pulls the plug on the Rhode Island operation and regroups. Worst case, well, I do not want to think about it.*

Sorin's cell rang. Looking at the caller ID he said, "It's Shashenka."

"Hello, Shasha."

"Anthony, I have arranged a meeting with some of my partners in the venture. We believe we can still salvage the most important aspects. We need to speak with you and the Senator; it will get him out of the limelight for a bit. Meet me at the private airfield, tomorrow morning. We will fly together to the meeting and I can fill you in. Make sure no one knows who you are meeting."

"Of course, Shasha. We will be there. What about Karen, do I bring her?"

"Yes, she has a part to play in this as well."

Sorin hung up.

Collucci, hands clasped together, leaning toward Sorin, said, "Well?"

"He's arranged a meeting with the others," Sorin said. "We fly with him tomorrow to a meeting."

"Where?" Collucci asked.

"Atlanta I would assume, but I'm uncertain. Shasha said they have a way to salvage the project."

"You see," Collucci said, wagging a finger at Sorin. "I told you they recognize my value to the project. This will all work out, you watch. I understand these things better than you."

"Let's hope you are right about that, Senator."

* * *

Early the next morning, the driver picked up Sorin and Karen, then drove to the Senator's brownstone building in Georgetown. The building was one of the original residences built as DC grew in prominence. The unremarkable facade concealing the ornate opulence of the interior.

Collucci rarely had guests over, but if he wanted to impress someone this was the perfect setting.

"So how long do you think we'll be there?" Karen asked.

"As long as is necessary," Sorin said, glancing up from his cell phone then resuming looking at email.

The car arrived at the Senator's home and the driver went to the door. As the Senator came out, he pointed inside for the driver to get his bags.

Collucci got in the car, surprised by Karen sitting there.

"What's she doing here?" he asked, ignoring her for the moment.

"Shasha says she has a part to play in this," Sorin replied. "I suggest you go along with it."

Collucci smiled. "My apologies, Karen. I meant no offense," Collucci said. "Just didn't expect anyone else."

"No problem, Senator. I was surprised myself when I Anthony invited me," she answered.

An hour later, they arrived at the private airfield. Dmitriev was already aboard the Gulfstream G-5. As the three got out of the car, Collucci said, "Once this is all done, I am going to get myself one of these."

Sorin, ignoring the Senator, climbed the stairs to the jet. As he entered the passenger compartment, the pilot came out.

"Bill?" Sorin said, surprised to see William Marshall standing in the cockpit door. "What are you doing here?"

"Shasha asked me to fly you to the meeting," Marshall answered. "He wants me to work with you guys on some new ideas to move things along."

"Great, we ready to go?" Sorin asked.

"Just waiting on the ground crew to finish the pre-flight. Go make yourself comfortable. Where's the Senator?"

Sorin motioned with his thumb, "Outside, probably waiting to be formally welcomed aboard."

Marshall laughed, "I'll see what I can do."

Karen looked at the Senator. Collucci motioned for her to go first and the two followed Sorin into the plane.

Marshall greeted them, directed them to the passenger compartment, and then closed the door behind them. He walked down the stairs to check on the pre-flight process. As they entered the compartment, they saw Dmitriev facing forward with Sorin seated next to him.

"Senator, Ms. Reynolds, welcome aboard. Please," motioning to the two seats across from him, "sit down and we can be on our way."

"Thank you, Mr. Dmitriev. I am looking forward to our discussions on this," Collucci said.

"Senator, I must apologize for my angry outburst the other day," Dmitriev said. "Please, Shasha will do."

The Senator smiled and nodded, glancing at Sorin.

Marshall came back into the passenger compartment. "Ready Mr. Dmitriev," he said, then left for the cockpit.

Dmitriev nodded, turning the others, he said, "One of the privileges of owning the plane is I can ride up front in the cockpit. I love the view from there. Once we are airborne, I'll come back and we can discuss things.

"Meanwhile, enjoy your drinks and the flight." Dmitriev walked to the front, closing the passenger compartment door behind him.

Marshall was waiting.

"Follow your last flight plan to the airstrip on the island. I'll have someone there to care for our guests."

Dmitriev walked down the stairs as his assistant security chief came aboard. Dmitriev took the man by the arm, "See that he follows the flight plan."

Dmitriev got into the limo, heading in one direction as the plane taxied in another.

* * *

Josh, Tommy, and the other members of the investigative team sat in the SIU office. Kennedy was on the phone with Washington. Tim Donahue was talking to the Superintendent of the State Police, updating her on the latest developments.

The door opened, and Chief Brennan rushed in. "Turn on CNN, there's something you might find interesting."

Flipping on the TV, they all shifted around so they could watch.

...Continuing our exclusive coverage of this breaking story. CNN has a crew on the way to the scene of a plane crash outside of Arlington, Virginia. The plane took off from a corporate airfield outside of Arlington and crashed moments later.

CNN confirmed that Senator Robert Collucci and his Chief of Staff, Anthony Sorin, were among the passengers aboard the aircraft.

Senator Collucci and Sorin are at the center of a huge corruption scandal arising from an investigation into money laundering, corruption, and fraud in Rhode Island. Law Enforcement sources tell CNN the plane is registered to Harriet Lane Enterprises, one business named in the corruption report. Sources close to the investigation tell CNN the business is a front organization for Russian organized crime.

The Senator had denied any involvement, blaming the problems on his political enemies.

Also reported onboard the aircraft was Shashenka Dmitriev, Chairman and CEO of ZMI Media. ZMI and ANM Media were in a merger pending FCC approval. The merger would create the largest cable news company in the world.

Preliminary reports are there are no survivors. Witnesses reported the plane on fire before the crash.

FAA sources tell us the pilot filed no flight plan and had taken aboard a full load of fuel. This aircraft has an operating range of 5000 nautical miles.

A CNN aviation consultant tells us this aircraft normally has a crew of two pilots but can be flown by one. The control tower at the private airfield declined our request to hear the departure recordings due to the pending investigation.

CNN will continue with live coverage of this breaking story...

"Well, I guess we put that down as a win, right?" Tommy Moore said, breaking the silence.

The room broke into laughter. "I suppose you can say that, son," Chief Brennan said. "It'll be interesting to see if anyone else on the plane was involved in this. Any ideas?"

"My guess is someone decided Dmitriev became too big a liability," Kennedy said. "I bet Collucci, Sorin, and Dmitriev were onboard thinking they were on the way to do damage control. Whoever set up the meeting sabotaged the plane. These guys don't take kindly to having things taken from them."

"Who do you think did this?" Josh asked.

"Someone with good intelligence," Kennedy speculated. "I'd say whoever is behind this decided none of those onboard were worth protecting. Dmitriev was the face of ZMI, not all the power behind it. It makes sense; they had to have some inside information. If whoever did this wanted to take them all out, they would have to get to the aircraft. Take out Dmitriev's security and ground crew and you own them.

"According to the FAA, the name of the co-pilot listed on the manifest is a corporate pilot for another company. FBI located him in Belize. He's been there a week. They're trying to determine how the impostor got past security at the airport FBO. He must have been the one to sabotage the engine."

"FBO? What's that?" Tommy asked.

"Fixed Base Operations," Josh said. "It's where private planes operate from at most airports. You'd know this if you hadn't joined the Marines and slept in the mud."

Tommy laughed. "That's true."

"But why would Marshall fly without the co-pilot?" Josh asked.

Kennedy shrugged his shoulders. "Who knows? It normally has a crew of two, but it's not required. Probably assumed it wasn't necessary. I bet the guy who placed the device, the fake pilot, just disappeared so they thought he was a no show and left without him. Who knows?" shrugging his shoulders.

"So now what?" Tommy asked.

"Now you have to go back to your real job," Brennan said. "Give me some time. I'll think of something useful you can do."

"Thanks, Chief. I appreciate your confidence in my abilities," Tommy said. "Hey, somebody's got to go tell Jennifer. She may not know yet."

Josh looked at Tommy, "Go. Take the rest of the day off and go."

Tommy was out the door.

"Pretty generous with the city's time aren't we, Lieutenant?" Brennan said.

Josh smiled, "He's got some things to deal with. I think we can cut him some slack."

Brennan patted Josh on the shoulder, "You're learning my boy. You're learning," he said. "Let's spend the next few days tying up loose ends, and then we'll have a little celebration of our accomplishments. Sound good?"

They all nodded in agreement. Josh then turned to trying to put this into an understandable report. One that would not read like an imaginative fiction novel.

* * *

Two weeks after the crash, NTSB released the report. There were five people onboard the aircraft on takeoff, including the pilot. They recovered and identified all five bodies. Senator Robert Collucci, Anthony Sorin, Karen Reynolds, Shashenka Dmitriev, and the pilot, William Marshall.

The NTSB reported evidence of tampering with the fuel line, causing fuel to spray inside the number two engine. As the fuel spread, a timing device triggered, igniting the fuel. Just before the aircraft reached 4000 feet, the pilot tried to shut down the number 2 engine. The aircraft went into an emergency descent attitude. The pilot attempted to return to the runway. As the plane turned, the fuel in the wing tank exploded.

Josh got off the phone after speaking to Zach Kennedy. The Justice Department had assumed responsibility for the investigation. Josh, Tommy, and the others planned to appear in a Federal Grand Jury starting next week.

The Department of the Attorney General launched their own investigation into the matter. They focused on the involvement of several members of the Rhode Island legislature, including the Speaker of the House.

The Governor, to no one's surprise, selected the Attorney General to fill the vacant Senate seat. Solicitations of campaign funds for a run for a complete term were already in progress.

The Governor fought to salvage the development program for the waterfront. The President, in appreciation for his new control over the Senate, made assurances that the project would continue.

There remained just a few things to conclude this matter.

PERSISTENCE OF JUSTICE

Chapter 45

"All rise," the Deputy Sheriff intoned. "Hear ye, hear ye, hear ye. The Superior Court of the State of Rhode Island and Providence Plantations is now in session. All having business before this court draw near and you shall be heard. The Honorable Justice Michael Patrick Campbell, presiding."

The small group in attendance rose.

Campbell assumed the bench, shuffled papers, and then turned his attention to the court. "It is my understanding there is a petition before this court to dismiss charges against defendant, Darnell Grey. Is that correct, Ms. Williams?"

Keira rose from her seat, "It is your Honor. On behalf of Mr. Grey's daughter, we submitted a petition to the court to dismiss these charges. We recognize the unusual circumstances in place, but believe the court has the jurisdiction and authority to grant this motion."

"I have reviewed your motion. While it is a bit unusual, under the circumstances the court is inclined to allow it to proceed. Would you like anything read into the record?" Campbell inquired.

"We would, your Honor," Keira answered. She then read a concise version of the circumstances leading to Grey's arrest and indictment by the Providence County Grand Jury. "In light of this information, your Honor, we respectfully move to have all charges dismissed. In addition, we request an order issued to the Rhode Island Department of the Attorney General to destroy any and all related arrest records of Darnell Grey arising from this case."

"Does the Attorney General have any objection to this motion?" Judge Campbell asked.

Deputy Attorney General Michael Webster rose from his seat. "You Honor, the State supports this motion," turning to look at Loren Grey. "On behalf of the many fine members of the Department of the Attorney General, I wish to extend our sincere apologies this took so long to come to light."

Judge Campbell also took a moment to look at Loren. "Ms. Grey, I know this is woefully inadequate, but the court also extends its apology for the way the system was perverted against your father. I hope this small, symbolic gesture brings you some measure of comfort."

Grey nodded her head, sobbing into a tissue, as she held her father's picture tight to her heart.

"With that said," Campbell continued, "the court grants the motion. All charges against Mr. Grey are dismissed and all records in this matter concerning him are ordered destroyed," banging the gavel.

Keira turned and hugged Loren as Chris Hamlin and Maggie Fleming joined in the embrace.

* * *

Josh pulled up to the front of Kathleen Lakeland's home. He could see her looking out the window. As he got out the car, the front door opened. Kathleen came outside.

"I was wondering if you would come back to see me."

"I said I would," Josh answered, "once I knew the truth."

"And do you?" she asked.

"I think I am as close as I am ever going to get," Josh said. "Can we go inside and talk?"

"Of course, I'm sorry," she said. "Come on in."

Settling into their seats, Josh said, "He wasn't the one, Kathleen. The picture the detectives showed you was not the guy who raped you. We believe the man who attacked you was the guy caught by Massachusetts State Police a month or so later. Unfortunately, he raped two more women, killing one, before they caught him."

Tears formed in her eyes, "I knew I should have made them listen to me, I knew it." She sobbed.

"This is not your fault; none of this is your fault. The cops didn't do their job. We're supposed to look for the truth, not assume things we want to believe," Josh said, trying to comfort her.

"I wasn't supposed to be working that night you know," Kathleen said, regaining her composure. "I was covering for a friend who needed the night off. I did not usually work on Tuesdays. The rape happened right after I left the store."

"I didn't know that," Josh said. "It must have been hard on your friend, knowing it could have been her."

"She was distraught over it. I told her it wasn't her fault," clutching the tissue in her hands. "Her father had friends who helped me. They got me in to see all sorts of doctors. Took care of moving me out of my apartment and even let me stay with them for a while."

Josh listened, letting her talk.

"Gino made sure they took good care of me. My family was all gone. I had no one except for Stella and her family."

"Gino?" Josh asked. "Gino who?"

"Stella's father," Kathleen explained, "Gino Bellofatto." Seeing the reaction on Josh's face, she explained, "I know, I know he's supposed to be some big Mafia guy or something, but he helped me more than anyone else."

Josh, trying to get his mind around this, looked past the woman. Her words faded into the background in the turmoil of his thoughts.

"Lieutenant? Lieutenant?" Kathleen said, touching his arm. "Are you okay?"

"What? Oh, sorry," Josh said. "Kathleen, you may have just added a bit more to the story."

"I did?" Kathleen asked.

"I am sorry it took so long for us to find out the truth for you. I apologize for the way the detectives treated you back then," Josh said. "If there is ever anything I can do," handing her his card, "please call me. Thank you for all your help, and patience."

Josh walked out. He had one more stop to make, then he would go talk to Bellofatto.

Driving to the East side, he called ahead and make sure Mary Lyons was home.

"Hello."

"Dakota? It's Lieutenant Williams from the East Providence Police."

"Oh yes, Lieutenant. How are you?" Dakota Jones answered.

"I am well. I was hoping to come speak with your mother, will she be home?" Josh asked.

There was a pause on the line, "I'm sorry Lieutenant. My mother suffered another stroke several days ago. She... she didn't survive...."

"Oh, I am so sorry to hear that. I wanted to tell her the story in person but there was so much going on," Josh said. "I wish I had tried sooner."

"Oh no, Lieutenant. My mother was grateful for what you did. She was glad you sought her out."

"I wish there was something else I could do, Dakota. I am sorry for your loss."

"Thank you, Lieutenant. My mother was glad she was right all those years about the investigation. You made it all seem worthwhile to her," Dakota said.

"She was a strong woman. I'm glad I had the chance to meet her. You have my number. If there is ever anything I can do for you, please call me. Take care, Dakota."

Then there was one; off to get more answers.

* * *

339

Josh drove up to the gate in front of Bellofatto's house. As the security camera examined his face and the gate opened, Josh wondered what he would say.

Bellofatto stood on the stairs, arms folded, waiting. No bodyguard in sight.

Josh walked over to him; Bellofatto motioned for him to follow. He led Josh to an enclosed deck overlooking the Turner Reservoir. The leaves were just fading, the diffusion of colors diminishing to brown.

Bellofatto said, "Sit please, Lieutenant. I suppose you have some questions. Would you like a drink?"

Josh hesitated a moment. What the hell. How many honest cops can say they had a drink with the consigliere of the Patriarca crime family? "Sure, got any vodka?"

"Of course," Bellofatto said, grabbing the bottle out of the freezer. "Ice cold like my friends recommend."

Josh watched as Bellofatto poured the drinks. The man had changed. His movements slowed by age and lifestyle. His face now creased with lines. He was an aging, dying shell of what once had been a powerful man. Josh almost felt sympathy for him.

Handing Josh the glass, he took a seat next to him. "I love the view. I sit out here often when I need to think..." sipping from his glass.

"How is your family, Gino?" Josh asked.

"My wife is ill, she is in a wheelchair now," Bellofatto said, staring into his glass. "She spends most of her time at our daughter Carla's house in Miami. My other daughter, Stella, is in New York. She and her husband have a restaurant there."

"Grandkids?"

"Three, two girls and a boy. Stella has the girls and Carla has the boy. Joys of my life," Bellofatto smiled. "I wish I saw them more often."

"How about you, Lieutenant? Any kids?" Bellofatto asked.

"Not yet," Josh smiled, sipping the drink.

Bellofatto nodded, and then tipped his glass toward Josh. "But you didn't come here to talk about such things. What can I do for you?"

"You knew about the rapes because it could've been your daughter instead of Kathleen Lakeland, right?" Josh asked.

Bellofatto, sipping his drink, showed no reaction. "My daughter, Stella, worked with Kathleen. They knew each other from Bay View, had several classes together. Kathleen got her the job. I didn't want her to work, I wanted her to focus on studying, but she is as stubborn as her mother is. She wanted to have a job, earn her own money. I respected that.

"The night Kathleen was attacked was the date of my wedding anniversary. Stella and Carla surprised my wife and took her out to dinner, since I was still in prison. Stella came to visit me in the prison a few days before, told me what they had planned. I tried to convince them not to do it. I thought it would be too hard on my wife," pausing to take a drink. "If that had happened... if they had listened to me... well, who knows?"

Bellofatto walked to the bar and refilled his drink, "Need more?"

"No, I'm good right now."

Bellofatto returned to his seat, continuing the story. "Later, when I found out about Kathleen, I realized it could have been Stella walking out of the business that night. If they did not stop him, it could happen to Carla also. When Grey showed up in the prison, they made sure I knew who he was. They made sure everyone knew who he was and that he attacked white women. The rumor about the trooper's daughter, they made sure we knew that as well."

"So, you arranged to have him killed?" Josh asked.

"If that was your daughter, what would you do?" Bellofatto asked, staring into his drink. "The cops made a big deal about the case, about the evidence they had. It wasn't until I talked to Jimmy Calise that I found out the whole story. The other guy, the one that the State Police caught in Seekonk, he was the guy that did the rapes. Grey had nothing to do with any of it," draining his glass and refilling it once again.

"Besides, I didn't have to do anything," Bellofatto said. "There were guys in there looking to make a name for themselves. They figured if they killed the nigger, no one would care, and they might even get a little slack from the troopers when they got out. I just let them loose."

Josh closed his eyes and shook his head. Holding up his glass he asked, "Do you mind?"

"Help yourself," Bellofatto said, nodding toward the bar.

Josh walked to the bar, opened the freezer door, and took out the vodka bottle. As he poured the drink, he noticed the label bearing Cyrillic lettering. "What kind of vodka is this?" he asked. "It's excellent," examining the bottle.

"It's made by the producer of Russian Standard Vodka, but you can't get it in this country. It's a private reserve label only available to certain people. I have many friends, Josh," Bellofatto said, watching Josh's reaction.

Josh sat back down and sipped the vodka, "So, how did you get it?"

Bellofatto smiled. "As I told you once, you have your ways and we have ours. Would you excuse me a moment?" putting his drink on the table.

Josh waited, sipping his drink, looking at the water. Bellofatto came back after a few minutes, reclaimed his drink, and returned to his seat.

The two sat in silence for several moments, enjoying the drinks and admiring the view. Josh stood up, placed his glass on the bar, and turned to look at Bellofatto.

"Thanks for the drink, Gino," Josh said. "I have one more question."

Bellofatto's expression didn't change.

"Do you know anything about planes?"

Bellofatto locked his eyes on Josh. "I know this. People who threaten to hurt our friends should not fly in them," holding Josh's stare as he sipped his drink.

"And Maurio Bartoletti, what might he know about them?"

The name caused a small reaction in Bellofatto; his eyes grew wider. But he regained control. "Maurio, yes, he is a good man. Loyal, sympathetic, and discrete." Bellofatto's eyes now displayed a more intense level of concern. "I am sure he has no knowledge of such things. Why do you ask?"

"Idle curiosity," Josh smiled, and turned toward the door.

"Does the FBI share this, how'd you say, idle curiosity?" Bellofatto asked, rolling the drink around in his glass.

Josh shook his head, "I doubt it. We've all moved on," watching as Bellofatto drained the glass.

As he walked from the deck, he stopped for a moment. Images swirled through his mind, morphing into one. Remembering now what he could not before, it all fit together. Josh looked at Bellofatto. "I saw his picture." Josh wasn't certain, but he tried to bluff

Bellofatto narrowed his eyes, "You saw whose picture?"

"Where's your bodyguard?" Josh asked. "Not back from Virginia yet?"

Bellofatto faced betrayed no emotion. "He is around, when I need him."

Josh studied Bellofatto for a moment; looking for some emotional reaction to what he set in motion. There was none. Josh walked out of the house, got into his car, and drove off. He followed the winding driveway past the security gate and onto the road. Stopping at the intersection with Pawtucket Avenue, he heard a text message come through. The message, from a blocked caller ID, read, "No more visits, my friend. Problem solved. Look under your seat."

Reaching under the seat, Josh felt a box. He pulled it out and threw it on the passenger seat. Stopping at the next red light, he opened the box and pulled out a bottle of the Russian Vodka. Guy is a real piece of work.

Chapter 46

November 14, 2009
Gate of Heaven Cemetery
East Providence, Rhode Island

"The arc of the moral universe is long, but it bends toward Justice."
Dr. Martin Luther King

The group arrived at the cemetery. Chris Hamlin, Maggie Fleming, Vera Johnson, Loren Grey, Keira Williams, and Josh walked from their cars to the small grave on the hill. They met Chief Brennan, Zach Kennedy, the two troopers, Candace Ferguson, and Harrison 'Hawk' Bennett.

On the Wampanoag Trail in East Providence, Gate of Heaven cemetery is a quiet, peaceful setting not far from the Massachusetts border. Thousands of cars pass by each day. Few pay much attention to those buried there, lives lost.

Josh took the small wooden box, bearing the insignia of the 1st Cavalry Division, and handed it to Loren.

She took the box, hugged it to her chest, and then placed it in the open grave. The workers lowered it gently down.

The East Providence Police Color Guard came to attention. They carried three flags, the flag of the United States, the State flag of Rhode Island, and the Division Colors of the 1st Air Cavalry. The family of Gordon 'Ray' Reynolds, a deceased member of the East Providence Police and fellow Vietnam veteran, provided the flag.

Distant commands broke the silence; a trio of rifleman fired three volleys.

As the echoing report of the rifles faded, the mournful sounds of taps rose from the bugler of American Legion Post 10. Under the tearful eyes of those who loved him, one more veteran laid to rest.

As the last of the notes drifted away, the group began the slow walk back to their cars.

"I hear you enjoy Russian Vodka," Hawk said, coming up alongside Josh.

"How would you know that?" Josh asked, taken aback by the statement.

"Fatso and I go way back. I represented a few of his crew in the 80s and 90s. We've remained in touch," Hawk said, staring at Josh.

Josh looked into his eyes; he could not tell if it was relief or regret he saw. "Something you're trying to tell me?" Josh asked.

Hawk shook his head. "Some things are best left alone, my boy. Leave it be."

"There isn't much for me to do is there?" Josh said. "Not my jurisdiction."

"Do you know what happened on this date, Josh?" Hawk asked.

Josh looked at him for a moment, "No, what?"

"Ia Drang," Hawk replied, looking Josh in the eye. "The battle in the Ia Drang Valley in South Vietnam started on November 14, 1965, forty-four years ago today. It's splendid timing to lay one of the participants of that battle to rest if you ask me." Hawk patted Josh on the shoulder, linked his hands behind his back, and walked away.

Josh broke from the group, went over to another marker, and stopped. Remembering what he could never forget.

Loren Grey came over and stood next to him. She read the words on the gravestone,

Staff Sergeant Anthony 'JoJo' Machado
United States Marine Corps
June 6, 1983 to March 15, 2006
Semper Fi

"Was he a friend of yours?" Loren asked.

Josh turned to her, a sad smile on his face, eyes brimming with tears, voice quivering. "No, but I wish he had been."

Keira came over, took Josh by the hand, and walked with him back to their car.

"You did a good thing here, Josh," putting her arm around him as he fought back the tears, "a good thing."

Regaining his composure, he said, "A little late though…"

"Finding the truth is what is important. You did that for her. That's all anyone could ever expect, the truth."

Josh turned to look at the graves one last time, watching the sun setting behind the small rise in the cemetery. Truth? He wondered if there was any such thing.

Epilogue

"Dr. Howard, can I speak with you a moment?" the assistant Fairfax County Medical examiner, Dr. Samuels, said.

"Of course, what is it?" Dr. Howard replied. Howard had been the Chief Medical Examiner for almost 30 years. He wanted to retire, but three ex-wives made that impossible.

"There is a problem with the tissue samples from the aircraft accident."

"What do you mean a problem?" the ME asked.

"I decided to re-run the DNA analysis using our new thermo-cycler. When I ran the samples recovered from the aircraft against the known exemplars, I found an error." He handed the ME a report.

Reviewing the document, the ME could feel his heart rate rising. Calming himself, he tried to smile. "Ah, I see your point. Perhaps it is just your unfamiliarity with the new equipment. I will redo the analysis myself. Verify my original results. I am sure it was a harmless error."

"Doctor," Samuels, said, "I have been doing DNA analysis for over twenty years. I came here from the FBI lab where we used these devices all the time. It is no error. The DNA from the aircraft for one of the subjects is not a match for the exemplar. We need to notify the police."

Howard saw it all fading away. He was losing his chance to get out. Nobody would stand in his way.

"Dr. Samuels, I will call the FBI and tell them of your findings. Would you be so kind as to gather all the samples and prepare them for transfer to another lab? I would assume the FBI will conduct an independent analysis."

Samuels left the office and went to the lab. Howard reached into his brief case, took out a cell phone, and dialed a number.

"Da?"

"We have a problem."

* * *

One month later
December 17, 2009
3:00 PM
SIU Office
East Providence Police Department

Josh sat at his desk, the events of the last few months no longer part of his daily thoughts, his phone rang. Using the speakerphone, he answered, "SIU, Lieutenant Williams."

"Josh, Zach Kennedy. How are you?" The familiar voice of FBI Agent Zach Kennedy came over the line.

"I just manage to put all that shit behind me and you call," Josh chuckled, "other than that, fine. What's up? Where you been the last month?"

"Well, I have some more to share, something you might find interesting. We have been busy here at the FBI. You gonna to be around this afternoon? I'm flying to Providence to meet with the US Attorney and bring them up to speed. If you're free, how about we meet for a couple of drinks and I fill you in?" Kennedy asked.

"I never turn down an opportunity for the Feds to buy me a drink. Can I bring Tommy? He's sitting here with puppy dog eyes begging for a bone."

"Of course. What the hell, give the two troopers a call, I'll expense the whole thing on the US Attorney," Kennedy said. "Where and when?"

"Hmm, let me think," Josh said. "Someplace nice, how about Andrea's, just up the hill from the park where Donahue saved your ass? We can pretend to be Brown professors. Five o'clock work?"

"It does indeed, never knew a US Attorney that stayed in the office past happy hour. I'll find it. See you then," Kennedy hung up.

"Oh goody," Tommy said, "more perks from our tour with the Feds, I love it."

"Call Donahue and Moreira, see if they can make it," Josh said. "I'm gonna tell Brennan. He may want to come along."

"Brennan?" Tommy said. "If he's there, I'll have to behave."

"Yes, you will," Josh replied, waving his hand motioning Tommy away. "Now make the call."

A few moment later, Tommy said, "Good news, bad news. Donahue can make it, Moreira can't. He's stuck with some detail for the Colonel. He must be up for a promotion or something. Donahue said, and I quote, Moreira's head is stuck up the Colonel's ass, end quote."

"Ah well," Josh said. "I've good news for you, Brennan isn't coming either. Said he wants to have a solid alibi," smiling as Moore fist bumped him.

Josh's phone rang again. He put his feet up on his desk, hands behind his head, and hit the speakerphone. "SIU, Lieutenant Williams."

"Yes, this is Dr. Porter's office from Dana Farber. Is this Joshua Williams?"

Josh almost fell out of his chair reaching for the handset. He turned away from the staring Tommy Moore. "Yes, this is Josh Williams," his voice just above a whisper.

"Yes, Mr. Williams, I spoke to your wife and we've scheduled an appointment for you next week, Monday at 9:00," the caller said.

"Ah, well I am not sure—,"

The caller interrupted Josh. "That's what your wife warned me you would say. I am just telling you about the appointment. She told me to tell you to discuss any problems with her. Have a nice day, Mr. Williams." The call ended.

Josh hung up the phone. Avoiding looking at Tommy, he headed for the office door.

"Whoa there big fella, where do you think you're going? We have no secrets. Don't you remember that little talk we had when you found out about Jen and me? Everything is in the open. What's up, you dying or something? Can I have your truck?" Tommy smiled, trying to make light of the situation.

Josh sat back down. "It's nothing. My wife worries too much and wants me to have some tests done. That's all," Josh replied. "But if I do check out, you can have my truck."

"Great," Tommy smiled, "can you keep it washed? And don't drive it so much until then, okay?"

Josh laughed. "Okay, deal."

They left the office, heading to the back lot.

"One more thing, Tommy."

"What's that, boss?" as he followed Josh out to the car.

"In the office, there are no secrets," Josh said, stopping on the last step to look back at Tommy. "Out here, there are. Understand?"

Tommy winked. "You got it, brother."

* * *

Two hours later, the four men, Josh, Tommy, Zach Kennedy, and Tim Donahue stood at the bar at Andrea's on Thayer Street, near Brown University. They took over the whole back area of the bar, so they could watch the door; the paranoia of police officers ingrained deep in their DNA.

"Hey LT, remember the time we came here last summer? You glued quarters up and down the sidewalk with Superglue."

Josh chuckled.

"You guys should have been here," Tommy said, looking at the other two. "There were rear-end collisions with people bending over to pick up the quarters and others plowing into them; some were almost sodomized. It was freaking hysterical," Tommy laughed.

Josh took up the story. "The owner of Andrea's came out. Saw what we were doing and threatened to cut us off if we didn't come inside. He was not amused. Some of those quarters were there for a month."

"Ah, I so miss the intellectually stimulating environment of working with you guys," Kennedy chuckled. "We need to find another case to work together."

"Speaking of cases, fill us in on the latest with the Russians, anything new in Rhode Island?" Josh asked.

"Couple of things," Kennedy said, glimpsing around the bar. "We found some interesting banking transactions that point to a few local politicians here. One reason I came here is to coordinate with the local FBI office and the Rhode Island Attorney General on grand jury subpoenas. We'll be ruining the day for a few state senators next Monday, with a bunch of document subpoenas and a search warrant or two for some local law firms."

"Anybody we know?" Tommy asked.

"Let's say there may be some openings in the leadership positions in the House and Senate." Kennedy smiled, finishing his drink and motioning for another round.

"Anything more on the plane, or who brought it down?" Josh asked.

"Well, there it gets rather murky," Kennedy said.

"Murky?" Tim Donahue asked.

Kennedy paused as the bartender delivered the drinks. "We think someone other than the Russians did this."

"Who?" Donahue asked.

"Not sure, but here's what we found," Kennedy replied. "There were no images at the airport hangar because someone disabled the cameras.

We did get video from a security firm next to the airfield. Their cameras spotted a vehicle near one of the access gates the night before the Senator's flight. The video showed a male get out of the car and someone from inside the gate let him in. The images were low-quality, and we couldn't clear them up," Kennedy paused for another drink.

"Didn't the security guy go check on the car?" Tommy asked.

"We talked to the guy," Kennedy said. "He worked the overnight shift. He said he was making a building check and didn't see the car until he reviewed the tapes a few hours later. By then, it was gone. My guess is he was asleep."

"You get anything else?" Josh asked.

Kennedy smiled. "Two days after we got the images, DC police found the body of the maintenance supervisor from the hangar. He had called in sick the day of the flight. 911 call reported a body floating in the Potomac. Two in the head, through and through wounds. Hands tied behind his back. No identifiable ballistics recovered." Kennedy let the information sink in, "and there's more."

"More as in...?" Josh asked.

"Remember the unidentified guy in the photo when Bartoletti met with Dmitriev? The forensic guys compared the physical size of the two men in the photos. Similar, almost exact, height and build," Kennedy said. "The guy with Bartoletti and the one at the airport, one and the same. Contract killer. We think Bartoletti decided to cancel the merger with extreme prejudice."

"Did you interview Bartoletti?" Donahue asked.

"Tried to," Kennedy said. "You needed a scorecard to keep all the lawyers straight. Gave us nothing. Wouldn't even admit meeting with Dmitriev even after we showed him the pictures. Just sat and smiled, surrounded by a defensive line of lawyers answering for him."

"So, all you have is two pictures of an unidentified guy?" Donahue said.

"Yup," Kennedy nodded, two hands on his drink, staring into the glass.

"I know who that was. The guy in both photos," Josh said. "At least, I think I do."

The other three turned to look at him.

"Care to share?" Tommy said.

Josh hesitated a moment, "I think it's Bellofatto's bodyguard."

Donahue said, "Gino Bellofatto? The mob guy? Holy shit."

"Yup," Josh said. "I'm not sure, but it looks like him."

"Who's this Bellofatto guy?" Kennedy asked.

"He's the consigliere of the Patriarch crime family, or what's left of it," Josh explained. "He's an old school type. When this case started, I talked to him because he was in the prison at the time Grey died. Turns out he had a lot more to do with that case than I knew," Josh said. "And it looks like he's had more to do with this case as well."

"But why would the local mob have anything to do with the Russians?" Kennedy asked.

"I think you may have underestimated the local mob," Donahue said. "They may be nowhere near as powerful as they once were, but they still exist. My guess is they have some hooks into Bartoletti and used him to get them close to Dmitriev."

"That explains how," Kennedy said, "but not why."

Josh shook his head, "Believe it or not, I think they were doing us a favor. At least in their eyes," he said. "I know Hawk Bennett represented some of Bellofatto's crew. He told me so at Grey's memorial. I think he reached out to Bellofatto. I suspected the bodyguard was the one in Virginia, but I wasn't sure. It didn't click until I talked to Bellofatto after we had closed the Grey case. Bennett said I should just let it go."

"You know what?" Tommy said. "Who gives a fuck? They did do us a favor."

"There's the voice of reason," Donahue chuckled, tapping Tommy's glass with his own.

Kennedy was quiet for a moment, trying to make sense of things. "So, the local mob has the reach to take out a Russian organized crime guy and does it because of some odd sense of what, justice? Retribution? Greed?"

"Family," Josh answered. "They protect their own and those they care for. Hawk must have convinced them that going after his wife, and mine, crossed a line. They handled it their way. Bellofatto once said to me, 'you have your ways and we have ours.'"

The four sat in silence, lost in their own thoughts.

"Should we go have a chat with this bodyguard and Bellofatto?" Kennedy asked.

"Waste of time," Donahue said. "They wouldn't talk even if you had high quality video of them shooting the guy and planting the device on the plane. Gino did nine years in the can and never gave up anybody, that whole code of silence thing."

"What about Hawk? Can we talk to him?" Kennedy asked.

"You met him," Josh said. "What do you think?"

"Oh yeah, good point." Kennedy said.

Donahue ordered another round. "You know, something is still bothering me."

"What's that?" Josh asked.

"Why kill Dmitriev? The others I can understand, but not him. Doesn't make sense to me."

"I suppose we may never know," Kennedy said. "So now what?"

Josh looked at each and smiled. "We let it go," he said, "we just let it go."

Then lifting his glass, his voice rising above the crowd, he said, "Here's to us and those like us, the hell with everybody else."

Kennedy's cell rang. He spoke on the line for a few moments then hung up.

"Bad news?" Josh asked.

"No, just another one of those coincidences," Kennedy answered.

"How's that?" Tommy asked.

"They just pulled the body of the Fairfax County assistant state medical examiner out of the Potomac. He's been missing for a month. Two bullets in his head…"

* * *

Acknowledgments

Writing a novel is a solitary process, turning the novel into a book that people want to read takes the efforts of many.

I want to acknowledge the invaluable assistance of the following people. Without their dedication, creativity, and help this book would not be possible.

Lifetime friends, Dolores (dos Santos) Cohen, Jane Auger, Susan Pincince Hyman, and Walter Barlow offered their time and effort in reading, reviewing, correcting, and making suggestions for molding the story into what it is today. Mike Campbell, for his reading the manuscript and offering his helpful perspective. Special thanks to Jim Taricani, who graciously offered his vast experience in journalism helping me understand the inner workings. Geri Anderson, Owen Parr, and Todd Anderson (and his wife Debbie Grenier for volunteering him) for reading the pre-release version and giving their insight and feedback.

There is no more valuable thing to offer a fellow human than time out of your life. For their kind assistance, I am forever grateful.

To my daughter Kelsey Broadmeadow, Esq., for her assistance (and tolerance) in answering my unending questions on the law and for my brother-in-law, Dr. Edwin Pont, for his diligent and thorough help in finding answers to the medical questions I posed. I cannot adequately express my gratitude and thanks.

If there are errors in the book, they are mine and mine alone.

To my long-suffering wife, Susan, for tolerating my obsession with writing I am forever thankful and fortunate.

Thanks for reading, Silenced Justice, please take the time to write a review. It is very much appreciated.

About the Author

Joe Broadmeadow was born in Pawtucket and grew up in Cumberland, Rhode Island.

He retired with the rank of Captain from the East Providence, Rhode Island Police Department after twenty years. He served in the various divisions within the department, including Commander of Investigative Services. He also worked in the Organized Crime Drug Enforcement Task Force (OCDETF) and on special assignment to the FBI Drug Task Force.

Silenced Justice is his second novel in the Josh Williams series. His first novel, *Collision Course,* continues to garner rave reviews and is available on Amazon.com

When Joe is not writing, he is hiking or fishing (and thinking about writing). Joe completed a 2,185-mile thru-hike of the Appalachian Trail in September 2014. After completing the trail, Joe published a short story, *Spirit of the Trail,* available on Amazon.com in print and Kindle versions.

In the fall of 2015, Joe will release *Saving the Last Dragon,* a young adult novel also set in the backdrop of Rhode Island.

Joe lives in Lincoln, RI with his wife Susan.

Contact the author at joe.broadmeadow@hotmail.com
I encourage my readers to send me their thoughts and reactions to my writing. Thanks for reading!
Amazon Author page
http://www.amazon.com/Joe-Broadmeadow/e/B00OWPE9GU
Twitter: @JBroadmeadow
Author Blogs:
www.joebroadmeadowblog.wordpress.com
www.jebroadmeadow.wordpress.com

Books by Joe Broadmeadow
Collision Course (A Josh Williams Novel)
Spirit of the Trail (An Appalachian Trail Short Story)
Saving the Last Dragon (coming Fall 2015)

Made in the USA
Lexington, KY
22 November 2019

57450474R00224